WITH

A KISS WE

DIE

ALSO BY L. R. DORN

The Anatomy of Desire

WITH

A KISS WE

DIE

A Novel

L. R. DORN

WILLIAM MORROW

An Imprint of HarperCollins*Publishers*

WITH A KISS WE DIE. Copyright © 2023 by Matthew R. Dorff and Suzanne L. Dunn. All rights reserved. Printed in the United States of America. No part of this book may be used or reproduced in any manner whatsoever without written permission except in the case of brief quotations embodied in critical articles and reviews. For information, address HarperCollins Publishers, 195 Broadway, New York, NY 10007.

HarperCollins books may be purchased for educational, business, or sales promotional use. For information, please email the Special Markets Department at SPsales@harpercollins.com.

FIRST EDITION

Library of Congress Cataloging-in-Publication Data has been applied for.

ISBN 978-0-06-320509-3

23 24 25 26 27 LBC 5 4 3 2 1

For those who know better than to try
to get away with murder

O true apothecary! The drugs are quick!

Thus with a kiss I die.

—William Shakespeare,
The Tragedy of Romeo and Juliet, Act V, Scene III

MEG CHOI: I'm here with crime journalist Ryanna Raines, host of *The Raines Report*, which became an audio sensation last October when it shot to number one on the true-crime podcast charts. Her investigation into the De Carlo–Berne murder case has drawn a record number of listeners, not only in the U.S., but in Canada, the UK, and Australia, making it an international phenomenon.

Welcome to *CBS This Morning*, Ryanna.

RYANNA RAINES: Thanks for having me. You know, we're often categorized as a true-crime podcast. But we think of ourselves as an audio crime-investigation series. We're a core team of five, including my producing partner, a researcher, a sound engineer who does our mixing, and an editor. We conduct independent investigations and present them as serialized audio episodes.

MEG CHOI: *Independent* meaning?

RYANNA RAINES: We're not affiliated with a traditional news organization like the *New York Times* or NPR or CBS. We're partnered with the podcast network Amplify. We do our own investigating, recording, and production, and deliver the network finished episodes that they market and distribute.

MEG CHOI: Before we get into the case itself, tell us about your background as a journalist.

RYANNA RAINES: I've always had a passion for journalism. While my friends were watching *Buffy the Vampire Slayer*, I was watching Barbara

Walters specials. I edited my high school newspaper, majored in journalism in college, got my master's from Columbia. From there, I landed a job as an on-air reporter for WESA, Pittsburgh's local NPR station. I covered everything from city politics to human-interest stories, even the occasional crime story.

Then I met someone, fell in love, and altered course. My husband and I had two children, and when they started school, I started *The Raines Report*. We've put out six seasons and over a hundred episodes in the last four years.

MEG CHOI: And what do you think it was about the De Carlo–Berne case that caught such fire with listeners?

RYANNA RAINES: The crime isn't just murder, it's parricide. Which goes back to ancient Greek tragedy and the Bible—the murder of one's father, mother, or in this case, both. And at the center of it all are these charismatic young drama students.

MEG CHOI: In those first few weeks, the hashtag RealRomeo&Juliet got hundreds of millions of views. I tuned in after the fifth or sixth episode dropped and, like a lot of other people, found myself hooked by this couple's story as they were telling it.

RYANNA RAINES: Jordan and Victoria seemed like the iconic star-crossed lovers. Keep in mind, because our investigation was unfolding in real time, I was getting to know them just twelve to twenty-four hours ahead of everyone else.

I

EMBED

S6:E1

RYANNA RAINES: "It is better to risk saving a guilty person than to condemn an innocent one."

JESS MONAY: Amen, sister.

RYANNA RAINES: I'm Ryanna Raines. And welcome to *The Raines Report*, an audio crime-investigation series produced in association with Amplify. This is Episode 1 of a new season, a season so new and spontaneously put together, we don't have a title for it yet.

JESS MONAY: Yep, this is all on the fly. You're hearing it as it happens.

RYANNA RAINES: That's my producer, writing partner, cohost, and professional bestie, Jess Monay. We're recording ourselves in our downtown Pittsburgh studio because of a new message we found on the tip line of our *Raines Report* website.

JESS MONAY: Our tip line is a contact point for listeners who have information about crimes we're working on, as well as crimes we haven't reported on. We've received tips that have helped advance police investigations on a number of cold cases and unsolved murders.

RYANNA RAINES: What came in today is something different. Let's play the message.

JORDAN DE CARLO: Hi, Ryanna Raines. This is Jordan De Carlo. You might've heard about me in connection with a murder case in San Diego—my mother and father were stabbed to death inside our family home back in June. I'm with my girlfriend, Victoria Berne, and we'd like to speak to you as soon as possible. Please do not forward this message or tell anyone about it until we've had a chance to speak. Thank you. Love your podcast.

RYANNA RAINES: And he left a mobile number. Does the name Jordan De Carlo ring a bell?

JESS MONAY: No shame googling it. Okay, I do remember this.

NEWS ANCHOR: We begin tonight with the discovery by San Diego sheriff's deputies of a gruesome double homicide in the affluent North County community of Rancho Santa Fe.

NEIGHBOR: Hasn't been a murder or even an assault here in years. This is a peaceful, friendly place. The De Carlos were nice people, though they did keep mostly to themselves. We're hearing rumors about what happened up there, and it's shocking. So shocking.

SPOKESMAN: We've doubled the number of private security officers and added several more patrol vehicles. All residents should exercise caution, but please know that Rancho Santa Fe remains one of the safest places in the world.

JESS MONAY: Got attention from news outlets in Southern California. Nationally, not so much.

RYANNA RAINES: Anthony and Lauren De Carlo were days from celebrating their twenty-third wedding anniversary when their lives were abruptly and horribly cut short. The killings took place inside their Rancho Santa Fe estate in North San Diego County. It's an area where large luxury properties are nestled across hundreds of acres of rolling hills and green pastures. The homeowners' association describes the central commercial district as "a plush yet tranquil village." Residents here include tech billionaires, sports stars, music idols, hedge fund tycoons, and many of them own sprawling ranch homes at the end of long, gated driveways.

The De Carlos' only child, Jordan, a recent graduate of the University of California at Santa Barbara, went from being a figure of sympathy in his parents' deaths to a person of interest for homicide detectives to the main suspect in the crime. Also under suspicion is his eighteen-year-old girlfriend, Victoria Berne. Both Jordan and Victoria were theater majors at UCSB, where they met. As far as we know, police have yet to obtain arrest warrants for them. But according to local news sources, the couple continues to be the focus of the investigation.

JESS MONAY: Publicly, investigators are keeping their cards close to the vest. They seem to be building their case one brick at a time. It's been only four months since the murders, so not that long.

RYANNA RAINES: Prosecutors like it when police go beyond mere probable cause and hand them a slam dunk conviction.

JESS MONAY: I looked up the mobile number he left on the tip line, and it is registered to a Jordan De Carlo, currently a resident of Santa Barbara. Given this is an active homicide investigation, and it appears someone under suspicion is reaching out to a journalist who specializes in crime reporting, I'd say it's your professional duty to at least return his call.

RYANNA RAINES: Hello, is this Jordan De Carlo?

JORDAN DE CARLO: This must be Ryanna Raines. I recognize your voice.

RYANNA RAINES: It is, and I'm responding to the voice message you left on our tip line. First of all, may I have your permission to record this conversation?

JORDAN DE CARLO: Yes, you have my permission to record me. I'm here with my girlfriend, Victoria. We have you on speaker. Do you give your permission to be recorded?

VICTORIA BERNE: Hi, Ryanna. Yes, I give my permission to be recorded.

RYANNA RAINES: Where am I reaching the two of you?

JORDAN DE CARLO: In Los Cabos, Mexico.

RYANNA RAINES: Okay. Is the San Diego sheriff aware you're out of the country?

JORDAN DE CARLO: Yes. We didn't ask permission to leave, but we made it clear we aren't trying to escape or hide from anybody.

VICTORIA BERNE: It's been incredibly stressful. They—the police—were spying on us, following us around, harassing our friends. They got search warrants, tore through all our stuff, took away our phones and laptops. They interrogated us three times, individually and together. We had to get away just to get our lives back.

JORDAN DE CARLO: Victoria's been staying in touch with her mom and keeping her current. We've been taking a vacation. That's all.

RYANNA RAINES: Have you been in communication with detectives or the prosecutor?

JORDAN DE CARLO: Our attorneys have. They know we're coming back. We just haven't told them exactly when.

RYANNA RAINES: Do you know if law enforcement plans to arrest you when you return?

JORDAN DE CARLO: All we know is we're their only suspects and they say they have some kind of evidence.

VICTORIA BERNE: But they won't tell our attorneys what that evidence is. It's like they're playing mind games with us—blowing up our lives to see how far they can push us.

RYANNA RAINES: Who's representing you?

JORDAN DE CARLO: Natalie Bloom from San Francisco. She's a family friend.

RYANNA RAINES: I know of Natalie, haven't met her. Very accomplished defense attorney.

VICTORIA BERNE: My attorney is AJ Novick out of L.A.

RYANNA RAINES: I do know AJ. Excellent attorney. So, you both have high-end legal counsel. And what is it I can do for you?

JORDAN DE CARLO: We're being set up for this. And we want you to tell our side of the story.

VICTORIA BERNE: You're a truth-teller, someone who's not afraid to dig deep. Our attorneys will be advocating for us—that's their job. We want someone from the outside to see what's really happening here.

JORDAN DE CARLO: Someone who's not biased. Whose word is trusted.

RYANNA RAINES: And how do you see me telling your story?

JORDAN DE CARLO: When we land back in San Diego, we'd like you to meet us at the airport and stay with us until the moment we're arrested. We'll tell you everything there is to know about who we are and give you proof that we had nothing to do with this.

VICTORIA BERNE: We'll answer any question. We have nothing to hide. We need to get our voices out there before . . .

JORDAN DE CARLO: . . . before they separate us and put us in jail. By then it'll be too late.

RYANNA RAINES: Why not have me come out and interview you both? I could fly to California and we could talk it out over a couple of days.

JORDAN DE CARLO: We want you to get to know us, to hang out and share meals. To experience us when we're just being ourselves. If you were doing formal interviews, we'd be in presentation mode the whole time.

VICTORIA BERNE: We want to leave a record of the real us, so you and your listeners and the world will see we're not capable of committing such a hideous crime.

RYANNA RAINES: As a journalist, I need to keep some distance between me and my subjects. I'd want to be clear up front. I wouldn't be telling just your side of the story.

JORDAN DE CARLO: Great! Ask the tough questions. Talk to other people about us. We'll be totally transparent.

VICTORIA BERNE: We want to document the injustice here. Two people getting torn apart by the legal system and having their lives changed forever.

RYANNA RAINES: Have you mentioned this idea—of my getting involved—to your attorneys?

JORDAN DE CARLO: No, because they'll be against it. They don't want us talking to anybody.

RYANNA RAINES: There are good reasons for that. I'm sure you know the line in Miranda that says, "Anything you say can and will be used against you."

JORDAN DE CARLO: We're adults, we don't need our attorneys' permission to talk to you. Look, Victoria and I thought about posting TikToks to explain what's happening to us and why it's harassment. But how is that not going to look self-indulgent and desperate?

VICTORIA BERNE: People will want to hear our story *before* we're in custody. After that, our voices will be turned into lawyer and law enforcement speak.

JORDAN DE CARLO: A lot of true-crime podcasts are about people already found guilty and sent to prison. Like Adnan Syed in *Serial*. If you were reporting on that case, wouldn't you want the chance to interview him before he got arrested and went on trial?

RYANNA RAINES: You make a good point. After you fly back in, where will you be staying?

JORDAN DE CARLO: At my family home.

RYANNA RAINES: In Rancho Santa Fe? Where your parents . . .

JORDAN DE CARLO: It's my home. It's where I lived during my high school years and where I came back to during college. I know there's a plan to sell it, but not until next year.

VICTORIA BERNE: It's the normal place for Jordan to go. He still has clothes in the closet, all his stuff from growing up.

RYANNA RAINES: Okay, I hear that. Who else will be meeting you at the airport or at the house?

JORDAN DE CARLO: We're only telling you. We're going to the airport tomorrow with cash to buy tickets for the flight back. The only person we want to see when we get off the plane is you. Also, would you mind renting a car and driving us to the house? It's only a half hour away.

RYANNA RAINES: So there are people on this end I need to check in with, like my producer and our podcast partners. In order to jump into this, I'd have to drop everything else. I'm not saying I won't. But I need a minute to prepare.

JESS MONAY: Wow. There is a lot there. Initial thoughts?

RYANNA RAINES: Natalie Bloom is one of the highest profile criminal attorneys in Northern California. She's represented a lot of prominent clients in Bay Area courtrooms, including Elmer Gordon, the Silicon Valley CEO she got acquitted for the murder of his wife. Her counsel is not inexpensive. AJ is Beverly Hills stylish, loves his Rolexes and fast cars. He's also smart, highly experienced, and has a great trial record. These two have A-plus defense teams. That means something.

JESS MONAY: So you go meet Jordan and Victoria without alerting their attorneys or law enforcement. Are you breaking a law? Crossing an ethical line? We'll confirm there's no warrant out for their arrest. If not, I see no legal reason against meeting them at the airport and driving them to the De Carlo home. Ethically, since you explained your obligation to stay neutral, I also don't see a problem.

But why would they want to stay in the house where his parents were stabbed sixty-five times? I checked that number. Mr. and Mrs. De Carlo weren't just killed, they were massacred.

RYANNA RAINES: I can see why Jordan might still consider it his home. The murders happened months ago. Forensics must have been through it inside and out.

JESS MONAY: Another answer we need—has the lab finished processing the crime scene?

Now, how are *you* going to feel being inside that home with the two main suspects? Might it be, I don't know, a little unsettling to be in the space where one or both of these folks may have committed a savage act of violence?

RYANNA RAINES: Not my perfect comfort zone, but it could add a compelling tension to the interviews.

JESS MONAY: I don't disagree. I just want you as ready as possible, given we'd have to get you on a plane in the next twelve hours. What's the downside of not meeting them at the airport? What if we take another day or three to get up to speed on the case?

RYANNA RAINES: They could be arrested before I get to them. And that's a game-changer. When Jordan mentioned the Adnan Syed case, it hit home. There's an opportunity for exclusive access here, and we don't know how long that window will stay open.

VICTORIA BERNE: We've watched videos about you, we've listened to you, we've read about you. You are the person we'd most trust to play fair with us.

RYANNA RAINES: My reporting would be based on what I see and hear, not what you want the world to see and hear.

JORDAN DE CARLO: Ryanna Raines, you're one of the most conscientious journalists out there. You really care about people getting justice. That's why we want you to come be with us and tell it like you see it.

RYANNA RAINES: Okay then. You'll be hearing back from me.

S6:E2

UPLOADED THURSDAY, OCTOBER 13

RYANNA RAINES: I am married with two children. We live in an Allegheny County suburb twenty minutes outside of Pittsburgh. Our home is not far from the Mary Roberts Rinehart Nature Park, a lovely little three-acre green space named after the bestselling mystery author. She was in her prime during the early decades of the twentieth century. She's all but forgotten in the twenty-first, but was a badass in her day. In addition to becoming a famous writer, she was a registered nurse, a war correspondent, an avid outdoorswoman, and a breast cancer survivor. While launching her career, she continued in her homemaking roles, taking care of her physician husband and their three rambunctious sons. When things quieted down in the evenings, she sat at the kitchen table and composed her popular novels and hit Broadway plays. She specialized in crime fiction, often writing about cases involving murder.

Mary Roberts Rinehart is one of my working mom inspirations.

I'm Ryanna Raines. And welcome to *The Raines Report*, an audio crime-investigation series produced in association with Amplify. This is Episode 2 of our new season, which came upon us so suddenly, we don't even have a title yet.

JESS MONAY: We're working on it. Said the podcast producer.

RYANNA RAINES: I do a fair amount of my work from home, which is nice, but travel is inevitable. When I'm on a case, I can be gone for weeks at a time. My husband also works from home, so when I'm gone, he has to cover the parenting duties on his own. Anytime I sense a business trip in my future, first thing I do is talk it over with him.

When I get home in the late afternoon, I find him at the kitchen table, on his phone, working out his fantasy football picks. Our daughter and son are upstairs doing their homework. I let him know I have something to discuss. He sets the phone down and gives me his attention.

"Had a call today with Jordan De Carlo and Victoria Berne," I say. "They're suspects in—"

My husband interjects: "In the murder of his parents. I've read about it. Have they been arrested?"

My husband constantly surprises me by how up he is on current crime cases. "No," I tell him. "Not yet. Long story short, they're flying from Mexico to San Diego tomorrow and want me to do a podcast about their case. Interview them *before* they're arrested."

My husband says, "Have you checked out the murders they're suspected of? Hyper-violent stabbing, massive overkill. A bloody, gory mess."

"Yes," I say. "*Butchered* was a word used a lot in the reporting."

He says, "So you'd be embedding with them?"

I hadn't thought of that word, but it's the right one. Like a reporter in a war zone, I'd be embedding myself with troops on the front lines of a murder case. To my husband I say, "I would be interviewing them and observing them during their last days of freedom."

"What if it's weeks or longer before they get arrested?"

"Excellent question. I'd be playing it mostly by ear, but if nothing's happened after a week or ten days, I can come back and monitor the situation from here."

"Is it me," he says, "or is getting stabbed with a sharp steel blade two dozen times an even worse thing to imagine than getting shot or beaten to death?"

"Any of those would be horrible, but yeah, getting stabbed like that would be a seriously unpleasant way to go. I'll have to fly out early tomorrow morning to meet them. Your thoughts?"

"About you being alone with those two? It doesn't thrill me."

"So you think they're guilty?"

"I'd say it's probably fifty-fifty."

"Well, they want me to be the one to tell the story of their innocence, so killing me would not be a very smart thing to do."

"Unless you find reason to believe they're lying to you, and they actually did it."

My husband is expressing concern for my safety, and I keep that in mind as we go back and forth. Bringing things to a resolution, he says, "I see how this could be a big story. And if you work it out with your team and your partners, I guess you shouldn't turn it down."

I say, "The first team is you, me, and the kids. I always want you on the field with me, calling the plays together."

"Now you're trying to win me over with football metaphors. Go meet them, see what they have to say, apply your considerable powers of observation. I know you'll take extra care."

He stands up to embrace me. I embrace him back. It feels good.

Next, I need to get on the phone with Jess and our executive from the podcast network, Carmen Faro. She is our liaison at Amplify, which distributes and promotes the podcast, leads social media initiatives, manages subscription services, and handles advertiser relations. I go into our home office where I have my recording closet, and which my husband and I share, and dial Jess. She connects our exec to the call.

JESS MONAY: Carmen, we see this as a way to put out episodes that are closer to real time. Ryanna reports from the field with two high-profile murder suspects. I'll be in the studio with our team as she sends updates. We'll be working around the clock, taking in assets, cutting and mixing them, and getting you finished episodes.

CARMEN FARO: The episodes wouldn't be regularly scheduled? We'd get them out to the platforms as they come in and adjust our promos accordingly?

RYANNA RAINES: Right. We can't really know how this story is going to play out, but we've been talking about finding an opportunity to do the nearest thing to live podcasts. Episodes that have a sense of immediacy, in sync with the day's headlines.

CARMEN FARO: Or *making* the day's headlines.

JESS MONAY: It's tricky because we won't be live, but only eight to ten hours behind the breaking news cycle.

RYANNA RAINES: And therein lies one of the downsides. If a knock comes at the door and Jordan and Victoria are taken into custody, a hundred outlets will break that news before we can.

JESS MONAY: But we'll have positioned ourselves as the *inside source* for De Carlo/Berne news, so those breaking news clips will become like teasers for our next drop. Even if that drop comes eight hours after the news first breaks, it'll still feel fresh because of our direct access.

CARMEN FARO: Sounds pretty exciting, guys. Let me run it by Gary.

JESS MONAY: She's off the line. "Let me run it by Gary," aka "Let me run it by the man in charge."

RYANNA RAINES: We love you, Carmen and Gary. Sometimes we bend toward irony here at *The Raines Report*. Now I've got to break it to my kids that Mom has to go away on a business trip.

JESS MONAY: Tell them Auntie Jess sends her love.

RYANNA RAINES: Our daughter and son are two years apart. I bring them into the living room and have them tell me about their days. My husband offers to make dinner. We follow him to the kitchen. The kids sit up on barstools at the counter. As their dad and I collaborate on making the family meal, I explain that my work is taking me to California. We talk a little about California. We do not talk about my work.

> Dispatcher: 911. What is your emergency?
>
> Caller: They're dead! Both dead! Help! I need help!
>
> Dispatcher: Okay, please try to stay calm. What's your name?
>
> Caller: My name is Dolores! Send police! Oh my god!
>
> Dispatcher: Dolores, are you calling from a house? Are you inside with the bodies?
>
> Caller: It's 130 Colina Conchita! I can't stay in here! The smell! The blood!

RYANNA RAINES: Jess sends me a batch of articles and news stories about the De Carlo murders, my reading and listening homework for the flight out to San Diego. This is the first time I've heard the De Carlo 911 recording. No matter how many 911 calls I listen to, I hope never to get desensitized to the raw anguish expressed in so many of them.

Mystery Surrounds Stabbings was the dominant theme of early media reports. The medical examiner determined that the victims had been dead more than sixty hours before they were discovered. So that's pretty eerie. My mind goes to the interior of the home and the awful silence and stillness as the blood from two human beings dries ever so slowly on the walls and floors. Two inanimate bodies are just lying there, horribly violated by knife wounds, gradually passing through the stages of decomposition.

For hour . . . after hour . . . after hour.

During that time, a landscaping crew tended the De Carlo grounds. Mail and packages were delivered. Phones rang, unanswered. Texts pinged, unopened.

It was the housekeeper who found them. She had the code to the front gate and a key to the front door. Within two minutes of entering the home, she was dialing emergency services.

There are no direct flights between Pittsburgh and San Diego, so I have to make a connection in Phoenix. Looking out my window, all I see is blue sky. The flight attendant announces that temperatures on the coast are in the mid-seventies. Well, at least the weather will be nice. Beyond that, I have no idea what the day will bring. As the plane begins its descent into San Diego, I feel my adrenaline rise. I reach under the seat and lift up my equipment case. My ever-dependable Sony recorder with its searchable sixteen gigs of memory, check. RØDE microphone with windscreen attachment, check. One pair of Sennheiser noise-canceling headphones for playback, check. Charging cords, check. This Sony recorder is my second brain. My first brain asks the questions, my second brain records the answers.

Jordan has texted me their arrival info and I'm getting in ninety minutes ahead of them. Enough time to go rent a car, park it in short-term parking, and head on foot to meet them as they emerge from the terminal. I check the flight board and see their plane has landed. They'll be required to go back through TSA and might have been placed on a watch list, which could delay their exit. I glance around to see if anyone waiting to greet arriving passengers looks like a family member or a reporter tipped off that the couple was inbound. Seems like just the regular group of hired drivers holding up name signs.

I admit, I feel a fluttering in my stomach. Why? Am I fully prioritizing my safety? These are a couple of college students, not infamous outlaws or convicted killers. Both had been living lives insulated from the real world, attending an idyllic seaside university, immersed in theater studies. By all accounts, they are smart, passionate creatives with a talent for drama. Okay, I see how that cuts both ways—pardon the metaphor.

I have given them a description of me: five-four, medium-brown neck-length hair, light brown eyes. I'll have my sunglasses up on top of my head. When I first catch a glimpse of the pair approaching the revolving doors, I know instantly it's them. They walk hip to hip, arms slung around each other, weighed down by backpacks. Do I see an aura of doomed romance about them, of lovers condemned to an inescapable fate? Or am I projecting that, given all I've crammed into my mind over the last twelve hours? They come out the doors one at a time, rejoin arms, and march toward me with smiles that convey a dark but vibrant kind of . . . the word that comes to my mind is *glamour*.

"Hello," calls out the twenty-two-year-old directing and playwriting graduate. "I'm Jordan, nice to meet you." He's a natural blond and tall, deeply tanned by the tropical sun. He strikes me as the type who gets mobbed at airports by fangirls.

"Yes," says his eighteen-year-old companion and BFA student. "I'm Victoria, thank you so much for meeting us here." She's black-haired, with fairer skin, delicately boned but wide shouldered. She gives off a mix of fragility and resilience. And has a way of staring so deeply into my eyes it's borderline intimidating.

Before I can return the greeting, Jordan looks sharply at a stranger who is staring at us and reaching for his phone. Jordan immediately shields Victoria from this person's line of sight and says, "Let's keep moving."

As we make it out to the sidewalk, I say, "Nice to meet both of you, too. My car's over in Lot B, not too far." I lower my sunglasses and walk a step ahead, leading our undercover procession of three. As we go, I notice people glancing at the beautiful bohemian couple behind me with looks that say *Aren't they somebody?* That's the moment it hits me. Season 6 of *The Raines Report* will be different from any case I've ever reported on.

S6:E3

RYANNA RAINES: Do I have each of your permissions to record our conversation?

JORDAN DE CARLO: You have mine.

VICTORIA BERNE: Mine too.

JORDAN DE CARLO: We'll let you know if we want to go off the record.

RYANNA RAINES: I'm Ryanna Raines. And welcome to *The Raines Report*, an audio crime-investigation series produced in association with Amplify. We still don't have a title for the season, but this is Episode 3, and we're calling it "The House at the Top of the Driveway."

This is being recorded during my drive with Jordan De Carlo and Victoria Berne as we travel from the San Diego International Airport to Jordan's family home in Rancho Santa Fe. I'm not too familiar with Southern California—last time I was here was five years ago. My impressions of my surroundings are ones of a lifelong Pennsylvanian.

We've gotten on the main north-south highway—excuse me, *freeway*—Interstate 5, which spans 800 miles from the border of Mexico all the way up to the border of Oregon. Contrast that with my home state's longest road, the 360-mile Pennsylvania Turnpike, which, as a "way" that's far from free, will cost you over a hundred bucks in tolls between Ohio and New Jersey. We are moving at 20 to 30 miles an hour in what I'm told is moderate traffic. I'm at the wheel of a rented Ford Explorer and my backseat passengers are the suspects in a double murder. Right now we're headed to the scene of the crime.

So for the time being we'll keep it informal, recording on the go. First of all, how does it feel to return to the U.S. after almost a month in Mexico?

JORDAN DE CARLO: I could have stayed a lot longer. But we had to come back to deal with this thing.

VICTORIA BERNE: Our plan was to slip in under the radar. To get us a few more hours of peace before the heat gets turned back on.

RYANNA RAINES: You think the De Carlo home in Rancho Santa Fe will be an *under-the-radar* place to stay?

JORDAN DE CARLO: There's a gate you can't get past without a code. Up a long curving driveway to the house that isn't visible from the street. It's the most private place we could be.

RYANNA RAINES: How long had your mom and dad lived there?

JORDAN DE CARLO: Almost seven years. We moved down the summer I was going into my junior year at Torrey Pines High.

RYANNA RAINES: Where did your family live before that?

JORDAN DE CARLO: Atherton in Northern California. From one over-priced, overprivileged zip code to another.

RYANNA RAINES: And where does your family live, Victoria?

VICTORIA BERNE: My mom lives in a suburb south of Seattle called Issaquah. That's where I grew up. We're the least expensive house on our block—she got it in the divorce from my dad.

JORDAN DE CARLO: Get off at Via de la Valle. Turn right. You'll be on this for about six miles.

RYANNA RAINES: Jordan, what was it like living in Rancho Santa Fe?

JORDAN DE CARLO: Like being inside an American fantasyland. It's a rustic paradise for the one-percenters. There's zero social or economic diversity. You're not even allowed to walk on the sidewalks if you're not a resident. I'm not kidding.

RYANNA RAINES: We are passing a sign that says WELCOME TO RANCHO SANTA FE. I am seeing lush grassy hills and driving along gently winding two-lane roads. Hardly any street traffic here.

VICTORIA BERNE: First thing I noticed was these tall trees lining the roads. The air is fragrant with eucalyptus.

RYANNA RAINES: The homes are all surrounded by greenery that looks immaculately maintained, in compliance with the rules of a community covenant. That's what they call it here, a *covenant*.
   I thought California was in a drought.

JORDAN DE CARLO: They'll pay whatever it costs to keep their lawns green and their gardens lush. Left at the next street.

RYANNA RAINES: I am turning onto a no-outlet road and going uphill. We pull into a driveway with a ranch-style iron gate across it. No house is visible from here. The driveway curves up out of sight beyond terraces filled with vegetation. Jordan gets out of the car and goes to the call box to enter the code. The gate electronically swings open. Jordan gets back in.

JORDAN DE CARLO: Just follow the driveway.

RYANNA RAINES: And up we go, winding our way past blooming bushes and leafy trees.

JORDAN DE CARLO: It's two acres with an acre and a half of gardens and orchards. The crews come three times a week. The monthly landscaping bill is more than most people's mortgages.

RYANNA RAINES: We've reached the top of the driveway to find a Mediterranean-style mansion.

VICTORIA BERNE: I think the word they use is *estate*.

RYANNA RAINES: Mediterranean-style *estate*. Thank you.

I park the Explorer between a marble fountain and a stone archway. Jordan gets out and goes to a tall double door made of carved wood and custom stained glass. I try not to think about what happened on the other side of those doors on that night back in June.

JORDAN DE CARLO: All right, that sucks. They changed the locks.

VICTORIA BERNE: They locked you out of your own house?

JORDAN DE CARLO: Let's go around the side. I might be able to find another way in.

RYANNA RAINES: Jordan and Victoria go together around one end of the building and leave my sight. I start taking photos of the house exteriors. The facade is made of natural stone tiles with arched windows across two levels. We checked the comps and when the house—estate—comes on the market, the price should be north of five million. Even after becoming a "murder house."

Oh, now I hear another car coming up the driveway. Whoops, looks like a police car. No, it's a private security vehicle and it is pulling up behind my Explorer. A single officer, wearing a uniform and carrying a holstered firearm, gets out of the driver's seat and approaches me. I face him, smiling.

Hello! Hi!

RSF SECURITY GUARD: Excuse me, this is private property. Are you authorized to be here?

RYANNA RAINES: My name is Ryanna Raines, I'm a journalist. I'm here with Jordan De Carlo, whose parents live—*lived at* this house.

RSF SECURITY GUARD: Where is Mr. De Carlo?

RYANNA RAINES: He went around to look for another way inside. His front door key didn't work.

RSF SECURITY GUARD: Does Mr. De Carlo have authorization to be on the property?

RYANNA RAINES: You'll have to ask him.

The security guard is calling someone on his cell phone. I wonder if I should toot my car horn to alert Jordan. He'll need to deal with this situation. Before I can toot, Jordan and Victoria come around the opposite side of the house, having circled the building.

A neighborhood security officer is asking if we have authorization to be here.

Jordan goes to talk to the security officer. Victoria comes over next to me.

VICTORIA BERNE: It's all locked up and the hide-a-keys are gone. We thought about breaking a window, but that would set off the alarm. Jordan knows the code, but they probably changed it.

RYANNA RAINES: I think not breaking a window was wise. You've been here before?

VICTORIA BERNE: Jordan and I came down for a night the weekend before—you know. For me, it was just that once. If you think it's nice out here, you should see the backyard and the pool. It was the first time I've been up close to this kind of wealth.

RYANNA RAINES: How did it make you feel?

VICTORIA BERNE: It worked for his parents. Personally I don't think I'd ever be comfortable living in a home like this.

RYANNA RAINES: Victoria and I head over to where Jordan is speaking to the security officer.

JORDAN DE CARLO: Until it gets sold, this is still my home.

RSF SECURITY GUARD: Sir, my commander called the real estate agent involved with the property. She's coming right over.

JORDAN DE CARLO: Do you have a key to get in?

RSF SECURITY GUARD: No, sir. But Ms. Winkler will.

RYANNA RAINES: The four of us stand there awkwardly. Then Jordan takes Victoria aside and embraces her. He speaks into her ear in a voice that neither the security guard nor I can hear. Within ten minutes a third car comes up the driveway, this one a white Range Rover. A well-dressed, nicely accessorized blond woman in her mid-forties gets out and goes to Jordan.

SHERI WINKLER: Hi, Jordan, I'm Sheri Winkler. I've been contracted to sell the home under the supervision of the estate attorney, Jacob Latimer.

JORDAN DE CARLO: I'm aware it's going to be sold. But my understanding is it won't go on the market until next year. While my family still owns it, I intend to stay here with my girlfriend.

SHERI WINKLER: I'm not sure that will be possible.

JORDAN DE CARLO: What do you mean? This is my family home. I still have a bedroom here with all my stuff in it.

SHERI WINKLER: I'm sure we can arrange getting your stuff to you. But my instructions are not to let anyone inside the house at this time. Sorry, that's just the way it is.

JORDAN DE CARLO: I'm calling Aunt Frances.

RYANNA RAINES: Showing his annoyance, Jordan steps away, taps a number, and puts the phone to his ear. Victoria looks after him with sympathetic eyes. I ask her:

Aunt Frances?

VICTORIA BERNE: His dad's sister. Jordan and she are very close. I've never met her.

RYANNA RAINES: And you and Jordan have been together how long?

VICTORIA BERNE: Since March of this year. It feels like we've known each other our whole lives.

RYANNA RAINES: What do you mean by that?

VICTORIA BERNE: I'm not some starry-eyed teenager. I may be young in age, but I've lived long enough to know what true love feels like.

RYANNA RAINES: Her reply seems a bit defensive. I nod, silent for the time being. It's better not to be in a rush. Jordan finishes his call and comes back to us.

JORDAN DE CARLO: She's telling me not to fight it, it's legally compli- cated. So getting inside right now isn't happening. Not a problem, we'll continue on to the Santa Barbara house. That okay with you, Ryanna?

RYANNA RAINES: Help me with my geography. How far is Santa Barbara?

JORDAN DE CARLO: About two hundred miles north of here. Three-to- four-hour drive depending on traffic. Otherwise I guess we'll Uber it.

RYANNA RAINES: Let me make a quick call.

JESS MONAY: I've been staring at my phone, willing it to ring. How's it going there?

RYANNA RAINES: Pickup fine, drive to Rancho Santa Fe fine. We're at the De Carlo house—I mean *estate*. The De Carlos' attorney had the locks changed, Jordan can't get in. A private security officer drove up and so did the real estate agent. Jordan is being denied entry. So he's asked me to drive him and Victoria up to his house in Santa Barbara. Checking in with my producer before I agree to that.

JESS MONAY: Google-mapping it. Oh, that's kind of far.

RYANNA RAINES: If I decline, they'll call an Uber. I'd just be following them up there in my car. That's where Jordan left his car parked.

JESS MONAY: Right, I get it. You're driving them to where their vehicle is and you're going there anyway to record them at their request. What does your gut tell you?

RYANNA RAINES: No sense of danger, if that's what you're asking. I can use the drive time to establish a rapport with them.

JESS MONAY: I can always trust you to read a room. Text me a street address, I'll book you into the nearest hotel.

RYANNA RAINES: I probably won't get to the hotel until late, past midnight your time.

JESS MONAY: Doesn't matter what time it is here, text me every hour so I know you're okay. And call me when you're in your room.

RYANNA RAINES: Will do. Thanks, Jess.

Jordan is approaching me, his eyebrows arching with concern.

JORDAN DE CARLO: The security guard said he has to call in a report to the sheriff's department. So if you're driving us, we should get going.

RYANNA RAINES: I'm driving you, so let's get going.

We take a different route back to the I-5 and get on northbound toward Los Angeles. I notice my passengers have gone quiet. In my rearview mirror, I see them leaning against each other, lost in their own thoughts.

How are you guys doing back there?

VICTORIA BERNE: I feel really bad that Jordan got locked out of his family home.

JORDAN DE CARLO: Truth is, it's not my home. Never was. Anthony and Lauren were the owners.

VICTORIA BERNE: But that's where you have your memories with your mom and dad. To completely shut you out is cruel.

JORDAN DE CARLO: It's a cruel world and only getting crueler.

RYANNA RAINES: The house in Santa Barbara is where you were living when you two met?

JORDAN DE CARLO: Yes. A day I'll never forget. Flashback to your audition for Abbie Putnam in *Desire Under the Elms*. Life-changing event!

VICTORIA BERNE: For two people.

JORDAN DE CARLO: I never believed in the idea of a muse until I met you. And now I have no vision for a life without you.

RYANNA RAINES: In the rearview, I see them gripping each other's hands. Someone's vibrating.

VICTORIA BERNE: It's my mom.

JORDAN DE CARLO: Answer it. You don't want her to worry.

VICTORIA BERNE: Hi, Mom. Yes, we just got back. What? Where? She's saying she read we were back from Mexico in her news feed.

JORDAN DE CARLO: There goes my phone. My attorney, what a surprise. Hello, Natalie. It's true. We're headed up to my house in Santa Barbara. Yes, we plan on staying there—for now.

RYANNA RAINES: My phone starts ringing. It's Jess. I'm driving and would have to put her on speaker, but with two conversations going on in the back seat, I decide to call her later. Then I hear Jordan tell his attorney they're being driven to his house by Ryanna Raines, "the podcast host." I can hear Natalie Bloom shout on the other end, "Ryanna Raines!"

Uh-oh, cover blown.

VICTORIA BERNE: Let's turn off our phones for the rest of the trip.

JORDAN DE CARLO: I love that idea. Off and out of sight.

RYANNA RAINES: What did Natalie say when you told her I was driving you?

JORDAN DE CARLO: "Oh my god, you're with a reporter? Do not talk to her until you talk to me first! You have no idea what you're getting into!"

Chill, Natalie. We know what we're getting into.

RYANNA RAINES: On my phone comes a text from AJ Novick, Victoria's attorney. I interviewed him during our Season 2 investigation and we got along well. I felt a mutual respect between us. On this occasion, his message to me is five words punctuated by periods:

Ryanna. What. Are. You. Doing—question mark.

S6:E4

RYANNA RAINES: Under normal circumstances, an inquiring text sent to me by a prominent criminal defense attorney involved in a major murder case would get my immediate attention. But these aren't normal circumstances. So AJ Novick will have to wait until I have more space to engage with him.

In the meantime, I am in the driver's seat headed northwest, crossing through the San Fernando Valley and all the way out to the Pacific coast. It's getting into the late afternoon as my rented Explorer passes small sunshiny beach communities with ear-pleasing names like Rincon, Carpinteria, Summerland, and Montecito.

I should probably mention here that my two passengers, both sitting behind me in the back seat, are the prime suspects in a particularly gruesome murder case. They've just come back into the country from a month-long getaway in Mexico.

The term *getaway* may be misleading here. A better term might be *time-out*. The suspects felt the need to step away from the intense scrutiny on them by San Diego homicide detectives. But today they have returned to California. And I am embedding with them.

I'm Ryanna Raines. And welcome to *The Raines Report*, an audio crime-investigation series produced in association with Amplify. This is Season 6 and we're calling this episode "Two Criminal Suspects."

JORDAN DE CARLO: This part of the drive always relaxes me. Nothing but ocean on one side and sea cliffs on the other.

VICTORIA BERNE: It'll be a beautiful sunset. Despite everything, I'm feeling peaceful right now.

RYANNA RAINES: I look in the rearview mirror and see my passengers snuggling each other. I'm a little surprised to feel a momentary ache in my heart for these two.

JORDAN DE CARLO: There's zero food at the house. Mind if we stop at a market to get some essentials?

RYANNA RAINES: I haven't eaten all day, sounds like a plan.

VICTORIA BERNE: We're both vegans. We'll eat nothing consciously where the harming of animals was involved.

RYANNA RAINES: Well, I promise not to eat any steaks in front of you. That's a joke.

We have gotten off the freeway just west of Santa Barbara and are pulling into the parking lot of a Sprouts Farmers Market not far from Jordan's house.

JORDAN DE CARLO: This is where we buy groceries. Their produce is locally sourced—shortest distance between farm and table.

RYANNA RAINES: You guys go ahead. I'll tag behind and grab a few snacks for myself.

I watch the two of them enter the store holding hands. Like any normal college couple—yet their circumstances are so far from normal.

Following them inside, I get a sudden craving for a juicy medium-rare Standard Deluxe from Burgatory with bacon and avocado. Avocados are a vegetable, right?

As I watch Jordan and Victoria move to the checkout line, I notice another shopper, a young man with spiky hair and neck tattoos—let's call him Spike—recognize and approach them. It's too noisy and I can't get close enough for clear audio, so I'll describe what happens.

Spike acts surprised to encounter the couple and says in a not-quiet voice, "What are you guys doing back here? I heard you were headed for South America."

Jordan and Victoria respond politely in quiet voices. Spike doesn't lower his voice and asks if they're worried about going to jail. This attracts the attention of other shoppers in line. Jordan shrugs and tries to wave Spike off, but the young man persists. "Hey, listen," he says, "I think you guys are innocent. But the question is, if you didn't do it, who did?"

To me, it looks like Spike is being a jerk on purpose. Jordan turns away from him, but Victoria gets in his face and tells him to mind his own business, or words to that effect. This clash is now causing a bit of a scene. I see one shopper take out her phone to record the incident. Victoria turns to the woman, imploring her to *please* not invade their privacy. To which Spike says in his not-quiet voice, "Oh, your privacy days are over."

Victoria turns to him and says, "Why are you being such a dick?" She looks like she's ready to escalate when Jordan puts his hand on her shoulder and says something in her ear. He turns back to the clerk, pays cash, takes the grocery bags in one hand, grabs Victoria's hand with his other, and leads her out the exit. I hang back to hear Spike tell the shoppers around him some details of the De Carlo murders, including the misinformation that the victims were stabbed over a hundred and fifty times. I feel an impulse to correct him, but think better of it.

JORDAN DE CARLO: We can't control what people say, only how we react to it. Turn right up here. It's at the end of the block.

VICTORIA BERNE: He's got a giant chip on his shoulder because he didn't make it into the BFA program. He's jealous of us.

RYANNA RAINES: We're in a residential neighborhood a couple of miles north of the UCSB campus, driving up to the two-bedroom house Jordan has been renting since the start of his senior year. It's got white stucco walls, a low-pitched tile roof, and fits right in with the other homes on the block.

VICTORIA BERNE: Uh-oh.

JORDAN DE CARLO: Oh, no.

RYANNA RAINES: They are reacting to the presence of what looks like a news van and two video cameras on tripods positioned on the sidewalk in front of Jordan's house.

JORDAN DE CARLO: Pull into the driveway. I'll hop out and open the garage.

RYANNA RAINES: Victoria sinks down in the back seat as I pull past the van and cameras and turn into the driveway. Jordan gets out and goes in the front door of the house. In the rearview, I see a reporter calling out questions to him. From the inside, Jordan opens the garage door. I drive in, parking next to a black Jeep Wrangler. Jordan closes the garage door. Victoria and I get out of the car and follow Jordan through an inner door leading to the kitchen. Jordan goes through the house, turning on lights and making sure the front window shades are down. I take in the theatrical and modern design posters on the walls and the stacks of art books and play scripts on counters and tables.

VICTORIA BERNE: So you'll stay for dinner? We're making tofu vegetable curry.

RYANNA RAINES: Sure, that'd be nice. I got a message from your attorney that I should return. I don't want him to think I'm ducking him.

Victoria points me down the hall to a bedroom that's been converted into a home office. I step inside and gently shut the door. I take out my phone, go to my AJ Novick contact, and tap it.

Hi, AJ. It's been a while. Before we start, do I have your permission to record this call?

AJ responds "Absolutely not." Which I more or less expected. So I'll describe our exchange in my own words. Victoria's attorney starts out by asking a variation of his earlier text:

What's going on?

"I'm doing my job," I say, trying not to sound like a smartass. AJ has a reason to be surprised and, yes, even unhappy with this turn of events. I go into the brief history here, stretching back less than forty-eight hours, when we found Jordan's message on our tip line. I explain that I received permission to record my initial conversation with Jordan and Victoria and have been recording our interactions since picking them up at the San Diego airport earlier that day. I also say that we plan to start dropping new episodes as soon as tomorrow, creating a near real-time chronicle of my reporting. He asks why I didn't call him before going down this road. I'm tempted to say, "Because I don't need your permission," but instead I inform him that I did caution his client about making statements that could be used against her in court. "I didn't exactly Mirandize them. I did let both know there may be unforeseen consequences to speaking on the record without their attorneys present. But that's no reason for me not to interview them, when they're the ones offering to tell me their story."

AJ softens a bit and asks if I have a take on the story I want to tell. I say I'm in uncharted waters, having jumped in and learning as I go. "It's an experiment, embedding with suspects in a murder case prior to arrest and letting them tell their side." AJ asks if I've thought through the risks of real-time reporting in a high-stakes case like this. That without deeper reporting and the benefits of time and hindsight, I could get things wrong. And by then the podcasts will have been downloaded by all those people with my mistakes in plain sight, immortalized for the rest of time. Even on the phone, AJ speaks with the flair of a big-time trial attorney.

Then I ask if he knows what kind of evidence the prosecutors have against his client. He responds that the D.A.'s office has not provided specifics but has assured both him and his colleague Natalie Bloom that they have sufficient probable cause to obtain arrest warrants.

I hear raised voices from the other end of the house. I tell AJ I don't want to be in an adversarial position with him. I hear him take a breath and say, "Let's stay in touch." We end the call on a more or less cordial note, and I head back to the living room.

VICTORIA BERNE: They are violating our right to privacy!

RYANNA RAINES: I find an agitated Jordan and Victoria at a window facing the street. I look out and see a Santa Barbara county sheriff's vehicle parked directly opposite the house. I can make out two officers in the front seat—just sitting there.

JORDAN DE CARLO: I'm going out and asking them what they're doing here. That's within my rights.

VICTORIA BERNE: What if Ryanna goes out and asks instead? As a neutral person. A journalist.

RYANNA RAINES: Again, I ask myself about crossing boundaries. I mean, given that law enforcement is playing a major role in this story, going out to ask questions probably fits my job description.

So I say okay, step out the front door, and immediately draw attention from the reporters. There are two now calling out questions to me, but I merely smile and walk past them toward the sheriff's SUV. The officers inside watch me approach.

SB SHERIFF'S DEPUTY: Can we help you?

RYANNA RAINES: I'm curious why you're parked here.

SB SHERIFF'S DEPUTY: We're parked here because we're parked here.

RYANNA RAINES: Do you intend to serve any warrants at this address?

SB SHERIFF'S DEPUTY: Who wants to know?

RYANNA RAINES: Sorry, I should've introduced myself when I walked up. My name's Ryanna Raines, I'm a journalist and I'm investigating the De Carlo murders in Rancho Santa Fe. Has your office been in contact with the San Diego sheriff's department?

SB SHERIFF'S DEPUTY: We're in contact with county sheriffs all over the state.

RYANNA RAINES: Back to my prior question. Do you intend to serve any warrants at this address?

SB SHERIFF'S DEPUTY: For the moment we are monitoring the activities of two criminal suspects. A call from our commander could change that assignment at any time.

RYANNA RAINES: No warrants, only monitoring. Helpful to know, thank you.

I turn away and head back to the house. The reporters stop calling out and are tapping out notes on their phones. Once inside, I report my exchange with the officer to Jordan and Victoria.

JORDAN DE CARLO: They want us to know they're watching.

VICTORIA BERNE: And if we try to go anywhere, they'll be all over us.

JORDAN DE CARLO: The cat-and-mouse of it all is making me hungry.

RYANNA RAINES: I sit at the kitchen counter and watch Jordan wrap a block of tofu in a cloth, place it on a dish, and set a heavy pan on top of it. I ask what he's doing, and he shares that Victoria taught him how to press the moisture out of tofu before cooking with it. As I watch, I think about how it took me and my husband years to get in cooking sync with each other. These two seem to have mastered it in less than eight months.

Victoria washes the eggplant, zucchini, and green beans, peels the onion, then sets the vegetables on the cutting board and starts chopping. I try not to fixate on the knife blade and her dexterity with it.

VICTORIA BERNE: We like a glass of wine with dinner. Would you like one, too?

RYANNA RAINES: Thank you, no.

JORDAN DE CARLO: Not a drinker?

RYANNA RAINES: Not on the job.

We sit at the table and I'm served my first ever tofu and vegetable curry over brown rice. Jordan and Victoria tear off small pieces of flatbread and eat with their fingers, which I'm told is authentic to India. I ask for a fork.

This is good. Very good.

JORDAN DE CARLO: We're trying to eat only really healthy food right now. Because who knows what kind of slop they serve in jail.

RYANNA RAINES: And here Jordan falters, showing a surge of emotion. It's the first significant sign of how the stress of their predicament is impacting these two. Victoria gets out of her chair, comes behind Jordan, and embraces him supportively.

VICTORIA BERNE: It's okay, Jordan. It's okay, baby.

JORDAN DE CARLO: You guys keep eating. I'll be right back.

RYANNA RAINES: He gets up and heads toward the back bedrooms. Now it's just Victoria and me at the table.

VICTORIA BERNE: We promised each other we'd put on our bravest faces. But it's not easy.

RYANNA RAINES: You seem to be holding up okay. Is that the acting training?

VICTORIA BERNE: We're not acting, though.

RYANNA RAINES: I meant your ability to control your emotions.

VICTORIA BERNE: There's controlling and there's channeling. When I start feeling panic about what may lie ahead, I redirect those impulses into living my present moment. My present moment is having a meal with my boyfriend and a famous investigative journalist and enjoying their company.

RYANNA RAINES: I can appreciate all that except the "famous" part. But thank you.

Jordan returns to the table after a reset and we continue the pleasant, though at moments strained, dinner chat. It's easy to see that these two are very bright. They're engaged in cultural and social issues and seem politically responsible. As the plates are cleared, I get a text from Jess. I announce I have to go check in at my hotel. I'll be back in the morning. If anything happens during the night, I'll have my phone on and will respond ASAP. As we say our good nights, Jordan and Victoria tell me how much they appreciate what I'm doing for them. I reply that it's not for them. "It's for the audience to listen to and make up their own minds." We part smiling.

The hotel Jess booked me into is 4.3 miles from Jordan's house, an eight-minute drive with stops and traffic lights. Check-in is accomplished and I'm in my room by 9:30 Pacific Time, half past midnight on the East Coast.

JESS MONAY: I'm still at the studio with Alec and Hailey. Before we do a final mix, we want you to record a few more lines of commentary.

RYANNA RAINES: I record these using my RØDE microphone and send the audio file directly to the editing program we use in our Pittsburgh studio. I do each line three times with slight variations, trusting Jess and the team to pick the best fit. I'm sure I'll be recording commentary every night when I get back to my room.

JESS MONAY: While they're mixing in the new lines, catch me up.

RYANNA RAINES: I tell her about the encounter with the Santa Barbara sheriff's deputies and my perfectly domestic, vegan dinner experience with our murder suspects. Then Jess loads up the Episode 1 final, and I listen to it straight through on my headphones.

Technically it's great, Jess. But here's a quick discussion I need to have with you, reporter to producer. I had a conversation with AJ Novick, who's representing Victoria. We knew the attorneys would not be happy about the fact that their clients are doing interviews for a podcast, and I told him I'd discussed those concerns with them. At the end of the day, their clients can exercise their free speech rights however they wish. Then he said that without deep reporting and the benefits of time and hindsight, we could get things wrong—and that could hurt our credibility. I just want to bring it up to you before we're fully committed. I've got to ask the question: Are we sacrificing responsible reporting for opportunistic scheduling?

JESS MONAY: This method of "record-edit-drop" does increase our chances of making mistakes. But that's part of what will make it compelling. Should we pull back for a few days to see what unfolds? Then we risk those two getting arrested and the judge issuing a gag order. If we stay transparent and play fair with our listeners, I think we may end up with something special, even groundbreaking. That's my producer's two cents.

RYANNA RAINES: Once we drop this first episode, there's no going back.

And drop it we do, at 5:00 A.M. Eastern, into thousands and thousands of listener feeds across multiple audio and streaming platforms.

S6:E5

NEWS ANCHOR: We begin tonight with the discovery by San Diego sheriff's deputies of a gruesome double homicide in the affluent North County community of Rancho Santa Fe.

DISPATCHER: 911. What is your emergency?

CALLER: They're dead! Both dead! Help! I need help!

JORDAN DE CARLO: It was a Wednesday morning. Victoria and I were just getting up. My phone rang and the ID said *San Diego Sheriff*.

VICTORIA BERNE: I'd gone online and was seeing reports. It was so surreal. I was like, "This can't be happening, this can't be happening."

RYANNA RAINES: I'm Ryanna Raines. And welcome to *The Raines Report,* an audio crime-investigation series produced in association with Amplify. This is officially Season 6 and we're calling this episode "Romeo and Juliet Meet Bonnie and Clyde."

I fall asleep in my hotel-room bed with my notebook resting on my chest. I dream that I'm standing at the bottom of the driveway leading up to the De Carlo home. I can hear distant screams coming from beyond those immaculately landscaped terraces. My legs feel paralyzed, my vocal cords numb. I am powerless to do anything about the violence I know is taking place inside a luxury estate that's invisible to me. My ringing phone wakes me up a few minutes before my 7:00 A.M. alarm.

Good morning, Jess—maybe that should be a question. Is it a good morning, Jess?

JESS MONAY: I just got off with Carmen. New subscribers and downloads are already outperforming the early episodes of our first five seasons. By a lot.

RYANNA RAINES: I'll take that as a good morning. Are we getting any backlash?

JESS MONAY: Not too much, but it's early. We'll have a better view after Episode 2 drops. Good morning, Ry. Did you get some sleep?

RYANNA RAINES: Enough—I guess. Got a whole lot swirling inside my head.

JESS MONAY: Welcome to tightrope walking without a net.

RYANNA RAINES: A shower and a cup of hot coffee will snap me back. Didn't I see a Starbucks in walking distance?

JESS MONAY: Your caffeine fix is less than a block away. Snap back and call me to discuss today's schedule.

RYANNA RAINES: I check to see if I received any messages from Jordan and Victoria—nothing. Then I discover the best thing about my room is the showerhead. It provides a firm yet relaxing stream with a nice wide spray pattern. When you need that morning shower to help you out of a grog, spray patterns are important.

That first cup of coffee is the best of the day. Dark roast, large cup, and extra hot please. The barista asks if I'd like to try oat milk instead of cow milk. No thank you, I'm still a dairy girl. On my walk back to the hotel, I breathe in temperate sixty-eight-degree air and see green foliage that shows no sign of seasonal change. At home, green is turning orange and yellow.

Back in my room, I call my husband and ask how school drop-off went. "Without a hitch," he answers. Then he asks how my day with *The Real Romeo and Juliet* went. I ask where he got that phrase. He says it's a new hashtag being pasted into comments on our first episode of Season 6. "I listened to it, by the way. Great start, Ry. The only downside is I can't binge it."

"You'll only have to wait a day until the next episode drops."

"What are they like?" he asks, a perfectly normal question.

"So far, they're both engaged, articulate, affectionate with each other—and they make an outstanding tofu and vegetable curry."

I sign off with my husband, affectionately.

JESS MONAY: I left word for the lead detective on the case, Paul Sanchez. I want to set up a call between you two.

RYANNA RAINES: Good luck with that. Our track record for getting homicide detectives to return our calls isn't great.

JESS MONAY: He might be a fan of *The Raines Report,* you never know.

RYANNA RAINES: I'm starting the car and you're on speaker. Got eight minutes to wrap up.

JESS MONAY: I would think that Jordan and Victoria will have listened to Episode 1. Maybe start there? Ask how it feels to hear themselves on a podcast.

RYANNA RAINES: Good idea.

JESS MONAY: Be prepared for feedback. Theater majors are trained to critique each other's work.

RYANNA RAINES: Bring it on.

JESS MONAY: The reality of having their voices out there may cause them to pull back.

RYANNA RAINES: Or embolden them to go deeper.

JESS MONAY: This is where your interviewer empathy helps. They need to know you're not judging them. You want to get to the truth with that gentle persuasiveness you do so well.

RYANNA RAINES: Are you quoting that Season 3 rave from *USA Today*?
 I pull into Jordan's driveway and text him. I look over to see another camera has set up on the sidewalk. The Santa Barbara sheriff's vehicle is still parked across the street. At a glance it appears the officers in the car are different from the ones parked there last night. The garage door goes up, and I drive in. It closes behind me. For a moment I'm in the dark. I look around, but my view is blocked by Jordan's black Wrangler. I don't see or hear anyone.
 Now the garage light pops on and I see Jordan beckoning to me from the kitchen door.

VICTORIA BERNE: How's that hotel? My mom stayed there once. She liked it pretty well.

RYANNA RAINES: The shower is excellent and it's close to a Starbucks, so I'm good.

VICTORIA BERNE: We don't drink coffee. Would you like tea?

RYANNA RAINES: I'm fine right now. I was thinking we might sit down and chat for a little bit.

JORDAN DE CARLO: How's the living room? You can sit there, we'll sit here. Set your recorder on the coffee table. That's me, always directing.

VICTORIA BERNE: So, we listened to the first episode.

RYANNA RAINES: And? What did you think?
 They exchange a quick glance, with Jordan deferring to Victoria.

VICTORIA BERNE: The episodes are going to be shorter than the ones you usually do?

RYANNA RAINES: We want to get them out on a compressed schedule, so they'll be more about a single event or a conversation I record. The daily drops will add up. After a week there'll be a few hours that can be listened to straight through.

JORDAN DE CARLO: I was listening with two sets of ears. One as the person trying to get our voices out there. The other as someone who's a fan of investigative journalism and true crime. If I didn't know about our case, I'd definitely want to keep listening.

VICTORIA BERNE: When will you know how many listens it gets?

RYANNA RAINES: Our podcast network tracks those numbers. The major listening apps have different ways of counting, so they aggregate the data across a number of platforms. Another gauge is social media. Tracking hashtag views and other metrics. And news media mentions, but those usually don't show up right away.

JORDAN DE CARLO: I've already heard from Aunt Frances. She didn't love it. Predictably.

VICTORIA BERNE: The people I've heard from *are* loving it. They get why we're doing it.

RYANNA RAINES: So, as we start out Day 2, will you restate your reasons for contacting *The Raines Report* and asking me to cover your story?

VICTORIA BERNE: The police are trying to make us into the killers of Jordan's parents. We want a chance to speak out before we're arrested and charged with a crime we did not commit.

JORDAN DE CARLO: It's traumatic enough to see my mom and dad's mutilated bodies and know I've lost them forever. But to have the police focus on me and my girlfriend, it piles on more trauma. The only thing worse than losing your parents like that is to be falsely accused of doing it.

RYANNA RAINES: You haven't been accused—officially. Can you think of reasons why the investigators are focused on you to the exclusion of everything else?

VICTORIA BERNE: They ruled out robbery and a stranger killing from the start.

JORDAN DE CARLO: The only son stands to come into a big inheritance. I'm the sole family member within 200 miles. Maybe we were too smug when they interviewed us.

RYANNA RAINES: How did you first hear of your parents' deaths?

JORDAN DE CARLO: It was a Wednesday morning. Victoria and I were just getting up. My phone rang and it said *San Diego Sheriff*. A lot of stuff flashed through my mind, but not about my parents. I answered, and the man introduced himself as Detective Sanchez. He asked if I was Jordan De Carlo and if my parents were Anthony and Lauren De Carlo. I said yes and he said, "I'm sorry to inform you of this, but your parents are deceased." Not dead, *deceased*. And then it was like a bad movie where everything goes into slow motion and the sound gets slurred. I said, "What happened?" And he said they'd been murdered. Not only deceased, but *murdered*.

VICTORIA BERNE: Jordan repeated that word out loud and time just stopped.

JORDAN DE CARLO: Within five minutes I was taking off for Rancho Santa Fe. I have no memory of that drive, zero.

RYANNA RAINES: Did Victoria go with you?

JORDAN DE CARLO: No, I went alone. I just thought it was my responsibility.

VICTORIA BERNE: I wanted to go with him. I mean, I was in shock, too. Murdered? Who can get their head around that? I'd just been down to their house. It's like a fortress. You've been there. People don't get murdered in houses like that. It was hard to be here alone while he went down.

JORDAN DE CARLO: I'm sorry, babe. I should've taken you with me.

RYANNA RAINES: What do you remember about arriving at your parents' house that day?

JORDAN DE CARLO: I got there around noon. There was a crowd of people on the street and yellow tape across the bottom of the driveway. I parked down below and ran up to the house. My heart was pounding. There were officers and crime lab people everywhere. Someone from the coroner's office asked me to identify the bodies. I saw my mom and dad and I—I collapsed.

RYANNA RAINES: Victoria leans over and rubs Jordan's shoulder. Then she rests her head there. I see Jordan's chest rise and fall as he takes a long breath.

JORDAN DE CARLO: The rest of that day felt like I was walking around in a fog.

VICTORIA BERNE: I do remember you calling me. You were sobbing. I'd gone online and was seeing reports. It was so surreal. I was like, "This can't be happening, this can't be happening."

JORDAN DE CARLO: I didn't want to stay down there, but the detectives wanted to talk to me. I honestly don't know what I said to them, but they were taking notes.

RYANNA RAINES: Are you concerned you might've said something that raised their suspicions?

JORDAN DE CARLO: I think it was just the basics. When did you last speak to them? Did they mention any concerns about their safety?

Do you know anyone who might have a reason to harm them? Did my parents keep cash in the house? I showed them the safe in my parents' bedroom. I knew the combination and opened it and there was about twenty thousand in cash along with passports and that kind of stuff. They asked me to look around to see if I noticed anything missing. Their devices were all there. Artwork that I knew had value was still there.

RYANNA RAINES: So you understood that robbery hadn't been the motive?

JORDAN DE CARLO: There was no breaking and entering. My mom and dad felt safe there. They'd lock the front door when they went to bed, but other entrances might be left unlocked. My dad did keep a gun in the nightstand next to their bed. But I never knew him or my mom to go to a gun range and practice shooting it. He got it after I left for college. I guess because it was just Mom and him, he thought he should have some protection. We never really talked about it.

RYANNA RAINES: What else did the detectives ask you that first day?

JORDAN DE CARLO: About how well I knew the housekeeper. I mean, Dolores was hired when I was living at the house. Nice lady, trustworthy—I never heard anything to the contrary.

RYANNA RAINES: Do you know if Dolores came under suspicion at any point?

JORDAN DE CARLO: No, not really. That's the thing, the detectives were grasping at straws.

RYANNA RAINES: Jordan's phone vibrates. He says it's his attorney, Natalie Bloom.

JORDAN DE CARLO: She might have information from the sheriff. I'll take it in the other room. You guys keep going.

RYANNA RAINES: Jordan leaves the room to take the call. Now it's just Victoria sitting across from me with the recorder between us.

What was going through your mind while Jordan was down in Rancho Santa Fe?

VICTORIA BERNE: I just worked really hard to center myself and not panic. I've never known anyone who got murdered. I was so worried about Jordan. It was awful.

RYANNA RAINES: Do you have a car?

VICTORIA BERNE: I did. At the time it was in the body shop getting fixed. After I got it back, I ended up selling it. Jordan and I only need one car.

RYANNA RAINES: I make a mental note to ask Jess to confirm with the body shop.

When did you learn the details of how Jordan's parents died?

VICTORIA BERNE: While Jordan was gone, I went looking online, and one of the San Diego news sites was reporting they were both stabbed multiple times. It literally made me sick to my stomach. I mean, who does that? An insane person, right? Mental health is such a critical issue. I'm not saying mentally unwell people are murderers, not at all. But a person who'd do something like that would have to be seriously disturbed.

RYANNA RAINES: Did you have any fears that whoever it was might come after you and Jordan?

VICTORIA BERNE: Sure. We were at his parents' house seven days before it happened. What if this person had shown up then and attacked all four of us? The imagination goes to some dark places in situations like that.

JORDAN DE CARLO: Okay, Natalie said the sheriff is still not giving a firm date. But they said if we try to leave the house, we'll be arrested.

VICTORIA BERNE: What?!

JORDAN DE CARLO: Natalie wants you to call her, Ryanna. Like, now.

RYANNA RAINES: Text me her number and I'll take it in the other room.

    I am a bit surprised when Natalie gives me permission to record our call.

NATALIE BLOOM: I'm a fan of your podcast. I think you're doing good work.

RYANNA RAINES: I appreciate that, Natalie. I've been anticipating some pushback from you, or does that come next?

NATALIE BLOOM: Jordan explained he was the one who solicited you, so I can't blame you for taking the assignment. You know what makes a good crime story, and this one has an embarrassment of riches. Also, my colleague AJ Novick speaks highly of you.

RYANNA RAINES: That's good to hear. As I told AJ, I don't want to be in an adversarial relationship with defense counsel here. I understand and respect what you guys do. But Jordan and Victoria believe that once they're arrested, their voices will be silenced for the sake of legal strategies and court politics. They want a chance to speak before the system swallows them up.

NATALIE BLOOM: I get it. And if I were them, with what they're facing, I'd want to be heard, too. But every word they speak, down to the tiniest detail of whether they had an omelet or scrambled eggs on a given morning, will be going under a microscope and create all kinds of opportunities for the prosecutor to discredit them. This case is going to come down to credibility.

RYANNA RAINES: You don't have to worry about them remembering between an omelet or scrambled eggs—they're vegans.

    Natalie laughs. I'm encouraged to hear she has a sense of humor.

    Is there anything you can tell me about the timing of Jordan and Victoria being arrested, or why they're still waiting on a warrant?

NATALIE BLOOM: I can't comment on the conversations I'm having with the sheriff's department right now. I can say we're all trying to stay in sync with each other. The worst thing that Jordan and Victoria could do right now is to leave that location. If they bring it up, I would ask you to strongly discourage them from going anywhere. For their own safety.

RYANNA RAINES: As far as I know, their only plan is to stay hunkered down here.

NATALIE BLOOM: Will you let me know if that changes?

RYANNA RAINES: I'll do my best. Given my role here is to be an observer.

NATALIE BLOOM: Your podcast will be stirring up social media and increasing the demand for news coverage. That will only add to the pressure on those two. So while I wouldn't expect you to intervene in a way that crosses any professional boundaries, these are two human beings with a lot to lose and they are putting all their trust in you.

RYANNA RAINES: I hear that. If I have any concerns about them leaving the house, I'll check in with you.

We end the call and I go back to the living room. I find Jordan and Victoria on the couch, leaning their heads against each other. When I sit back down, I see Victoria is teary-eyed.

JORDAN DE CARLO: This is brutal on us. When one starts to lose it, the other tries to prop them up. The scary thing is imagining the other not being there—because we're locked in separate jail cells.

VICTORIA BERNE: We have to stay in the present. And trust the universe that things will work out.

RYANNA RAINES: I give them their moment. Then I ask my next question.

So we were talking about how you found out about your parents and your experiences of that day. Now I'd like to back up to June fifth—

the night of the murders. Can you walk me through where you were and what you were doing that evening?

JORDAN DE CARLO: This is what's so crazy to us. We were here in Santa Barbara the whole night. Two hundred miles from my parents' house. When we were interviewed by the detectives, we walked them through our every move.

VICTORIA BERNE: They couldn't refute anything we were telling them.

JORDAN DE CARLO: We'd booked a study room at the Davidson Library for three hours on that evening. We were working on a new play together.

VICTORIA BERNE: An original, for Jordan to direct and me to play one of the leads.

JORDAN DE CARLO: It's a period piece set in the 1930s. The library had research books that either aren't available online or are too expensive to buy.

RYANNA RAINES: Can you tell me a little more about the play you were writing? I don't think I've heard anything about it.

VICTORIA BERNE: It's a crime drama about two young lovers.

JORDAN DE CARLO: The elevator pitch is *Romeo and Juliet* meets *Bonnie and Clyde*.

RYANNA RAINES: This is new information I need to take in before asking my next question. Suddenly a knock comes at the front door, a few feet from where we're recording. All three of us are startled.

Are you expecting someone?

JORDAN DE CARLO: No. Would you mind answering it?

RYANNA RAINES: I can do that.

So I get up and go to the door. I think, if these are deputies serving a warrant, wouldn't they announce themselves? At the same time, I fully expect to be met by a SWAT team with guns drawn. I center myself, throw back the bolt, grip the knob, and pull it open.

The person standing there is someone none of us expected.

S6:E6

RYANNA RAINES: Opening the front door, I find a woman standing there, mid-forties, with tired eyes, a worried frown, and a suitcase. Seeing me, she takes a defensive posture, as though she expects a dog or cat to come leaping out.

VICTORIA BERNE: Mom!

RYANNA RAINES: The woman looks past me and comes inside, rolling her bag and going straight to Victoria, who is on her feet, eyes wide with surprise.

GAIL BERNE: I'm sorry, I couldn't stay away. I needed to be here with you. And for you.

RYANNA RAINES: I realize I'm still holding the door open and glance out at the cameras and reporters. I quickly close and bolt it.

By the way, I'm Ryanna Raines. And welcome to *The Raines Report*, an audio crime-investigation series produced in association with Amplify. We're calling this episode "Clearly, I Have Touched a Nerve."

VICTORIA BERNE: Mom, this is Ryanna. She's a journalist.

GAIL BERNE: I know, I listened to the first episode on the way to the airport. Do you think this is a good idea, all things considered?

VICTORIA BERNE: You've been talking to AJ.

GAIL BERNE: Yes, but I'm speaking as a concerned parent. Sorry, sorry. Hello, Ryanna, nice to meet you. Jordan, nice to see you. That sounds like such an inadequate thing to say.

JORDAN DE CARLO: Surprised to see you, but—welcome! Can I get you something to drink?

GAIL BERNE: No . . . Okay, water's fine. Sorry for interrupting. I can go and come back later.

VICTORIA BERNE: Why didn't you tell me you were coming?

GAIL BERNE: Because you would've told me to stay home. I'm so worried for you.

VICTORIA BERNE: Mom, let's go to another room to continue this. Jordan, why don't you and Ryanna keep talking? I'll rejoin in a little while.

RYANNA RAINES: Jordan hands Gail a glass of water. Victoria whisks her off down the hall to the office and shuts the door. I turn back to Jordan and let my next question be expressed in my eyes.

JORDAN DE CARLO: So, I don't know Gail all that well. We met on opening night of *Desire Under the Elms*. We had breakfast with her the next morning, and that was pretty much it.

RYANNA RAINES: How do you feel about her showing up right now?

JORDAN DE CARLO: We said we'd answer all your questions, but I'm going to pass on that one. And if we're going to tell you about the night of June fifth, it should be Victoria and me together.

RYANNA RAINES: There are other things we can talk about. Your relationship with your parents?

JORDAN DE CARLO: Right. Instead of me generalizing, you want to be more specific?

RYANNA RAINES: Were you close? Did you have warm feelings for them?

JORDAN DE CARLO: We weren't an outwardly affectionate family. I mean, my mom and I would hug, but Dad was more a handshake, squeeze-your-shoulder guy. He liked a good strong grip. We didn't have a super close relationship, but it was low conflict. After I went away to college, I saw them maybe a half-dozen times a year, including birthdays and holidays. For the last four years I've been really focused on my theater work.

RYANNA RAINES: What did your parents think about your theater work?

JORDAN DE CARLO: They were happy I found something I was so passionate about.

RYANNA RAINES: Were they theater people? Did they go out to see plays?

JORDAN DE CARLO: Not really. My mom would talk about the one college drama class she took and how much she loved it. My dad was into history, I remember discussing Sophocles and Euripides with him. I'm not going to lie, I'm sure he would have preferred me to be an athlete. He was very into Stanford football, Golden State basketball, and pro golf.

RYANNA RAINES: Were there times you fought, like most teens fight with their parents?

JORDAN DE CARLO: Sure. But nothing that dramatic. They had their own things going. My mom was into riding horses. Dad played a lot of golf. He belonged to multiple country clubs. He'd also travel to watch tournaments. Like up in Pebble Beach and out in the desert. I went with him—once.

RYANNA RAINES: How did being an only child affect your relationship with them?

JORDAN DE CARLO: I have a much older half brother, Steven. From Dad's first marriage. Steven never lived with us, so yeah, my experience was as an only child. But my parents were like, "Live and let live." Which is a weird thing to say now. I have some photos on my phone. Want to see?

RYANNA RAINES: I go sit next to Jordan as he scrolls through his phone screen. I see photos of him at various ages with one or both parents. All smiles and domestic tranquility. Christmas, birthdays, goofing around in the backyard pool. And a nice-looking pool it is. This is certainly a curated album. Has it been put together in tribute by a grieving son? Or to paint a picture for an outsider of happy normality?

JORDAN DE CARLO: Here's a voice mail my mom left me a few weeks before she—died.

Hi, honey. Just checking in on you. Hope all is well. I watched an old movie called Act One *and it made me think of you. Call your mother when you get a chance. Love you, sweetheart.*

RYANNA RAINES: It's spooky to hear the cheery affection of a mother who would soon be violently murdered.

I know you said you and Victoria spent the weekend before the murders at your parents' home. Had they met Victoria prior to that weekend?

JORDAN DE CARLO: Yes. We had a dinner with them before that.

RYANNA RAINES: Did they know you two were serious with each other?

JORDAN DE CARLO: It wasn't like I took them aside and said, "Mom and Dad, she's the one." But I did let them know what a talented actor she is and that we work incredibly well together. Speaking of which, do you mind if I go check on her?

RYANNA RAINES: You check on Victoria, I'll check with my team. Okay if I step into the backyard?

JORDAN DE CARLO: It's all yours.

RYANNA RAINES: I go out the French doors onto a redwood deck. It's surrounded on three sides by an overgrown lawn and enclosed by wood plank fencing. The deck furniture and glass-top table show an abundance of dust. Another thing in abundance back here is California sunshine.

JESS MONAY: They're super pumped at Amplify. Carmen's asking if we could put out two episodes a day.

RYANNA RAINES: Of course she is. We're worried about going too fast, and the network wants us to go faster. By the way, an unexpected visitor arrived this morning. Gail Berne, Victoria's mom.

JESS MONAY: She just showed up at the front door?

RYANNA RAINES: Yep. Said she couldn't stay away from being at her daughter's side. Which I find admirable. First thing she said to Victoria was: Are you sure you want to be talking to that journalist woman? It's changed the vibe in the house.

JESS MONAY: It could be interesting to get Mama Berne to speak on the record.

RYANNA RAINES: Great minds think alike. Oh, hey, I see a furry black creature climbing over the top of the backyard fence.

JESS MONAY: You mean like a cat? A skunk?

RYANNA RAINES: No, it's a subspecies of us. A hunter-gatherer from the news family is hanging a microphone with a windscreen over the fence, no doubt recording my every word. I'm going to step back inside the house.

I get off with Jess, shut the back door, and go looking for Jordan. He's not in the front room. I go down the hallway, find the office door shut, and hear voices coming from inside. I knock. Jordan opens the door. He and Victoria are with Gail, all three trying to smile past their tension.

Sorry to interrupt. Just wanted to say I noticed someone hanging a microphone over your back fence. And that's probably not the only one being set up to eavesdrop.

JORDAN DE CARLO: They're turning this house into its own prison.

VICTORIA BERNE: Ryanna, we were thinking you might interview me and my mom together—as long as she's here. To get some background on me and her perspective on things. Would that be okay?

RYANNA RAINES: Actually, I think it could add an important dimension. If you're okay with it, Gail.

GAIL BERNE: Just don't be too tough on me.

VICTORIA BERNE: That's not Ryanna's style, Mom.

JORDAN DE CARLO: Why don't you do it in here, I'll give you some privacy.

RYANNA RAINES: Jordan steps out and shuts the door. I take a seat on the desk chair, which swivels. Victoria and Gail sit side by side on the sofa. Gail looks a bit stiff. She may be a reluctant participant, pressed to convert from supportive mom to character witness.

First let me say, I'm a mother, too. Though my kids are still pretty young, I can imagine the terrible stress I'd feel if one of them got into trouble with the law. How are you managing?

GAIL BERNE: It's been really tough. There's a helplessness, like nothing I can do will make it better. You know, when your child is suffering, a mom's first instinct is to make it better.

VICTORIA BERNE: It's okay, Mom. We'll get through this. We will.

GAIL BERNE: That's what I'm supposed to be saying to you.

RYANNA RAINES: We can circle back to the present, but I'd like to know a little history. Your home is in a suburb south of Seattle. That's where Victoria grew up?

GAIL BERNE: We moved to the house in Issaquah when Victoria was five. We thought it would be a great neighborhood for the kids and the schools are really good.

RYANNA RAINES: I know it's cliché to ask a mother, but it's the only way I can think to phrase it—what was Victoria like growing up?

GAIL BERNE: Where do I begin? You know she's gifted, don't you?

VICTORIA BERNE: Mom.

GAIL BERNE: Well, when someone asks what you were like growing up, there's no way around that. She tested off the charts for IQ in first grade. She'd be embarrassed if I stated a number.

RYANNA RAINES: How did that show up in her early years?

GAIL BERNE: She seemed more like a baby alien than an Einstein. And I say that with all love. She was a very *serious* child. I always felt like she was observing me. She did that with everyone. My friends would come over and she'd watch them from her high chair, to the point they'd feel self-conscious. "Why's your baby staring at me like that? Did I do something?"

Her teachers figured it out pretty quick. Because I never wanted her to feel like she was "other," at home and at school I didn't allow the *genius* word. It's just a label. All it does is create a sense of separation between the child and her peers. A lot of gifted children spend their early years feeling like freaks and outsiders. I didn't want that for Victoria.

VICTORIA BERNE: For me, it showed up in being painfully shy.

GAIL BERNE: I tried my best to socialize her. Made friends with other moms, got her involved in swimming and jujitsu, gave her birthday parties with twenty kids invited. One day she came to me and said, "Mom, if I'm okay not having many friends, you should be okay with that, too." I said, "I don't want you to be lonely." And she said, "I'm not lonely because I get to be my own friend." That broke my heart.

RYANNA RAINES: And how was her father with it?

A conspicuous silence descends. Clearly, I have touched a nerve.

GAIL BERNE: Here's how I'll answer that. One day, out of nowhere, her father pulled a rented van into our driveway and started loading up his stuff. I asked what he was doing. He said he was moving out. I said, "I can see that. Why?" He said he'd met someone else and wanted to be with her. I'm not kidding, it was that abrupt. The kids were devastated. After ending up somewhere in Florida, their dad would call maybe once a month. On Victoria's thirteenth birthday he sent a card. It said *Love, Dad* and had a fifty-dollar bill inside. You know what she did with that money? Took a lighter, lit it on fire, and watched it burn in the bathroom sink.

The problem was, she wouldn't talk about her feelings. I got her to see a therapist, but she refused to say anything about her dad. My daughter can be extremely stubborn. When she doesn't want to talk about something, no one's getting it out of her. FYI to you.

VICTORIA BERNE: Our agreement with Ryanna is to tell her whatever she wants to know.

GAIL BERNE: I wish I'd had that agreement with you.

RYANNA RAINES: You mentioned *kids* plural. Does Victoria have siblings?

Mother and daughter exchange a look conveying more shared trauma.

GAIL BERNE: She had a little brother, James, two years younger. When Victoria was fourteen, James got hit by a car while skateboarding and was killed. They hadn't been all that close when they were younger, but they bonded over their father leaving. They wouldn't talk to me about it, but I'd notice them talking together secretly. One time I stood outside his bedroom door and listened. James was blaming himself, saying he'd gotten bad grades and been mean and that's why their dad left. Victoria told him that wasn't true. Their dad left because he was a "weak person." Those were her words. She was adamant that none of us, not her, not James, not me, had caused their dad to leave. I loved her for saying that.

RYANNA RAINES: Victoria reaches over and gently takes Gail's hand. It's an emotional moment.

I'm so sorry for that. I also have a boy and girl. Losing either would be devastating to me, but I can't imagine the impact on the sibling left behind. Victoria, do you want to say anything?

VICTORIA BERNE: No, this is my mom's perspective. I can tell you mine later.

RYANNA RAINES: How did you first learn about the De Carlo murders, Gail?

GAIL BERNE: I saw it on my news feed. I didn't know the De Carlos, never met them. But I knew Victoria was dating Jordan, and that last name is kind of unique. So I knew it was his parents. I called Victoria and she wasn't answering. I left voice messages. I texted her. I didn't hear back for twenty-four hours. Finally the phone rang and it was her. She apologized for not calling sooner, said she'd been totally absorbed in consoling Jordan. I told her how sorry I was and asked her to call me when she had more time to talk. I didn't hear anything from her for several days. I spent hour after hour online searching for updates about the murders. It was my only source.

VICTORIA BERNE: I'm really sorry for that. I was so caught up in helping Jordan, I couldn't think about anything else. I should've communicated more with you. Must've been so hard, seeing all the news and not hearing from me.

GAIL BERNE: That's okay, I understand. I do.

And then I got a call from one of the detectives on the case. Got a few calls from him, in fact. He asked me everything about Victoria you could imagine. And then some.

RYANNA RAINES: At any point did he tell you she was a suspect?

GAIL BERNE: Not directly, not until she went to Mexico. Then the floodgates opened. Detective Sanchez started calling every day. I became a sort of liaison between my daughter and the San Diego homicide unit.

RYANNA RAINES: There's a knock on the door and Jordan pokes his head in. He asks Victoria if he can see her for a moment. She goes out, shuts the door. Leaving Gail and me alone together.

GAIL BERNE: Look, I may get in trouble for this. But the truth is, I don't know Jordan that well. The first time I met him was on the opening night of their play. I do know my daughter. And it's absolutely impossible that she was directly or even indirectly involved in . . . that crime. Might she be covering up something? People do crazy things when they're in love.

RYANNA RAINES: And Jordan would be her first real love? I mean, she's so young.

GAIL BERNE: That's my point. She didn't have a single boyfriend in high school. She was friends with some boys, but nothing romantic. This is a life-changing relationship for her.

RYANNA RAINES: I'm feeling good that Gail has showed up. Hers is an important perspective to get into the mix. Jordan and Victoria invite me to stay for lunch, but I tell them I have to run back to my hotel to record commentaries and send them to the team.

JESS MONAY: Episode 2 is ready to go up at 5:00 A.M. Eastern. We're in good shape on 3, which has the encounter at the Rancho Santa Fe house. We're all thinking it's the strongest so far.

RYANNA RAINES: Let's remind ourselves we're doing a crime investigation, not a thriller. I get wanting to build momentum from one episode to the next, but we can't predict the future or look like we're *trying* to predict the future. What if it's another month till a warrant's issued?

JESS MONAY: Then this will all have been an exercise in hurry up and wait.

RYANNA RAINES: To our listeners, we want to be transparent about our process. There's a spontaneity we need to embrace here, which is different from how we usually put these podcasts together and get them out to you. You are being brought inside our experiment doing audio journalism in the present tense.

When I return to Jordan's that afternoon, I sense more stress in the crowd outside, now covering both sides of the street. A group of neighbors are appealing to the sheriff's deputies about the news crews blocking traffic, making noise, trespassing on private property. Jordan and Victoria have been home less than twenty-four hours, and the number of spectators and media personnel keeps growing. I text Jordan and he opens the garage. As the door rises, a group of neighbors approach up the driveway. Jordan comes to the threshold of the garage to meet them.

NEIGHBOR 1: Hey, we were wondering how long you're planning to stay here?

JORDAN DE CARLO: As long as I want to stay here. It's my home.

NEIGHBOR 2: The home you're *renting*. We heard you're behind on your payments.

JORDAN DE CARLO: What the fuck business is that of yours?

NEIGHBOR 1: Look, we don't want to make more trouble than you already got. But this is a quiet neighborhood. We can't have our block turned into a circus. That's not fair to the homeowners.

JORDAN DE CARLO: My life is upside down, my family is gone, I can't go home. So, breaking news—we're here and this is where we're staying. You got a problem, take it up with the circus.

RYANNA RAINES: Jordan clicks the remote and the garage door shuts out his neighbors. They can still be heard, complaining about the disruption to their lives. The media and law enforcement are camped out on Jordan's doorstep, and the disruption is to his neighbors' lives? Hmm. We step into the house, where Victoria meets Jordan with a hug of solidarity.

VICTORIA BERNE: I can't believe what an asshole that guy is. Like any of this is your fault?

GAIL BERNE: Oh god, I'm getting a call from Detective Sanchez. Should I answer it?

RYANNA RAINES: All attention turns to Gail, who is sitting at the kitchen table. Sanchez is the lead investigator on the case for the San Diego sheriff's homicide unit.

JORDAN DE CARLO: Let it go to voice mail. See if he leaves a message.

RYANNA RAINES: Victoria nods her agreement and Gail complies. A few moments later, a ping comes through announcing she has a new voice message. She clicks play and we all listen.

> *Hello, Gail, it's Paul Sanchez from the San Diego sheriff's department. I understand you've flown down to join your daughter and her boyfriend in Santa Barbara. Okay. Well, we have an issue and you may be able to help us with it. Call me back as soon as you can. Thanks.*

GAIL BERNE: What should I do?

RYANNA RAINES: After a brief discussion between the three, a decision is made.

DETECTIVE SANCHEZ: Hello, Gail, thanks for returning my call.

GAIL BERNE: Before you start, I need to let you know you're on speakerphone. I've got Victoria and Jordan here. And also Ryanna Raines, who's doing a podcast.

RYANNA RAINES: Detective Sanchez agrees to be on speakerphone but declines to have his voice on the podcast. So we'll have Jordan, Victoria, and Gail's side of the call, and I'll read from my notes to fill in what Sanchez is saying.

He greets the three of us. Jordan and Victoria have been down to the sheriff's station for interviews, so they know him already. To me, Sanchez declares his respect for my work as a crime journalist. But in this particular case, he has *concerns*. He does not think it's in Jordan's or Victoria's best interest to be speaking publicly about the case.

JORDAN DE CARLO: Why not? Because your department is catching so much heat now for persecuting innocent people?

RYANNA RAINES: Sanchez won't take that bait. He reminds the couple they have no editorial control over how their statements are presented on the podcast, and despite the best intentions of the journalist, their words can take on meanings they didn't intend.

VICTORIA BERNE: We have to get our voices out there before you arrest us.

JORDAN DE CARLO: You are planning to arrest us, aren't you?

RYANNA RAINES: Detective Sanchez says that decision does not lie with him alone. He and his fellow investigators are responsible for gathering evidence and presenting it to the city attorney. His voice carries a sympathetic tone, considering this is the man leading the effort to pin a double murder on them.

VICTORIA BERNE: If things we're saying now come back to hurt us, that would only help your side win a conviction. So why do you care?

RYANNA RAINES: Sanchez explains that pretrial publicity cuts both ways, especially in high-profile cases. He's aware that Mr. Novick and Ms. Bloom are advising them against doing the podcast, and notes the rarity of defense attorneys and law enforcement being on the same page.

JORDAN DE CARLO: Are you looking for other suspects, Detective? Following other leads, tracking down other possible killers? If the answer is no, you're the ones forcing us to speak out.

RYANNA RAINES: Seeing his lack of progress, Sanchez asks Gail to take him off speaker. Despite the conflicts, the detective and Victoria's mom seem to have a friendly rapport. Gail ends the call and there's silence for a few moments. I'm the one who breaks it.

Listen, I want these interviews to be one hundred percent an exercise of your most well-informed free will. If you'd like to step away and discuss it out of my presence, please do. You both need to believe you're doing the right thing here.

Jordan and Victoria stare at each other a moment, then excuse themselves and head to the back bedroom. That leaves Gail and me sitting across the kitchen table from each other.

GAIL BERNE: That's very decent of you to give them a chance to talk it out. It's funny, all I hear about is how unethical the news media is.

RYANNA RAINES: I can't speak for the news media. I can only tell you we're one small team doing the best we can to find interesting stories, seek out the facts, and report what happens in an interesting way.

GAIL BERNE: What if in the end you still can't be sure what's fact and what's fiction?

RYANNA RAINES: At that moment, I don't have a good answer to Gail's question.

S6:E7

JORDAN DE CARLO: *It's the middle of the night and I can't sleep. I've come out to the kitchen to record this, so I don't wake up Victoria. So many feelings stirring inside of me. I can't hold a thought for more than a few moments. I want to call Mom and Dad, but I can't. Ever. I'll never hear their voices or see them. Dammit! So a big part of what I feel is anger. I'm really freaking mad at the person or people who did this to them. I'm not a hater, but whoever held that knife and did this horrible thing, I hate you. I'm not a violent person, but if I find who did this, I'll do violence to you. You don't deserve to live. Who did this? Why? And we're about to go down for your crime? Fuck you! I'm so messed up. I'm destroyed inside. Thank god for Victoria. Thank the universe for Victoria. I love you, baby. I love you so much.*

RYANNA RAINES: This is a voice memo from Jordan De Carlo that I wake up to. It was sent to me at 3:26 A.M. I had no idea he was going to send it. As you can hear, it's full of raw emotion, much more than he's expressed since I greeted his arrival in San Diego. Before I left yesterday, Jordan and Victoria told me they were fully committed to participating in our podcast investigation of the murders they will likely be charged with.

VICTORIA BERNE: We are trusting you to present us as we are. Not as characters who best fit your commercial true-crime narrative.

RYANNA RAINES: Our team is constantly looking with a critical eye at what the story is versus what we want the story to be. Do we always get it right? Probably not. But I can promise you every step of the way we strive to be fair and reasonable.

I arrive at Jordan's house at 9:00 A.M. sharp. The media presence is even bigger than when I left last night. I text Jordan. The garage door opens, I drive inside. The garage door comes back down, shutting out the media circus, the pissed-off neighbors, and the ever-present sheriff's deputies.

I'm Ryanna Raines. And welcome to *The Raines Report*, an audio crime-investigation series produced in association with Amplify. We're calling this episode "The Alibi."

I tell Jordan I received his voice memo and I assume he's okay with me inserting it into the podcast.

VICTORIA BERNE: What voice memo?

JORDAN DE CARLO: I recorded it last night when I couldn't sleep.

VICTORIA BERNE: What did you say?

RYANNA RAINES: I hear a degree of concern from Victoria I haven't heard before.

JORDAN DE CARLO: That I was sad and missing my parents and mad at the person who did that to them. I'm trying to hold it together, but sometimes I feel so lost. I was going to tell you.

RYANNA RAINES: Victoria gives him a look that to me shows an edge of annoyance.

JORDAN DE CARLO: Is this a good time to talk about the night of the murder?

RYANNA RAINES: We move into the living room. Gail is sequestered in the office. I sit in an armchair, and they sit on the sofa, the coffee table between us. Victoria and Jordan settle in hip to hip. He puts his arm around her shoulders. She rests her hand on his thigh.

JORDAN DE CARLO: After this thing happened to my parents and the suspicion turned on us, Victoria and I researched a lot of different real-life murder cases. Seems to us the most critical evidence in any criminal case is the suspect's alibi.

VICTORIA BERNE: We've both thought and talked a lot about what we were doing that day, June fifth. The details are very clear in our minds.

JORDAN DE CARLO: That afternoon we whipped up an early dinner because we planned to spend the evening at the library. We'd reserved a late-night study room. There's a record of that.

VICTORIA BERNE: We were working on a play about two bank robbers who are also lovers. One comes from a family of gangsters, the other from a family of cops. It takes place during the Depression in the west, maybe San Francisco, maybe Portland.

JORDAN DE CARLO: We drove over to campus about five-thirty and parked in lot 22 on the west end. From there we walked to the main library, took the elevator to the seventh floor, and set ourselves up in the study room.

VICTORIA BERNE: For the first hour or two, we went around gathering reference books. About 1930s American culture, the fashions, the justice system. We dug out everything we could find that mentioned Bonnie and Clyde and other gangsters like Pretty Boy Floyd and Ma Barker.

JORDAN DE CARLO: We also mapped out the families of the Montagues and Capulets from *Romeo and Juliet*. We were still at an early stage, just researching and making notes.

RYANNA RAINES: Out of curiosity, did you have a title?

VICTORIA BERNE: *With a Kiss We Die.* That's a variation on Romeo's last line in the play, "With a kiss I die."

JORDAN DE CARLO: We worked together in the study room until around ten-thirty. Then we left and went down the stairwell because it was the closest exit and we'd been sitting so long. It was a clear night, and pretty warm, so instead of going back to my car, we went out to the Commencement Green, which is the big lawn on the backside of Theater and Dance. It was a Sunday night in summer, so it was deserted.

VICTORIA BERNE: There's a big magnolia tree in the middle of the lawn that looks out on the lagoon and the ocean. It's a great spot for studying and chilling. It's not like a single trunk kind of tree. There's a cluster of thick trunks that branch up and out into this big wide canopy.

JORDAN DE CARLO: We stepped inside the cluster, which gave us some cover. Not that we needed it, because no one was around to see us.

VICTORIA BERNE: We made love standing against the tree trunks. We really got into it. It felt forbidden, having sex in this spot where hundreds of people pass every day. This lawn is where the university holds graduations, where families come to watch the ceremonies. Where Oprah Winfrey stood to give her commencement speech.

JORDAN DE CARLO: We were there awhile, having outdoor sex. We lost track of time. After that, we lay down on the grass, holding hands and staring up at the stars. Fully blissed out.

VICTORIA BERNE: We fell asleep on the grass. When we woke up, it was after one. We held each other, made out some more, then got up and walked back to the parking lot. We got into Jordan's car about twenty to two. Then we drove back to his place and went to bed.

RYANNA RAINES: Did anyone see you, a witness who can place you on campus during that time?

JORDAN DE CARLO: Here's the thing. We're pretty sure there's security cam footage of us going up the elevator in the library around five-thirty. But the cameras in the stairwell weren't working or got erased or something—no time stamp showing us leave the library. As we said, campus was deserted that time of night, it was dark, and we were doing our own thing. The next time we would've been on-camera was in the parking lot when we got back to my car around one-forty in the morning. And the security cameras would show my car was parked there the whole time.

VICTORIA BERNE: We'd left our phones in Jordan's car, too, so we'd have no distractions. The pings from cell towers can prove they were there the whole night and into the next morning. So how did we travel two hundred miles to the De Carlos' house, commit the murders, then travel two hundred miles back without a car?

RYANNA RAINES: You could've left Jordan's car there and taken another one. What about your car, Victoria?

VICTORIA BERNE: In the body shop, as I told you.

RYANNA RAINES: The investigators must've checked the car rental places in the area. And with car services like Uber and Lyft. And with your friends to see if you'd borrowed someone's car.

JORDAN DE CARLO: No record of us renting a car or borrowing a car. Nothing. Because we didn't.

RYANNA RAINES: The police must have something they see as disproving your alibi.

VICTORIA BERNE: If that was true, wouldn't they have arrested us by now?

JORDAN DE CARLO: They can't disprove our alibi. That's why it's taking them so long to make a case against us. It's common knowledge how police do investigations. Their procedure is based on process of elimination. Once they ruled out everyone else, in their minds it has to be us.

RYANNA RAINES: Do you have any ideas about who else it could be?

JORDAN DE CARLO: I don't think that's something we should be commenting on right now.

RYANNA RAINES: Without naming names, you have thoughts about other possible killers?

JORDAN DE CARLO: Not ready to talk about it.

RYANNA RAINES: I catch Victoria averting her eyes from mine. It's a little thing, but a journalist gets sensitized to little things in a subject's behavior.

I hear that. Then, between you being on-camera in the library elevator and on-camera getting back into your car in the parking lot, how much time elapsed?

VICTORIA BERNE: We timed it out. Eight hours and ten minutes.

RYANNA RAINES: Long enough for you to drive down, commit the crime, and drive back?

JORDAN DE CARLO: Technically, I guess. But how'd we do it without a car? I mean, c'mon.

RYANNA RAINES: Were there any witnesses who saw you on the seventh floor of the library?

VICTORIA BERNE: We're still hoping somebody comes forward.

RYANNA RAINES: Because if anyone can place you in the library at even, say, 8:00 P.M., that would not give you enough time to get to Rancho Santa Fe and back. It's physically impossible. Did you write anything down that night? You said you were making notes about the new play?

JORDAN DE CARLO: We had to turn all that over to the detectives. But we were writing in pen on legal pads, there's no time stamp.

VICTORIA BERNE: I wrote down everything I remembered from that night in my Mexico journal.

RYANNA RAINES: Mexico journal?

VICTORIA BERNE: We both kept journals while we were down there. It really helped me to track my thoughts and feelings day to day.

JORDAN DE CARLO: I wrote in hers. She wrote in mine. Both together we probably wrote two hundred pages.

RYANNA RAINES: Have you shared the journals with anyone?

VICTORIA BERNE: Not yet. We talked about maybe self-publishing them someday.

JORDAN DE CARLO: They're a deep dive into what was going on in our hearts and minds.

RYANNA RAINES: Would you mind letting me see the journals? I won't copy them or share them without your permission. It would be helpful to have an understanding of what was in your minds while you were down there.

Jordan and Victoria check in with each other. They nod tentatively, then agreeably.

GAIL BERNE: I'm going to make my special comfort casserole. You just sit and relax, I got this.

RYANNA RAINES: Coming up will be my second dinner with Jordan and Victoria. And tonight we have the addition of Victoria's mom, who has offered to make the meal while the three of us sit around the kitchen table and chat.

JORDAN DE CARLO: My mom was prideful about her cooking. She belonged to a recipe club, always trying new dishes. My dad considered himself a master of the barbecue. I grew up eating a lot of barbecued ribs and chicken. It makes me shudder to think about.

GAIL BERNE: I'm sorry I didn't get a chance to meet them.

RYANNA RAINES: You said you were at opening night of *Desire Under the Elms*?

GAIL BERNE: I was. But the De Carlos were a no-show.

RYANNA RAINES: I glance at Jordan. He avoids my gaze.
Did your parents come to any of the performances?

JORDAN DE CARLO: No. They did not.

RYANNA RAINES: I expect Jordan to follow with some explanation. But he offers none, at least not at that moment. Once again, I see Victoria glance away, as though reluctant to meet my eyes.

GAIL BERNE: Ahh!

RYANNA RAINES: Gail suddenly shouts—we see her pointing out the window over the kitchen sink. We all go there and see an unidentified flying object hovering above the backyard lawn.

JORDAN DE CARLO: Fucking camera drone!

RYANNA RAINES: He snaps the shade down. Then does the same with the shade over the French doors. He marches through the rest of the house, shutting the shades on the windows that face the backyard. When he comes back into the kitchen, he is sullen.

VICTORIA BERNE: Flying cameras into people's backyards to spy in their windows? Is that legal, Ryanna?

RYANNA RAINES: I look it up on my phone and read a sentence from a page called *Drone Laws of California*: "No drone pilot can enter the airspace of persons to capture images without consent." When Jordan looks out the window again, the drone is gone. Still, a defeated gloom descends over the table. Gail tries to brighten things by serving her fresh-out-of-the-oven vegan pasta casserole. It has layers of spaghetti, marinara sauce, non-dairy cheese, and meatless meatballs. But Jordan politely bows out, saying he's lost his appetite. Victoria follows him and we hear their bedroom door shut. Once again, it's just me and Gail.

GAIL BERNE: I'll save theirs to heat up later. How is it?

RYANNA RAINES: Comforting and delicious. I'll get the recipe from you. My kids would love this.

When I leave later that night, Victoria tells me Jordan has fallen asleep, otherwise he would see me out. She hands me a manila envelope containing both of their Mexico journals.

VICTORIA BERNE: We're okay letting you read them, but as Jordan said, they're deeply personal. We didn't put on any filters, it's a direct window into our feelings. We know you have integrity. If these got out in snippets, people could take things we wrote out of context and make us look different from who we are.

RYANNA RAINES: I won't put anything from your journals into the public space without your permission.

Victoria thanks me. Then she opens the garage door so I can back my car out.

JESS MONAY: Do you know where they stayed in Los Cabos? Encontrada, a luxury resort with rooms in the $2,000- to $3,000-a-night range. I spoke to the manager, she told me they were there six nights. With food, drinks, and gratuities, they had to have spent twenty grand.

RYANNA RAINES: Maybe they put it all on a credit card, figure out how to pay for it later. Do you know where they spent the other twenty nights?

JESS MONAY: We're searching. I'm guessing some of that information will be in their journals.

RYANNA RAINES: I'll be cracking them tonight. I'm curious to see what's there. I can fill you in later.

It's too late to call home. So I put on sweatpants and a T-shirt, then text my husband that I'd like to FaceTime him and the kids in the morning. He texts right back to say he's still awake.

"Hey," I say, "what are you doing up so late?"

He says, "Hoping to talk to you."

"Aw, you're sweet. It's a little crazy here. But right now I'm alone in my hotel room wearing my comfy sweats and talking to my favorite guy, so no complaints."

He says, "Your audio crime investigating seems to be building a lot of heat. Good for *The Raines Report*."

"In my other cases, I knew where the story was going before we started putting out episodes. On this one, I have no idea. That scares the heck out of me."

"To quote my wife, 'Growth comes when you're out of your comfort zone.'"

When I'm on the road reporting a case, talking to my husband grounds me. No matter how insane things get, knowing he and the kids are there keeps me sane. We stay on another ten minutes, then say good night. I stack all four bed pillows against the headboard and take the two journals out of the envelope. They have faux leather covers and lined pages. With a pad and pen to make notes, I open Victoria's, and start at her first entry, dated September fourteenth.

VICTORIA BERNE: "As I write this date, I'm aware summer's almost over. I met Jordan in winter. Fell in love with him in spring. Suffered with him through summer. Will fall bring redemption? Or damnation?"

RYANNA RAINES: When I sit down to record Jordan and Victoria the next morning, I ask them to read aloud from their journals. I have marked several passages that I found striking. They talk it over briefly, then agree to having these excerpts, spoken with their own voices, published through *The Raines Report*.

VICTORIA BERNE: "May we be allowed a few more moments of happiness? More delicious bits of time together to dream big dreams with positivity and hope? Our love story was too brief. I want our future back."

JORDAN DE CARLO: "We floated in the infinity pool without a word. I held her. She held me. We floated away. We floated back. The trick is to focus everything on the floating, being suspended in water, mind and body drifting, no concern for direction or destination. Let the water, rotation of the earth, and gravity of other galaxies carry us where they will. Trust the drift."

VICTORIA BERNE: "We stopped at a fish taco truck and there were three American couples ahead of us. They were mid-twenties, and I so envied their carefree attitudes. They were laughing and acting silly. One asked me to take a group photo. The guys lifted up their girl-friends and they all made silly faces. I clicked a few shots, handed back the phone. I had to step away. Jordan could see the tears in my eyes. He didn't have to ask why."

JORDAN DE CARLO: "The nights are warm and we spend them out on the deck, together on the same chaise. The moon is so bright I can still see it when I shut my eyes. This is what it feels like to have life's essentials— love and freedom. You can exist without them. Your heart still beats, your lungs still breathe. But you can't be truly *alive* without a special person in your heart and air to breathe from an open sky."

VICTORIA BERNE: "First the play, Jordan and I feeding off each other's energy and challenging each other to go bold, bolder, boldest. And the highs of opening night and the audience's applause and our castmates and crew toasting us. And then the numbing horror after Jordan saw the San Diego sheriff on his caller ID. Those hideous words: *Your parents have been murdered.*"

JORDAN DE CARLO: "Day and night I see their mutilated bodies. The greenish tinge of their skin, the stab wounds edged with congealed blood, their mouths twisted in the physical agonies that were the last sensations they ever felt. Those images are burned into my brain. Will I ever be able to block out the sight of those death masks from that terrible day? Or will they haunt me till the end of time?"

VICTORIA BERNE: "I look at this beautiful man asleep next to me and ask the universe 'How can I live in a place where I can no longer reach out and touch his cheek, brush back a lock of his hair, kiss his forehead?' Must focus on this precious moment with him asleep beside me. Past, present, future, they're all here. Nothing exists outside of this moment. So pure. So perfect."

JORDAN DE CARLO: "I can't imagine a fuller heart than when I cradle her precious head to my chest."

VICTORIA BERNE: "We took a long walk on the beach and I fantasized that we found a magical sea cave where we could bliss out together and no one would ever find us."

RYANNA RAINES: This next run is Jordan and Victoria writing in each other's journal, conversation style.

JORDAN DE CARLO: "I want to stay with you in this space forever. But we have to go back."

VICTORIA BERNE: "We will fight and we will win and we will come out the other side with stronger bonds and a brighter future."

JORDAN DE CARLO: "And go on to make all our dreams come true."

VICTORIA BERNE: "I have to believe that. Or I'll fall apart. The only thing holding me together right now is your love and our passion."

RYANNA RAINES: Thank you. I found those passages to be especially poignant. Reading them gives me insights that I might not have gotten through a straight Q&A.

As we finish the morning session, Jordan peeks out a corner of the front window shade.

VICTORIA BERNE: Are the sheriff's deputies still there?

JORDAN DE CARLO: Round the clock in three shifts. Welcome back to reality.

RYANNA RAINES: We go into the kitchen, where Gail sits at the table. She starts playing our latest podcast on her phone. We seat ourselves around the table and listen as Episode 3 unfolds.

> *Oh, now I hear another car coming up the driveway. Whoops, looks like a police car. No, it's a private security vehicle and it is pulling up behind my Explorer.*

RYANNA RAINES: I'm struck by the strangeness of listening to an episode of my reporting in the same room with the subjects of that reporting.

> *On this occasion, his message to me is five words punctuated by periods: Ryanna. What. Are. You. Doing—question mark.*

JORDAN DE CARLO: Nice cliffhanger.

VICTORIA BERNE: Have we officially gone viral?

RYANNA RAINES: Seems to be heading in a viral direction.

Jordan gets up and goes to the door of the backyard. He opens it. All four of us can see to the back fence, where cameras and microphones are being lifted up and aimed at the open doorway. Now we can hear a helicopter fly over the house. Jordan slams the door in anger.

JORDAN DE CARLO: This is insane! We're trapped in here! We can't even go in the backyard to get a breath of air!

RYANNA RAINES: Now Victoria goes to the door, throws it open, and strides to the middle of the back lawn. She throws herself down on the grass, spreads her arms, and stares up into the sky. When the news helicopter flies back over, she holds up both hands and gives it a pair of middle fingers. Jordan follows her out and repeats her gesture, aiming two middle fingers at the sky. Then he helps Victoria up off the grass. They come inside, shut the door, and snap down the shade.

GAIL BERNE: Maybe I should go out front and try to appeal to their common decency.

JORDAN DE CARLO: I don't think any of them are motivated by common decency.

RYANNA RAINES: Actually, it's not a bad idea. I mean, if you're up for it, Gail. Who can fault a mother asking to get breathing room for her innocent-until-proven-guilty daughter and her innocent-until-proven-guilty boyfriend?

GAIL BERNE: What should I say?

RYANNA RAINES: The theater majors offer Gail ideas about how to grab her audience. I offer her insights about what would most impact reporters' mindsets.

Gail steadies herself for her performance. Then she goes to the front door, opens it, and steps out to meet the press. Jordan, Victoria, and I go to the front window to peek out the shades. Once Gail is seen emerging from the house, a wave of cameras and microphones surge in her direction. We can see her only from behind and can't hear what she's saying. The following recording is by another source that we're using with permission.

GAIL BERNE: Hi, I'm Gail Berne, Victoria's mom. I am not a spokesperson for my daughter or for Jordan. I've come out here on my own initiative to ask you in the news media to give these two the space to step into their backyard without being filmed or recorded. You've surrounded them on all sides—and from above—by cameras and microphones. Can you give them one small free zone? Just their backyard, that's all.

RYANNA RAINES: The reporters burst out with questions, most being a variation on "Do you think your daughter's a violent killer responsible for butchering her boyfriend's parents?"

GAIL BERNE: I'm speaking for myself and just asking you to consider that anyone who's not been charged with a crime should be allowed the privacy of their own backyard. Please back off enough to let them breathe the outside air. I'm asking you to find a little compassion. Please.

RYANNA RAINES: As she turns away and heads back to the front door, we can hear the collective clamor of the American news media demanding answers. When Gail comes back inside and shuts the door, she's met with an emotional hug from her daughter.

VICTORIA BERNE: That was the bravest thing I've ever seen you do.

RYANNA RAINES: I experience this mother-daughter moment in a way that feels personal to me.

S6:E8

RYANNA RAINES: Five hundred thousand downloads? Jess, you're freaking me out.

JESS MONAY: Our podcast network is freaking out, too—in a good way. These numbers are off the charts.

RYANNA RAINES: And then come the metrics of social media engagement.

JESS MONAY: We're surging across all our platforms. I'm sending you a sample of tweets and IG comments. Give them a glance. I'll include some less-than-positive ones—because I know you have a thick skin.

RYANNA RAINES: *"Jordan and Victoria are stone-cold killers. Too bad they stopped the death penalty in California. Those two deserve to fry."*
   O-kay.
   "Those two are adorable together. They are what true love looks like. God bless them, and God save them from a miscarriage of justice."

All right.

"*Bruh, you gettin' played by two college students. You smarter than that.*"

I assume *bruh* refers to me?

"*Shame on the sheriff's department for crucifying these innocent young people who have wonderfully productive lives ahead of them.*"

I've never seen Romeo and Juliet as a crucifixion story, but hey.

"*Here are a pair of skilled actors taking on the roles of their lives to save their lives.*"

There's my sampling of Jess's larger sampling. To give an overview, the Jordan/Victoria believers seem to far outnumber their disbelievers. But it's only been forty-eight hours since Episode 1 dropped, and this story has a long way to go.

On that note, I'm Ryanna Raines. And welcome to *The Raines Report*, an audio crime-investigation series produced in association with Amplify. This is Episode 8, which we're calling "A Full-Throttle Rage Machine."

AJ NOVICK: Hello, Ryanna, am I catching you at a good time?

RYANNA RAINES: I've just finished recording my latest commentaries in my hotel room during the midday break, so this unexpected call from Victoria's attorney is well-timed. He gives me permission to record our conversation.

You still upset with me?

AJ NOVICK: Look, you're doing your job and attaching yourself to a hot story. I have a job to do, too, and I'm thinking it may be best to work *with* you. That will put me in a better place to advise my client. I need a face-to-face with her, so I'm on my way up to Santa Barbara.

RYANNA RAINES: Be prepared to run the media gauntlet.

AJ NOVICK: Doesn't bother me. I would like your help, though. I can't get Victoria to return my calls and her mother Gail is also being unresponsive. I'm hoping you can get there ahead of me and let them know I'm coming. And not to worry, I won't be dropping any bombshells.

RYANNA RAINES: Are you going to advise her to stop doing the podcast?

AJ NOVICK: As I said, I want to work with you now. My client is clearly committed to this path.

RYANNA RAINES: Why the change in course? A few days ago, you wanted to wring my neck.

AJ NOVICK: As one of my long-ago mentors counseled me, you've got to judge between when to buck the tide and when to ride it. And when the tide becomes a tidal wave, the goal is to stay on the surfboard as long as you can.

RYANNA RAINES: I was wondering when you'd start with the surfing metaphors. Well, I'm glad to know we'll be sharing this wave, AJ. And yes, when I return to Jordan's, my first order of business will be to let Victoria know to expect you.

I stay offline and write out lists of new questions to ask Jordan and Victoria. Just before heading back, I get a text from Jordan asking if I'd pick up some herbal teas and coffee for Gail. Hmm. Not the usual job of a journalist, running errands for their subjects. But they are housebound, and having coffee to make while I'm embedded there would be a good thing. So, sure, I'll make a quick store run for them.

As I come down Jordan's street, I see two canopy tents have been set up on the front lawns of neighboring homes. Underneath are media people using folding tables for their equipment. I wonder what the homeowners are charging for those spots. I see a line of beach and camping chairs with spectators sitting along the opposite sidewalk. Are they news crew people or locals coming to join the circus? Probably both.

Turning into the driveway, I text Jordan, and seconds later the garage door opens. As I roll inside and put it in park, the garage door comes down behind me. The sight of the spectacle disappears, but the sound of the spectacle continues as a low buzzing.

JORDAN DE CARLO: Thanks, Ryanna. Victoria and I feel like we're both coming down with something. Peppermint tea is great for clearing congestion.

GAIL BERNE: Thank god I found that French press. My headache already feels better.

RYANNA RAINES: As a coffee gal myself, I'll second that. Cheers.

Gail and I lift our mugs and clink them together.

Victoria, I got a call from AJ Novick. He wanted me to let you know he'll be stopping by this afternoon to meet with you.

I see her stiffen and blanch. This is not happy news for her.

VICTORIA BERNE: I didn't ask him to drive up here. Can't we do it by Zoom?

RYANNA RAINES: He said he was having trouble reaching you. I think he just wants to check in and give you an update on what's happening in San Diego.

JORDAN DE CARLO: Think of the media coverage he'll get just by walking up to our front door.

VICTORIA BERNE: What if he's coming to make a case for me stopping the podcast?

RYANNA RAINES: He's accepted this is something you've decided to do. It's more about seeing you in person and talking things through, counsel to client.

After we've sat down in the living room, we hear the noise level outside rise. There's a knock at the front door. It's AJ looking his dapper self, in a designer shirt and jacket, with his perpetual tan. He greets us all with warm words and a smile. He tells us he was tempted on the drive up to pull off at Rincon beach and paddle out to catch a few waves.

VICTORIA BERNE: You carry a surfboard in your car?

AJ NOVICK: My six-foot Lightning Bolt goes wherever I go. Along with flip-flops, a pair of surf shorts, and a half wetsuit.

RYANNA RAINES: When offered coffee or tea, AJ asks for tea. He tells us he starts every day with a cup of Yogi peppermint and loves the "minty zing." He also approves that Yogi tea bags are compostable. I'm reminded of how silky smooth this man is, and it takes practically no time for Victoria to let down her defenses. She agrees to step into another room with him so they can talk privately. I ask if I can sit in, knowing what his answer will be.

AJ NOVICK: I need some one-on-one time with Victoria. We won't be long. And Jordan, this would be a good time for you to put a call in to Natalie. She and I briefed each other on my way up here. We were hoping to have these client conversations in parallel.

RYANNA RAINES: Jordan heads to his bedroom to call Natalie while AJ and Victoria go into the office. Gail and I sit across from each other at the kitchen table.

GAIL BERNE: That neighbor who confronted Jordan in the driveway came back and knocked at the front door. Jordan didn't open it, had to shout at him to go away. It's getting hostile out there.

RYANNA RAINES: Actually, that gives me an idea. I think I'll go out front to chat up some of my fellow reporters and maybe a bystander or two.

Taking Gail's comment as inspiration to go meet the circus, I step out and aim for the heart of the crowd, my Sony in hand. Cameras and mikes swing toward me. Here she comes, folks!

I'd like to interview some of you for our podcast. Who's game?

REPORTER #1: Hi, I'm John Lee Scott, a staff reporter for KSBY 6, the NBC affiliate in San Luis Obispo, about ninety miles north. We cover the news for California's Central Coast.

RYANNA RAINES: And what do you find newsworthy about this story?

REPORTER #1: Violent murder, two attractive young suspects. Did they or didn't they? We're in the golden age of true crime. People can't get enough of this stuff.

RYANNA RAINES: What's your name?

TIKTOK SLEUTH: Jennifer Fergus. I don't work for a news company. I'm an internet sleuth.

RYANNA RAINES: And for our newer listeners, remind us what that is?

TIKTOK SLEUTH: I post on social media to share updates about different murder and missing person cases. I discuss my theories with other sleuths, and do whatever I can to help solve mysteries.

RYANNA RAINES: What is it that draws you to this particular case?

TIKTOK SLEUTH: Jordan and I are the same age. I was a theater major at San Diego State. And because I want to be you someday.

RYANNA RAINES: Hah!

RESIDENT: Can I say something? My name is Don Madsen and I live a few doors down. Those two are the reason all these people are camping out on our street. I caught a guy trespassing on my property and relieving himself on my rosebushes. He's lucky I didn't run him down and beat his ass.

RYANNA RAINES: To be honest, not so interested in talking to disgruntled neighbors right now.

Then I meet the eyes of a young man with a black beard and the deep, questioning gaze of a philosophy student. As he emerges from the crowd and approaches me, I sense the look in his eyes is actually more specific and intentional. "Excuse me," he says, "I have something to tell you," and it hits my reporter's radar that he's someone I should listen to. Suddenly I hear a commotion. I turn to see AJ emerging from Jordan's house, alone. He heads for the cameras as the cameras head for him and it appears he's going to address the media. This will be something I need to record. I turn back to Blackbeard but I see him heading away. Did he change his mind about talking to me? I start to call out, but he disappears behind the line of news vans. Hmm.

AJ NOVICK: Hello, I'm AJ Novick, the attorney representing Victoria Berne in this matter. Just going to make a brief statement and won't be taking questions.

RYANNA RAINES: Like my press colleagues, I move in close to AJ and hold up my microphone to record him.

AJ NOVICK: Right now there's a lot of wild speculation regarding this case. The fact is, no person has been charged with the murders of Anthony and Lauren De Carlo. This is still an open homicide investigation. As for a certain podcast that has been releasing episodes about the case, my client is simply exercising her First Amendment rights. Like every citizen in this country, she deserves the presumption of innocence. At this time, I would ask you all to keep in mind that Victoria Berne has not been accused of anything. She is just a hardworking theater arts student who is trying to live her best life. Please respect her privacy and give her the benefit of the doubt. If any one of you were in her shoes, you'd be asking for the same. That's all for now.

RYANNA RAINES: AJ looks at me and gives a little nod. Then he strides off to one of those big boxy Mercedes SUVs, metallic silver. Enough room for ten surfboards in there. He hoists himself into the driver's seat, fires up the engine, and peels out on his trek back down the coast. I wonder if he'll stop along the road to catch a few waves.

VICTORIA BERNE: The D.A.'s office is "acutely aware" of what an "explosive case this could be," so they're "proceeding with an excess of caution." AJ's phrases.

JORDAN DE CARLO: I said to Natalie, if we haven't been charged, we should be able to go wherever we want. But no, we're being held hostage by arrogant authoritarians with badges.

VICTORIA BERNE: "Oh, we're not charging you, but if you try to leave your house, we'll throw you in jail." That's the same as being under house arrest.

JORDAN DE CARLO: Mr. Prosecutor, do you have a case against us or not?!

RYANNA RAINES: As their frustrations spill over, I suggest we take a ten-minute break. When Jordan and Victoria come back to the sofa, I turn to a more welcome subject.

I've been wanting to ask more about your work together on *Desire Under the Elms*. It sounds like your creative collaboration fueled your emotional relationship and vice versa. How did that journey begin?

JORDAN DE CARLO: Probably back to me first discovering Eugene O'Neill. *Man is born broken! Embrace your suffering! Jump off the cliff into your deepest, darkest places!*

I decided early in my senior year to do an O'Neill as my spring honors project.

RYANNA RAINES: What drew you to his work?

JORDAN DE CARLO: He's an artist who never wrote for money or fame, but got tons of both. From the beginning, he was a take-no-prisoners revolutionary. He didn't just disrupt the culture of his time, he took an axe to it. They tried to censor him. They had protests in front of the theaters. Police threatened to throw his producers in jail. He got death threats—from the Ku Klux Klan—before that was even a thing.

For Gene, it was all about taking his most profound pain and funneling it through his art.

RYANNA RAINES: This is the most creatively engaged I've seen Jordan yet. And why did you choose *Desire Under the Elms*?

JORDAN DE CARLO: It's ferocious. A full-throttle rage machine. Rage over land, over family, over sexual lust. Gene never compromises. Not a single word is in there to give the audience relief. His characters love passionately and hate passionately, no middle ground. The New York district attorney said the play was obscene and tried to shut it down. Gene made them put it on at one of the biggest theaters on Broadway, and it ran for over four hundred performances.

VICTORIA BERNE: Success is the best revenge.

RYANNA RAINES: Did you personally identify with the main characters in the play?

JORDAN DE CARLO: One of them is a son who hates his father. But I'm guessing you knew that.

RYANNA RAINES: I had to ask the question.

JORDAN DE CARLO: You don't need to be a theater major to understand that a director needs to find an emotional connection with his characters. The stronger that connection, the more the work comes alive. By the way, Eben doesn't kill his father.

RYANNA RAINES: I wasn't a theater major, but I know how important casting is. Talk about what that process was like for *Desire Under the Elms*.

JORDAN DE CARLO: I wanted to cast the father and son before the stepmother role. And I knew who I wanted for Eben. An African American BFA actor named Thaddeus Baylor. O'Neill originally wrote the part for a white actor. I didn't change a single line.

RYANNA RAINES: Wouldn't that casting alter O'Neill's original themes?

JORDAN DE CARLO: If Gene were restaging *Desire* today, that's how he'd do it. The play he wrote before *Desire Under the Elms* was about interracial marriage—in 1924! He insisted on casting Black actors in Black roles, not whites in blackface. One of the main themes in *Desire* is land ownership, who gets to claim property rights. The character of the father *is* the patriarchy. The son is all Americans of color who've been locked out by generations of white privilege. The faculty loved the idea so much they let me put it on at our main stage, the Hatlen.

RYANNA RAINES: You cast your two male leads. Then it was all about finding Abbie Putnam, Eben's stepmother. Victoria, how did your audition come about?

VICTORIA BERNE: I saw it was casting, but I felt intimidated. See, I already had a huge crush on Jordan. We hadn't been officially introduced, but I'd noticed him at events and in the halls. I thought he was so hot—and a director! So when the audition notice came out, I just collapsed into myself. I mean, it wasn't good. I was completely frozen.

So I thought I'd missed out on it. Then Thad—Thaddeus Baylor— took me aside one day and said they were having trouble finding the right Abbie. He wanted me to read for Jordan. Thad's a sweet-talker and kept saying, "You can do this, I know you can do this." He's also a brilliant actor. To play opposite him in my first spring production would be huge. So I wiped Jordan out of my mind and agreed to do the audition in three days. I made my roommate Gwen rehearse with me the whole time and almost broke her. "Once more." "Once more." "Once more, *please.*"

I went to the audition, stepped onstage, and my instincts took over. I didn't even look at Jordan. It felt like I was channeling this other person through my voice and body. I just stood aside and let Abbie take control.

You know what's crazy? I'm pretty sure I blacked out for those ten minutes. I didn't remember anything—except not looking into Jordan's eyes until the very end. I surrendered to the larger consciousness. Victoria checked out. Where she went is anyone's guess.

RYANNA RAINES: How did you find out you got the part?

VICTORIA BERNE: I stepped outside to get a drink at the fountain. When I looked up, there was Jordan. He said, "You ready to start rehearsing tonight?"

I said, "I am."

He said, "And so it begins," or words to that effect. I reached out to shake his hand. He took it and I felt this tremor go through my body. It was the first time we had skin-to-skin contact. I couldn't believe the electricity I felt. I looked in his eyes and saw he felt it, too.

So after my regular classes I went to room 1507 and we started with a table read of the entire play. Everyone else was already cast and had been for a while, so they knew the text and I was playing catch-up. I had to work that much harder.

RYANNA RAINES: Jordan and Victoria look at each other with a deep wistfulness. It strikes me that they're too young to be this wistful.

JORDAN DE CARLO: I really miss Thad. You know, I'm going to call him and ask him to come over. We'll have him for dinner. He's great. Not only a talented actor, but a quality human being.

RYANNA RAINES: Jordan picks up his phone and calls Thaddeus Baylor.

JORDAN DE CARLO: Hey, man. What's going on? Right, I heard that. Very fucking cool, so happy for you. Yeah, I know. It's been *interesting*. Oh, you listened to the podcast? We are going to win at trial—if it even gets that far. Listen, I'd love to see you and so would Victoria. We're kind of stuck here, as you know. So come over for dinner. What? Oh. Okay. No, right, I get it. Makes me sad, but I get it. Okay, well, I'll come visit you in London. Or you come visit me in jail. Sorry, bad joke. Love you too, man. Bye.

VICTORIA BERNE: What's wrong?

JORDAN DE CARLO: He doesn't want to come here because of all the fucking cameras. Just by coming to the front door he'd end up all over social media. Who can blame the guy? This is so messed up!

RYANNA RAINES: Jordan slams his fist on the coffee table. The suddenness startles both me and Victoria. Then he pops up from the sofa and strides off down the hallway. We hear his bedroom door slam shut.

VICTORIA BERNE: I'm so sorry.

RYANNA RAINES: You don't have to apologize, Victoria.

VICTORIA BERNE: He rarely loses it like that. Sometimes I just don't know how to console him.

RYANNA RAINES: That's not your job, you know. It's his responsibility to keep himself together.

VICTORIA BERNE: He's under so much stress. They were his parents, his family. If someone did that to my mom and I got blamed for it—

RYANNA RAINES: Don't minimize the stress you're under. We all process it differently.

I see a glimmer of gratitude in Victoria's eyes. Then she goes back to the bedroom to console her boyfriend. I sit back down at the kitchen table with Gail, who makes me another cup of coffee. We scroll our phones.

GAIL BERNE: You don't put out episodes on the weekends?

RYANNA RAINES: That's a bit of a dead zone for us. Our next drop will be Monday morning. Which reminds me, I've got some more recording to do in my hotel room. I don't want to disturb Jordan and Victoria. Would you mind letting me out of the garage? I'll check in with them later.

I back out, thread my way through the ever-growing mob, and drive to my hotel. At the front desk, they give me messages left by five reporters requesting interviews with me. Am I ready or willing to go from telling the story to being the story? No thanks.

I call Jordan in the evening and it goes to his voice mail, which is full. Probably a good idea to let them have their space for now. When they want me, they know how to reach me.

I go to a nearby hamburger joint and order a cheeseburger. After my nights of eating vegan, I feel a twinge of guilt as I bite into that juicy beef patty. And the melted cheese, a dairy product. And the bun, high in gluten. The French fries I feel only slightly better about.

I get on the phone with Jess and we walk through my commentaries for Episodes 5 and 6. It takes me most of an hour to get all of them right. Then I do a brief check-in with my husband. He's good, kids are good, pets are good. At home, all is good.

Friday night I get my best sleep of the week, a solid seven hours. Getting enough sleep is a challenge when I'm on the road for an investigation.

On Saturday morning I do a FaceTime with my daughter and son. They set up the phone so I can watch them watching our home TV, where *Frozen* is playing for the zillionth time. But I never tire of seeing and hearing our kids react to the animated travails of Anna and Kristoff.

I call Jordan Saturday morning to see if he and Victoria are up for talking today. Again my call goes to voice mail, and again his voice mail is full. I decide to keep giving them their space.

At midday, I drive down to the UCSB campus for the first time. I park in the same lot where Jordan and Victoria parked the night of June fifth. Using a school map, I take the most direct route to the main library in the center of campus. It's Saturday, but even with no classes there are quite a few students riding around on cruiser bikes. Though it's mid-October, most are wearing shorts and flip-flops. I enter the library and take the elevator to the seventh floor. There I find the private study rooms, all in use. It's as quiet as a crypt in here. I descend the stairwell, seven flights, where I do see security cameras—installed since or not working that night? I reach the ground floor and step outside. Then I take the path that I imagine Jordan and Victoria would have walked as they made their way down to the Commencement Green. I pass through the outside of the theater and dance complex, closed on weekends. I'll be coming back here at some point to look inside the classrooms and performance spaces.

I step onto the big sprawling lawn that looks out on the thirty-acre UCSB Lagoon, which is lime green because of a type of algae that grows in there. A hundred yards beyond it, I can see the sparkly blue of the Pacific Ocean. I go over to that magnolia tree, where two students are sitting in the shade, eyes glued to their phones. I take a look inside that cluster of trunks and my mind conjures images of two people making love at midnight. Because of the cramped space and vertical angles, they had to be on their feet the whole time. I click off a few reference photos.

Then I feel the hairs prickle on the back of my neck. I turn around and see him. Blackbeard. He's standing on a hill above the lawn. And he's looking at me. Or not just looking. He's watching me.

My mind does some fast processing. He approached me on the street outside Jordan's house, said he had something to tell me, then shied away and disappeared. And now here he is again. Did he follow me to campus? Is he—stalking me? Given it's broad daylight and we're out in the open, I start toward him. I'm focused on learning two things—who is he and what did he have to tell me? Seeing me come toward him, he just stands there. Still as a statue, watching me approach.

I hear the ping of an incoming text. I glance at my phone screen and see it's from Jordan. Right now, he's the only person whose message I would stop to look at:

We're laying low today. Let's touch base later to discuss next steps.

"Next steps," I repeat to myself. Interesting choice of words. When I look up from my phone screen, Blackbeard is not there. I rush forward to where I saw him standing and don't see him anywhere. This is beyond weird. Then I hear the vroom of a motorcycle and I catch sight of Blackbeard racing off down the street, away from campus.

I send a text to Jess describing the encounter. This is part of our safe practices protocol. Whenever I feel there might be a threat to my safety, I document it ASAP and loop her in. She texts back within a minute:

I purchased you a can of pepper spray at the nearby Target. Curb-side pickup. Go now and text me when it's in your hand.

Good ol' Jess. I follow her instructions and then send her a photo of me holding my new self-defense tool.

I don't hear from Jordan or Victoria the rest of Saturday. I end up taking a little tourist trip to downtown Santa Barbara in the late after-noon. It's beautiful here. Note to self: a future vacation spot for the family. I stay on alert, though, pepper spray close at hand, glancing warily at men with dark beards.

Sunday morning I call Jordan again. It goes to voice mail again. Which is full again. I do a FaceTime with my husband and kids, then spend a few hours scanning comments on our first four episodes. As with everything social media, opinions run from triple A to triple Z. Mostly, though, I see an outpouring of sympathy for the couple. Which is a direct result of the way they're coming off on our podcast. Jess calls in the afternoon and we do a final check on Episodes 5 and 6. I ask if she's feeling anxious about the week ahead.

"Anxious how?"

"I don't know, that this will explode in our faces, we'll make some mistake and get canceled."

Jess says, "As long as we stick with our process and stay vigilant on our standards, we'll be fine." Thank you, my producer, I needed that reassurance.

Later that afternoon I go back to Sprouts Farmers Market and pick up a green bean casserole from the deli. That's my dinner. Yes, it's vegan. And it's very tasty.

Around eight in the evening, I call Jordan and get the "voice mail box is full" message. I consider driving over to check on them. Maybe they turned off their phones for the weekend? It's okay, Monday morning we'll pick up where we left off. Despite reassuring myself, I do not get a good night's sleep.

Monday morning I'm up early checking social media reactions to

Episodes 5 and 6, both having dropped at 5:00 A.M. Eastern. Seventy-five thousand likes already on Instagram. Wow. We even get a mention on *Good Morning America*. *The Raines Report* goes mainstream!

I leave a few minutes earlier than the other mornings and drive a route I've gotten to know well. I turn down Jordan's street and see the media mob has grown over the weekend. Now there are two Santa Barbara sheriff's SUVs parked across from the house. Filled with anticipation, I pull into the driveway. Just as on the other mornings, I text Jordan that I've arrived so he can open the garage door. Usually the door starts rising within a few seconds of my text. Thirty seconds pass and the garage door stays shut. After a minute, I text Jordan again. Another full minute passes. The garage doesn't open. And I receive no reply text.

Two more minutes go by. It feels like two hours.

My pulse quickens and sweat pops out on my forehead. Behind me I am hyperaware of being watched by the global media and four eagle-eyed sheriff's deputies. Of course, it's possible that Jordan's phone is off and he hasn't gotten my texts. But here's my dilemma. If I go to the front door and it's locked and no one answers my knocks, that could set off big-time alarm bells. Not only with the media but with law enforcement. I can foresee a situation that quickly spins out of control. The longer I sit here in my car, the more suspicious it looks. I have two choices, calmly drive away or try the side gate that leads into the backyard. There is a chance the gate is locked. And it would not do for me to climb over it. But if it's unlocked, I can get in and make this look semi-normal. Whatever I decide, I have to do it fast.

I open my door and step out, barely managing not to trip and fall. I show confidence—despite my shaky legs—as I go to the gate on the side of the garage. I reach for the handle and turn it—the gate opens! Huge relief! I enter and shut it behind me. Now hidden from the authorities and camera lenses, I exhale. Then I brace myself for what lies ahead.

I walk around to the backyard and the French doors off the kitchen. All the shades are drawn, no way to see inside. I check the sky for drones, then knock. No answer. I try the knob. Locked. I turn and look around, wondering if there's a hide-a-key somewhere. My eyes fix on the Weber grill in a corner of the deck. I go lift the lid and check underneath. I find a hide-a-key magnet under the air vent. Just where people who never use the barbecue might put it.

I take the key out, go to the French doors, slide the key into the lock, and push it open. I step inside the house and shut the door behind me. Now what?

Hello? Jordan? Victoria? Gail? Anyone?

I go through all the rooms. I open closets. I look behind doors and under beds. I go to check the garage. Jordan's Wrangler is there, locked. I look in the windows. Nobody inside.

I am now reasonably sure that Jordan and Victoria, who were warned they would be arrested if they attempted to leave this house, have left this house.

Without drawing the attention of the media mob or those ever watchful deputies, and under the nose of their embedded journalist, the prime suspects in the De Carlo double murder have made a clean getaway.

S6:E9

JESS MONAY: Hey, Ry. How's the morning going?

RYANNA RAINES: Not so great, Jess. I'm at Jordan's house. And they're gone. Jordan, Victoria, Gail. They are nowhere to be found. I'm the only one in here.

JESS MONAY: *What?*

RYANNA RAINES: Over the weekend I was letting them have their space. I called Jordan a few times, but it went to voice mail, which was full. I got one text from him Saturday afternoon. I'll read it from my phone.

"We're laying low today. Let's touch base later to discuss next steps."

That was it. Didn't hear from him all day Sunday. But I'm thinking, okay, no need to overreact, we'll just resume Monday morning. And now no one's here, and I realize I don't have Victoria's or Gail's contacts.

JESS MONAY: Could they have been arrested?

RYANNA RAINES: The sheriff is still parked outside and so's the media. If they'd been arrested and hauled away, we would have heard about it.

JESS MONAY: Where are you exactly right now? Inside the house?

RYANNA RAINES: Yes! I've been all through it, the rooms, the closets, the bathrooms. I checked the garage and Jordan's car is still here. Other than me, there are no people in this house. Unless they're hiding in some attic or basement I don't know about.

JESS MONAY: How could they vanish without anyone seeing anything?

RYANNA RAINES: You are correct. This is nuts.

JESS MONAY: You said the mother took an Uber from the airport?

RYANNA RAINES: Yes, she did not have a car. Jordan and Victoria have friends around campus. Maybe one drove over here and picked them up.

JESS MONAY: But not from the front of the house, they would've been seen. I know there's a backyard and a fence. What's on the other side of the fence?

RYANNA RAINES: An alley, I think. I don't think it's a street.

JESS MONAY: So the only way they could've gotten out unseen would be through the backyard.

RYANNA RAINES: I guess that's right. They did not go out the front. The whole world thinks they're still inside here, including law enforcement.

JESS MONAY: Have you been texting Jordan?

RYANNA RAINES: I texted him when I pulled up to let me in the garage. He hasn't responded.

JESS MONAY: How did you get into the house?

RYANNA RAINES: The side gate was unlocked. The back door to the kitchen was locked, but I found the hide-a-key. I can't go back outside right now. Everyone will know something's wrong.

JESS MONAY: So you arrive at the house, they're not there. It's reasonable to give ourselves a little time to think this through. Did you check to see if their travel bags are still there? Passports, credit cards, cash?

RYANNA RAINES: Right. Good. I can check that. Sorry, my mind is a bit blown.

JESS MONAY: It's okay, I got you. Let's switch to FaceTime so I can see what you're seeing.

RYANNA RAINES: By the way, I'm Ryanna Raines. And welcome to *The Raines Report*, an audio crime-investigation series produced in association with Amplify. This is Episode 9 and we're calling it "Lights On, Nobody Home."
     I'm texting AJ:
     Call me ASAP.
     We have to let the attorneys know. They might have information. Okay, Jordan's bedroom. Looking for the backpack that he had when he got back from Mexico. Not finding it. Let's check the office. No backpack here, either. Front room, no.
     You know what I just realized? They left some lights on. The nightstand. The hallway.

JESS MONAY: Because they left when it was dark? Speaking of the nightstand, check the drawer.

RYANNA RAINES: Not seeing his passport, or wallet, or cash. Or anything that looks like it belongs to Victoria.

JESS MONAY: Top of the dresser?

RYANNA RAINES: Pair of Jockey shorts and T-shirt. I won't speculate on whether they're clean. Opening a dresser drawer. This must be Victoria's. A lavender-scented candle. Drugstore sunglasses. Sunblock, lip balm. Striped socks. Some face lotion. Things she didn't take because she didn't think she'd need them.

JESS MONAY: I'm Watson to your Holmes. Go, Sherlock.

RYANNA RAINES: So the bed is neatly made. That suggests they didn't leave in the morning after having slept in it. If you're making a getaway and thinking you may never come back here, why take the time to make the bed?

JESS MONAY: Right, so they left at night, before going to bed.

RYANNA RAINES: It could've been last night or Saturday night. All four bed pillows are here.

JESS MONAY: They expect to land in a place that has bed pillows, like a motel or hotel.

RYANNA RAINES: Or someone's guest bedroom. Now I'm kneeling down to look under the bed. Dusty down here.

JESS MONAY: They were gone a month and in no mood for housecleaning when they got back.

RYANNA RAINES: I'm seeing pieces of broken glass under here. They have a curve to them. From a drinking glass that broke on the floor? They missed sweeping up these pieces?

JESS MONAY: Do they have dust on them? I mean, can you tell if it was broken before they left or after they got back?

RYANNA RAINES: The dust seems to be underneath the pieces, so this was recently. I'm checking the wastebasket in the bathroom. Yep, here are other pieces. It's a drinking glass. Bottom is cracked, too. Doesn't look like it was broken by accident, more like it was purposely smashed.

JESS MONAY: Blood on the glass?

RYANNA RAINES: I thought of that—no.

JESS MONAY: While we're in the trash, anything else of interest?

RYANNA RAINES: Used tissues. Jordan and Victoria said they were coming down with something.

JESS MONAY: Ick.

RYANNA RAINES: Here's a receipt. From a pharmacy, a prescription—that's private medical information. Strands of hair, from a hairbrush, dark like Victoria's. A cardboard thingy you get at the end of a roll of toilet paper. Used Q-tips. Nothing of note.

I'm going back to the bedroom nightstand to look more thoroughly. Cloths for cleaning eyeglasses. A pair of wired earbuds. Note cards, blank. Pens, pencils. A receipt from Andersen's restaurant. For two bowls of pea soup. Maybe Jordan and Victoria went together?

JESS MONAY: I'm searching it. Two locations, one in Santa Nella, one in Buellton. The Buellton restaurant is thirty-five miles north of the UC Santa Barbara campus. This describes their pea soup as vegetarian and gluten-free.

RYANNA RAINES: Wait a second, I just found a second receipt from Andersen's. Also for two bowls of split pea soup. One is dated June . . .

JESS MONAY: Don't tell me—June fifth, the night of the murders?

RYANNA RAINES: Nope, June ninth. The other is from July first.

JESS MONAY: Driving thirty-five miles each way for a bowl of split pea? Must be darn good soup.

RYANNA RAINES: If they went together, maybe there's something sentimental to it?

JESS MONAY: Where else? Closets are where people keep things of value. Or things to hide.

RYANNA RAINES: We know detectives already searched this house, twice. But they weren't looking for the same thing we are. Jordan's closet, okay. T-shirts on hangers, black, white, gray. A couple of hoodie sweatshirts. A few collared shirts.

JESS MONAY: Those hoodies, do they have kangaroo pockets in front? I remember my brothers would stick things in there and forget about them. I was in charge of the laundry at our house, and I'd find cash, condoms, dime bags.

RYANNA RAINES: Checking. Got something. You'll never guess.

JESS MONAY: A receipt for Andersen's pea soup?

RYANNA RAINES: Oh, Watson, you are good.

JESS MONAY: Elementary, Ms. Holmes. What's the date?

RYANNA RAINES: July nineteenth. Okay, there's AJ calling. I'll call you back.

AJ NOVICK: Your text said urgent?

RYANNA RAINES: I'm inside Jordan's house, and Jordan and Victoria are not here.

AJ NOVICK: Where are they?

RYANNA RAINES: I have no idea. I was hoping you might know.

AJ NOVICK: No. Okay. Did anyone see them leave?

RYANNA RAINES: The media and sheriff's deputies are all out there acting like they're still inside.

AJ NOVICK: I'm calling Victoria on my other line.
    Voice mail:
    Hello, Victoria, AJ here, nine-thirty Monday morning. Call me as soon as you get this. It's urgent. Thanks.

Sending her a text marked urgent. Also texting Natalie to call me. How did they get out of the house without anyone noticing?

RYANNA RAINES: Got to be through the backyard. Probably late at night. Gail's gone, too.

AJ NOVICK: What were they driving?

RYANNA RAINES: Not Jordan's car—it's still in the garage. And Gail did not have a car—unless she rented one over the weekend. I wasn't here Saturday or Sunday.

AJ NOVICK: What else can you tell by looking around the house?

RYANNA RAINES: Both Jordan's and Victoria's backpacks are gone. I looked for their passports, credit cards, cash, and haven't found anything. When I was here Friday afternoon, Jordan was very upset about being trapped inside the house. He called a friend who declined to come over because of all the media outside. That kind of sent him into a spiral.

AJ NOVICK: This will force the prosecutor's hand. Unless we can find them before anyone realizes they're gone.

RYANNA RAINES: The only other person who knows about this right now is my producer, Jess.

AJ NOVICK: There's Natalie. I'm going to put her on the line and have you tell her.

Hi, Natalie. I've got Ryanna on with us. Ryanna, please repeat for Natalie the news you just told me.

RYANNA RAINES: I'm inside Jordan's Santa Barbara house right now, and Jordan, Victoria, and Gail Berne are not here. They didn't tell me they were leaving and I haven't seen a note anywhere. Jordan is not responding to my texts.

NATALIE BLOOM: Where's his car?

RYANNA RAINES: Parked in the garage.

NATALIE BLOOM: So they're on foot? Maybe they walked a few blocks to get breakfast?

AJ NOVICK: That's a hell of a risk for a stack of pancakes. And they wouldn't have made it ten steps before the media was all over them.

NATALIE BLOOM: Not to mention the sheriff. What are you thinking, AJ?

AJ NOVICK: They felt trapped and justified leaving because they haven't been charged with a crime. They could be headed anywhere. But like when they left for Mexico, they aren't running. They snuck off to get some privacy back while they still can.

NATALIE BLOOM: I doubt the D.A.'s office is going to sympathize with that justification. They're going to see this as a trigger event. The state now has a green light for putting those two in jail.

RYANNA RAINES: Which one of you is calling the D.A. to tell him your clients are missing?

AJ NOVICK: When we admit we can't find our clients, it signals we've lost control. And that's when things get dangerous.

RYANNA RAINES: Between my resources and yours, let's try to find them before anyone notices them missing. At some point, I'm going to have to leave this house, and it would be good to have an idea of where they are before that.

NATALIE BLOOM: We have access to Jordan's bank and credit card accounts. We can monitor them to watch for new charges.

AJ NOVICK: I have Gail's number. I'll keep calling her.

RYANNA RAINES: And I'll keep searching the house to see if they left any clues. You want to say we'll get back on the phone at 12:00 noon unless something breaks before then?

The attorneys agree and we hang up. Next, I call Jess back and give her a rundown.

JESS MONAY: I put Hailey on locating Thaddeus Baylor to see if he knows anything.

RYANNA RAINES: We have to be careful not to disclose that Jordan and Victoria have left the house. Once that gets out, it's going to unleash a crap storm.

JESS MONAY: You know what the social media knee-jerk will be? That we helped them escape.

RYANNA RAINES: A lot of folks will gleefully point the finger of responsibility at *The Raines Report*. And at me personally.

JESS MONAY: So we've got some time. We'll find them.

RYANNA RAINES: I check the hallway closets, which hold a couple of extra bath towels and a set of bedsheets. I look into the kitchen pantry, which is close to bare. I go into the second bedroom, converted into a drama-school student's office. Gail's bags are gone and the sleeper bed is folded back into the sofa. I think about Gail's mindset, knowing the risks of helping her daughter secretly escape from this house. Did she surrender to pressure from Victoria? Gail didn't get dragged along against her will. But against her better judgment?

There are two shelves packed with books on playwriting and directing. I see a volume titled *Staging O'Neill*. I find it well-thumbed with many sections highlighted. Here's one: "The play's director was very protective of his actors' feelings, as well as their freedom to create as individual artists. He would not try to impose his own ideas upon his actors and never raised his voice with them. He insisted on a spirit of collaboration."

I check my phone. Ten past eleven. Fifty minutes till high noon—and a decision point. No sooner do I set the phone down than an incoming text pings.

My heart stops.

It's from Jordan. It says:

Are you alone?

After steadying myself, I type out these words, aware Jordan can see my blinking ellipsis:

I am alone. Inside your house. Where are you?

He comes back with:

We are safe. We want you here with us. If we tell you where to meet us, you must promise to come alone and not tell anyone.

I text back:

The media and sheriff think you're in the house. My car is parked in the driveway. I can try to leave casually and not attract attention. But I may be stopped or followed.

Jordan replies:

Drive away and head for 101 North. If no one follows you, text me and I'll send directions. Otherwise we can't take the chance.

I want to write *Take the chance??* but instead I text:

Leaving now. You'll hear from me shortly.

Jordan replies with a thumbs-up.

Do I alert Jess, AJ, or Natalie? There's still over forty minutes before our deadline expires. This may be my only chance to hook back up with those two before they're in police custody. How do you feel about your acting abilities, Ry?

I go into the kitchen and open the drawer where I saw Jordan put the extra garage door opener. Then I prepare myself for a performance. Is this what an actor feels before making an entrance? Pushing aside my stage fright, I press the button and drop the opener in my pocket. The garage door rises on an audience that now numbers well over a hundred. I take a breath and here I go, out to the driveway and one step after another to the driver's side of my rental. I unlock it and get inside and turn on the engine, pretending not to be someone in a hurry. The garage door has been open all of ten seconds, allowing the spectators a good look at Jordan's Jeep. Then I roll down my window, stick out my left hand, and give a friendly wave to an imaginary person inside the garage. At the same time, my right hand presses the button on the concealed garage opener. In another six seconds the garage is shut. I shift into reverse and back out of the driveway, an expression of nonchalance pasted on my face. I feel more anxiety behind the wheel than when I was sixteen taking my first driver's test. I do not meet anyone's eyes, especially not the sheriff's deputies.

After backing up, my trembling hand shifts into drive and my wobbly foot touches the gas pedal. At fifteen miles an hour I roll down the street, spectators flanking both sidewalks. I reach the stop sign at the end of the block and turn right. I drive for half a block and pull over to the curb. I wait here to see if I'm being followed.

No other car comes after mine. I text Jordan that the coast is clear and wait for instructions. They come right back. With a slightly steadier hand I shift into drive and head for the 101 freeway, northbound.

S6:E10

RYANNA RAINES: Jordan's directions say: "North on 101 to Old Coast Highway, turn right. To Alisal Road, turn left. Continue to park entrance. Go to southeast corner of lot. Wait there."

I input Alisal Road into the navigation app. It's thirty-five minutes away. I should arrive before noon—then what? Jordan and Victoria have gone to a public park and are guiding me to them. Can I convince them to come back to the house before they're discovered missing? Have they gone on the run, with plans to hide out in the wilds of the Santa Barbara hill country? I have no idea what to expect, and the clock keeps ticking.

I'm Ryanna Raines. And welcome to *The Raines Report*, an audio crime-investigation series produced in association with Amplify. This is Episode 10, which we're calling "The Waterfall."

I exit the freeway and find myself on a pleasant rural road with a winery to one side and signs pointing to a horse ranch down the way. A few miles up I see the sign for Nojoqui Falls Park—maintained by the County of Santa Barbara—and turn down the entrance road. I find the public parking lot and drive into the far left corner. Mine is the only car in the immediate area. It is five minutes to noon. I am about to text Jordan when a car—a rental, it turns out—pulls up and parks beside me. Gail is at the wheel. Jordan and Victoria are in the back seat. They both get out and through opposite doors climb into my back seat. I turn around to face them.

JORDAN DE CARLO: Open your window and breathe the fresh air. How about this for a setting?

RYANNA RAINES: Setting for what?

VICTORIA BERNE: Our last hours of freedom.

RYANNA RAINES: You want to tell me what's going on?

JORDAN DE CARLO: Couldn't take that confinement anymore. If all that's going to happen is the sheriff comes to the door and drives us to jail, we'd just be going from one prison to another.

VICTORIA BERNE: This reminds me of where I grew up in the Pacific Northwest, always close to nature.

RYANNA RAINES: When I found the house empty, I contacted your attorneys. I'm advising you both to call them and let them know you're okay. And what your plans are going forward.

JORDAN DE CARLO: Sure, we'll talk to them. As for our plans, we rented a room up the road.

RYANNA RAINES: Near Andersen's?

JORDAN DE CARLO: You know Andersen's?

RYANNA RAINES: I came upon some receipts in your bedroom. You're a fan of their pea soup.

JORDAN DE CARLO: The waterfall here is our nirvana. We try to come once a week. Andersen's is the next exit, so it became our ritual. A hike followed by a bowl of split pea.

VICTORIA BERNE: This is where we get away from the pressures of school and the world. Come with us and we'll show you the falls. It's really peaceful up there.

RYANNA RAINES: If you two do not go back to the Santa Barbara house, arrest warrants will be issued, possibly today. They'll be coming for you.

VICTORIA BERNE: You didn't tell anyone we were here, did you?

RYANNA RAINES: No, but AJ and Natalie are expecting to hear back from me. I don't think you want to force the authorities to launch an operation to come get you. That would A, be dangerous, and B, show the court you're not cooperating. And they will penalize you.

JORDAN DE CARLO: What, lock us in solitary confinement? Give us a dozen lashes?

RYANNA RAINES: Deny you bail.

JORDAN DE CARLO: They're not giving us bail. We're already considered a flight risk because of Mexico. Or they'll set a ridiculously high amount, and maybe I can get Aunt Frances to put it up for me, but Victoria can't afford it. You think I'd let her stay in jail while I get out? Can't do that.

VICTORIA BERNE: This is it for us. The end of the line.

RYANNA RAINES: I get that. Just keep your advocates in the loop. Please call them. Now.

Jordan and Victoria look at each other. Without another word, they climb out of my car and step away to talk things over privately. I get out and go over to Gail's side of the car.

GAIL BERNE: I shouldn't have helped them get away. That's what you're going to tell me, right?

RYANNA RAINES: One mom to another, I'm not going to tell you that. I give you a ton of credit for flying down here to be with your daughter.

You showed up for her. I don't know how much she appreciates that right now. But she will someday.

I see Jordan and Victoria separately getting on their phones. That gives me some relief.

GAIL BERNE: I was listening to the podcast. They were right to call you. It's helping their case.

RYANNA RAINES: It's giving them a public hearing. But there's another side of the story that needs to be heard, too.

Gail looks away. Can you hear the awkward silence?

JORDAN DE CARLO: Okay, Natalie and AJ know we're safe, and that we're not on the run.

VICTORIA BERNE: Come to the waterfall. It's just a mile up the path. It's an important place to us.

RYANNA RAINES: At that exact moment my phone rings, AJ calling.

Hey, I'm with Jordan and Victoria. They're fine, I'm fine, let me call you back.

I click off and turn to my subjects. Hike to the waterfall with two soon-to-be fugitives, escapees from lockdown, who may be cold-blooded murderers? I fire off a quick text to Jess, then turn off my phone. The truth is, I don't feel unsafe with these two. I'm going to trust my instincts here. Gail decides to stay with the car. So off we go as a trio, two criminal suspects and a crime journalist, embarking on a nature walk. The dirt trail we climb is lined on both sides with thick trees and twisty branches filled with fluttering leaves.

VICTORIA BERNE: It's best on weekdays, when there aren't many people here. I love the way the sunlight comes through the trees.

RYANNA RAINES: Jordan reaches out and pulls Victoria close as they go up the trail. They move hip to hip, arms around each other's shoulders. I'm reminded of when I first saw them coming out of the airport terminal. Were they glowing then, or was that my imagination? Are they glowing now, or is that the California sunlight filtering through the leaves?

VICTORIA BERNE: I love you. No matter what, that will never change.

JORDAN DE CARLO: We can never give up the dream.

RYANNA RAINES: May I ask what the dream is?

VICTORIA BERNE: Changing the world through opening people's hearts . . .

JORDAN DE CARLO: . . . and expanding their capacity to feel.

RYANNA RAINES: We pass a warning sign: ALTHOUGH MOUNTAIN LIONS ARE SELDOM SEEN, THEY ARE UNPREDICTABLE AND HAVE BEEN KNOWN TO ATTACK WITHOUT WARNING. Hey, we have mountain lions in Pennsylvania, too!

VICTORIA BERNE: "I feel the cool, moist air on my skin. I hear the rustle of leaves and the trilling of birds. I breathe in the woodsy smell of tree bark. I taste air that is fragrant with nature. I see flashes of sun above the tree branches, and my lover's profile as he walks next to me." That's an exercise we do in performance studies. When I'm not here and can't be here, I'll be able to access my sense memories.

RYANNA RAINES: Victoria leans her head on Jordan's shoulder, he strokes her hair.

JORDAN DE CARLO: Can you hear the waterfall? C'mon!

RYANNA RAINES: They run ahead through a tunnel of gnarled tree trunks. I speed up my walk and arrive at the falls a few moments after them. In front of me is a wall of rock rising sharply upward—eighty feet, according to a guidebook. Deep veins of moss stripe this wall. A light stream of water falls down from above and splashes into a shallow pool. Jordan and Victoria take off their shoes and step into this pool. They meet in the center and embrace. My instinct is to get a photo. Then Jordan turns and tosses me his phone. Surprised, I almost drop it. He and Victoria face me and pose together. Like two of the happiest people on earth.

JORDAN DE CARLO: Make it a keeper.

RYANNA RAINES: Under pressure, I take several from varying angles. Given how photogenic these two are, it would be hard to screw up any photo with them in it.

JORDAN DE CARLO: I'm airdropping them to you. Will you post them on your page after we're in custody?

RYANNA RAINES: I'm not saying no. It's about the context.

VICTORIA BERNE: We'll send you permissions to use the photos. And you will or you won't.

JORDAN DE CARLO: Just curious, what will you do on the podcast when we're in custody?

RYANNA RAINES: I haven't thought too far beyond this experience of embedding with you. I'm taking it one step at a time—literally.

VICTORIA BERNE: We're glad we could help you stay more present in your work life.

RYANNA RAINES: We hear voices and see four other hikers arrive at the falls. Jordan and Victoria stop talking and turn away, worried they'll be recognized. I reflexively angle my face away from the newcomers. They are three men and a woman, early twenties, laughing and joking. Their loud voices change the intimate vibe between the three of us. As the hikers take off their shoes to step into the pool, Jordan and Victoria step out and back into their shoes. One of the other hikers says to me, "Not much of a waterfall, is it?"

I shrug and say, "You should see it in the rainy season." I have no idea what it's like in the rainy season. Does California even have a rainy season? I turn around and start back down the trail. I go slowly, waiting for Jordan and Victoria to catch up.

VICTORIA BERNE: Nothing lasts. Nothing.

RYANNA RAINES: I feel their discouragement at not getting more time at the waterfall. We move down the trail at three-quarter speed, squeezing every precious moment out of this hike.

Suddenly from behind we hear, "Jordan? Victoria?" We turn around to see one of the hikers coming after us holding up his phone. He barks a jubilant "I knew it was you guys!"

JORDAN DE CARLO: Hey, that's not cool. Don't do that, okay?

RYANNA RAINES: The hiker ignores Jordan, continues holding up his phone and recording. He says, "Aren't you two supposed to be locked down in your Santa Barbara house?"

VICTORIA BERNE: We're just like you, we came here to enjoy nature. Can you give us a break?

RYANNA RAINES: Jordan suddenly lunges at the man and tries to grab his phone.

VICTORIA BERNE: Jordan, don't! He's an asshole, let him be!

RYANNA RAINES: There is a momentary scuffle. Then Jordan abruptly backs off.

JORDAN DE CARLO: Let's get out of here.

RYANNA RAINES: The walk down the trail speeds up and turns even more somber. We get to the parking lot and Jordan says he'll ride with me. Next stop, Andersen's. Jordan and Victoria have brought "disguises," knit caps and sunglasses. We leave the park and five minutes up the road we pull into the restaurant parking lot. I ask Jordan to go ahead inside. I'll join them after I call AJ back.

JORDAN DE CARLO: You're not going to tell him where we are, right?

RYANNA RAINES: No, but we need to stay informed of what law enforcement knows, when they know it, and how they react.

Jordan gives a submissive nod. He gets out of the car and goes with Victoria and her mom into the restaurant. I lift my phone and tap AJ's contact.

AJ NOVICK: Are you going to tell me where you are?

RYANNA RAINES: Your client asked me not to disclose that information and I agreed.

AJ NOVICK: When arrest warrants are signed at the San Diego Superior Court, will it change how you answer that question?

RYANNA RAINES: If it reaches that point, I will strenuously encourage them to give themselves up on the spot. And everything I've seen indicates they will do exactly that. The immediate question is, how to let the sheriff know they've left the house and do not intend to go back?

AJ NOVICK: The safest, most predictable way would be to have Jordan and Victoria come to my office in west L.A. When the warrant is issued, I'll arrange for the San Diego deputies to pick them up here while keeping the operation under wraps.

RYANNA RAINES: I could recommend that.

AJ NOVICK: It's crucial to keep the lines of communication open between these two and their counsels. I know I don't have to tell you that.

RYANNA RAINES: Can the disclosure that they left Santa Barbara be delayed until morning? That would give me this afternoon and evening to talk to them about a safe and sane plan of surrender.

AJ NOVICK: Theoretically we can wait, but we would then need to disclose being aware they departed twenty-four hours earlier—which will not go down well. If in the same breath I tell them the suspects are in my office and are consenting to being transported down to San Diego, that will ease their minds a lot.

RYANNA RAINES: I'll explain to them the benefits of arriving at your office by noon tomorrow.

AJ NOVICK: Ten A.M. If you're anywhere north of Santa Barbara, they need to leave before dawn.

RYANNA RAINES: I tell AJ I'll do my best, and with that I go inside the restaurant to join Jordan, Victoria, and her mom. I find them in a booth with brown leather seats. I slide in next to Gail and glance at the menu. But there really is only one choice. Gail orders four bowls of split pea soup.

JORDAN DE CARLO: Boyfriend, girlfriend, girlfriend's mom, podcast host. This feels so normal. Only it's so not.

VICTORIA BERNE: For the rest of my life, I'll never take normal for granted.

RYANNA RAINES: Jordan and Victoria keep their faces turned toward each other and I can tell they're holding hands under the table. After some uneasy small talk, our soup is served steaming hot in white ceramic bowls. Old-school style.

You're right, this is delicious.

VICTORIA BERNE: All organic ingredients, no ham or bacon, gluten free.

JORDAN DE CARLO: I'm dreading how bad the food will be in jail.

RYANNA RAINES: I think I read that Vista Detention Facility does a "meatless Mondays."

I mean that to be a comfort, but it comes off like gallows humor. Jordan and Victoria hit one of those sudden shifts into melancholy. Their courage falters. Then they look into each other's eyes to find a mutual jolt of strength. This getaway of theirs has altered the dynamics of my relationship with them and caused their personal doomsday clock to move a lot closer to midnight. Yet, whatever their sins or the sins against them, their feelings for each other keep coming out in these touching bursts of heartache. If this were video instead of audio, you might see my eyes getting misty.

RYANNA RAINES: I'm Ryanna Raines. And welcome to *The Raines Report*, an audio crime-investigation series produced in association with Amplify. This is Episode 11, and we're calling it "Hold Me and Don't Let Go."

VICTORIA BERNE: My mom went into the office and paid for two rooms with cash. Sixty-five each. The reviews said "clean and convenient." So.

RYANNA RAINES: We have gone from bowls of soup to a small, no-frills motel about two minutes down the road from the restaurant. This is where Jordan and Victoria plan to spend the night. It's now past four in the afternoon. There have been no further calls from the attorneys. Jordan and Victoria take this as a sign that no warrants will be issued today. The four of us gather in their room, with the single window open and looking out to an empty parking lot. A breeze flutters the yellowed curtains. Jordan and Victoria are side by side on the bed, backs against the vinyl headboard. Gail and I sit in plastic chairs. Our phones are out in case someone gets a message.

JORDAN DE CARLO: We're going to finish our play.

VICTORIA BERNE: And stage it off-Broadway to rave reviews.

RYANNA RAINES: These may be exceptional students of the theater arts, but their optimism feels a tad strained right now.

JORDAN DE CARLO: From the day we go to jail until the day we're acquitted, it'll take a year, maybe eighteen months. We'll have our whole lives ahead of us.

VICTORIA BERNE: With so many more life experiences to share.

RYANNA RAINES: I want to ask this again. What makes you so confident you'll be acquitted?

VICTORIA BERNE: Our alibi. When the murders happened, we were two hundred miles away.

RYANNA RAINES: They'd have to make the case to a judge that there's enough probable cause to arrest you.

JORDAN DE CARLO: Like security camera footage near my parents' home from that night? Not possible. Because we weren't there.

VICTORIA BERNE: When will the prosecution tell us their evidence?

RYANNA RAINES: I'm not giving legal advice, but I believe there'll be a preliminary hearing where the prosecution has to declare why you should go to trial. And there's always a discovery phase before a trial starts. The state is legally compelled to show the defense everything they have against you, even the things in your favor.

JORDAN DE CARLO: What they have against us is that they have nothing against anyone else. This is all about making us guilty so they can show voters they caught the killers of two fine, upstanding high-net-worth citizens.

VICTORIA BERNE: I want to stop talking about it. I'm so tired of feeling helpless and doomed.

RYANNA RAINES: Jordan reaches out and draws Victoria to his chest. Her mother and I watch as he strokes her hair. It's another intimate moment that part of me feels embarrassed to be observing.

Would you like time alone?

VICTORIA BERNE: Later. Right now it feels good to be with people who believe in us.

RYANNA RAINES: I consider clarifying her statement for the record, but in the next moment, both Jordan's and Victoria's phones ring.

VICTORIA BERNE: AJ.

JORDAN DE CARLO: Natalie.

RYANNA RAINES: As they answer, I get up to leave. This is going to be attorney-client privilege time and I can wait. Gail follows me out. I don't get three steps when my phone pings with a text. It's from Jess:

San Diego Superior Court just issued arrest warrants for Jordan De Carlo and Victoria Berne on first-degree murder charges.

GAIL BERNE: So this is when everything changes.

RYANNA RAINES: In separate conversations, Jordan and Victoria are informed that warrants have been formally issued. AJ asks that Gail and I be included on the call to discuss their latest communications with law enforcement. And next steps.

NATALIE BLOOM: According to a San Diego sheriff's website posting from four minutes ago, officers called on the suspects at their Santa Barbara home and discovered both suspects were gone. As of now, the two of you have been declared fugitives from the law. Before AJ and I get back to the detectives, we need to map out a plan. A very specific and safe plan.

JORDAN DE CARLO: We want one last night together. Non-negotiable.

VICTORIA BERNE: We may never get to spend another night with each other.

NATALIE BLOOM: And if the sheriff balks?

JORDAN DE CARLO: We'll run.

VICTORIA BERNE: We're prepared to go into hiding. That will extend this for days, if not weeks.

AJ NOVICK: Guys, that's a really bad idea.

JORDAN DE CARLO: Then negotiate one more night for us. We'll surrender in the morning.

VICTORIA BERNE: Jordan and I are unwavering on this. We'll wake up, shower, and my mom will drive us straight down to the Vista jail. Right, Mom?

GAIL BERNE: Right, yes.

AJ NOVICK: Okay, I see a problem with that.

NATALIE BLOOM: So do I. Gail, I am not questioning your good intentions, but you were the one who helped them leave the house, knowing they'd be arrested if they did so. You're emotionally involved. That is going to weigh heavily against the sheriff trusting you to be the one who delivers them to a surrender point.

JORDAN DE CARLO: We'll drive ourselves.

NATALIE BLOOM: That's not going to work, Jordan.

RYANNA RAINES: And that's the moment both Jordan and Victoria turn to look at me.

VICTORIA BERNE: What about Ryanna?

RYANNA RAINES: Hang on.

AJ NOVICK: That might work.

NATALIE BLOOM: She's a neutral party, with a public reputation to uphold.

RYANNA RAINES: Wait, I have to agree to it first. That would put me in an awkward position, journalistically. I'd be intervening in the legal process.

JORDAN DE CARLO: How is it different from you driving us from the airport to Santa Barbara? You're transporting us from one location to another.

RYANNA RAINES: What's different is you've gone from being suspects to fugitives on the run.

AJ NOVICK: You'll have to give the sheriff a personal guarantee that you will drive them from wherever you are down to our office.

VICTORIA BERNE: We don't want to surrender at your office. We want to go all the way down to the jail.

AJ NOVICK: Why?

JORDAN DE CARLO: We're taking this to the front steps of the place they're going to lock us up. If we're picked up in an office building and driven in the back of a prisoner van to San Diego, our voices will be cut off, we'll turn invisible.

VICTORIA BERNE: We'll surrender at the jail. That's where we agree to be separated.

AJ NOVICK: Is it because you want extra time together? Arrive here at 8:00 A.M. and I'll give you my office. You can be alone until the sheriff arrives.

VICTORIA BERNE: We decided this, AJ. We'll give ourselves up only at the Vista jail.

AJ NOVICK: Ryanna, thoughts?

RYANNA RAINES: Quite a few, actually. Won't the extra hours on the road increase the chances of my car being spotted? And turning this into an O. J. Simpson white Bronco chase?

NATALIE BLOOM: Excellent point.

JORDAN DE CARLO: We'll be in the back hunkered down and you'll wear sunglasses and a hat. No one will recognize you.

RYANNA RAINES: But my rental car has been seen and recorded by the global media going into your garage. Now everyone knows you're missing. They'll be looking for my car.

VICTORIA BERNE: You can switch rentals with my mom. No one's seen her car.

AJ NOVICK: We'll need to connect with the sheriff and see if we can make any of this stick.

RYANNA RAINES: While waiting to hear back from the attorneys, Gail and I go into the second room to give Jordan and Victoria their privacy.

GAIL BERNE: I'm sorry you got caught in the middle of all this.

RYANNA RAINES: I put myself here. You didn't really have that choice. This is your kid's life at stake. How did you make the decision to leave the Santa Barbara house?

GAIL BERNE: They were both so upset. I could hear them crying in the bedroom. Then there's this loud crash. Jordan threw a drinking glass against the wall. I thought, *Someone is going to hurt themselves if I don't help them get out of here.* I went out through the backyard, walked down the street, and called an Uber to take me to the car rental lot. I parked a couple of blocks away, and they left through the backyard at three in the morning.

RYANNA RAINES: That explains the broken glass in Jordan's bedroom. Again, I don't blame you. And because it was prior to the warrants, I don't think you'll be in any legal trouble. When we were up at the park, those two seemed genuinely happy. That must have felt good to you.

GAIL BERNE: To see my daughter's face light up with a smile? You can't put a price on that.

AJ NOVICK: We got the sheriff to okay a 10:00 A.M. surrender at the Vista Detention Facility, which is next to their North County substation. *If* you agree to all their conditions.

RYANNA RAINES: I then call Jess to go over those conditions.

Make, model, and license plate of the vehicle. Only I can be the driver, and I must send updated locations every half hour. We all have to keep our phones on so they can match my reports with our progress via satellite. If we stop along the way—aka bathroom breaks—we have to provide exact information about where we're stopping and for how long. None of which is unreasonable. I personally spoke to the sheriff and promised not to deviate from the plan. Jordan and Victoria are staying in their room until we depart at 5:00 A.M.

JESS MONAY: And what will be the consequences to you if there is a deviation?

RYANNA RAINES: Unless Jordan and Victoria try to commandeer the vehicle, which I don't believe they'll do, as long as I stay in communication and we're making progress, I'll be fine.

JESS MONAY: So, does driving these folks to the jail so they can surrender constitute an ethical breach? Is it a *favor* you're doing in return for the access they've given you? Are you intervening in the legal procedures of the case by agreeing to and following the conditions set by law enforcement? Interesting questions, Ry.

RYANNA RAINES: And your opinion of my ethical choices?

JESS MONAY: I could debate either side, but we don't have that luxury. It's something you're doing, and as your producer, I support it. When and if the fallout comes, we'll deal with it. On a personal level, I worry about your safety. You're putting yourself in the crosshairs of law enforcement all across Southern California. Something goes wrong, there'll be consequences.

RYANNA RAINES: "Goes wrong" as in a tire blowout or our subjects change their minds?

JESS MONAY: Or you get in a fender bender, or you get off at the wrong exit, or someone recognizes you and sends a photo to TMZ of your car on the freeway. You'll be on some of the most heavily trafficked roads in the country, surrounded by some of the most aggressive drivers.

RYANNA RAINES: If I thought too much about all the things that could go wrong, Jess, I wouldn't be able to get out of bed in the morning.

JESS MONAY: I'll say this. It should make for riveting audio journalism.

RYANNA RAINES: Next, I call my husband. After I explain what's going on, he asks a question and I can hear him trying to contain his stress. "Are you going to be safe?"

"Yes. Or as safe as anyone can be driving the freeways of Southern California."

"Why are you doing it? For the podcast? For Jordan and Victoria? You're not their caretaker."

"True, but I see things getting messy if I don't this. I believe this is the best way to achieve a safe resolution for all involved, I really do."

"I'm not going to tell the kids until you're across the finish line."

"Thank you. By tomorrow at one-thirty your time, this part of my reporting will be done."

"And then?"

"And then I'll get on a plane and come home to my family."

Gail's room has two beds, and she invites me to stay the night. I say yes and reimburse her half the cost. The room shares a wall with Jordan and Victoria's room. As we turn off the lights—my alarm set for 4:15—we can hear through the wall the heartbreaking sound of Victoria sobbing. I can't see Gail's face and can only imagine her grief.

Sleep does not come easily. I drift off for what seems a few minutes at a time, then wake up in a panic that I've overslept my alarm. During one of these restless dozes, I have that same dream. Standing at the bottom of the De Carlo driveway, rooted to the pavement as I hear death screams coming from up inside their unseeable house.

When my alarm does go off, I bolt upright, disoriented. Then I remember where I am and why I'm here. I rise, put on my clothes, and go next door to make sure my passengers are awake. We've all agreed to leave the parking lot by 5:00 A.M. I knock at Jordan and Victoria's room. I don't expect them to open the door, but I do expect them to let me know they're up and getting ready. When I don't hear anything, I knock again. Still I hear nothing.

So I call out, "Are you up, guys? Almost time to go." No response. An icy chill runs down my spine. Will this be the second time in twenty-four hours they've escaped from under my nose? Or is it something darker, as in a pact to take their Romeo and Juliet doom all the way?

I start toward the motel office to get a key to their room when their door suddenly opens. A wet-haired Jordan stands there with a bath towel around his waist. He apologizes, saying he and Victoria were in the shower and didn't hear me knock. They're getting dressed and will be ready to travel in ten. I let go an exhale and shake the panic out of my body.

Victoria and Gail share a tearful parting. The daughter takes off her rings and bracelets and gives them to her mom for safekeeping. In their final embrace, I see how reluctant Gail is to let go of her daughter. But she does let go and the three of us get into Gail's blue midsize rental, then head south on the 101. It's still dark and few cars are on the road in either direction.

The first hour of the trip is uneventful. In the rearview I see Jordan and Victoria asleep in each other's arms. I've inputted our destination and leave the map screen on. Every thirty minutes I take a screen grab and text it to the lead detective and defense attorneys. By 6:00 A.M. we've gone seventy miles of the two-hundred-and-thirty. At this rate, we should arrive ahead of the deadline.

JORDAN DE CARLO: Did Episode 7 drop today?

RYANNA RAINES: It did. Forgot all about it.

VICTORIA BERNE: May we listen?

RYANNA RAINES: And then I start a crime investigation podcast on the car speakers, featuring the two people sitting right behind me. The podcast host is in the driver's seat, transporting the duo to a county jail, where they will give themselves up to the sheriff and be arraigned on first-degree murder charges. Perfectly normal, right?

RYANNA RAINES: *There are those points when things start looking black and white. Then here come those pesky shades of gray.*

JORDAN DE CARLO: Can you pause it? What are the shades of gray in this case?

RYANNA RAINES: I'll need to hear the other side of the story before I can answer that.

JORDAN DE CARLO: Either we were two hundred miles from the scene of the crime or we weren't. That's as black and white as it gets.

RYANNA RAINES: Would still love to hear your thoughts on who else may have committed the murders, either of you.

JORDAN DE CARLO: You'll come to the jail and keep doing interviews with us?

RYANNA RAINES: Seems like that would be the plan.

VICTORIA BERNE: In jail, we'd have to do interviews with you individually?

RYANNA RAINES: Probably. Right now, I'm trying to stay in the moment, aka keeping my eyes on the road and hands on the wheel.

Our second hour on the road alternates between quiet and brief exchanges. At one point, Victoria asks me to turn on the car's Bluetooth. She connects with her phone and starts playing a song list by Lorde, the New Zealand singer-songwriter. We listen to smoky electropop anthems with titles like "Meltdown" and "Fallen Fruit." We chat about our musical tastes and favorite recording artists. I'm a little bit country myself—give me some Carrie Underwood and Brad Paisley and I'm good. Jordan leans toward alt-indie bands with names like Black Honey and Wolf Alice. From his Spotify, he plays the songs "Beautifully Unconventional" and "Into the Nightmare." On that one, Jordan sings the lyrics—without irony. His voice is good and resonates with conviction. The musical interlude helps uplift the mood and take the focus off our destination.

After transitioning from the 101 to the 405, at the top of what they call the Sepulveda Pass, we come to a dead stop. It's sevenish during morning rush hour, so this isn't unexpected. I text AJ and Natalie the update, but no one is unduly alarmed. We've factored in stretches of traffic in the five-hour trip time. But after several minutes we haven't moved at all, so Jordan and Victoria check their phones, and, yes, there is an accident up ahead. Hard to tell how bad. The sheriff's department would be aware of freeway conditions, so we're okay, right?

As we're stopped and waiting to start moving, I notice a woman in the car to my left looking at me while holding a phone to her ear. I'm wearing dark sunglasses with my hair pulled back. Am I seeing recognition in the driver's eyes? Will she post our coordinates on social media? C'mon, Ry, dial down the paranoia and keep your eyes in front of you.

JORDAN DE CARLO: We could get out and pose for photos with drivers. Maybe sign a few autographs? We're famous now. For all the wrong reasons, but what the hell?

VICTORIA BERNE: I could perform a tap routine I learned in American Dance.

JORDAN DE CARLO: If you want to dance, let's tango.

RYANNA RAINES: And then Jordan opens his door, hops out, reaches back, and pulls Victoria onto the freeway turned parking lot. They stand facing each other on the asphalt and smoothly assume partnering positions, cheeks turned outward. Then they start to do a tango step, swiveling and swooping together around the perimeter of the car. I experience a range of reactions. Panic, mortification, dread—and admiration because they're excellent dancers. I look around and see drivers and passengers lifting their phones to record the couple. My heart sinks at how this may compromise the rest of the trip. If these images find their way to certain personnel in the San Diego sheriff's department, it will not go well. I barely hold back from lashing out like a high-strung mom at her misbehaving kids. As my anxiety goes to the next level, traffic starts moving. Jordan and Victoria complete a twirl, then hop back into the car and lower their heads.

VICTORIA BERNE: We're sorry. That wasn't a nice thing to do to you.

JORDAN DE CARLO: It was spontaneous combustion. Hope you're not mad.

RYANNA RAINES: I've put myself on the line for both of you. If something goes wrong, the focus will be on me and how I failed to keep my promise to the sheriff and your attorneys.

VICTORIA BERNE: God, what's that?

RYANNA RAINES: We hear a thundering whoosh directly overhead. I roll down my window, stick my head out, and see a helicopter hovering over us. Does it have law enforcement markings? Because of this distraction, I almost rear-end the car in front of us, jerking to a stop within an inch of its bumper. I look up again and see the helicopter's local news station logo. Must be doing its regular reporting on morning rush hour.

Okay, boys and girls, the driver has to focus on not crashing the car. So let's just get through L.A. with minimal talking. And no more bolting out the doors, please.

VICTORIA BERNE: I promise.

JORDAN DE CARLO: I promise, too.

RYANNA RAINES: The heaviest traffic breaks up past LAX. At 40 to 50 miles an hour, I hope we can make up for lost time. It's now creeping up on 8:00 A.M.

JORDAN DE CARLO: Let's record statements for where we see ourselves ten years from today.

VICTORIA BERNE: I see us at a hotel in Paris, celebrating the run of our third Broadway show together and your second Pulitzer. We spend the day wandering through sidewalk art shows in Montmartre and get serenaded by street musicians.

JORDAN DE CARLO: It's a double celebration—you just won your first Best Actress Oscar. I'm only as successful as I am because of your inspiration. You've done so much to open my heart.

VICTORIA BERNE: Not that we're into awards. We don't believe making art should be a competition.

JORDAN DE CARLO: I see us at a mountain cabin, surrounded by wilderness, with two—no, three dogs. We're kicked back in a sunlit window nook, with all these big soft cushions, and we each have a book we're loving. We just laze the day away, looking at the view and reading and thinking and talking about our ideas.

RYANNA RAINES: The closer we get, the more I feel the mood change in the car. As we approach nine o'clock, my skin prickles at the air of rising desperation. In the rearview mirror, I glimpse Jordan and Victoria brushing back tears, clinging to each other. I hear them speak in low, urgent voices.

JORDAN DE CARLO: I love you so, so, so-o-o-o much.

VICTORIA BERNE: I love you today, tomorrow, forever. There will never be anyone else for me.

JORDAN DE CARLO: I've never felt so loved by anyone. You make me the best version of myself.

VICTORIA BERNE: I am in awe of your passion, your commitment, your incredible gifts. I will do everything I can to make the world know how talented and amazing you are.

RYANNA RAINES: This is the countdown to, if not the end of their relationship, then a profound change in it. They are hanging on to every bittersweet moment. My fingers grip and regrip the steering wheel as I try to manage my own apprehension of what awaits.

Looks like we're going to get an escort.

VICTORIA BERNE: Oh my god, is that for us?

JORDAN DE CARLO: Wow.

RYANNA RAINES: As we approach Route 78, which will take us inland to Vista, we see about ten sheriff's SUVs stopped, emergency lights spinning. They are holding back traffic at the turnoff. We are the only car they allow to swing around the overpass. We find ourselves part of a multiple vehicle convoy. This next stretch of highway runs only a few miles before we exit. There are red-and-blue flashing lights in front, to the sides, and behind us. I hear Jordan and Victoria quietly moaning. My legs tremble and I've got raging butterflies in my belly.

VICTORIA BERNE: This is a little too real.

JORDAN DE CARLO: Is it too late to change our minds?

RYANNA RAINES: I look in the rearview to make sure Jordan's not about to jump out of the car. The intensity builds as I take the freeway exit, go down the ramp, and turn onto a wide boulevard. I see the stoplights blinking and a sign ahead says COUNTY COMPLEX. But signage is unnecessary because a group of sheriff and police vehicles form a gauntlet to guide us into the facility. I see SWAT officers in riot gear holding shotguns, as though anticipating the second coming of Bonnie and Clyde.

VICTORIA BERNE: I can't believe they're going to separate us. Hold me and don't let go.

JORDAN DE CARLO: I've got you.

RYANNA RAINES: Entering the parking lot, I drive slowly and cautiously toward the far end, where the sheriff's station and county jail stand next to each other. A group of command-staff officers awaits our arrival.

One of these commanders steps forward and sharply motions to us. "Stop the car! Everyone out with your hands in the air! No fast moves!"

Now I see several shotguns being leveled at us and I say a prayer in my head, something I don't do very often. I step out of the driver's seat, hands raised. I look over my shoulder to see Jordan and Victoria still clinging to each other, not budging from the back seat.

"You two, out of the car now! Do not make us come in to get you!"

I call out to the commander that they are unarmed and not dangerous. He pays no attention to me and signals his deputies. They open both passenger doors and aim their shotguns inside. They are yelling at Jordan and Victoria to get out of the car. I have a sudden vision that this might all go horribly wrong.

So I speak up in my most urgent voice. I scream "Hey, guys, c'mon! Please do what they ask! It'll be okay, just get out of the car!"

Jordan and Victoria climb out the same door, holding hands. The commander shouts at them to let go of each other. They keep their eyes locked and hands clasped. I see each heave a sigh and then let go. Instantly, the officers pull them apart, frisk them, and handcuff them. Two deputies escort each down the path and through the front door of the station. I go to follow them, but an officer blocks my way. He declares that I will be allowed no further.

It's the end of the line for me. I stand there alone, hugging myself. The reception personnel begin to disband and return to their regular duties. I look at my phone: 10:06 A.M.

The phone rings in my hand. Caller ID tells me it's AJ.

AJ NOVICK: You played your role perfectly, Ryanna. Thank you on behalf of Natalie and me and the San Diego sheriff's department. Mission accomplished.

RYANNA RAINES: I see AJ wave to me from inside the doorway of the sheriff's station. Both he and Natalie are on-site to attend their clients through jail processing and their formal arraignment. In just two hours at the Superior Court, in the same complex as the jail and the sheriff's station, Jordan De Carlo, twenty-two, and Victoria Berne, eighteen, will be charged with two counts of murder in the first degree, which carries a penalty of life in prison without parole. Then they'll be locked in separate cells, in different buildings, to begin the long wait until the start of their trial. They will not be allowed to see each other except at preliminary hearings, when they'll be brought into court individually to face their accusers.

JESS MONAY: Welcome back, Ry.

RYANNA RAINES: It is midday on Friday, October twenty-first. Yesterday was a family day for me. Today I'm back in the studio for the first time since October tenth—the day Jordan De Carlo left a message on our tip line. Earlier this morning, our Season 6, Episode 10 dropped, and we have assembled the team to put the final touches on Episode 11, which will drop on Monday.

JESS MONAY: So we're picking this up after your tension-filled five-hour drive with two murder suspects in the back seat. Jordan and Victoria surrendered to authorities in front of the Vista Detention Facility. Within the hour, their mug shots were released publicly and seen in all four corners of the earth.

RYANNA RAINES: Since they'd come under suspicion for the murders, there were few photos of Jordan and Victoria online that showed them up close. Now these flatly lit outlaw portraits snapped during their intake at the jail are coming out and putting human faces to the voices that so many listeners have become emotionally involved with.

JESS MONAY: Social media's doing a collective swoon over those mug shots.

RYANNA RAINES: Contrast those faces with the charges against them, read at their arraignment. "In the matter of the State of California v. Jordan De Carlo and Victoria Berne, the district attorney of San Diego County hereby charges each, under California Penal Code 187, with the unlawful killing of Anthony and Lauren De Carlo, two human beings, with malice aforethought."

JESS MONAY: "Malice aforethought," premeditated. You were in court. How did they plead?

RYANNA RAINES: With their strongest stage voices. "*Not guilty.*"

JESS MONAY: How did they act?

RYANNA RAINES: Mostly they stayed quiet and respectful of the court. But they did keep looking at each other and mouthing *I love you* and *We'll be okay.* The hearing lasted only ten minutes. They tried to embrace at the end, but the deputies kept them apart.

JESS MONAY: Our fact-checker, Hailey, just handed us a printout of a court order issued by a San Diego judge moments ago. Whoa, this is big.

RYANNA RAINES: First pretrial motion by the prosecution. Not a surprise. Here's the ruling:

"The prosecution sought an order to restrict all publicity on the case, specifically referencing the podcast *The Raines Report*. Prior to arrest, defendants provided a series of interviews for said podcast in which they not only proclaimed their innocence but spoke in detail on matters of evidence to be presented at trial. The episodes of this podcast have gone viral on social media and are inflaming public opinion against the prosecutors before they can begin to put on their case. Prosecution contends publicity from this podcast may prejudice potential jurors against the state. Furthermore, there is the risk of the defendants exacerbating the media spectacle by continuing to publicly argue their case while awaiting trial. After reviewing counsel's arguments, and given the cooperation of the defense, the court grants the motion and places a temporary gag order on both defendants. At this time, Jordan De Carlo and Victoria Berne are barred from making further public comment on anything related to their case. This order does not extend to *The Raines Report*, which is free to continue producing episodes about the case, but absent new interviews or statements from the defendants."

JESS MONAY: Sounds like we can use anything we recorded prior to Jordan and Victoria being taken into custody. From that point on, they're prohibited from communicating with us.

RYANNA RAINES: This changes everything. Whatever direction we thought this season was going, this will cause us to pivot. In how we investigate, how we report, how we present episodes to come. While being denied access to our subjects poses a challenge, we'll roll up our sleeves and keep bringing this story to you as it unfolds. We're not going away, folks. In fact, we've just begun to report on what has officially become *The People of California v. De Carlo and Berne.*

We've heard Jordan and Victoria's side of the case but very little about the case against them. That will be coming in future episodes. Our team needs to step back and do a reset, but we'll be returning here very soon. Until then, this is Ryanna Raines, signing off.

MEG CHOI: Being with Jordan and Victoria for those eight days and developing a personal relationship with them, then seeing them separated and arrested, how did that affect you?

RYANNA RAINES: As a journalist, I knew one part of the story was ending and another was about to begin. I also had a sense that what was to come would be very different in terms of the reporting. Personally, I felt sympathetic to both of them. It was difficult to watch.

MEG CHOI: Did you believe what they'd been telling you?

RYANNA RAINES: I thought they seemed credible. But I also knew there would be a counternarrative coming from the police and prosecutors. I needed to be open to exploring that. Wherever it took me.

MEG CHOI: The judge's gag order prevented you from going back and getting the defendants to comment on the new information you began uncovering.

RYANNA RAINES: We wanted to test the gag order legally, so we had a First Amendment attorney petition the court on our behalf. At the same time we were going out to gather testimony from people who'd been close to Jordan and Victoria.

MEG CHOI: You also returned to doing regular weekly episodes of the podcast. Even without the voices of the two main suspects, your listener numbers continued to grow.

RYANNA RAINES: Which surprised us because, in terms of the investigation, some weeks it felt like we were just treading water. But we were determined to press on and keep searching for new information. We hit a few dead ends. People kept calling our tip line and messaging us with new leads, and we had to check those out, because you never know when something comes in that might be valuable.

MEG CHOI: During the weekly episodes, you presented witnesses who had conflicting opinions about the defendants and their relationship. Then things took a dramatic turn.

RYANNA RAINES: They did indeed.

II

RECAP

A warning. The following episodes are intended for mature audiences. They contain descriptions of violence, sexual behavior, and psychological abuse that some may find triggering.

S6:E33 RECAP (PART 1)

UPLOADED MONDAY, APRIL 3

RYANNA RAINES: I'm Ryanna Raines. And welcome to *The Raines Report*, an audio crime-investigation series produced in association with Amplify. You're listening to *The De Carlo Murders*, and this is Part 1 of our season-to-date recap.

JESS MONAY: This is where I ask—for the benefit of listeners—why are we doing recaps?

RYANNA RAINES: Well, Jess Monay, podcast producer and investigative partner extraordinaire, our sixth season is about to change course once again. And that change will be announced following our second recap episode that we'll put out on our regular schedule, a week from today. In preparation for that, we've been editing together the most relevant pieces from my interviews and summarizing the evidence we've uncovered since Jordan De Carlo and Victoria Berne were arrested and charged with the murder of his parents six months ago.

JESS MONAY: These next two episodes will be highlights, strung together with our commentary. Our goal is to synthesize what we've learned so far and get everyone in sync with where our investigation presently stands. Ready to jump in?

RYANNA RAINES: I am. So let's go.

After Jordan and Victoria's surrender to the San Diego sheriff last October eighteenth, our podcast team took some time to get our bearings and plan our next steps. Prevented by a gag order from continuing to interview our two main subjects, we decided I would head back to Santa Barbara to talk to faculty and students in the UCSB Department of Theater and Dance. That's where Jordan and Victoria first met and where their relationship developed. I'd ask questions of the people who worked most closely with them, who knew them individually and as a couple.

JESS MONAY: A note: these interviews have been edited down from how they were originally presented. You'll find the prior episodes in their entirety on our website, TheRainesReport.com.

RYANNA RAINES: To some, the University of California at Santa Barbara is an idyllic seaside setting for scientific research and academic study. To others, it's an idyllic seaside setting for the lively social interaction native to people in their late teens and early twenties.

UCSB STUDENT: This place is about diversity and inclusion and learning, but also about hanging at the beach and playing beer pong with your bros.

RYANNA RAINES: My first trip to Santa Barbara was under very different circumstances. I had just met Jordan De Carlo and Victoria Berne, the main suspects in the killing of Jordan's parents. They were riding in the back seat of my rental car at the same time law enforcement, news outlets, and social media were finding out about their return from Mexico. Now they are in jail awaiting trial for murder. I drive out to the peninsula on the Pacific Ocean where the university they attended sprawls across nearly a thousand acres of California beachfront. I head to the parking lot closest to the school's Arts District and the department of theater and dance. Jess has gotten me an appointment to meet with Cheryl Dean, a professor who is herself a Yale School of Drama graduate with a long list of artistic achievements. Outside her office I find a bulletin board with photos from a dozen student productions, mostly of young actors and actresses at a dramatic high point in their performances.

I don't see Jordan or Victoria in any of the photos. I assume those have been taken down.

CHERYL DEAN: Welcome to our little enclave for the performing arts.

RYANNA RAINES: Professor Dean, with her abundant sweep of silvery hair and round-rimmed glasses, looks more "artist" than "academic." She takes me on a tour of the department. The Hatlen is the performing space with the largest capacity, a theater with a traditional proscenium stage and seating for up to three hundred and fifty. There is a smaller studio theater next door, used mostly as a lab for acting and directing classes. Surrounding the theaters is a split-level complex of offices, classrooms, and dance studios. After getting to see the spaces where Jordan and Victoria worked together and interacted with fellow students, I am led by Cheryl back to her office, where we sit down to talk.

CHERYL DEAN: Let me start by saying the murder of Jordan's parents and the arrests of Jordan and Victoria have traumatized our department. While Mr. and Mrs. De Carlo were not directly connected to Theater and Dance, their son is one of our most talented and accomplished graduates. When we first heard about what happened to them, we were all shocked and heartbroken for Jordan. Victoria is an extremely talented actor in our BFA program and was enrolled here up until her arraignment. Sheriff's investigators have been on campus to question the faculty, staff, and students. Everyone has been cooperative. It's all terribly, terribly tragic.

RYANNA RAINES: As a journalist, I'm not on the side of the prosecution or the defense. I'm here because this is where Jordan and Victoria met and it was under the auspices of this department that their relationship developed.

CHERYL DEAN: Their relationship as fellow theater students and artists developed here. Obviously, there was another dimension to their relationship that was formed *outside* these auspices.

. . . Jordan made a proposal to our theater committee to put on *Desire Under the Elms* as his senior honors project. He has a special passion for Eugene O'Neill, and it was a natural evolution for him to adapt and direct a work that he could bring his own creative vision to.

. . . The play is O'Neill at his fiercest and still one of his most controversial works. And yes, it's about family dysfunction and a father's cruelty to his son. The San Diego detectives went through the text line by line. They know it better than most theater teachers by now.

. . . Opening night of *Desire* was the pinnacle for Jordan. His final student project, in the department's premier showcase. He'd worked on the play his entire senior year, analyzing and reinventing every detail. First performance was a full house. Only two seats were empty. Anthony and Lauren De Carlo did not attend.

. . . After the final curtain, I asked Jordan why they hadn't come. He just gave a shrug and showed me this sad expression. I didn't pursue it. Maybe I should have.

. . . Yes, those two did show an emotional connection during readings and rehearsals. That's not so unusual, given the nature of a director-actor collaboration. Now, if Victoria had come to me and said Jordan's attentions were making her uncomfortable, or vice versa, I would've stepped in. But what I witnessed was mutual and consensual.

. . . After being accepted into the BFA program—which was the reason she came to UCSB, we're the only UC school that offers a Bachelor of Fine Arts in acting—Victoria appeared socially shy and introverted. She was younger than her fellow students because she skipped a grade in school. Highly intelligent, focused, but lacking in confidence. Until she got the role of Abbie Putnam.

. . . I was at her audition. It was one of those remarkable moments when an actor connects with a character and everything she's been learning and thinking and visualizing comes together. That carried all the way to her public performances. She just blossomed.

RYANNA RAINES: Do you think either or both of them could have killed Jordan's parents?

CHERYL DEAN: To me, it is unimaginable that this young man or this young woman could have done something so monstrous.

RYANNA RAINES: Professor Dean was helpful in painting the bigger picture—from the faculty point of view. We also needed the perspective of fellow students, Jordan's and Victoria's peers.

THADDEUS BAYLOR: My friends call me Thad.

RYANNA RAINES: I meet Thaddeus Baylor at a coffee shop in Isla Vista, a neighborhood of mostly student apartments and houses, adjacent to the UCSB campus. At six-three and 220 pounds, with muscled arms and legs, I'd assume he was a star athlete before a Bachelor of Fine Arts.

You graduated from the BFA acting program last spring? Same class as Jordan?

THADDEUS BAYLOR: Yes. I decided to stay in town to do a season at the Granada Theatre. I start my MFA in the fall at the Royal Academy of Dramatic Art.

RYANNA RAINES: In London? Good for you. That's an adventure to look forward to. Tell me about your relationship with Jordan before working on *Desire Under the Elms*.

THADDEUS BAYLOR: I met Jordan first quarter freshman year. We hit it off and started working on stuff together. We're from different backgrounds, but we have this natural creative juice between us. We spin each other up, make each other better. I love the guy.

. . . When Jordan got the idea for *Desire*, he came to me before pitching it to the faculty. He said, "I want to do this only if you play the son. If you don't want to do it, I'm not doing it." I read the play that night and said, "I'm your son." We went together to formally propose it to the scheduling committee. And they were like "Hell yeah."

. . . For the role of Abbie Putnam, Jordan auditioned every woman in theater and dance, then went outside to film studies and journalism. When he couldn't find one who fit his vision, Jordan started auditioning men. Then he was thinking of casting a trans actor, which would've been fine with me. But he still wasn't satisfied, and Jordan is not the type who settles. We were going back through the list of first-year BFA students and he caught her name.

"Victoria Berne? Have we seen her? I don't remember her."

Turned out she hadn't auditioned because she didn't think she was ready for such a big role. Jordan sent me over to talk to her. Her face went bright red as I begged her to read a scene with me. Wasn't easy getting her to the audition room. But the moment she launched in—*boom*. From wallflower to tower of power.

. . . By the end of her monologue, Jordan's eyes were tearing up. He said, "She's our Abbie" and off we went. The cast did a full reading that night, and a week later we were in rehearsals. I felt the weight on my shoulders because I'm a Black man playing a role written for a white man, created by one of the greatest white American playwrights.

RYANNA RAINES: When did you know Jordan and Victoria's relationship had become romantic?

THADDEUS BAYLOR: Look, I tried to tell him to cool it. If he wanted to get down with her, okay, just wait until we're through the performances. But he went into a *Victoria trance*. He shut off every part of his brain except the part working with her on the play. Their romantic relationship and creative collaboration were fused together, no separation.

. . . I'll be the first to praise Victoria's talent. Her acting is so pure, it comes out of her with no filters or self-consciousness. But she's also *savvy*, know what I mean? Jordan had the highest profile of any student in the department, he was golden. And from the moment she got cast, Victoria wrapped herself around him.

. . . If we were onstage or in the rehearsal room, Jordan was available. Outside of there, he wouldn't respond to my texts. My calls would go to voice mail and not be returned. One night at rehearsal I took him aside and said, "What up, man? Talk to me." He said, "I found my muse. She's making me a better artist. I'm doing the best work of my life because of her."

The glow in his eyes was like someone in a religious cult. Sent a chill down my spine.

. . . He was first to arrive at rehearsals and last to leave. Victoria always came and left with him. If you were in that room, you could feel the chemical pull between them. Kurt Nall, who played Ephraim, the father, started calling it Desire Under the *Palms*.

RYANNA RAINES: In your role as Eben, you have several intense encounters with Abbie Putnam. What was it like to rehearse and act those scenes with Victoria?

THADDEUS BAYLOR: Yeah, wow, okay. Here's an example. Act Two, Scene Two is when Abbie makes her first move on Eben. O'Neill wrote detailed stage directions. She comes into Eben's bedroom, "her eyes burning with desire." Then she sexually assaults him: "Throws her arms around his neck, pulls his head back, covers his mouth with kisses." Eben doesn't respond at first, but then can't help himself and starts kissing her back. O'Neill wrote, "Suddenly aware of his hatred, he hurls her away from him, springing to his feet. They stand staring at each other, panting like two animals."

It's a big physical moment. When we first started blocking it, I took it easy on the "hurls her away" part. Victoria is a hundred and ten pounds. I could throw her the length of the stage if I wanted to. So she turns to Jordan and says "The text says 'hurls her away.' Thad isn't hurling me. I need to be hurled. I need to feel that physicality."

I said, "If I really hurl you, you might break something."

She got right in my face. "Pick me up and *hurl* me." I appealed to Jordan. He doesn't want her to get hurt, a director's first job is to keep the cast safe.

He says to me, "Pick her up and hurl her."

What is this, some fucked up S&M game you guys are playing? I turned back to Victoria and said, "I will *toss* you, but I will not hurl you." I tossed her like four feet and she smacked down hard on her butt. Jordan rushed over to see if she was okay. She's yelling, "I don't want to be tossed, I want to be hurled!"

And right before the curtain went up on opening night, she comes over to me. I expect a hug, a "break a leg," something constructive. She slaps me with an open hand across the face. With force. Then she just leaves and next time I see her is onstage in front of three hundred people. I get it, my character's supposed to hate her at first sight. But really?

RYANNA RAINES: Did you see Jordan after he found out about the death of his parents?

THADDEUS BAYLOR: Soon as I heard, I went straight to his place. Victoria answered the door. She stood there telling me he didn't want to see anyone. I'm like, "Tell him it's me. I just want to hug him and let him know I'm here for him." She's like, "Nope, sorry, he's too deep into his grief." So I left and texted him. "I love you, man, I'm here for you." No response. Next thing I know he's a suspect in the killings. Then he's arrested and charged with first-degree murder. Last time I saw him was backstage after our final performance. How crazy is that?

RYANNA RAINES: Any other incidents with Jordan or Victoria stand out in your mind?

THADDEUS BAYLOR: I wasn't directly involved, but I heard about it from Kurt Nall. It happened with Victoria in Stage Combat class. That's where they teach fighting with weapons in a performance so it looks real but no one gets hurt. You know, I'm heading over to the department to meet someone, I can show you where it happened. If Kurt's around, he can tell you firsthand.

RYANNA RAINES: Thad takes me to room 1507, a large ground-floor studio where the group spent six nights a week rehearsing *Desire Under the Elms* and where Stage Combat class meets twice a week. I get to see the equipment they use. The dagger blades are steel. The tips are only slightly blunted. Being stabbed with one might not kill you, but it would certainly hurt.

While I'm checking out the broadswords, Thad calls Kurt Nall.

THADDEUS BAYLOR: How you doing, man? I'm in 1507 with Ryanna Raines. I mentioned your little incident with Victoria in Stage Combat. Would you be okay talking to her? Uh-huh. Right. How about off the record? Yeah, I can respect that. Sure. Okay, man, see you around.

Kurt said he doesn't want to speak to the media right now. He already talked to the police and is probably going to be called as a witness at the trial. So he'd rather not comment. Sorry.

RYANNA RAINES: Oh. Okay. You mind giving me his contact so I might check in on him?

Given Kurt's reluctance to talk to me, Thad is not keen on giving me his information. But a reporter has to ask. I make a note to track down Kurt Nall and get the Stage Combat story.

On my way out of the theater and dance building, I notice a female undergrad locking her bike to the bike rack. I recognize her from photos I'd seen online and know she is on our list of key interviews. I intercept her as she's heading to class.

Hi, aren't you Gwen Phan?

GWEN PHAN: Yes?

RYANNA RAINES: My name is Ryanna Raines, I'm a journalist looking into the De Carlo/Berne case. Could you spare a few moments to talk to me?

GWEN PHAN: Well, I have Voice from two to three-thirty.

RYANNA RAINES: After that? At the Starbucks in Isla Vista? I'll buy the coffee.

GWEN PHAN: Make it the IV Bagel Café. It's more private. I can meet you there in ninety-six minutes.

RYANNA RAINES: I notice these acting students try to be precise in their communications. Which someone like a reporter can really appreciate.

JESS MONAY: Gwen Phan and Victoria were roommates during their sophomore year. Her parents are Taiwanese and she's a first-generation Chinese American. I couldn't get her to return my calls or texts about setting up an interview, so good work by you.

RYANNA RAINES: I'm just hoping she shows up at the Bagel Café.

And she does—ninety-six minutes after she said she would. Her jet-black hair is styled in a bob with sky-blue tips, her expressive brown eyes framed by cut-glass cheekbones.

Thanks for meeting me, Gwen. Do I have your permission to record our conversation?

GWEN PHAN: Um, okay.

RYANNA RAINES: If you want to say something off the record, ask me to pause the recorder and I will. So, how did you and Victoria first meet?

GWEN PHAN: At the auditions for the BFA acting program. We were scheduled to present back to back. We met outside the theater to compare notes and support each other. After we both got accepted, I invited her to live with me at my apartment.

. . . I would describe her as quiet. Private. Pretty without knowing it. Serious about her acting. Capital S serious.

. . . Yes, she was ambitious, you have to be to make it into the BFA program and work through this curriculum. It's a massive commitment of time and energy. We go to classes all day, then rehearse for shows every weeknight and on weekends. It becomes your whole life.

. . . Never saw her get violent. Never even saw her get mad. She's a complex person, but no way is she someone who could stab a human being fifty times, or however many it was.

. . . She got hyperfocused on the Abbie Putnam role. She lived that character inside and out. I'm sure she's on the spectrum, undiagnosed. I know a few kids in theater who are undiagnosed. Or diagnosed, but won't admit it.

RYANNA RAINES: Did you notice any changes in Victoria during the run-up to opening night?

GWEN PHAN: She started spending nights up at Jordan's place, so I'd only really see her on campus. Maybe two or three nights she came back to the apartment and slept in her own bed—alone. She was pretty tight-lipped about what was going on personally between them. One of the nights she came back, I could hear her crying in her room. I knocked on the door, and she let me in. She wiped her tears and said, "I just needed a break."

I said, "So you guys are pretty intense with each other?"

She gave this helpless little smile. "Pretty intense," she said.

It was like she wanted to say more but couldn't get herself there. With total sincerity I said, "If you want to talk, I'm here for you. Anytime."

This light came into her eyes and she said, "He's a beautiful man."

I said, "And . . . ?"

"And—I just needed to take a break for the night."

. . . I sat in on their early rehearsals for *Desire*. Then Jordan closed the studio, so it was only him, Victoria, Thad, and Kurt. He was in there with them every night, doors locked. Jordan could get away with that because the faculty loves him and believed in his vision for the play.

RYANNA RAINES: Some people I've talked to said Victoria cast a spell on Jordan. Did you see anything like that?

GWEN PHAN: No, I saw the opposite. Jordan was the one who cast a spell on Victoria. She was insanely in love with the guy. Ugh, not the best word choice. *Passionately*—she was *passionately* in love with Jordan. To an extent that might not have been healthy.

RYANNA RAINES: How so?

GWEN PHAN: It was her first time to be involved in something like that. She didn't get explicit, but she let it be known they were having a lot of sex. Like a lot. She went from this shy, first-year BFA student to the top of the department, the one everyone was talking about and watching. All because of Jordan. I think she would've done anything for him. I mean, within reason.

RYANNA RAINES: Anything else stick in your mind about Victoria's behavior?

GWEN PHAN: One thing—it's pretty minor. Victoria didn't talk much on her phone, but a few times I could hear her talking in her bedroom with the door closed. I didn't hear her words, but there was something secretive in her voice. And intimate, like she was talking to a best friend. I thought it might be a girlfriend from high school, someone from home.

RYANNA RAINES: Could it have been Jordan?

GWEN PHAN: This happened before *and* after she met Jordan.

RYANNA RAINES: Her mom?

GWEN PHAN: I heard her on the phone with her mom. That was different. I didn't get the impression she was super close with her mom.

JESS MONAY: You interviewed other students and faculty, but we chose to focus on these three because they were the people closest to Jordan and Victoria. You also did another tour of campus and again traced the course of their alibi.

RYANNA RAINES: And I went to some of the establishments Jordan and Victoria were known to frequent, to get a feel for where they spent time when not on campus. Gwen Phan had mentioned a coffeehouse downtown where Victoria would go to study. Café Bloomsday is a block off State Street and has a laid-back, cultured vibe, with window-seat tables on either side of the front door. Victoria hunkered down here with her theater books and laptop and ordered the house specialty, a Mayan Mocha. The menu lists the ingredients: fresh-brewed Guatemalan coffee, raw cacao powder, coconut oil, cinnamon, and cayenne pepper.

I sit at the single unoccupied table and order one. My server tells me he's ending his shift and that *Daniel* will now be taking care of me. I've got to say, this Mayan Mocha is the zestiest coffee drink I've ever had. I know that cacao contains the "bliss molecule," which raises serotonin levels in the brain. After a few sips, I'm feeling quite mellow. "Can I get you anything else?" I hear from behind me. I turn to the voice—and freeze.

The server taking over the shift is *Blackbeard*. The man who approached me in front of Jordan's house and who followed me to the UCSB campus. He reacts as surprised as I am. But a moment later he regains control and looks at me with blandly inquisitive eyes.

"You remember me," I say.

He shakes his head. "I don't."

"Well, I remember you. I'm the journalist who was up here with Jordan De Carlo and Victoria Berne before they got arrested. You came up to me and said there was something you had to tell me."

"Sorry, I think you're mistaken."

"Were you in front of his house when all the media was camped out there?"

"No."

"On the UCSB campus a couple Saturdays ago, watching me?"

"You must be confusing me with someone else."

"Do you drive a motorcycle?"

He hesitates, then says yes, he does drive a motorcycle. With that, he shrugs to demonstrate innocence, then excuses himself to tend to other customers.

JESS MONAY: And you're sure it's the same guy?

RYANNA RAINES: A hundred percent. He knew me, too. He was lying, I could see it.

JESS MONAY: We checked out Daniel Mazzoli. No arrest record, employed at Café Bloomsday for two years, attended Santa Barbara City College, where he majored in political science. Found no connections between him and Jordan or him and Victoria or anyone in their circle.

RYANNA RAINES: Though he'd know Victoria, because of the time she spent at the café.

JESS MONAY: Weird. Well, to summarize your first round of interviews at UCSB, what emerged was two very different pictures of the defendants.

RYANNA RAINES: Some saw Jordan as being dominant, some saw Victoria. It's easier to visualize Jordan in that role because he was Victoria's director, the senior to her sophomore, the more experienced and accomplished.

JESS MONAY: He's also four years older. That's a lot at their age. In the eight days you spent with them, what was your read on who was dominant?

RYANNA RAINES: I went back and listened to the tapes. Jordan was the more expressive, quicker to anger and change moods. I had a few interactions with Victoria when Jordan wasn't there. I sensed a vulnerability about her. I'm not even sure that's the right word. Her guard was up. She was focused on Jordan and every bit the attentive lover. But I also felt there was a naiveté, an ingenuousness. I wish I'd had more time alone with her.

JESS MONAY: We knew that Jordan had grown up in Atherton in Northern California. His parents didn't move to Rancho Santa Fe until between his sophomore and junior year in high school. We hadn't found much about his childhood, other than he was an only child, and intellectually gifted, with a half brother who was sixteen years older and lived on the East Coast. Hailey and I googled "child therapists in Atherton" and came up with a short list. The town has fewer than eight thousand residents, so we thought we'd start with the top five in the area and see what came up.

Second call, I connect with an office assistant who logs into a database of patients and says, "Yes, Jordan De Carlo, age thirteen. He saw Dr. Sheldon for six sessions."

RYANNA RAINES: Kids that age usually don't go into therapy unless there's an issue and the parents think it's necessary. What was the issue? It could be significant.

JESS MONAY: Turns out Dr. Sheldon passed away two years ago, and the records from Jordan's sessions—i.e., the therapist's notes—are confidential. The assistant told me there had been no other inquiries she knew of. The investigators and defense attorneys missed it, apparently.

RYANNA RAINES: Is it possible to get those notes?

JESS MONAY: If the patient is eighteen or older and requests them, the therapist is legally obligated to hand them over. They would give them to Jordan—but he'd have to ask in writing.

RYANNA RAINES: Since there was a court order prohibiting us from speaking to him, we passed this information on to Natalie Bloom. She said she'd speak to Jordan. That's where we left it.

JESS MONAY: After you got back from Santa Barbara, we decided to do an episode on the victims.

RYANNA RAINES: Almost all our focus had been on the suspects. We felt it was important to try to humanize Anthony and Lauren. To see them as living, breathing people, not just these gruesomely violated deceased people. We gathered photos posted on social media and reached out to the De Carlos' family, friends, and associates.

Anthony had been a pitcher for his college baseball team at Stanford and had stayed in pretty good shape at sixty years old. We found far fewer photos of him than of his second wife, Lauren Bridger, who was forty-six, and had modeled professionally during her college years. She posted pictures of herself fairly regularly on social media. Many of them were selfies. Anthony had only a Facebook account, where he rarely posted.

JESS MONAY: They'd eloped to the Bahamas the year before Jordan was born. The wedding was just the two of them, no guests. Despite the age difference, they were an attractive couple. He was tall and broad-shouldered, she blond and petite. Jordan gets his blond hair from his mom's side of the family.

RYANNA RAINES: We spoke to some of Anthony's former business associates, to social friends of the couple, to some of their neighbors in Rancho Santa Fe. We talked to Anthony's regular golfing partners and to Lauren's riding instructor.

JESS MONAY: And here I want to apologize for a comment I made in reference to the De Carlos during that episode. Here's the clip:

They were pretty much your standard white, privileged, California rich people.

We got blowback for that, and it was insensitive of me. I wasn't making a value judgment as much as stating that the couple seemed to fit a certain stereotype. But no matter, it came off as condescending. And if it offended you, I'm sorry.

RYANNA RAINES: We found holiday photos posted by Lauren over the last four Thanksgivings and Christmases. Jordan was noticeably absent. In fact, we looked through all the photos posted from her account and didn't see any with Jordan past around the age of seventeen. Then I remembered the family photos he showed me on his phone in Santa Barbara. They were of him and his parents when he was younger. He didn't look much older than seventeen.

JESS MONAY: Here's their only son, who happens to be more than presentable, and is a star of his university's drama department. The kind of kid parents brag about. But the last few years we're not seeing mentions of or photos with Jordan. Possibly some were posted that she deleted.

RYANNA RAINES: And they were no-shows on opening night of *Desire Under the Elms.*

JESS MONAY: Mr. De Carlo does seem to be holding either a cocktail glass or a beer bottle in many of Lauren's pictures. What was his blood alcohol at time of death?

RYANNA RAINES: It was .12. Based on his weight of 190, he'd had about five drinks or the equivalent. On the other hand, Lauren had no alcohol in her blood. Though we did hear she would enjoy a glass or two of a good Cabernet.

According to his golf partners, Anthony liked to gamble on the course. He might win or lose up to ten thousand a round.

JESS MONAY: Which he could afford. He cashed out of his venture capital firm for a quarter of a billion dollars. Not Bill Gates–level money, but still rich, very rich.

RYANNA RAINES: We found a source that quoted Jordan saying his parents had stopped him from going to Juilliard. This is from the *San Diego Union Tribune* two weeks after the murders: "I got accepted to Juilliard in high school, but my parents said I wasn't ready to move away from home."

JESS MONAY: This hasn't been verified. Juilliard won't release any of their records.

RYANNA RAINES: Someone who might shed more light on the De Carlos and their relationship with their son would be Jordan's aunt Frances, Anthony's younger sister. She's the one who retained attorney Natalie Bloom and is paying for Jordan's defense.

JESS MONAY: Frances proved a little elusive at first. I sent her a half-dozen messages without a response. So we asked Natalie Bloom to be our go-between.

NATALIE BLOOM: I spoke to Frances—she goes by Frances De Carlo Riche, R-I-C-H-E. She married into an old-money San Francisco clan and spends most of her time doing philanthropy. She's fiercely protective of the family and her brother's legacy. And she adores Jordan. She's been reluctant to speak publicly, but I got her to agree to a half-hour Zoom interview.

RYANNA RAINES: I admire people who are "fiercely protective" of their families. I'm fiercely protective of mine.

FRANCES DE CARLO RICHE: Hello there. I've been listening to *The Raines Report* Season 5, about the female judge in Texas who was murdered. You're very good at this podcasting thing.

RYANNA RAINES: Oh, thank you. Our team is deeply committed to this work. I'll let them know we got your thumbs-up.

The Zoom screen frames her head—hair pulled back in a tight bun. Kelly green sweater, cashmere I'm guessing. We exchange pleasantries. Then she mentions that Jordan has been calling her from the Vista Detention Facility.

FRANCES DE CARLO RICHE: It's criminal the junk they're feeding him there. He's turning to skin and bones, he's sick all the time. That is the definition of cruel and unusual punishment. He's innocent until proven guilty and they're treating him like he's been convicted and sentenced to prison. It's a scandal.

RYANNA RAINES: You know there's a gag order, so I haven't spoken to him.

FRANCES DE CARLO RICHE: I'm beside myself over this. So are his uncle and cousins. It's not enough that my brother and sister-in-law were horrifically murdered, now my nephew is going on trial for doing it. This is a lot for our family, a lot.

RYANNA RAINES: I should've started by giving my condolences for the loss of your brother and sister-in-law. I'm so sorry.

FRANCES DE CARLO RICHE: Thank you. It's one thing to lose a sibling prematurely, it's another to lose him—like that.

RYANNA RAINES: As the family member closest to Jordan, tell me your perspective on him.

FRANCES DE CARLO RICHE: My nephew is brilliant. He's in Mensa, though he probably didn't tell you that. He never wanted to be known for his IQ, but for his creativity. I was having fully adult conversations with that boy when he was eight. The first thing I need to declare is there is not the slightest chance Jordan could have done that to his parents.

RYANNA RAINES: Tell me why you feel that way.

FRANCES DE CARLO RICHE: I was at the hospital when Jordan was born. When his parents were away, he stayed at our house, with his cousins, who he's still very close to. We did birthdays together, holidays. I knew his school friends and teachers. I know Jordan as well as I know my own children. Even if he didn't have that alibi—which he does—I would say the same thing. He's not guilty of this. He can't be.

RYANNA RAINES: What about Jordan's relationship with Anthony and Lauren? There's usually some kind of conflict between parents and children, right? My oldest is seven, and I'm already dreading her teenage years.

FRANCES DE CARLO RICHE: Were there tensions from time to time? Yes, and as you said, that's normal. But there was nothing that would come close to justifying or explaining an act like that. The person who murdered my brother and his wife had to be severely ill.

RYANNA RAINES: Were you aware Jordan had gone to a psychotherapist when he was thirteen?

FRANCES DE CARLO RICHE: Where did you get that information?

RYANNA RAINES: From the office of a child therapist in Atherton.

FRANCES DE CARLO RICHE: Did they tell you why he was in therapy?

RYANNA RAINES: The records are sealed. I thought you might have some insights on that.

FRANCES DE CARLO RICHE: Sorry, I don't. I guess all families have a private side, things that stay within their walls.

RYANNA RAINES: What do you know about Jordan's relationship with Victoria Berne?

FRANCES DE CARLO RICHE: I've never met her or spoken to her, so I can't really say.

RYANNA RAINES: Did your brother or sister-in-law ever mention her to you?

FRANCES DE CARLO RICHE In passing. Jordan and his *new girlfriend* this or that. I had been looking forward to meeting her. I understand she's quite talented.

RYANNA RAINES: Do you know of any reason Victoria would want to harm Anthony and Lauren?

FRANCES DE CARLO RICHE: You mean like, so Jordan could get his inheritance and take her to a five-star resort in Mexico? I don't know the young lady. I can't give you an informed answer.

RYANNA RAINES: You know of any person or group that may have wanted to harm your brother?

FRANCES DE CARLO RICHE: Anthony started a venture capital firm, which is a very high-stakes business. But he'd been retired for five years, and he and Lauren lived a quiet life. I don't know of a single enemy they had in the world. When I first heard about the murders, I thought it had to be a mentally sick person or someone on a powerful mind-altering drug. Remember angel dust? When I heard the details of how they died, the words *angel dust* popped into my mind.

RYANNA RAINES: Have you known Jordan to take any kind of psychoactive medications or recreational drugs?

FRANCES DE CARLO RICHE: No. I mean, when he was younger, I remember his parents thought he might be ADHD, so he may have been prescribed Ritalin or Adderall for a time. Believe me, I've known druggies among our own kids' friends. Jordan was no druggie.

RYANNA RAINES: Were you close to your brother, Anthony?

FRANCES DE CARLO RICHE: Very much so. He was a man of a certain upbringing, so he wasn't effusive with his feelings. But we had a special bond. I . . . I'm sorry, my heart still really hurts. And with Jordan being accused, it's just compounding the tragedy of it all.

JESS MONAY: After Jordan's aunt, we turned to Victoria's family to dig deeper into her background.

RYANNA RAINES: I'd already done one interview with Gail Berne. But that was under tense conditions with Victoria in the room and Jordan in the same house. Her daughter was anticipating getting arrested and the media was gathered outside the front door. The next time I spoke to Gail was a month later, in Vista, California, where she'd rented a small casita in order to be closer to her daughter, who was sitting in the county jail a few blocks away.

GAIL BERNE: I took a leave of absence from my job. I get in-person visits with Victoria twice a week, thirty minutes at a time. And we talk on the phone every other day. I just couldn't be far away from her during this time. My daughter is the only family I have left.

RYANNA RAINES: I can understand, as a mother and as a daughter.

Since Victoria's arrest for the murders of Anthony and Lauren De Carlo, Gail has only communicated to the media through Victoria's attorney. To pay for AJ Novick's services, Gail started a GoFundMe page, but she still must be racking up a lot of personal debt. She serves me a mug of coffee, knowing just how I like it.

How are you holding up?

GAIL BERNE: When I start to feel the crushing weight of it all, I think of how much tougher it is for Victoria. I mean, I can get up, walk out the front door, go anywhere I want. She's lost her freedom. She's locked in a tiny cell every day and night. That's a hardship I struggle to imagine.

RYANNA RAINES: Tell me what you can about your communications with her.

GAIL BERNE: I try to keep it relaxed. We chat about news from home. TV shows I'm watching. I'll clip stories about what's happening on Broadway and the theater scene in Seattle.

RYANNA RAINES: How's her mood?

GAIL BERNE: She tries to act upbeat, but I can tell she's depressed. How could she not be?

RYANNA RAINES: You told me about Victoria being intellectually gifted as a child and that it caused her to be socially shy and a bit of a loner. Do you remember her going to parties or out on dates when she was in high school?

GAIL BERNE: She didn't really date in high school. She had a girlfriend who was also into drama—*theater*. Linette. She would come to our house on weekends and the two of them would watch movies together. They'd keep pausing the TV to critique the acting and the story.

RYANNA RAINES: Why do you think Victoria was so drawn to acting?

GAIL BERNE: I know what she wasn't drawn to—celebrity. She was very clear that it was about mastering the craft and not about getting famous. Pretty ironic, given what's going on now.

RYANNA RAINES: You said her father moving out was traumatic for Victoria. Can you say more about that?

GAIL BERNE: It caused her to withdraw even more into herself. Many times I'd catch her just staring out the window. I tried to get her to talk to me about her feelings, but she wouldn't go there. Acting was an outlet where she could channel the stuff going on inside her.

RYANNA RAINES: What was her relationship with her father like prior to him leaving?

GAIL BERNE: Good. I remember they would goof around with each other, tease and tickle. They were probably more physically affectionate than I was with Victoria. I can't think of one time they had a falling-out or got mad at each other. He would talk to her about her school, help her with her projects. There were times I felt jealous of how close they were. She was absolutely devastated when he left.

RYANNA RAINES: I know the importance of that bond between a daughter and her father. This is a sensitive area, I'm sure, but what else can you tell me about why Phil left?

GAIL BERNE: It was another woman. He fell in love with someone else, plain and simple.

RYANNA RAINES: But moving away from his kids is another order of magnitude, especially if he had a loving relationship with them.

GAIL BERNE: You'll have to ask him. After he moved out, we spoke only three or four times. Everything else was through our attorneys.

RYANNA RAINES: Did he attend your son's memorial service?

GAIL BERNE: No. Not that he didn't want to, but Victoria did not want him there. She said she wouldn't go if he came. So he decided to stay away. He did send flowers and a card.

RYANNA RAINES: After she got the part in *Desire Under the Elms*, what did Victoria tell you about her relationship with Jordan?

GAIL BERNE: She did not tell me they'd become boyfriend and girlfriend. I knew she was excited about getting the role. I knew she had a lot of respect for Jordan as a director. But I didn't find out they were *together* until I came down for opening night of the play. I asked Victoria why she hadn't told me. She said that she knew I'd be coming down, so she wanted to tell me in person.

RYANNA RAINES: What was your impression of Jordan the first time. you met him?

GAIL BERNE: I could see how she got swept off her feet. He's very hand-some, a real charmer.

RYANNA RAINES: Did she say that Jordan had been the initiator of their romantic relationship?

GAIL BERNE: Not in so many words. My daughter is brilliant, talented, and complicated. In many ways she's mature for her age. But she was still only eighteen. She'd never been in love before.

RYANNA RAINES: Were you concerned she was getting in too deep? That she might get her heart broken?

GAIL BERNE: Of course. First love, I mean—we know how life-changing that can be.

JESS MONAY: In more ways than one. Now, while you went to interview Gail, I was trying to contact Victoria's father to ask if he'd do an inter-view with you. When I first got ahold of him, he was reluctant. He said he fully supported his daughter, and I said if he wanted to show that support, he should talk to you. Eventually, I got Phil Berne to yes.

RYANNA RAINES: Thanks for speaking to me. Do I have your permission to record this call?

PHIL BERNE: You're not going to spring any gotchas on me, are you?

RYANNA RAINES: I'm not sure what you mean. I want to give you the opportunity to speak about your daughter and the situation she's in.

PHIL BERNE: Okay, you can record.

RYANNA RAINES: Have you spoken to Victoria since the murders of Anthony and Lauren De Carlo?

PHIL BERNE: I've been trying to communicate with her, unfortunately without much luck. I wrote to her at the jail. I have a copy of my letter here. You want me to read it out loud?

RYANNA RAINES: If you're okay with that, sure.

PHIL BERNE: "Dear Victoria. I know we haven't talked for a while, but I had to write to you to let you know I am one hundred percent in your corner. I know in my heart you are innocent. There is no chance you could have committed the crime they're accusing you of. These are shameless prosecutors looking for maximum publicity. I am ready to do anything I can to help you. I know you are in trouble and I am showing up for you. Please let me know how I can best aid you in this difficult time. All my love, Dad."

RYANNA RAINES: Has she responded?

PHIL BERNE: Not yet. Maybe you can help me by asking her to break the ice and call her dad?

RYANNA RAINES: I haven't been in touch with her lately because of a judge's order.

PHIL BERNE: Victoria and I were really close when she was younger. Until the breakup. I don't blame her for taking her mom's side. But that was six years ago. It's time to move on.

RYANNA RAINES: According to both Victoria and her mother, you left the family abruptly and moved far away.

PHIL BERNE: Then my ex turned our kids against me. Whenever a marriage breaks up, there are two sides to the story. I love my kids. I would've done anything for them.

RYANNA RAINES: Can you see that the manner in which you left the family would have been traumatizing to Victoria?

PHIL BERNE: When a marriage ends, one of the spouses has to move out. I wish it didn't have to be me, but that's the way it worked out. I tried to make it up to Victoria, but she broke off all contact. It's times like this a family should pull together, no matter what's in the past.

RYANNA RAINES: Have you reached out to your ex-wife Gail?

PHIL BERNE: Not yet, but I plan to. I hope she can set aside all the negativity and do what's best for our daughter. Victoria needs her father, now more than ever.

JESS MONAY: So let's take it back to the first news release on the De Carlo murders posted by the San Diego sheriff on the morning of June eighth: "Deputies responded to the 100 block of Colina Conchita in Rancho Santa Fe after the report of a double homicide. When they arrived, they found a deceased male and a deceased female inside the home. The sheriff's homicide unit reached the scene shortly thereafter and has assumed responsibility for the investigation."

RYANNA RAINES: We stayed in touch with Jordan and Victoria's lawyers through Zoom calls. At the same time, we continued trying to connect with the San Diego sheriff's homicide unit, but their media contact, Lieutenant Davis, continued to rebuff those efforts—politely. "Thanks for your inquiry, we won't be making comment at this time. But please check back later."

JESS MONAY: "Check back later" gave us a sliver of hope.

RYANNA RAINES: Then we got a request from AJ and Natalie to hop on a Zoom call.

AJ NOVICK: The sheriff's department has decided they want to show some goodwill to *The Raines Report*. They've given permission for the lead investigator in the case, Detective Sanchez, to give you a walk-through of the crime scene. And to let it be recorded on audio.

RYANNA RAINES: That's fantastic.

NATALIE BLOOM: There are caveats, of course. He will answer questions about their theory of what happened inside the De Carlo home on the night of June fifth, but will not discuss either of the defendants or any of the evidence against them.

JESS MONAY: What's motivating this change in policy? For the last nine weeks all we've heard is "Thanks, no thanks."

AJ NOVICK: They're getting hammered on the news and social media for their lack of responsiveness. Someone with sway must've said, "Let's show we're engaging in the discussion without compromising the case."

RYANNA RAINES: In other words, "Throw Ryanna a bone!"

NATALIE BLOOM: Albeit a bone where they control the narrative. You need to agree to the terms before they'll send out Sanchez.

RYANNA RAINES: Here's my intro to the episode where I'd be guided through the interior of the house and the crime scene by the lead investigator.

Rancho Santa Fe in north San Diego County is described in real estate brochures as "an enchanting, upscale equestrian community." It's where Anthony and Lauren De Carlo bought a five-million-dollar home and where they retired after Anthony made his fortune from the venture capital firm he founded. It was the home they would both die in, victims of a frenzied knife attack. Arrested and charged with the murders were the couple's son, Jordan De Carlo, and Jordan's girlfriend, Victoria Berne. By invitation, *The Raines Report* received exclusive access to the couple for the eight days prior to their arrest.

DETECTIVE SANCHEZ: From the kitchen floor and the island and the countertops to halfway across the living room, blood was everywhere.

RYANNA RAINES: As I drive out of the motel parking lot at eight-fifteen that morning headed south toward Rancho Santa Fe, I am feeling some anxiety. This was a terribly savage crime, and even though the scene has been thoroughly cleaned and the house is being prepped for sale, I know we'll be getting into details that will be disturbing. Even for a veteran homicide detective.

DETECTIVE SANCHEZ: Ms. Raines? Hi. Paul Sanchez, San Diego sheriff's homicide unit.

RYANNA RAINES: We meet in front of that wrought-iron gate with the stone walls on either side—an image already embedded in my subconscious. Paul Sanchez is a handsome Latino archetype of a big-city homicide detective, straight out of an HBO cop series. He has a masculine gravitas and eyes that are equally alert and exhausted.

I watch Sanchez enter a code on the keypad and the iron barrier starts to swing open. I leave my rental car on the street and ride in the passenger seat of his unmarked SUV as he winds his way up past that immaculate landscaping. At the top of the driveway, we approach the front of the De Carlo estate, which looks even more grand and impressive than the first time I came here.

DETECTIVE SANCHEZ: A custom build in 2000, designed by well-known California architect Basil Christos. In the early 2010s, the previous owners did a major remodel to keep pace with the market. High-end home buyers were wanting more open floor plans, larger bedrooms, closets, bathrooms. They made a killing on the sale.

RYANNA RAINES: I suppress a cringe at his metaphor.

DETECTIVE SANCHEZ: The De Carlos didn't make any significant changes to the structure. They mostly redecorated the interior. Eight thousand square feet on a 2.4-acre elevated parcel. Panoramic views of mountains and coast. All the open space and unobstructed views give a feeling of seclusion and serenity. There's a reason they call it an *estate*.

RYANNA RAINES: If you ever change jobs, you'd make a great real estate agent.

The detective says he'll save the area where the stabbings took place for last and walk me through the other parts of the home to get a sense of how the De Carlos lived.

I should mention here our agreement with the San Diego sheriff is that I will not take any photos of the house, inside or out. I am permitted to record the audio of my conversation with the lead investigator. The family's furnishings have all been moved out and replaced by furniture from a staging company. Nothing personal of the De Carlos remains in the house—or so I'm told. I'll do my best to describe the experience of going inside.

A double eight-foot door of glass and mahogany opens into a vaulted entry hall. The flooring is sand-colored stone tiles, the interior walls a creamy white, with high open-beamed ceilings throughout. Detective Sanchez leads me up a curving flight of stairs to the second floor, where the main bedrooms are. There's also a separate maid's quarters downstairs off the kitchen.

As we start down the upper hallway, I ask where Jordan's bedroom is. He points to the third door on the right. Just then the detective's phone rings and he steps away to take the call. I continue to the third door on the right and enter the room.

It's bigger than most owner's suites, with its own fireplace and en suite bath, and there's a view of the San Marcos Mountains through French doors that lead out to a private deck. The staged furnishings give it all an impersonal feel. I see no signs that a teen boy actually lived here.

I step inside the walk-in closet, which appears empty. I notice that one of the upper shelves runs into a small recess extending past the doorframe. My curiosity, both natural and occupational, gets me up on my toes trying to peek back there. I see something leaned against the inside of the nook. I lift up as high as I can, stretch out my arm, and drag down a big, heavy book. On the cover is a drawing of Freddy the Falcon—the mascot for Torrey Pines High School. I open the cover and realize I'm holding a yearbook from the year Jordan graduated high school. The first several pages are filled with handwritten inscriptions from his classmates.

Several things shoot through my mind at once. This had to have been overlooked when they cleaned out the house. Did Jordan hide it there on purpose? It would be considered evidence, or potential evidence, because the personal messages from his friends could offer insights into Jordan's state of mind before he moved away to college. I'll be obligated to show my find to Detective Sanchez, and I am certain he'll take it away to examine with his team.

Automatically, and it truly is more reflex than thought-out action, I grab my phone and click off photos of the inscription pages. As I'm doing this, I hear Detective Sanchez entering the bedroom. I drop my phone on the floor and nervously scoop it up.

"Ms. Raines?" the detective says, looking for me. He's about to stick his head inside the closet when I meet him at the threshold.

Holding up the yearbook, I say, "Look what I found."

DETECTIVE SANCHEZ: Oh. Where was it?

RYANNA RAINES: Inside that little nook up there. I guess the people staging the house missed it.

He opens the cover, sees the inscriptions. Then he shuts the book, tucks it under his arm.

DETECTIVE SANCHEZ: Okay. Well, thanks. I'll show you Anthony and Lauren's bedroom.

RYANNA RAINES: The owner's suite is huge, nearly six hundred square feet. A massive fireplace, with his and hers closets and bathrooms. The outdoor deck is big, too, with two lounges, a teak dining table, and a view that extends out to the coastline, six miles due west.

We go back downstairs and he leads me out to the "resort-style" backyard. There is a covered veranda with an outdoor fireplace, a full outdoor kitchen, and a built-in barbecue. The swimming pool has an infinity edge overlooking landscaped fruit groves and flower gardens. A Jacuzzi that could comfortably fit twelve is attached.

"It's all about the outdoor living," the detective says, letting me gawk a few minutes. Then comes, "Ready to see where it happened?"

I grit my teeth and motion him to lead the way.

DETECTIVE SANCHEZ: As you know, the housekeeper found them. The first responders got here within ten minutes, those being our North County patrol officers. Homicide was contacted just after those officers arrived, and I entered the home forty minutes after the 911 call.

RYANNA RAINES: What were your first impressions?

DETECTIVE SANCHEZ: Well, there are ten pints of blood in the human body, I knew that. And here are two stabbing victims—but it looks like a lot more than twenty pints got spilled here. With the sunlight and warm temperatures and passage of two and a half days, it had all turned from red to brown to gray.

RYANNA RAINES: As we go into the kitchen, I wonder how long it took to clean up all that gray.

DETECTIVE SANCHEZ: Six-by-eight-foot center island, Italian marble countertop. This is where the killing begins.

RYANNA RAINES: He squats down on the floor to show me the position of Lauren as he found her. I'd looked at some crime scene photos provided by the defense attorneys, but this gives me a three-dimensional perspective.

DETECTIVE SANCHEZ: Mrs. De Carlo is down below the island, right cheek against the floor. She's wearing a white spaghetti-strap top that's covered in dried blood. Multiple knife wounds in her back are visible, as is a deep slit across her throat. All around her upper body is curdled blood.

RYANNA RAINES: Despite my general lack of squeamishness, his descriptions are making me queasy.

DETECTIVE SANCHEZ: I could see the blood spray on the island counter, which indicated she was stabbed while standing there. There was a plate of food, a chicken breast with bite marks that matched Anthony De Carlo's teeth. Three glasses on the counter. A half-drunk vodka tonic with Anthony's fingerprints on the glass. An iced tea with Lauren De Carlo's lipstick on the rim. The third was filled with water from the purifier. That glass had only Mrs. De Carlo's prints on it. It's likely she was the one who poured it and set it there.

RYANNA RAINES: The third glass indicated what to you?

DETECTIVE SANCHEZ: That there had been a visitor standing with them at the island when the stabbing started. Someone they were familiar with, who they'd allowed into their home at nine o'clock on a Sunday night, who they'd given something to drink.

RYANNA RAINES: Detective Sanchez steps over into the great room, a large space adjacent to the kitchen in the open ground-floor layout.

DETECTIVE SANCHEZ: Anthony De Carlo was here, halfway between the kitchen and front door. Lying on his left side, wearing a polo shirt, shorts, and deck shoes. He had even more blood around him than his wife. The larger the person, the greater the volume of blood. He had defensive wounds on his hands and forearms. Multiple stab wounds in his upper torso—what the medical examiner calls *sharp-force injuries*. His throat had been cut ear to ear. The throat slashing was done to both victims, to be sure they died from exsanguination.

RYANNA RAINES: *Exsanguination* is the medical-examiner term for blood loss. To be honest, not my favorite word in the English language. If the stabbing started in the kitchen, how did Anthony end up out here?

DETECTIVE SANCHEZ: If he was trying to get away, the door to the backyard is a lot closer than the front door. Now, the couple did keep a handgun in their bedroom. He may have been headed to the stairs with the intent to go grab his weapon.

RYANNA RAINES: Jordan knew his parents owned a handgun . . .

DETECTIVE SANCHEZ: I'm not going to comment on the defendants in this case, as they have yet to stand trial. I'm here to tell you what I can about how the victims died.

RYANNA RAINES: Fair enough.

A note for listeners. What follows is a graphic theory for exactly how Anthony and Lauren De Carlo were murdered. If you want to skip this part, fast-forward three minutes.

What about the murder weapon?

DETECTIVE SANCHEZ: We inventoried all the knives in the house and matched them against the victims' wounds. The knife that struck them did not belong to the house. We believe the assailant brought the weapon into the home and was concealing it until the attack started.

RYANNA RAINES: Could you determine whether it was a single assailant or multiple assailants?

DETECTIVE SANCHEZ: Our county medical examiner and an independent forensic pathologist agreed the sharp-force injuries to both victims came from the same instrument. The stabs came in rapid succession, penetrating deep enough and impacting bones to an extent that it showed the assailant had good upper body strength. The weapon could have been handed off to a second person, but they'd have to have been of comparable height, strength, and in a similar state of frenzy.

RYANNA RAINES: The upper body strength indicates the assailant was male?

DETECTIVE SANCHEZ: That would be your gender assumption, not ours.

RYANNA RAINES: What tells you the attack was committed in a state of frenzy?

DETECTIVE SANCHEZ: The sheer number of wounds. Forty-three to Mr. De Carlo. They weren't all stabs—some were slashes, the sharp edge slicing the skin rather than going in knifepoint first. Nearly every organ in the man's upper body was damaged, including penetrating wounds to his lungs and heart. Mrs. De Carlo received twenty-two separate wounds.

Imagine you had a side of beef hanging in front of you and you took a steak knife and with all your strength slashed and stabbed it sixty-five times in under three minutes. That requires a tremendous amount of physical energy.

RYANNA RAINES: Setting aside the who, what's your theory of *how* it happened?

DETECTIVE SANCHEZ: No entry was recorded on the keypad at the front gate, so whoever it was parked on the street below, hopped the wall, and walked up the driveway. I'll refer to this person in the singular, though it may have been more than one person who entered the home.

If the De Carlos were surprised by a visitor, they still welcomed the person. They walked them into their kitchen, served them a glass of water, and faced them across the center island. The serology shows both victims were initially struck at the island. The first wounds were to their front torsos, inflicted by a right-handed attacker. Both victims were looking at their killer when the person struck.

RYANNA RAINES: I admire how nimble Detective Sanchez is at avoiding gendered pronouns.

Was Anthony or Lauren struck first?

DETECTIVE SANCHEZ: In our reconstruction, Anthony takes the first blow. The blade penetrates mid-abdomen at an upward angle. An under-handed stab, with the assailant concealing the weapon, then getting close enough to stick the blade in before either of the De Carlos have time to react. With Anthony immobilized, the assailant turns to deliver the next blow to Lauren, at a steep downward angle into her upper chest.

Despite suffering that first critical and painful wound, Anthony tries to defend his wife. Their blood gets mixed together on the kitchen tiles. His rush forward causes the assailant to spin back and stab Anthony overhand, the blade entering above his right clavicle. Anthony raises his left hand to ward off the next blow. The blade glances off his forearm and hits his left cheek, opening a three-inch gash. The assailant delivers three more overhand strikes, one slicing into Anthony's right shoulder, two puncturing his upper chest. All of this happens very rapidly and at close range.

RYANNA RAINES: The assailant must have gotten covered with blood spray.

DETECTIVE SANCHEZ: After taking the fifth stab, Anthony lurches sideways. The assailant turns back to Lauren, who's on her knees. Now comes an underhand swing for sharp-force injuries two and three, striking under her sternum. Then the assailant stabs downward, into the top of her spinal column. Lauren falls forward on the floor and doesn't get up again.

Meanwhile, Anthony's on the move. He's critically wounded, spilling blood, staggering across the floor toward the front of the house. The assailant catches him in the great room, strikes an overhand blow to the back of his neck. Anthony was not a small man, five-eleven, 190 pounds. He stops, turns around, and lunges at the assailant. The assailant sidesteps him, Anthony slips in his own blood and falls. The assailant sticks him several more times in the side ribs. Anthony stops moving.

RYANNA RAINES: The killer was so relentless. Could he—or she—have been on some psychoactive drug?

DETECTIVE SANCHEZ: We searched the residence, the grounds, and the street below and found no residues or paraphernalia. That doesn't rule out drugs, but again, everything started out peacefully. If the De Carlos were confronted by someone in a drug-induced psychosis, would they have calmly stood in the kitchen and served them a glass of water? And while the attack was frenzied, it was also controlled. After it was over, the assailant did not run out of the house. The person stayed around and cleaned up after themselves. That shows presence of mind, someone in possession of their faculties.

RYANNA RAINES: Were shoeprints found?

DETECTIVE SANCHEZ: That's information I can't discuss.

JESS MONAY: As the tour was ending, did you feel guilty about snapping those photos of Jordan's yearbook and not telling Detective Sanchez?

RYANNA RAINES: I did. Here's the tape:

RYANNA RAINES: I really appreciate you taking the time to walk me through all this and allowing me to record it—now I have a confession. Up in Jordan's closet when I found his yearbook—I took photos of some pages inscribed by his classmates. I knew I had to hand the book over to you, but I wanted those pages for our investigation. Those were the only photos I've taken.

DETECTIVE SANCHEZ: Would you stop the recorder, please?

JESS MONAY: When I heard that I was like, "Uh-oh, he's pissed!"

RYANNA RAINES: He actually praised me for coming clean. He said he would be within his rights to confiscate my phone. But he wasn't going to do that. He asked that we not publish anything about the yearbook inscriptions until he got back to me. I asked how long that would be. He said he would expedite it with his team. When we parted, I felt it was on friendly terms.

What happened next is where we'll start our Recap Part 2, which will be in your feeds one week from today. That will catch us up to the present moment and will be followed by an announcement from *The Raines Report* that you will not want to miss.

Because everything is about to change.

S6:E34 RECAP (PART 2)

UPLOADED MONDAY, APRIL 10

RYANNA RAINES: Here is Jordan De Carlo's high school senior year-book, inscription from Tim: "Remember: 'It is in despair that we find the most acute pleasure. Especially when we are aware of the hopeless-ness of our situation.' Keep that as your mantra and go kill it in college."

JESS MONAY: Inscription from Emily: "Some will say go forth and make a dent in the universe. To you, Jordan, I say go forth and blow a hole in it. If anyone has the firepower to do that, it is you, my dear, sweet boy genius."

RYANNA RAINES: Inscription from Ruben: "Jordan, when you're a fa-mous Broadway playwright, all I ask is you cast me in your next Pulitzer Prize winner."

JESS MONAY: Inscription from Hannah: "Hey, Jordan, the real tragedy of my high school career is that you and me never hooked up. But where there's life there's hope. Have a great summer."

RYANNA RAINES: A gruesome murder at a multimillion-dollar estate in Southern California. Two prime suspects, twenty-two and eighteen years old, college lovers and theater school standouts. Was this a conspiracy to commit parricide, the murder of one's parents? This season we're looking into the emotional extremes between impassioned lovers, toxic family relationships, high-stakes legal maneuvers, and the startling crossovers between art and life.

I'm Ryanna Raines. And welcome to *The Raines Report*, an audio crime-investigation series produced in association with Amplify. You're listening to *The De Carlo Murders*. This is Part 2 of our Season 6 recap.

JESS MONAY: Is the adjective form of parricide *parricidal*? Never mind.

We covered a lot in Recap 1, but there's so much more to come.

RYANNA RAINES: Including our big announcement at the end of this episode. We don't recommend fast-forwarding to it, but if you must, we forgive you.

Oh yes, Jordan's high school yearbook inscriptions. From the pages I secretly took photos of—before handing my discovery over to the lead homicide investigator.

JESS MONAY: In a demonstration of your journalistic integrity.

RYANNA RAINES: Those pages gave us another window into this bright and shiny theater school graduate. Jordan De Carlo seemed equally popular with boys and girls, and already had a reputation as someone destined for big things. With him now languishing in jail and awaiting trial on first-degree murder charges, many of the notes contain cringey ironies that could not have been foreseen five years ago. "Slay them, Jordan," says one, intending the metaphorical meaning. "And never, ever show mercy." It's written in the delicate hand of a girl named Tory. That, it turns out, is short for Victoria.

No, not the same Victoria who's been charged as Jordan's parent-killing accomplice.

JESS MONAY: And then there was this inscription from a classmate named Omar: "Jordan, love the way we keep it real with each other. I feel you and your struggles with your parents. You will always find a listening ear with me."

RYANNA RAINES: Detective Sanchez had asked me to wait before bringing the yearbook inscriptions into our reporting. After not hearing back from him for two weeks, we decided it was time for us to pursue this and sent the detective a note to say we were moving forward.

JESS MONAY: The investigators asked for a head start on questioning Jordan's classmates—we gave it to them. They're doing their job. And we're doing ours.

RYANNA RAINES: When we reached out to Tim, Emily, Ruben, and Hannah, each said they'd been contacted by San Diego sheriff's homicide detectives. However, the classmate we first reached out to was Omar, who had mentioned Jordan's "struggles" with his parents. We're identifying him by first name only.

OMAR: Yeah, I got a message the detectives wanted to talk. But I didn't call them back.

RYANNA RAINES: Why not?

OMAR: I'm not giving my voice to the people who want to put my brother Jordan behind bars.

RYANNA RAINES: So you and Jordan were close when you were at Torrey Pines High?

OMAR: We were in drama together. All the talking we did about the lives of characters in plays led to us talking personally about our own lives. It was a natural progression from the fictional stuff to the real stuff.

RYANNA RAINES: You wrote in his yearbook, "I feel you and your struggles with your parents." What did you mean by that?

OMAR: There were conflicts. But it wasn't a secret. I wasn't the only one he talked to about his parents. I won't go into the details he shared with me friend to friend. Like I said, there were conflicts. Some of it was about Jordan wanting a career in the theater.

RYANNA RAINES: His parents didn't support his aspirations?

OMAR: Not so much. I also got to say, I never once saw Jordan lose his temper or get violent. The tensions with his parents made him more sad than anything else. I don't know the young lady involved, but my brother Jordan could never harm another human being that way. Least of all his parents, no matter how difficult they were.

RYANNA RAINES: Did you ever meet his parents?

OMAR: No. They never came around the school, and Jordan didn't want me coming over to his place. He was embarrassed by his mom and dad's pretentiousness.

RYANNA RAINES: Was that Jordan's word, *pretentiousness*?

OMAR: Yes, and other words. *Snobbish. Elitist.* Some were more derogatory. I mean, I've got friends who're embarrassed because their families are poor and live in trailer parks. But Jordan's my only friend who was ashamed of his family because of how rich they were.

JESS MONAY: His parents *weren't* happy with Jordan's passion for the theater, his high school friends said. That contradicts what he told you in Episode 6.

JORDAN DE CARLO: *They were happy I found something I was so passionate about.*

RYANNA RAINES: Though, it should be noted, we did not find any of Jordan's *college* friends who heard him be critical of his mom and dad or say they disapproved of his major. In college, he apparently avoided talking about his parents and where he came from.

JESS MONAY: That episode didn't make Natalie Bloom happy. Which we get. Detective Sanchez cut off communications with us, despite you owning up to taking the photos and giving him some lead time before reporting on them. This was the first time sources in our podcast revealed that Jordan had spoken of tensions between him and his parents. We'll be talking about the other backlash.

RYANNA RAINES: This is where you hear a heavy sigh from the host.

JESS MONAY: It was after this episode that we became aware of #FreeJDC, the online community whose self-declared mission is to actively call for Jordan De Carlo's release from jail and total exoneration.

RYANNA RAINES: *By any means necessary.* They started as a subreddit, then got a Twitter account and an Instagram and a TikTok. These are extreme Jordan partisans. When anyone posts a negative comment about him or makes a case for his guilt, the group goes into attack mode.

JESS MONAY: In the hours after the high school friends episode dropped, #FreeJDC followers flooded our social media with, shall we say, *complaints.* They accused us of putting words in the mouths of our sources to make Jordan look like he hated his parents. And they got pretty darn mean about it.

RYANNA RAINES: These are people who have not only taken up Jordan's cause but have put out a lot of hate against Victoria, casting her as the real villain. The #FreeJDC movement started taking on a life of its own. And we'll have more to say about that a bit later.

LINETTE: I'm not big on mainstream media. Never watch the news. When I go on my socials, it's to post my poetry and artwork.

JESS MONAY: We tracked down the high school friend Victoria's mom mentioned, Linette—we're using her first name only. Initially, she declined to talk to us. I went back and made it clear she wouldn't have to answer anything she didn't want to and could go off the record anytime.

We wouldn't attribute anything she told us in confidence. Finally she agreed to get on the phone.

RYANNA RAINES: For most of it she was on her guard, careful not to say the wrong thing. She spoke affectionately of Victoria, though they hadn't seen each other since Victoria graduated and moved to Santa Barbara. There was one story she told worth noting. It came out toward the end, when I asked if Victoria had any problems with other students at their high school.

LINETTE: There was a girl in our drama class, a mean-girl bully-bitch who I will not name. Her daddy bought her a red Corvette for her eighteenth birthday. Such a smug entitled asshole. We stayed away from her. She could be dangerous if you got on her wrong side. In class one day, Victoria did a monologue from the movie *Clueless* by the Cher character, the cute blond popular girl. And the bully-bitch raised her hand to give a critique. She basically called Victoria out for being a loser and "clueless" about what it was like to be a socially successful girl in high school. She kept on ripping into Victoria. I don't know why the teacher didn't stop her. I could see Victoria's face getting red, but she stood there and took it. She didn't even say anything back, just sat down and stared straight ahead. I felt horrible for her.

So two or three weeks later, the bully-bitch goes out to the parking lot after school and finds her Corvette completely trashed. Tires slashed, battery acid poured over the roof and doors, F-U-C-K and the letter U spray-painted on the hood. Now, I swear to you, to this day I couldn't tell you if Victoria had anything to do with it. She never said anything to me and I didn't ask. I do know they called like six different kids into the office to take lie-detector tests given by the police. Victoria was one of them. I heard through the grapevine that she passed and was cleared. Far as I know, they never caught the person who did it.

RYANNA RAINES: Why didn't you ask Victoria if she did it?

LINETTE: Because I didn't want to put her in a position where she might have to lie to me. And the evil skank deserved it anyway.

JESS MONAY: That was really interesting.

RYANNA RAINES: We found a source from the school that corroborated the Corvette trashing incident. But whether Victoria was suspected of it or took a lie-detector test, we did not get confirmation.

JESS MONAY: Does that behavior coincide with what we know about her?

RYANNA RAINES: I think about her quiet intensity and the hormone-fueled inner world of a teenage girl. There are people who describe her as shy and withdrawn. But there is also this supercharged performer inside who can get on a stage and light up an audience.

JESS MONAY: Then, big news, we received permission from the prosecutors to watch video of the interview that detectives conducted with Jordan and Victoria in mid July.

RYANNA RAINES: They were interviewed together just once, after both had been interviewed separately. Keep in mind, this is before they'd hired legal counsel. This double questioning is the only video we know of that shows Jordan and Victoria interacting between the night of the murders and their return from Mexico to the United States, 126 days later.

JESS MONAY: The murders happened on Sunday night, June fifth. On June twenty-first, Jordan had his first formal interview with San Diego detectives. Then, on the twenty-eighth, Victoria was interviewed by the same detectives. Two weeks later they were asked to come in for a double interview. Not standard procedure, but the detectives wanted to see if they'd get tripped up on what they had already said in their individual interviews.

RYANNA RAINES: And they wanted to watch the body language and behavior between them. So Jess and I sat there with the pause button between us.

When the video starts, we see the empty interior of a police interrogation room, with no windows and blank walls. The angle looks down from where the camera is mounted.

The door is opened by a deputy who lets Victoria and Jordan into the room. The deputy says the detectives will be with them in a few minutes and shuts the door, leaving the two of them alone. Right away Jordan goes over and looks into the lens of the surveillance camera.

JORDAN DE CARLO: *They're recording us.*

RYANNA RAINES: Victoria comes over, waves at the lens, blows it a kiss. Jordan pulls out one of the chairs at the table for her, and she sits down.

JESS MONAY: Glad to see chivalry is not dead for Gen Z.

RYANNA RAINES: Jordan drops into the chair next to her. Two chairs across the table are empty, awaiting the interrogators.

JORDAN DE CARLO: *How're you feeling?*

VICTORIA BERNE: *Like an innocent person about to be questioned by the police—nervous but confident.*

JESS MONAY: How are you reading their emotional connection?

RYANNA RAINES: Genuine. I want to root for them. Jordan's hand covers hers on the table. They gaze at each other, trying to bolster each other's spirit. He leans over and whispers in her ear. She smiles, leans against his shoulder. He puts his arm around her. They sit that way, neither talking, just leaning into each other. Given the stress of the situation, they seem pretty at peace together.

Then the door opens and a male and a female detective enter the room. The man is Detective Paul Sanchez, the lead investigator who gave me a tour of the crime scene, and the woman is Detective Stella Plunkett, a law enforcement veteran who is presenting as the "good cop." They sit down opposite Jordan and Victoria and start taking down identifying information for the record: full names, addresses, student status.

Jordan gives the address of his rented house in Santa Barbara, Victoria the address of her apartment with Gwen Phan in Isla Vista. Then the detectives acknowledge they've already questioned Jordan and Victoria individually and thank them for their cooperation.

JORDAN DE CARLO: *If you already got what you needed, why did you bring us back in?*

JESS MONAY: Jordan starts out by pushing back. Detective Sanchez explains they need more clarity on certain matters and talking to them together will hopefully provide "a sharper picture." Another interesting metaphor.

DETECTIVE SANCHEZ: *Walk us through what you were doing between 5:00 P.M. Sunday June fifth and 2:00 A.M. Monday June sixth.*

JORDAN DE CARLO: *Victoria and I were working on a new play and using UCSB's main library because it has research material that isn't available anywhere else.*

JESS MONAY: We have a transcript here of the interview you did with Jordan and Victoria in Santa Barbara on October twelfth, three months after this double interview was recorded. We can compare their answers in the interrogation to the same questions they answered for you.

RYANNA RAINES: Jordan's story about going to the main library, doing research with Victoria in a seventh-floor study room, then leaving by the stairs instead of the elevator—it's all consistent with what they told me.

JESS MONAY: They say they crossed campus and went to the Commencement Lawn, which they knew would be deserted late on a Sunday night in the summer.

RYANNA RAINES: Detective Plunkett asks, "What did you do when you got there?"
Jordan and Victoria exchange a look. Victoria sits forward.

VICTORIA BERNE: *We made love inside the tree.*

DETECTIVE PLUNKETT: *Can you be more specific?*

RYANNA RAINES: Jordan keeps his eyes on Victoria as she describes their tree-trunk encounter in graphic—I mean graphic—detail. Much more so than what they shared with me.

JESS MONAY: They were playing to our listening audience when they talked to you. In the interview room, they were playing to an audience of two.

VICTORIA BERNE: *It was a cool night, but we were both dripping sweat. I orgasmed three or four times, I lost count. We were swapping sweat, spit, body fluids. It was rad.*

RYANNA RAINES: We follow their accounts closely, pausing to check what they're saying against the transcript of our later interviews. This is the core of their defense, the alibi.

JESS MONAY: There's still that gap between five-thirty, when they were recorded going up the library elevator, and 1:40 A.M., when they were captured by the parking lot camera getting in Jordan's car.

RYANNA RAINES: I'll add here that on my last trip to Santa Barbara, I retraced this route in my rental car. On a Sunday night at 6:00 P.M., I left from the same parking lot, drove down to the De Carlo home in Rancho Santa Fe, waited forty minutes, then drove straight back to that parking lot.

JESS MONAY: And what time did you get there?

RYANNA RAINES: A little after 1:30 A.M. I made the trip at a different time of year, but on the same day of the week. The traffic conditions were similar to what they were on June fifth.

JESS MONAY: So it's definitely possible to make that trip during the period of time Jordan and Victoria's whereabouts can't be verified.

RYANNA RAINES: But the question remains, how did they travel back and forth across a distance of 400 miles if Jordan's car was in the parking lot and Victoria's was in the body shop?

JESS MONAY: That's what the two detectives want to know, but the suspects are sticking to their story and including lots of small details that would make it seem they're telling the truth.

RYANNA RAINES: Then the questioning turns to an event that Jordan and Victoria had provided no details on during the time I spent with them.

JESS MONAY: The weekend before the murders, the couple took a trip down to his parents' home together. A "family visit" that had been scheduled the week beforehand.

RYANNA RAINES: To the detectives, they downplay any significance to the visit. Jordan starts out saying it was "nice," Victoria upgrades that to "great." Then the detectives bring up that, according to Lauren De Carlo's calendar, the visit was scheduled for two nights. But Jordan and Victoria stayed only one night, heading back to Santa Barbara the morning of May twenty-ninth.

DETECTIVE PLUNKETT: *Did you or Victoria get into any arguments with your parents that weekend?*

JORDAN DE CARLO: *My parents tend to be—tended to be opinionated. I saw it as more like debating than arguing. Sometimes my mom would get sensitive and take my pushback as fighting with her. To me it was just a healthy discussion. But that weekend was completely mellow.*

JESS MONAY: The detectives ask in what bedroom did Jordan and Victoria spend that Saturday night. Jordan says in the maid's quarters downstairs. Why not in his bedroom upstairs? Plunkett asks. Victoria leans forward.

VICTORIA BERNE: *Because I wasn't comfortable being that close to Jordan's parents.*

DETECTIVE PLUNKETT: *Why not?*

VICTORIA BERNE: *I knew Jordan and I would be having sex, and I can be a bit loud. I didn't want anyone to feel awkward.*

JESS MONAY: Here again Victoria is pretty brazen to these detectives about the sex.

RYANNA RAINES: Then comes something else that's new to us. Detective Sanchez asks Victoria, "So tell us what happened in the kitchen."

VICTORIA BERNE: *I was cutting up a watermelon on the island and the knife slipped and sliced into my left index finger. It started bleeding, a lot. I was by myself, so I tried to clean it up before anyone found out. But then Lauren came in and I felt embarrassed, so I didn't tell her. I just wrapped my finger in a paper towel and excused myself. I went to the downstairs bathroom and looked for a Band-Aid. I dripped blood on the floor and on the sink. I couldn't find anything to stop the bleeding, so I went to the door of the back patio and waved to Jordan. He came in and got me a bandage from an upstairs bathroom.*

RYANNA RAINES: Jordan follows up to say that he told his mom what happened because she'd see the bandage on Victoria's finger. And he asked her to take a photo of Victoria's cut.

JESS MONAY: Why?

RYANNA RAINES: He thought his mom should have a record and his mom seemed fine with it.

JESS MONAY: Did the police find that photo on Lauren's phone?

RYANNA RAINES: According to AJ Novick, Victoria's attorney, yes. He said you can see the cut is deep. When Victoria got back to Santa Barbara, she went to the campus emergency room and they gave her three stitches.

JESS MONAY: And what do we think about this?

RYANNA RAINES: Like most things in this case, there are two diametrically opposed perspectives. One, it was a straight-up accident. Or Victoria did it deliberately, so she would have an excuse for why her blood would be found inside the De Carlo home a week later.

JESS MONAY: To keep their alibi intact.

RYANNA RAINES: The next part of the interview focuses on how the De Carlos felt about Victoria as their son's girlfriend. The detectives had been in contact with a neighbor who lived up the street from the De Carlos who told them Lauren didn't like Victoria. She felt she "wasn't good enough" for Jordan.

JESS MONAY: Not just not good enough, this witness said Lauren had referred to Victoria as "trailer trash." And that she was using Jordan to further her acting ambitions.

JORDAN DE CARLO: *That's not true, my mom never said that!*

VICTORIA BERNE: *Even if it was true, I would've won your mom over. Your dad, too.*

DETECTIVE PLUNKETT: *Did you have a conflict with Anthony?*

VICTORIA BERNE: *Not at all. His dad was nothing but sweet to me.*

JESS MONAY: As the questioning continues past the two-hour mark, how are you seeing the body language between Jordan and Victoria?

RYANNA RAINES: They're still touching hands, rubbing shoulders, showing physical intimacy. Making eye contact, checking to see the other is okay. Yes, these are star drama students and well-practiced at playacting. To my eyes, their mutual affection looks balanced and real.

What's harder to tell is how the detectives are reading all this—they're practiced at a different type of playacting. If this had been a contest, I'd say detectives and suspects fought to a draw.

JESS MONAY: Maybe with a slight edge to the suspects.

RYANNA RAINES: Agreed.

And then came the night I was back on the West Coast for some follow-ups, staying at an Airbnb in Oceanside. I was in bed, pillows propped up behind me, going over some police reports that had just been released. I dozed off.

My phone wakes me up. I see a call coming from a 617 area code—which I know is the Boston area because my husband's sister lives there. It's 11:00 P.M. local time, 2:00 A.M. on the East Coast. My reflex is to hit record as I pick up the call.

"Hello?"

STEVEN DE CARLO: Hello, is this Ryanna Raines?

RYANNA RAINES: Who's calling, please?

STEVEN DE CARLO: My name is Steven De Carlo. I'm Jordan's older half brother. Anthony De Carlo was our father.

RYANNA RAINES: Oh, hello.

No, I am not expecting this call.

STEVEN DE CARLO: I apologize for calling this late. I got your number from Natalie Bloom. Do you have a few minutes to talk?

RYANNA RAINES: I sit up in bed, fully alert.

Sure. Do I have your permission to record the call?

STEVEN DE CARLO: I'd rather not be recorded at this point. But I will give you permission to quote me.

RYANNA RAINES: Okay, I am grabbing my pen and notebook so I can take notes. Is that all right?

He says that's fine and starts off with some family history. His mom got pregnant when she and Anthony were twenty-one, still undergrads at Stanford. They eloped to Vegas so that Steven would be legitimate. But the marriage lasted less than two years. Steven's mom got custody and relocated with him to the East Coast. He'd spend a couple of weeks every summer in California with his dad—until Lauren came into Anthony's life. According to Steven, Lauren resented him because he'd been Anthony's "mistake." She was also jealous of Anthony's first wife. Lauren and Steven didn't get along, and he saw his dad less and less. After Jordan was born, Steven felt downright unwelcome, and didn't even meet his half brother until he was five. That's when Steven got invited to stay at the De Carlo home in Atherton while his dad and stepmom were on vacation in Europe. Steven was twenty-two, had just graduated from college, and didn't have a whole lot in common with a kindergartner. A nanny was taking care of Jordan, and the two brothers played in the backyard. Steven showed Jordan how to pitch and hit a softball. At night they ate dinner together and watched TV. Steven could see Jordan was super bright. His favorite movie at the time was *Night at the Museum*, and Steven was amazed that Jordan had memorized the dialogue and could act out all the action scenes without looking at the screen.

On the last night Steven was there, Jordan had a hard time falling asleep and kept calling Steven back to his bedside to read him another story. One of the storybooks was inside the nightstand. Steven opened the drawer, and under the book he noticed some photos that he said were, quote, "disturbing." They were different angles of Jordan nursing at Lauren's breast. Only it wasn't baby Jordan or toddler Jordan. It was five-year-old kindergartner Jordan. This was the era pre-selfies, so Steven assumed Anthony had taken the photos. Steven was confused. Lauren was still breastfeeding Jordan? And why would these photos be in her child's nightstand?

Next day, when Steven was leaving to go home, Jordan became hysterical and tried to stop him from going. At first Steven thought it was sweet, but then Jordan started really freaking out, flinging himself down on the floor and banging his head against the wall. Steven stayed until Jordan calmed down. Then he sneaked out the back to go catch his plane. When he got to the airport, he listened to a phone message from the nanny saying that Jordan had gone into convulsions when he found out Steven was gone. She'd taken him to the emergency room.

When Anthony and Lauren got back from Europe and asked Jordan how he'd gotten the bruises on his face, he told them Steven had hit him. Steven got on the phone with Anthony to say that wasn't true, they'd gotten along great until Steven had to leave, which the nanny corroborated. Anthony said he was sorry, but Lauren wanted all contact between the brothers cut off. It was at that point Steven mentioned the photos in Jordan's nightstand. Anthony reacted defensively, accused his elder son of snooping, and hung up on him. Steven and his dad didn't speak again for ten years.

Then Steven tells me he'd gotten a call from Jordan the previous spring—about a month before the De Carlos were murdered. Jordan said his mom always told him that Steven had hit him when he was a child and that's why he was forbidden from contacting his brother. But Jordan had no memory of that happening and wanted to know if it was true. Steven said no and explained what really happened. Then he asked if Jordan knew how long he'd been breastfed as a child. Jordan said he had no idea, so Steven told him about the photos. Apparently, Jordan became very angry on the phone—not at Steven, at Lauren. He called his mom a liar and other derogatory terms. Jordan told Steven he was going to confront her about the photos. At the end of the conversation, Jordan said he and his girlfriend were coming to New York that summer and he'd love to hook up with him. Steven said that would be great.

A few weeks later Steven got a call from his aunt Frances to say that his dad and Lauren had both been stabbed to death inside their home.

I asked if he thought Jordan had anything to do with their deaths. Steven said he didn't have an opinion because he didn't really know Jordan. But when Frances had told him about the murders, the first thing he said he flashed on was that angry reaction Jordan had toward his mom during their call. He had no intention of implicating Jordan, just wanted to clear his conscience.

When we hang up, it's almost midnight. I turn off the light, but sleep does not come easy. In fact, the rest of that night, sleep doesn't come at all.

JESS MONAY: It was after we put out the Steven De Carlo episode that the you-know-what hit the fan.

RYANNA RAINES: The #FreeJDC community was becoming increasingly hostile. They denounced Steven and me and declared his comments about the breastfeeding photos were part of a conspiracy by a pro-Victoria faction to paint Jordan as a sexually damaged mother hater.

JESS MONAY: Within forty-eight hours of that episode dropping, I opened an email sent to our *Raines Report* address.

If threats of violence or details of stalking are triggers for you, you may want to fast-forward about two minutes.

RYANNA RAINES: There were three attachments to the message. One was a photo of me entering the Airbnb where I'd been staying in Oceanside, California—no, I was not aware I'd been photographed. The second was a photo of the front of our family home in Pennsylvania with a current *USA Today* in the frame to show the shot was taken the day before. And the third was a video clip showing a pack of African wild dogs killing and eating a young gazelle.

The note that came with the photos read as follows:

> *To Ryanna Raines. This is to let you know that you are under our surveillance. We are tracking your every move, and have eyes on your husband, daughter, and son. If you value your and your family's safety, you will make a public statement within the next 72 hours declaring your investigation has found Jordan De Carlo 100% innocent of the murders of his parents. Additionally, you will state that you now believe it was Victoria Berne who committed the killings of Anthony and Lauren. If you have not publicly made these statements by the 72-hour deadline, you and your family will be targeted for reprisals—hear that, bitch? The clock*

*starts at midnight tonight. We urge you to take this extremely
seriously. If you ignore us or contact the authorities, we will take
swift and lethal action against you and your loved ones. Choose
your path wisely.*

It was signed #FreeJDC.

JESS MONAY: "Hear that, bitch?" That sent a chill down my spine. And
how specific it was, with the photos. The video of the wild dogs ripping
into a helpless animal, that's really messed up.

RYANNA RAINES: Was this something I should have foreseen? Even with
all the social media turmoil, I felt blindsided. This journalist received an
anonymous online threat against her and her family that shook her to
her core. Got to be honest, for a moment there I considered ending the
investigation.

JESS MONAY: When the doxing happened, I thought that might be it
for you.

RYANNA RAINES: Because I wasn't the only target of the doxing, it included my husband and children. That was the first time anything like
that had happened to me.

JESS MONAY: Doxing, by the way, is when someone posts your private information online, without permission, and with malicious intent. This
was beyond bullying, it was blackmail, and we reported it to the police,
the FBI, and the De Carlo/Berne defense attorneys right away.

AJ NOVICK: I've gotten a lot of death threats in my career. I'm sure
Natalie has, too. Pretty much comes with the territory.

RYANNA RAINES: I've been trolled and hated on out there, but no one's
directly threatened my family. That really, really sucks.
   The first thing I did, even before calling the police, was to call my husband. I told him everything I knew and urged him to be extra cautious,

especially with the kids. That night I didn't get home until the kids' bedtime. We got them down, and then my husband and I went into our bedroom, shut the door, and lowered the shades. What I said to him went something like this:

"I feel such guilt because I'm the one who put you guys in this position. If I hadn't gotten involved in this case, if I hadn't dug so deep, if I'd just been a regular mom and wife with a day job in a newsroom instead of running off to chase criminals and get justice for victims, then we wouldn't have these wackos putting a photo of our home next to video of wild animals making a kill. I'm sorry, I'm so sorry."

My husband said, "Chasing criminals and getting justice for victims makes you who you are. If that comes with people threatening you online—well, it's the price we have to pay."

JESS MONAY: Damn, I love your husband.

RYANNA RAINES: Me too.

We immediately contacted a private security company and took the responsible precautions. The De Carlo murders became personal to me in a way no previous case had. Was I going to let myself be blackmailed by cyberbullies? Would I grovel at the feet of trolls?

AINSLEY COLES: Thanks for picking up, Ry. I just heard about those creeps threatening you and your family. Whole lot of swear words I could use right now to express my outrage. But I really just want you to know I'm here for you, sister.

RYANNA RAINES: Ainsley Coles hardly needs an introduction on this podcast. She is my longtime friend, mentor, and colleague. As crime journalists with our own audio series, we're friendly competitors. I have great respect for her and her work, and she's the first one I'll reach out to when I need advice about a challenging work situation.

AINSLEY COLES: If there's anything I can do for you, name it. Even if it's just a shoulder to cry on.

RYANNA RAINES: Ainsley, I so appreciate you showing up. I hope you know how much it means to me.

AINSLEY COLES: I have experience with how alone one can feel in this job sometimes.

RYANNA RAINES: Alone while going globally viral. There are definitely times when it's *not* good to be trending on Twitter.

AINSLEY COLES: That's when I've felt the loneliest, being the subject of a breaking story, seeing my name everywhere. Then I tell myself to slow down and just focus on what I can control. Breathing, looking straight ahead, and putting one foot in front of the other.

RYANNA RAINES: This case has blown up like nothing I've ever been involved in.

AINSLEY COLES: I knew it would. It's got everything. A baffling murder mystery, two gorgeous young suspects, doomed romance, and that new category of media celebrity—the independent audio journalist.

RYANNA RAINES: Media celebrity is a double-edged sword. It opens doors and gets your calls returned. At the same time, it puts a big target on your back.

AINSLEY COLES: For what it's worth, I think these online troll gangs look a lot bigger than they really are. I'm not saying don't take their threats seriously. But my read on #FreeJDC is it's a tightly networked group of fellow obsessives who are really good at amplification. They're masters at creating an illusion of critical mass. In reality it all comes down to a dozen fanboys and fangirls, living in mom's basement or grandma's attic, channeling their social frustrations into making threats and attacking people online.

JESS MONAY: So cool of her to offer her support like that. We included Ainsley's call because we did get so much support from within our own community of crime reporters and from the wider world of journalists.

RYANNA RAINES: The message is "We stand up for each other and we'll never let the trolls win."

JESS MONAY: Oh, hang on, this is the office manager who works for that Atherton therapist.

RYANNA RAINES: Jess goes off into a corner and has an animated phone conversation.

JESS MONAY: Okay, so Jordan did request his therapy records from when he was thirteen, but didn't have them sent to him at the jail. He had them sent to a residence in Atherton. She couldn't give me the address, but she did say the last name of the addressee: "Riche with an e."

RYANNA RAINES: Which prompted me to reach out to Aunt Frances, who I'd had quite a good Zoom call with earlier in the season. She picked up and, without even a *hi*, said the following: "I do not want to be interviewed or questioned by you or anyone else from the media. Please do not try to contact me or any of my family members. I have nothing more to say." *Click.*

JESS MONAY: Wow. What changed? She read the therapist's notes and realized they might be damaging to her nephew's case?

RYANNA RAINES: Maybe. We can only speculate because Aunt Frances has shut the door on us.

JESS MONAY: And speaking of doors shutting.

RYANNA RAINES: Or staying shut. Remember the acting student Kurt Nall, who played one of the leads in *Desire Under the Elms*? The other male lead, Thad Baylor, had told us about some kind of incident between Kurt and Victoria in Stage Combat class. We were able to get Kurt's contact information, but he kept declining to talk to us.

JESS MONAY: Which is his right, we respect that. His not wanting to talk heightened our curiosity about this incident, but we couldn't get anyone to talk to us about it, not even the faculty member who taught the class.

RYANNA RAINES: Let's turn back to another source that we'd publicly been keeping quiet about. We knew we'd put it into our reporting, but wanted to make sure we got a confirmation first. I'm talking about the journals that Jordan and Victoria kept while they were in Mexico.

JESS MONAY: They were given to you by Jordan and Victoria, and they did so freely, willingly, and on the record.

RYANNA RAINES: Yes, and they specifically asked me to keep their journals for them in the event of their arrests. We knew these would be of interest to both prosecution and defense, and early on we were asked to hand them over. This led to some intensive negotiations between the San Diego D.A.'s office and the legal advisor we retain for our podcast. The issue came down to us wanting to maintain possession of the actual journals, while being perfectly willing to get all the pages scanned and provide those to the prosecutors. The prosecutors balked, saying they wanted the original physical notebooks so they could be analyzed by a forensic document examiner.

JESS MONAY: What would the examiner be testing for? From the scans they could do handwriting analysis, but the authorship of the journals is not in dispute. Jordan and Victoria stated it was all their writings.

RYANNA RAINES: The prosecutors wanted a lab to perform "indented impressions testing" to see if any pages had been written on and torn out. They would also examine the original pages under ultraviolet and infrared light to detect "alterations, obliterations, and erasures."

JESS MONAY: We showed the journals to the defense attorneys and they made their own copies. They advised us that the prosecutors would eventually subpoena the original documents, so we might as well show a little goodwill and hand them over sooner than later.

RYANNA RAINES: We had the highest quality scans made from the original pages, preserving the printing and ink colors, because Jordan and Victoria used a few different pens over the four weeks they were keeping the journals.

JESS MONAY: According to the dates they wrote down, the entries spanned from September fourteenth to October eleventh.

RYANNA RAINES: Back in Episode 7, I asked Jordan and Victoria to read passages from those journals. What they wrote was filled with a mix of romantic euphoria and melancholy. They spoke of "wrenching pain" and "precious, precious moments." That episode was one of the most downloaded and commented on of the first eleven. Listening to them read those passages was riveting.

JESS MONAY: And heartbreaking. Let's you and I read some of the other entries, to locate listeners inside the lovers' hearts and minds during their Mexico retreat.

RYANNA RAINES: I'll start. This is Victoria writing, dated September twenty-first:

"*Fue como un sueño*—it was like a dream. Today we visited a tiny town called Cuadano. We stopped at the one cantina and sat outside in rusty metal chairs. The tower of a long-abandoned sugar mill shaded us from the sun. We ordered two Coca-Colas that came in old bottles with faded logos—at least we were drinking from recycled glass. We heard bells start ringing and we walked down the road to a small Catholic church. Inside were six rows of pews and an altar with lit candles and fresh roses. Jordan and I both knelt there and silently prayed. He reached for my hand and said he wanted to marry me. Then and there. He found the priest, Padre Juan Pablo, and asked him if he'd do a quick ceremony. The priest spoke very little English and just kept smiling and shaking his head. So Jordan and I performed our own ceremony and exchanged vows. We are married now, one soul to another—*un alma a otra*."

JESS MONAY: This is in Jordan's journal, dated September twenty-fourth:

"Last night was magic. We sat on the beach and watched the moonrise. The light beamed down on the sand and we started dancing. Victoria would sing a song—she has a beautiful voice—then I would sing a song, and we danced barefoot by the light of the moon. We danced and made love, danced and made love again. Covered with sand, we jumped into the ocean and held each other in the shallows, emphatically, not wanting to let go."

RYANNA RAINES: From Victoria's journal, dated September twenty-fifth:

"I had a bad dream of being harshly separated from my beloved. Waking up, I saw him asleep next to me. I put my arms around him and pressed myself against his back. Sometimes I do feel like we should run, take off south and start a new life in some village in Panama or Ecuador or Bolivia. I'd miss my mom, I'd miss acting, but I'd have Jordan. At moments like this, he's all my heart wants. At the same time, I know we must go back to face the liars and prove our innocence. After we're exonerated, we'll come back here."

JESS MONAY: Jordan's journal, dated September twenty-fifth:

"Stayed in bed all morning, embracing, skin to skin, warm and safe from the terrors of this world. I keep asking the souls of my mother and father to come back and give the police a sign that it wasn't us who did this to them. Point our pursuers in the direction of the real killers. It's a cold, cruel universe that would compound the tragedy of my parents' deaths by the victimizing of their son and the woman he loves."

RYANNA RAINES: The two of them filled page after page with vivid descriptions of their feelings and experiences together. They told me they were thinking of publishing these journals someday. As a testament to their love under the strain of a corrupt system trying to tear them apart.

And then came the morning that Jess called me into a meeting with her and Hailey, our fact-checker and researcher.

JESS MONAY: Hailey and I had been trying to find the origin of the two journals that Jordan and Victoria wrote in. We knew they'd bought them in the gift shop of the resort where they spent the first five nights of their twenty-six-night stay in Los Cabos. We wanted to see if we could find the receipts from Encontrada. No gift-shop purchases on the room charges or on either of their credit-card statements for their time in Mexico.

RYANNA RAINES: So they paid cash?

JESS MONAY: Must have, right? Hailey and I called the Encontrada gift shop and happened to get a cashier who spoke excellent English. We texted her photos of Jordan and Victoria and asked if she remembered them coming into the shop and paying cash for the journals sometime in mid-September. She said they looked familiar but was fuzzy on the dates. The shop keeps its cash receipts in a separate file, so she went looking for a receipt for two journals and writing pens within our timeline. And guess what?

RYANNA RAINES: She found the receipt. What was the date on it?

JESS MONAY: October ninth. Two days before Jordan and Victoria flew back to San Diego. And this cashier said she did remember them, because October ninth is the day after her birthday, which she'd taken off. It was her first day back on the register.

RYANNA RAINES: Hold on, I need to process this. You found a witness and a receipt that shows Jordan and Victoria purchased the journals on October ninth? Which means any entry they dated before that—would've been faked.

I just got a chill down my spine.

JESS MONAY: For real.

RYANNA RAINES: I'm looking at our copy of the journals. I see entries dated September fourteenth, September fifteenth, September seventeenth—all of them *before* October ninth. Now we know the entries had to have been backdated and written over the two days before they got on a plane to come home.

JESS MONAY: And the question is—why?

RYANNA RAINES: What first comes to mind is they were deliberately scripting their narrative. To paint a picture of themselves that would make people sympathetic to their cause. That would make *me* sympathetic to their cause.

Oh, Jess. Wow. They gave me the journals knowing I'd find newsworthy material there. That I would possibly, even probably, put those entries into my reporting. That I might even ask them to read some and play them in the podcast so our listeners would let their judgment be guided by what they heard.

JESS MONAY: They didn't create #TheRealRomeo&Juliet. They influenced our listeners to create it for them.

RYANNA RAINES: I feel sick to my stomach. Apparently, they selected *The Raines Report* to be their primary influencer. Can you think of another reason they would have faked those journals?

JESS MONAY: I suppose they could claim everything they wrote was true and they just backdated the entries to match the timeline of their trip.

RYANNA RAINES: If they'd said that up front, maybe. But they darn well knew people would think they were authentic. The journals not only express their feelings for each other but declare their innocence of the murders. Now we know it was all cooked up over the last thirty-six hours of the trip, during the time Jordan called our tip line. Great detective work by you and Hailey.

JESS MONAY: Finding the receipts is what we do.

RYANNA RAINES: There has been a distinct pattern to this season. We began with two subjects—a young man and woman—who contacted us to ask that I meet them, talk to them, and investigate their story. I embedded with them for eight days, during which we spoke at length, took meals together, even went for a wilderness hike together. I was drawing almost all my impressions about them *from* them. Those eight days came to a dramatic climax for which I literally had a front-row seat.

At that point, I lost my connection to them, so our team turned the microphone around and looked for witnesses and sources that could bring other perspectives on our subjects. We discovered two camps, those who stood by Jordan and those who stood by Victoria. Not that one camp or the other was pointing fingers, but most sources knew one well and the other less so. A split image was forming, and these two people who had seemed so tightly bonded, so joined at the hip, started emerging as differentiated individuals, with separate strengths and vulnerabilities.

Then we came upon information that started creating doubt about our subjects' truthfulness. We encountered contradictions in their statements to us. We came across evidence that led to questions, questions we couldn't ask because of a court order. Our protocol at *The Raines Report* is to always take statements that conflict with what we've been told and give our subjects and sources a chance to respond. But in this case our hands were tied because our subjects were barred from responding to the new questions we wanted to ask them.

Well, that situation has now changed.

In the last few weeks, secret negotiations began that involved the defendants in the murders of Anthony and Lauren De Carlo, their attorneys, the San Diego district attorney, and the judge of the San Diego Superior Court where the murder trial will be held. Independently, Jordan De Carlo and Victoria Berne let it be known that they wanted to make statements—but insisted they would only speak to me. I have been out of touch with them for many months, so I had no personal influence in the matter. The legal team representing *The Raines Report* and our network, Amplify, has from day one been fighting to get the defendants' gag order lifted. We've made progress over the last months but still have a long way to go. Hearing that the defendants were reaching out to me—and had new information they wanted to disclose—caused our team to do another pivot. Pretty quickly all parties came to an agreement that would be kept confidential.

Until now.

I have been making visits to the Vista Detention Facility and recording separate interviews with Jordan and Victoria. A lot of new information has been coming out. I can't talk about it because our side, *The Raines Report* and our partner Amplify, accepted the condition of a news embargo on all matters related to my jailhouse talks with the defendants. We agreed not to release anything publicly until there is a legal resolution for both of them. A resolution defined as one of three outcomes in *The People of California v. Jordan De Carlo and Victoria Berne*.

One, the defendants are acquitted at trial by a jury of their peers.

Two, the defendants are found guilty at trial, and the judge issues their sentencing orders.

Three, a plea bargain is reached on behalf of both defendants, and the judge issues their sentencing orders.

All that leads to the announcement we promised you last week, and the reason we produced these last two recap episodes.

We are putting a pause on new episodes of *The De Carlo Murders* until one of those three conditions is met. At that time, in accordance with the legal settlement of this case, we will be dropping all the new episodes at once. These will include my full interviews with Jordan and Victoria from inside the jail. As I said, I agreed not to disclose any particulars from those interviews, but I can say this: they will be full of surprises and drama.

We'd love to be able to set a date for our return, we just don't know right now when that will be. Here's the heads-up I can give you for now. Everything you thought you knew about this case, and about these two defendants, is going to change. I'm Ryanna Raines, signing off for *The Raines Report*. We'll be back with you as soon as we can.

CBS THIS MORNING INTERVIEW WITH
CORRESPONDENT MEG CHOI

MEG CHOI: Such a difficult position to be in. You were receiving this explosive information and had to keep it all to yourself.

RYANNA RAINES: Well, I was sharing it with my producer and the defense attorneys. But I absolutely could not let it become public, or I'd be held in contempt of court.

MEG CHOI: And the circumstances were so different from when you first interviewed Jordan and Victoria. What was it like to see them again?

RYANNA RAINES: It felt like the masks were coming off and they were each showing me a different face than they'd been wearing before.

MEG CHOI: As an interviewer yourself, I'm sure this is a question you've asked before. How did that make you feel?

RYANNA RAINES: I felt a burden of responsibility. What was coming out of their mouths and being recorded on my little device would be determining their fates and defining their entire futures. As they continued to talk, the weight on my shoulders kept getting heavier.

MEG CHOI: Were you ever scared to be in a room alone with them?

RYANNA RAINES: I was too caught up in what they were telling me to feel scared. I've never been aware of time moving so quickly as I was sitting across from them inside that room. I wouldn't call it fear, but I was in a cognitive state of suspense during every moment I spent with them.

III

BINGE

A warning. The following episodes are intended for mature audiences. They contain descriptions of violence, sexual behavior, and psychological abuse that some may find triggering.

S6:E35

VICTORIA BERNE: So that night was a big turning point. I've never told anyone about what happened at the dinner—and afterward. Long exhale. Bear with me.

JORDAN DE CARLO: Maybe in my lowest moments, or when I was really angry at them, I'd fantasized about that, but I never crossed the line into actually planning it.

VICTORIA BERNE: Oh, don't worry. It gets worse.

RYANNA RAINES: I'm Ryanna Raines. And welcome to *The Raines Report*, an audio crime-investigation series produced in association with Amplify. We're in the last phase of our season on the De Carlo murders and we're calling this episode "All Anyone Sees."

JESS MONAY: It's really welcome *back*. We haven't put out a new episode in almost five months.

RYANNA RAINES: During that time, we recorded and produced nine new episodes. All nine will be dropping today. Our listeners will be able to start here and go straight through to the end.

JESS MONAY: The conditions that released us from our news embargo have now been met. Most of you know what's happened, because it's been all over the news and social media.

RYANNA RAINES: That said, going forward we will be spoiler free. We'll unfold the events for you as they unfolded for us, one dramatic turn after another. You'll be getting a look inside this case that has not been shared publicly anywhere or by anyone—until this moment.

A quick review of the series of events that got us here: Last October *The Raines Report* received a message on our tip line from Jordan De Carlo. I got on the phone with Jordan and Victoria Berne, who were in Mexico, and they said they wanted to get together with me so they could talk about the murder case in which they had become the main suspects. I met them at the airport when they arrived back in San Diego and spent several days in their company, recording our conversations and interactions. They told me of their love for each other and declared themselves innocent of the murder of Jordan's parents. On my eighth day with them, they surrendered to authorities at the sheriff's station in Vista, California, where they were separated and taken into custody. Shortly thereafter they were gagged by the San Diego Superior Court. That caused our investigation to shift focus, and we began interviewing the people closest to Jordan and Victoria. We went out, gathered our own evidence, and reported it in weekly episodes. We completed that phase with two recap episodes and brought the story current. In the meantime, I received permission to go into the Vista Detention Facility, where the defendants were being held for trial, and conduct separate interviews with them. Apparently, they had new information to share, and the only one they were willing to share it with was me. Here's a clip from a conversation I had with the defendants' attorneys, Natalie Bloom and AJ Novick.

NATALIE BLOOM: We have to follow the jail's policies. You'll be like any other visitor, restricted to one visit with one inmate per day. North San Diego County inmates are allowed only two thirty-minute jail visits a week.

AJ NOVICK: The visits have a hard stop after thirty minutes. The people in charge do not want Jordan and Victoria getting preferential treatment over other inmates. The one concession they'll make is letting you use the private attorney-client meeting room. And you'll be allowed to record audio, with the defendant's on-the-record consent.

RYANNA RAINES: Attorney-client privilege applies only to the individual defendant and their attorney of record. I agreed I would send each attorney their client's recorded interviews separately. It would be up to them to decide what to share with the other.

JESS MONAY: They requested that we upload those audio files to an encrypted website to protect them from being hacked.

RYANNA RAINES: So, the day after the deal for my jailhouse visits was concluded, I flew back to California, rented a car, and settled in at an Airbnb in Oceanside, just down the freeway from where the jail is located. It was arranged that I would visit Victoria first.

JESS MONAY: Not really knowing what to expect, we prepped you for a shorter interview. Focusing on the more urgent questions that came up during the second part of our investigation.

RYANNA RAINES: The north San Diego County city of Vista, seven miles inland from the beach, is a sprawling Southern California suburb. The jail there houses up to 825 inmates and, along with the sheriff's station and the Superior Court complex, is situated within a thicket of shopping centers, fast-food chains, and tract home developments. I'd been there once before, but that experience is somewhat of a blur.

I go over the visitor guidelines listed on the jail's website and check the attire restrictions. No khaki or army green. "Dress like you'd dress for church," it says. I wear a simple white blouse with gray slacks and no jewelry except my wedding band.

In the visitor processing center, a steely-eyed deputy sits behind bulletproof glass. After showing two forms of ID, I fill out an authorization form and sign it in three places. One of the first questions is my relationship to the detainee. I'm not a family member or a friend or a legal rep, but the sheriff has briefed the facility commander, who advised the staff to expect me. I write *journalist*, hoping that covers it. I slide the paperwork into the slot between me and the admitting deputy. The deputy checks his computer to confirm that the inmate I'm there to see is eligible for visits and that we'd been approved to use the attorney-client room. He stamps a single-use day pass and slides it back to me. The deputy informs me that I must carry the pass with me at all times. If I attempt to exit the facility or am found in a restricted area without my pass, I will not be allowed to leave. He says that last part with an Alpha male grin.

Next comes the search of my person and possessions. I empty my pockets and place my car keys, ID, and audio recorder into a tray to be sent through an X-ray machine. I'd left my phone in the car because I'm not permitted to bring it into the room. I have received prior authorization to bring in my Sony recorder. I remove my shoes and pass through the metal detector.

Then I go into a small waiting area and sit in a plastic chair. On one side of me is a sad-faced young blond woman. On the other is a heavily tattooed bail bondsman.

An armed corrections officer comes in, calls my name, then escorts me through a series of metal doors and down a concrete corridor to a private visiting room. This room is windowless except for the soundproof glass in the upper part of the door so a guard can visually monitor the visit. Two fluorescent bulbs inside a protective cage provide cold illumination. The table and chairs are bolted to the floor. I am told the inmate is on her way. Then my escort steps out and shuts the door. I am alone in an inner sanctum where all around me are people caught in the clutches of the criminal justice system. As in any jail, a few are innocent, many are guilty, and the majority are not having a good day. All are invisible to me, but I can almost feel their collective desperation through the cinder block walls.

Not having seen Victoria in six months, with all I've learned in the interim, I am feeling more than mild apprehension. Has this time in jail changed her? Would she be emotional? Stoic? Despairing? Defiant? All I know is she initiated this contact with me—because she has "new information" to disclose. I've come to this room ready to listen and record.

No knock, the door just opens, and Victoria Berne enters, locked in wrist and ankle restraints, followed by a female corrections officer. Victoria looks even tinier in the facility's standard khaki uniform, shapeless mid-sleeve top and baggy bottoms. *SD Jail* is stenciled across her chest. The jailer unlocks her shackles, then turns to me and announces, "The thirty minutes start now." She steps out and shuts the door, then stands outside to keep watch.

I'm alone with the now-nineteen-year-old BFA acting student accused of a double murder.

Victoria stretches her arms and legs, then seats herself across the table from me. She looks in my eyes.

Her pale skin has become nearly translucent. Her facial features, refined to begin with, look like they've been resculpted with a sharper chisel. Those expressive brown eyes are burning more brightly than I remember. There's intelligence there, which is familiar, but there's something else I don't recognize. "Hello, Victoria," I say, aware of the effort it takes to make my voice sound normal.

She does not return my greeting, instead asks me not to turn on the recorder yet, which sits on the table between us. She says she wants to explain her intentions for the interview.

I nod and sit back. I feel an impulse to cross my arms but refrain because I don't want to appear defensive or anxious.

She starts talking about how as an actor she learned the importance of constructing a biography for every character she plays. She takes the character's life history that's set down in the script, then fills in the gaps by imagining an additional set of life experiences. It is in these experiences that she discovers the character's inner truths. This becomes the foundation for her understanding of the character's behavior and psychology. She tells me she wants the world to understand her behavior and psychology. She wants to use our first thirty-minute session to lay out her own character biography. And to give a context for what will be coming in future visits.

She leans forward and with emphasis says she wants to be the one who gets to tell her story, not the courts, not the media, not other people. She says she's had a lot of time to think it over, and this is the right path forward for her. Her voice. Her words.

I say I'll need to relay whatever she tells me to her attorney. She says that's okay because he's bound by attorney-client privilege. I ask if she understands that whatever she tells me will eventually go out to the public through my podcast. She says she understands and will trust me not to edit her words in a way that changes their meaning. I promise her I will not do that.

She gives me permission to start recording.

VICTORIA BERNE: The earliest feelings I can remember are of being frustrated—by not having enough stimulation. I wanted things to be faster, bigger, brighter. I could feel my mind needing input, input, input. My mom will tell you I was *demanding* as a toddler. It's true. I demanded more activities, more mental exercise. My hunger for stimulation was stronger than my hunger for food.

I now believe there's an innate processing power in every human brain, and some of us are just born with more of it. Doesn't make me a better person. In many ways it's made my life harder. I've seen videos my mom took of me reading Shakespeare out loud at three years old. At school, I did not want to be that show-off kid. Sometimes things just leaked out, like when I was called on in class. I could see other kids resented me. I went through a period of trying to dumb myself down to fit in. I guess I wasn't very convincing. Most of my peers kept shunning me. Even the smart ones, girls *and* boys, didn't know how to be in relationship with me. And I didn't know how to be in relationship with them. Or with myself.

My brain felt like a birth defect. I had to fight back feelings of shame for being too quick. What hurt most was the isolation. My mom would set playdates, but other kids didn't want me around. I was too different. Gail did the best she could. She was adamant I skip only one grade, when the counselors were telling her that academically I could skip three. So I went from fourth grade straight into sixth. To be starting middle school at ten years old, that was—painful.

RYANNA RAINES: Was your dad involved in those decisions, too?

VICTORIA BERNE: I was just about to get to my dad. Phil Berne. A profound influence on my childhood years. And beyond. Yes, let me tell you about my father.

For my first twelve years, he was the center of my universe. He was constantly showing me affection, appropriately, and made me know I was loved and accepted. I can feel his beard stubble against my cheek when he kissed my face. I can smell his aftershave, that manly smell so foreign to young girls. I can hear his deep voice whispering in my ear, "You are the best." I can feel his strong arms wrapping around me and hugging me against his chest. Given my ongoing alienation at school, his arms were the safest place in my world.

Then came the summer I turned twelve. The summer my brother and I got a new babysitter—we'll call her Mandy. She lived around the corner and was going into her senior year of high school. Pretty sure she wasn't eighteen, but given how well-endowed she was in the chest area, to me she looked like a full-grown woman. I had no breasts yet and my mom had small ones, so our babysitter fascinated me. She'd wear these little tank tops without a bra that made her breasts look enormous. One night I asked her point-blank how I could grow breasts like hers. I remember her eyes getting a little sad when she answered:

"You don't want boobs like mine. Because then that's all anyone sees."

It was such an honest response and it made me think. Maybe having big breasts was like having a big brain. It caused you to stick out and made you a target for the mean kids.

I became emotionally attached to my babysitter. I fantasized that she was my big sister and would tell me all the secrets of navigating the world of bullies. Then one night my mom was off on a trip and my dad called Mandy to come babysit because he was going out with his guy friends to a Seahawks game or something. She'd put my brother and me to bed and I'd fallen asleep. Around midnight something woke me up. I listened and could hear these weird noises coming from somewhere inside the house. Suddenly my twelve-year-old radar snapped on. I got out of bed, went to my door, opened it. I could hear these low, strange vocal sounds, like mumbling or moaning. They felt ominous and made my heart start racing. I tiptoed down the hallway to find out where they were coming from.

Stopping before the living room, I peeked around the corner and saw something I will never unsee. Mandy was sitting on the couch and my dad was kneeling on the floor in front of her. Her top was pulled up, and my dad was kissing her breasts. I could see her face, and not only was she not resisting, she seemed to enjoy it. Those low moaning sounds were coming from her.

Did I rush in and scream at him to stop? Or scream at her because I thought she was my friend? Or sneak back to my room and pull the covers over my head? No. I stood there. And watched. I could not tear my eyes away. And then my dad stood up and pulled his pants down and I saw his penis, and it was hard, and he climbed up over Mandy's chest, and she pushed her breasts together, and he started thrusting. I vaguely knew this was something adults did, but to actually see it made me feel sick and mesmerized me at the same time. When my dad ejaculated on her, it was so—disturbing. The spell was broken and I crept back to my bedroom. I shut the door as gently as I could and climbed into bed. I lay there, shivering from full body chills.

Something had changed inside of me. Going forward, my life would be different. I wasn't sure how. What I was sure of, and absolutely crushed by, was that my relationship with my dad would never be the same.

RYANNA RAINES: I'm so sorry you had to experience that.

VICTORIA BERNE: Oh, don't worry. It gets worse.

Mandy came over to babysit another time when my mom was away and my dad was going out. After I went to bed, I stayed awake until I heard his car pull into the driveway. I waited a little while, then snuck out of my room and went to peek around the corner into the living room. They were together on the sofa and Mandy had her mouth on my dad's penis.

This time my dad looked up and saw me. I froze. I thought he'd jump up and start yelling at me. But he just stared in my eyes and shook his head, like he was disappointed in me. I backed away and ran to my room. I dove under the covers and curled into a fetal position. I was sure he was going to come in my room and say something to me.

He didn't come in. Didn't say anything about what happened. That night or ever.

RYANNA RAINES: Did you say anything to him? To anybody?

VICTORIA BERNE: No. Not until now. Within a year of that happening, Phil left my mom. Left our home for a younger woman, barely twenty-one. Moved to Florida and started another family with her. I really thought it was my fault. Catching him like I did was too shameful for him to deal with. It totally broke our family. My mom went into a long depression. My little brother had problems managing his anger. And me? I withdrew. From everyone and everything.

I started trying to numb myself by sneaking my mom's beer and wine out of the fridge, guzzling it in my bedroom, hiding the bottles, and lying my ass off. After my mom caught me red-handed, I figured out how to steal pints of vodka from Target and Walmart.

When I realized that alcohol was only making me feel worse, I switched to self-harming. I stole packs of single-edge razor blades. I cut myself on the inside of my thighs, where no one could see. I'd make a little cut, and when it started to bleed, I'd press a tissue against it until it stopped. I'd make another cut right next to it and do the same thing. It was horrible and disgusting and wickedly compulsive. But it didn't hurt as much as it made me feel some relief.

This went on for a while. I had no real friends. My grades were going downhill. I didn't care about anything. My mom was lost in her own problems. My brother joined a skateboard gang and was gone all the time. I was spiraling in slow motion and did not have the will to pull myself out of it. Every day I seemed to drift a little further away from myself.

And then, in my first semester of high school, I took drama as an elective. On the first day, the teacher asked me to get onstage and perform a monologue from *Alice in Wonderland*. He handed me a sheet of text and said: "Be Alice." Those two words unlocked something in me. *You mean, I don't have to be myself all the time? I can get onstage and be somebody different for a while?* It felt like I was Alice stepping through my own looking glass. For the first time in my life, I had permission to be someone other than myself.

"I wonder if I might follow him. Why not? There's no rule that I can't go where I please. I will follow him. Wait for me, Mr. White Rabbit! I'm coming, too!"

That was the turning point. The start of my all-consuming passion for becoming an actor. For escaping into other people and putting on the different faces they showed the world.

"Be Alice."

JESS MONAY: Did you get a chance to ask her about the Mexico journals?

RYANNA RAINES: You have no idea how fast thirty minutes goes by. Before I could check my clock, the knock came at the door. Victoria stopped talking and the guard came in saying our time was up. The whole visit was her in monologue mode. So the answer to your question is no.

JESS MONAY: Did she say anything as she was leaving?

RYANNA RAINES: Let's play the tape.

VICTORIA BERNE: For your next visit, the girl-meets-boy chapter of Victoria's biography.

JESS MONAY: Now she's serializing her life story to you!

RYANNA RAINES: After the door shut, I just sat there stunned. I mean, that was heavy stuff.

JESS MONAY: Her voice sounded steady. Did she show emotion in her eyes or body language?

RYANNA RAINES: There were moments when she had to pause and gather herself. We left some of those in and edited out others. I'd say she was more pensive and thoughtful than emotional.

JESS MONAY: She is experienced in the art of rehearsing and performing. Not that I don't believe her. I want to believe her.

RYANNA RAINES: We'll have to get back in touch with Phil Berne and ask him to comment.

JESS MONAY: Oh boy.

RYANNA RAINES: I know.

JESS MONAY: Have Jordan and Victoria been communicating with each other in jail?

RYANNA RAINES: Their attorneys say no. Because while they're allowed under the rules to write letters, whatever they exchange would be closely studied by the jail staff. Anything they see that violates the rules would be censored and the inmates subject to disciplinary action.

JESS MONAY: What about the timing of them asking for you to visit? Did they coordinate it?

RYANNA RAINES: According to AJ and Natalie, they came to that decision independent of each other.

JESS MONAY: Victoria started by telling you her history of sexual trauma and self-harm. Where will Jordan start?

RYANNA RAINES: Our listeners can find out by staying in their podcast app as it rolls over to the next episode. Coming up, my first jailhouse interview with Jordan De Carlo. See you on the other side.

S6:E36

JORDAN DE CARLO: Do you think we're guilty?

RYANNA RAINES: I've asked myself that every day since you left a message on our tip line last October. And my answer keeps changing.

JORDAN DE CARLO: What's your answer today?

RYANNA RAINES: On the website for the Vista Detention Facility in North San Diego County, you'll find this description: "VDF houses a special-handling inmate population, consisting of those with medical challenges, those under psychiatric care, an administrative segregation unit, as well as defendants facing high-publicity trials."

The inmates I've flown across the country to visit fall into the last category. Jordan De Carlo had been arrested and charged with the first-degree murder of his mom and dad. The case received tidal waves of attention from social and tabloid media. One reason is that Jordan is young and handsome and talented, and Gen Zs across multiple platforms and of all genders have been expressing a desire to have sex with him.

JORDAN DE CARLO: Did you know I'm not allowed to send Victoria a note that says "I love you"? Because those three words might contain a coded message meant to subvert the authority of the VDF staff. I'm completely cut off from expressing my feelings to her.

RYANNA RAINES: And if Jordan's heartthrob looks weren't enough to feed the media frenzy, his girlfriend was also charged as an accomplice in his parents' murders. "All the world loves a lover," said Shakespeare, or said someone, and there's a multiplier effect when those lovers are beautiful, brilliant, and notoriously star-crossed.

I'm Ryanna Raines. And welcome to *The Raines Report*, an audio crime-investigation series produced in association with Amplify. We're in the last phase of our investigation into the De Carlo murders and we're calling this episode "Heaven's Gate."

JESS MONAY: Your first jailhouse interview—first *visit*—with Jordan is taking place twenty-four hours after you met with Victoria. And you have the same ticking clock, thirty minutes from the moment he enters the room, not a minute more.

RYANNA RAINES: No time for chitchat. But I get it. Jails need strict security policies.

On this afternoon, in the visitor waiting room, a fellow visitor asks me if I'm there to see one of the "head cases" or one of the "hard cases." I am tempted to say, "Both."

For the second consecutive day, I am escorted by an armed officer through a series of metal doors and down a concrete corridor. He leads me to the same room where I'd visited Victoria. I seat myself, place my recorder on the table, fold my hands, and wait. I'm wearing the same Sunday church outfit I wore yesterday. But Jordan won't know that.

When I see Jordan through the glass in the door, he's laughing. The door opens and I see that the male officer and Jordan are both laughing. The officer stops laughing the moment he sees me. He then goes about the business of unlocking Jordan's shackles. When the officer shuts the door, Jordan faces me. In contrast to his apparently chipper mood, his natural blond hair is stringy and unwashed, his face gaunt, his eyes bloodshot. He gives me an appraising look as I rise from my chair in greeting. He holds out his hand and I notice it quiver.

"The rule is no touching between visitor and visitee," I say, aware we're being watched through the glass in the door.

Jordan shrugs.

I smile and sit back down. He takes a moment to match my smile. Then he sits down, leans forward on his elbows, and asks me to turn on my recorder.

JORDAN DE CARLO: This is Jordan De Carlo and I hereby grant Ryanna Raines permission to record our conversation.

Time is precious, but I have to start by letting you know that this fine institution fed me a baloney and cheese sandwich for lunch today. The cheapest brand of baloney, with more sodium per slice than a bag of pretzels. The processed cheese has a lethal fat-to-protein ratio. The bread, food-color white, stuck to the roof of my mouth. I had to reach in with my finger to dig it out.

RYANNA RAINES: I am genuinely sorry to hear that. Your aunt Frances mentioned you were pretty unhappy with the food here.

JORDAN DE CARLO: Look at me, I'm emaciated. I wouldn't eat any of the crap they serve, but I need the calories or I'll die. I thought the worst part of incarceration would be separation from Victoria and loss of freedom. Turns out it's the toxic cuisine. And they do it on purpose. If they can kill their inmates through daily sodium bombing, it saves the cost of putting them on trial.

RYANNA RAINES: I can't imagine.

JORDAN DE CARLO: So, look, I have a lot to say. I'm going to start by telling you a story about my father. And what set all of this in motion.

I'm going to tell you the dirty secret that he'd been keeping from the world for a long time.

RYANNA RAINES: Can you give me a context for how this fits with our earlier conversations?

JORDAN DE CARLO: I'll leave the contextualizing to you. Have you heard of the Heaven's Gate doomsday cult?

RYANNA RAINES: When I read up on Rancho Santa Fe, I saw a mention of Heaven's Gate.

JORDAN DE CARLO: Still the largest mass suicide on American soil. Between March twenty-second and March twenty-sixth, 1997, thirty-nine souls willingly departed this world after drinking a cocktail of vodka mixed with phenobarbital. In three successive groups the cult members dressed in identical outfits, down to the same Nike tennis shoes and matching armbands, lay down on bunks and mattresses, and killed themselves.

And you know where they all died? On the property that's right across from my parents' property on Colina Conchita.

RYANNA RAINES: The cult members believed a comet passing by earth would rescue their souls and take them to another planet?

JORDAN DE CARLO: Wacko, right?

The person credited with discovering the bodies was a former member of the cult. This person worked for a tech company in Beverly Hills. One day, without warning, he received a FedEx package containing a videotape that showed his friends from the cult saying, "By the time you see this, we will all be dead." He told his coworker and together they drove down to Rancho Santa Fe. The front door was unlocked. This former member went inside and saw it was true. He dialed 911 and reported the suicides, but left the scene because he was too distraught. When deputies arrived, they let themselves in. And over the next twenty-four hours, news of the Heaven's Gate suicides spread all around the world.

Now here's a detail no one knows. Someone else discovered those thirty-nine dead people before that former member did. This man worked for a local bank in Del Mar and came to the house earlier that morning to discuss financial matters with Marshall Applewhite, the leader of Heaven's Gate. When the man knocked at the front door, there was no answer. He saw it was unlocked, opened it, poked his head in, and called out. No response.

Then he stepped inside, and at the entrance to the living room, he saw a bunk bed with two bodies lying in it. After that, he started finding bodies everywhere. Imagine his shock. All those happy smiling people he'd seen when he came to the house for financial meetings were now laid out in every room, deceased and beginning to decompose. He went upstairs to Marshall Applewhite's bedroom and found the leader alone in bed, also dead.

This man knew that Applewhite kept a safe-deposit box on the cult's behalf at his bank. The man had access to a second key that opened the box. The owner's key was in the nightstand next to Applewhite's body. The man took the key and left the house. He drove to the bank, opened the safe-deposit box, and found a bag filled with cash. Hundred-dollar bills, three thousand of them, in neat little stacks. He took all the money out, put the box back, then drove out to the beach and threw the key in the ocean. He came back to work, and within a week had given the bank and his landlord notice that he was moving out of the area.

That man who first discovered the bodies and stole over a quarter of a million dollars from the Heaven's Gate cult was my father, Anthony De Carlo.

RYANNA RAINES: My hands stay folded on the table in front of me. I glance down to see my knuckles have turned white.

Was the missing money from the safe-deposit box reported?

JORDAN DE CARLO: The only people who knew of its existence were dead. After the suicides, my dad went underground for over a year. Letting time pass before he did anything with the money.

RYANNA RAINES: Anthony told you these things?

JORDAN DE CARLO: Here's how I found out. Soon after we moved to Rancho Santa Fe, I heard the story of the cult. I checked the address of the house where they died and realized their property was on the hillside next to my parents' property. I thought it might be an interesting subject for a play, so I did some research. I found this newspaper report from the day the suicides were discovered that an anonymous call came into the sheriff's office prior to the one from the former member. But the cops thought it was a hoax, so they didn't pursue it. I knew my dad had been living down the road when the suicides took place, and that he'd worked at a local bank. The Anthony De Carlo VC lore was that he invested $250,000 *cash* in his first tech start-up in 1999. That made a profit, so he invested in another company, made a profit, and bankrolled that into his own venture capital firm. Pretty soon my father had become a very wealthy man.

RYANNA RAINES: Did you ask him where that first investment money came from?

JORDAN DE CARLO: I did. I confronted him. With enough information so that he couldn't deny it. He ended up telling me everything that happened that day in excruciating detail. Then he made me swear never to tell anyone. And threatened he would kill me if I ever betrayed him.

RYANNA RAINES: A chill runs down my back.
    Why are you telling me this now?

JORDAN DE CARLO: It's time for me to let go of my father's lies. And to tell you the real circumstances that led to his death.

RYANNA RAINES: Do you think your dad taking that money played a role in his murder?

JORDAN DE CARLO: I know it did.

RYANNA RAINES: How?

Jordan pauses. He leans back in his chair and folds his arms.

JORDAN DE CARLO: You were up to our house in Rancho Santa Fe with Detective Sanchez?

RYANNA RAINES: I was.

JORDAN DE CARLO: So in the backyard, beyond the edge of the infinity pool, the view looks out north and west. Can you picture it?

RYANNA RAINES: Yes.

JORDAN DE CARLO: I remember many evenings when Dad would pull a chair to the edge of the hillside and just sit there staring out at the Heaven's Gate property. As he got older, I think he became obsessed with the shame he felt. He built his fortune on the backs of those thirty-nine souls. And that haunted him.

JESS MONAY: So we let that part of Jordan's interview roll without commentary. I just want to say, the first time I heard it, I had a whole lot of commentary going through my head.

RYANNA RAINES: Right? I'm thinking, *He's going to accuse people connected to the Heaven's Gate victims of coming back to get revenge and committing the murders.* Where else would he be taking this?

JORDAN DE CARLO: I kept my dad's secret a long time. Finally I did tell someone. I told Victoria. You visited her in here yesterday?

RYANNA RAINES: I did, yes.

JORDAN DE CARLO: Except for court hearings, where we can't talk or touch, I haven't touched or talked to her since the day we turned ourselves in. How's she holding up?

RYANNA RAINES: Physically she seemed okay.

JORDAN DE CARLO: Nice deflection. She say anything about me?

RYANNA RAINES: I'll tell you both the same thing. During these visits, whatever's said between Victoria and me and you and me will be shared only with your individual attorneys.

JORDAN DE CARLO: Meaning you can play us against each other. But you wouldn't do that. You'd never exploit your subjects. Your brand is integrity.

RYANNA RAINES: Nice sarcasm.

JORDAN DE CARLO: I'm just pointing out the dynamic has changed since the three of us were together. At that point, Victoria and I were speaking to you as one. This gives you the advantage now. You can ask me the questions you've asked her and compare our answers. If our stories don't match, you'll know one of us is lying.

RYANNA RAINES: I'm listening to both of you with an open mind. My agenda right now isn't to catch you telling lies.

JORDAN DE CARLO: Your agenda is to find the truth. How is that not the same thing?

RYANNA RAINES: Can we get back to the earlier thread? What was Victoria's reaction when you told her about your dad and Heaven's Gate?

JORDAN DE CARLO: First, I want to make a point about #FreeJDC.

RYANNA RAINES: This catches me off guard.

JORDAN DE CARLO: I have no connection with those people, none. They formed completely independent of me. I don't personally know anyone affiliated with them. Whatever they do or say has nothing to do with me or my stake in this. I mean, I'm happy they support my innocence. But I'm not responsible for their statements or actions.

RYANNA RAINES: You know about their threats against me and my family?

JORDAN DE CARLO: They won't let me get online here, but I'm allowed to receive snail mail and printouts from my *fans*. They can't send cash or sexually explicit photos. But they can send regular photos. One of these fans seems exceptionally passionate about my case. I have no direct knowledge of anything she's been involved in regarding FreeJDC. But if I were you, she's someone I'd keep an eye out for.

RYANNA RAINES: Jordan pulls out a printed photo from his waistband, unfolds it, and slides it across the table.

JORDAN DE CARLO: Her face is hidden—she's no dummy. But you can see her red hair and blue hoodie. She's probably the type who wears hoodies like it's a uniform. She hasn't stated she was involved in those threats against you, know that. She did make a pilgrimage to the Vista Detention Facility. They denied her request to visit me. I believe she may still be lurking out there somewhere. I don't imagine she's physically dangerous. But these days you never know.

RYANNA RAINES: I appreciate the heads-up. You'll let me know if you hear anything threatening from her? Or anyone?

JORDAN DE CARLO: I got your back, Ryanna Raines.

RYANNA RAINES: Do I believe him?

JORDAN DE CARLO: Flashback to the day of Victoria's audition for Abbie Putnam. As you know, she nailed it. I was completely blown away. Though, to be honest, at that moment I did not feel a sexual attraction to Victoria. I mean, she's beautiful, incredibly smart, and has this charisma—when she flips that switch. Up to the day of her audition, I was so deeply involved in the play that I'd basically been celibate for months. I wasn't thinking about sex—it was all *Desire, Desire, Desire*. That's a pun, ha ha. Anyway, Victoria let it be known that she was physically attracted to me. So after the audition I ended up driving her back to my place and we had what was for me a peak sexual experience.

I know some people look at me and think I must've had affairs with all these gorgeous young women. A straight guy in theater arts, he has no problem getting laid. The truth is, while I've had my share of hookups, I'd never been in love. The act of sex was something physical, of the senses. Fun, pleasurable. But I'd never felt a deep connection to anyone I'd had sex with.

In the afternoon between Victoria's audition and our table read, and on the days and nights to come, we had a type of sex beyond anything I'd known. Not only was she a fantastic actress who transcended my vision for *Desire Under the Elms*, she was a magical lover. She knew exactly where to touch me, how to move, what to say. She took charge. For the next forty-five days leading up to opening night, we had this wildly passionate sexual relationship at the same time we were having this wildly passionate creative collaboration. It was like being in an altered state.

She was as creative in the bedroom as she was on the stage. Creative work mixed with epic lovemaking produces some powerful brain chemicals. Oxytocin on steroids. I believe the erotic component enhanced my art and hers. Before, I'd thought too much sex would deplete me, leave me empty. But with her it was the opposite. I was never more confident in my choices. I'd never felt so creatively empowered.

RYANNA RAINES: Love is empowering. So you felt real love for Victoria?

JORDAN DE CARLO: Actually I bypassed real love and went straight to worship. With the totality of my being. Does that sound too dramatic? That's how I was experiencing it.

RYANNA RAINES: Was there a letdown after the last performance and you no longer had that shared pursuit?

JORDAN DE CARLO: Big-time. But that didn't last long. We found a new pursuit.

RYANNA RAINES: You mean the play you started writing, *With a Kiss We Die*?

JORDAN DE CARLO: I'd say we took our artistic collaboration in a more real-world direction.

JESS MONAY: And there's the guard knocking at the door! Just as Jordan sounded like he was ready to drop a bombshell! How was he as he left the room?

RYANNA RAINES: Polite. He smiled and said, "See you in forty-eight hours."

JESS MONAY: So much to unpack here.

RYANNA RAINES: And let's save that unpacking for the start of the next episode.

S6:E37

RYANNA RAINES: Jordan De Carlo dropped two bombshells in my first jailhouse interview with him. He stated that his father, Anthony, stole $300,000 in cash from the Heaven's Gate doomsday cult and used the money to fund his career as a venture capitalist. In addition, Jordan painted a picture of Victoria Berne as an experienced and "magical" lover who led him into a highly charged sexual affair during their run-up to opening night of *Desire Under the Elms* for the UCSB Theater Department.

JESS MONAY: Nothing wrong with a woman taking the lead and being the initiator in the giving or receiving of sexual pleasure.

RYANNA RAINES: Absolutely nothing wrong. The bigger question is, why was Jordan sharing this with me? Is he setting up some point of connection between the information about his father and Victoria's sexual sway over him?

JESS MONAY: What he said at the end to you was ominous.

JORDAN DE CARLO: *We found a new pursuit...*

RYANNA RAINES: It *was* ominous, as was his comment about their collaboration taking "a more real-world direction." He's someone who fine-tunes his words for his audience.

JESS MONAY: Coming up, not only do you have your second jailhouse interview with Victoria, we were able to get you on the phone with Phil Berne, Victoria's father.

RYANNA RAINES: I'm Ryanna Raines. And welcome to *The Raines Report*, an audio crime-investigation series produced in association with Amplify. We're in the last phase of our investigation into the De Carlo murders and we're calling this episode "All In."

Hello, is this Phil?

PHIL BERNE: Hi, Ryanna. Nice to talk to you again.

RYANNA RAINES: Thanks for taking my call. So, I've been conducting interviews with Victoria while she's in jail. She talked to me about her family history, and I wanted to see if you'd respond to something she told me. Our policy is to give people a chance to confirm or deny or explain statements made about them by other sources.

PHIL BERNE: Okay. Go on.

RYANNA RAINES: To start, have you been in contact with your daughter since you and I last spoke?

PHIL BERNE: I'm sorry to say she still hasn't replied to my letters.

RYANNA RAINES: Do you have any thoughts about why she's not responding to you?

PHIL BERNE: Honestly, her mom has put a lot of stuff in her head. And I know Victoria blames me for what happened to her brother. She told me if I'd been more involved in his life, he wouldn't have gotten so wild.

RYANNA RAINES: You moved out and relocated to another state, without your kids, when they were twelve and ten. From then on, you saw and spoke to them infrequently. Why was that?

PHIL BERNE: I love my kids from my first marriage, but things got messy with their mother during the divorce. She made it difficult for me to stay in communication with them.

RYANNA RAINES: Victoria told me, on the record, that you had a sexual affair with a neighborhood girl, the family babysitter. This was during the summer Victoria turned twelve.

PHIL BERNE: Victoria said that? No, that's absolutely not true. I don't even know who she's talking about. What babysitter?

RYANNA RAINES: The girl was possibly underage at the time, so Victoria didn't use her real name. You're saying you did not have sexual relations with a high school girl who was babysitting your kids at the family home in Issaquah?

PHIL BERNE: No, no, no way. Why would she even say that? How would she even know?

RYANNA RAINES: Victoria said she witnessed you and the babysitter engaging in sex on the living room couch.

PHIL BERNE: In our house? No. I did start seeing a woman while I was married to Gail, but she was over twenty, long out of high school. And we were never together in the family home. Never.

RYANNA RAINES: Can you think of a reason why Victoria would invent that?

PHIL BERNE: To make her life sound more dramatic? Because she's still angry and wants to hurt me? I have no idea.

RYANNA RAINES: I'm not an advocate here. I'm repeating to you what was told to me.

PHIL BERNE: But you'll be putting my daughter's words into a podcast and a lot of people will believe her.

RYANNA RAINES: Your denial will be in there, too.

PHIL BERNE: You know how it is these days, no one believes the man. If Victoria says it, that's how it'll be remembered. I have a wife and young children and a job. This will be terrible for me.

RYANNA RAINES: You can say whatever you want in your defense. We always want to hear both sides.

PHIL BERNE: Victoria is still furious about me leaving, and she's lashing out. I'm not trying to justify what I did, but I can own it. I fell in love with someone else, and the only way I could have a relationship with her was to go live where she was living. I did try to communicate with my kids, but they refused to talk to me. I sent cards and letters and money. Neither of them ever responded. I couldn't even attend my son's funeral because Victoria said she wouldn't go if I came. Okay, I understand she's bitter, but he was my son! I loved him! I was devastated by his death! I cried for days, ask my wife—my second wife.

JESS MONAY: Two statements in complete contradiction. Welcome to investigative journalism!

RYANNA RAINES: After getting off the phone with the father, I drive to the Vista Detention Facility for my next visit with his daughter. Should I start the conversation with Phil's denial of her allegation about sex with the babysitter? Given the thirty-minute shot clock, I'll have to improvise and see where Victoria wants to go.

VICTORIA BERNE: I give you permission to start recording.

RYANNA RAINES: Not a criticism, but you look a little pale. Are you feeling okay?

VICTORIA BERNE: That's irrelevant right now. I want to start by going back to the day I got the role of Abbie Putnam.

RYANNA RAINES: Victoria sits up straight and her eyes communicate she's on a mission.

VICTORIA BERNE: Remember I told you about the audition? That night we did a cast read-through. We got done pretty late, and Jordan said he'd walk me home to the apartment where I was living with my roommate Gwen. The more he talked, the more I saw how unbeliev-ably smart and creative he was. I'd ask him a question and he'd come back with three answers, each from a different angle. He said it wasn't his job to tell me how to play the role. His job was to help me discover the character and then apply my instincts to make her come alive on-stage. Everything he said was so supportive and made so much sense. When we got to the gate of my apartment building, he said he had just one concern and wanted to state it up front. "I feel incredibly attracted to you. It's my responsibility to keep that from becoming a problem. But I think I should disclose it. If you find me distant at times, it's because I want to respect the space between us."

I said, "Your concern goes double, because I'm incredibly attracted to you, too."

He said, "Then we should decide together how we're going to handle it."

I said, "What's the downside of leaning in?"

He considered a moment and said, "I'm in a power position as the director, as a senior, as the decision-maker who chose you. There's an imbalance here, and I would never want you to think I'd use that to take advantage of you."

I thought that was an awesome thing for him to say. I thanked him and said, "It's my choice whether I act on the attraction I feel for you." And then I stepped up and kissed him. He was passive for a moment. Then he leaned in. I ended up going with him back to his place that night and spent almost every night there until we premiered the play six and a half weeks later.

I was not a virgin when I met Jordan. I'd slept with two guys, one when I was a senior in high school, one in my freshman year of college.

Both were one-night stands and more about them getting off than anything mutual. I was very inexperienced in lovemaking. Not only was Jordan four years older, he'd slept with dozens of women. So he initiated me into a world of experiences that were completely new to me. I was fully willing, excited to learn, open to pretty much anything because I trusted him. I didn't orgasm the first night we were together. But I did on the second night, and every night after that. He helped me learn how to be multiorgasmic. We'd be down on campus, rehearse till ten, eleven at night, then go back up to his place and make love for hours, often till dawn. It was madness. And total bliss. Twenty-hours a day doing our creative work, advancing the production, talking about our dreams, and fucking each other's brains out. Nothing in my life prepared me for that. Jordan overwhelmed me in so many ways.

RYANNA RAINES: Sometimes *overwhelmed* can have a negative connotation.

VICTORIA BERNE: At the time, nothing seemed negative. The character of Abbie is a lusty thirty-five-year-old with no shame for her sexual appetite. I did see how our relationship was filling me up with emotional and psychological content that I could use in my performance. I asked Jordan if he was doing it deliberately, to make me better in the role. He said no, that was not his intention. What he wanted was to introduce me to a man's loving with a mix of "ecstasy and intimacy." *Ecstasy* and *intimacy* were the right descriptors for what I was feeling.

I was all in. And opening night for *Desire Under the Elms* was the greatest climax to the most intense and amazing forty-five days of my life. At the curtain call, Jordan and I stood together to take a bow and got a standing ovation.

After the cast and crew party, we went back to Jordan's, and I could tell something was wrong. I knew his parents hadn't showed up, even though he got them tickets. We really hadn't talked much about his parents up to that point. I asked if he was upset that they were no-shows.

He just shrugged and mumbled something. Then we started kissing and headed to the bedroom. I was anticipating sexual fireworks. But Jordan couldn't get an erection. That hadn't happened before, and I was kind of shocked. Maybe all the work and sleepless nights had finally caught up with him. I thought it best to let it be. We just cuddled together and fell asleep in each other's arms.

So on opening night of *Desire Under the Elms*, the emotional high point of this wild six-week marathon, we came crashing down on what I would find out was Jordan's family dysfunction and this hostility he'd been holding inside. Sucked under by the sins of the father. See how that would resonate with me?

RYANNA RAINES: Let me interject here—I contacted your father, Phil. I asked him to comment on your account of him having sex with the babysitter in your family home.

VICTORIA BERNE: He denied it.

RYANNA RAINES: Strenuously. I'm curious, did you tell Jordan about the incident with your father?

VICTORIA BERNE: I did, yes. I didn't describe the babysitter thing. I just said when I was younger, I caught my dad cheating on my mom. And how that fucked me up in ways I still hadn't processed. Jordan was so supportive. He didn't try to fix it. He just listened and held me.

Anyway, after our final performance, Jordan started sinking into a deep depression. It was like nothing I'd experienced with him. I wondered if he might be bipolar. We had been talking about everything, but suddenly he could barely express himself. I thought it would be emotionally supportive for me to meet his parents. So I could have my own perspective on Anthony and Lauren. I was confident they'd like me. I can turn on the charm—I'd nail the role of a great girlfriend. When I brought it up to Jordan, he was not in favor. I said once his parents got to know me better, they'd realize what a positive influence I am. Or not. But it was better to face them head-on than to hide out. Finally I got him to agree to a meeting. He called them with me on speakerphone and we set a dinner in L.A., halfway between San Diego and Santa Barbara.

Wow, okay, so that night was a big turning point. I've never told anyone about what happened at the dinner—and afterward. Long exhale. Bear with me.

Jordan's dad made reservations at a five-star restaurant in Brentwood and booked a private room. Which I thought was a little over-the-top, but all right, maybe it's good they don't want to be disturbed by other diners and have us all to themselves. We were on time, and the De Carlos were already seated. Both had cocktail glasses in front of them. Anthony stood up and greeted me with a limp handshake. Lauren stayed seated and said something like, "You're prettier than your pictures on social media." A compliment, I guess. I sort of expected them to say something about the play and why they missed opening night, but no, they immediately started asking about my family and background. As you know, not my happiest subject. Being as neutral as I could, I said my mom and dad divorced when I was twelve, my brother was killed in a skateboarding accident when I was fourteen, and my mom currently lived alone and worked in the office at our local high school. I could see they were thinking, *Oh, broken family, father ran off, dead skateboarder brother, mom a public employee, all red flags for our son.* Meanwhile, they're throwing back one cocktail after another. When the waiter came in to take our dinner order, Jordan and I asked for the gluten-free menu. I saw his mom roll her eyes.

Then Lauren asks, "So, Victoria, why do you want to be an actress?" Jordan jumps in and says, "She *is* an actress, Mom." And his mom's like, "Well, I haven't seen her in any movies or TV shows." And Jordan shoots back, "You could've seen her as the lead in a Eugene O'Neill play, but you and Dad didn't think it was important enough to show up."

It got uglier from there.

RYANNA RAINES: Seems like they came looking for reasons you weren't good enough for their son.

VICTORIA BERNE: They never gave me a chance. I stayed pleasant, kept my smile on—being a trained actor can come in handy. At a certain point, Jordan lashed out at his parents for not supporting his love for theater, for always belittling and undermining him. He berated them for not letting him go to Juilliard. His parents weren't even putting up an argument. They were just sitting there like they knew best and Jordan wasn't capable of making independent choices about life. Even though he warned me, their arrogance was quite a shock. Then Jordan hit his breaking point. He jumped up, grabbed my hand, and we left his parents there halfway through the main course.

RYANNA RAINES: So the meet-the-parents dinner did not go well. What happened afterward?

VICTORIA BERNE: As we were driving back to Santa Barbara, Jordan got so upset he had to pull off the freeway. That's when he told me about his dad and Heaven's Gate. You know about that?

RYANNA RAINES: I nod.

VICTORIA BERNE: He told me how his dad had stolen their money and that Jordan found out and confronted him about it. And then he told me that his dad threatened to kill him if he ever exposed the secret. Jordan's problem was more than overly judgmental parents. He believed his dad was capable of hiring people to kill him and make it look like an accident. I could see real fear in his eyes. I felt scared for him. And for us.

I tried to console him, rubbing his shoulder, asking what I could do to make him feel better. I didn't know what else to do, so I started massaging him between the legs and moved my head down to his lap. But he lifted my head up and stared at me. His eyes changed from fearful into this cold resolve. He said in a tone of voice I hadn't heard before: "Victoria, you really want to make me feel better? Help me kill my parents."

JESS MONAY: When I first listened to that, I basically spit out my sip of water.

RYANNA RAINES: And that was when the guard came in and ended the visit—as I'm hanging on the edge of the cliff! Victoria was escorted out and I sat there trying to take in what I just heard. Then I played back that last bit of tape to be sure A, I didn't imagine it and B, that it got recorded.

VICTORIA BERNE: *He said in a tone of voice I hadn't heard before: "Victoria, you really want to make me feel better? Help me kill my parents."*

JESS MONAY: I'm struggling to find the words.

RYANNA RAINES: Here are my words—a confession's coming. We don't know the what or the how, but before Victoria and I sit down again, I need to have a serious talk with her defense attorney.

S6:E38

AJ NOVICK: In my mind I'm hearing "The truth shall set you free." Only in this case, the opposite may end up happening.

RYANNA RAINES: That's defense attorney AJ Novick, who represents Victoria Berne in an upcoming trial where she faces two counts of first-degree murder.

AJ, as a defense attorney, isn't it always better to know the truth than not?

AJ NOVICK: Most of the time, but at this moment I'm trying to get past "Be careful what you wish for." Whatever you do, please don't forget to use our encryption service to send the audio files. You're making your own transcriptions, I take it?

RYANNA RAINES: Yes, and we have an encrypted server that I send the files to and then delete them from my recorder. It would not be good if those files were hacked.

AJ NOVICK: Because the D.A. and the sheriff are going to hold you responsible for any leaks—before the embargo is lifted.

RYANNA RAINES: As if there isn't enough pressure on me to ask the right questions and get the answers recorded during those fleeting thirty minutes?

Have you spoken to Natalie?

AJ NOVICK: Not since I listened to the last episode—I mean *interview*. See, the podcastification of my profession has become unavoidable.

RYANNA RAINES: You should start your own audio series.

AJ NOVICK: Believe me, it's under discussion. I just don't see how we can compete against *The Raines Report*. In the meantime, Natalie and I agreed to check in after we each had two interviews to listen to. Which will happen after you send her the next Jordan recording.

JESS MONAY: I wonder what the defense attorneys will and won't be sharing with each other.

RYANNA RAINES: It's tricky for them, because the question is suddenly shifting, from *They're both guilty* or *They're both innocent* to *One may be more guilty than the other*.

I'm Ryanna Raines. And welcome to *The Raines Report*, an audio crime-investigation series produced in association with Amplify. We're in the last phase of our investigation into the De Carlo murders and we're calling this episode "She's Not Joking."

JESS MONAY: Wait, what happened?

RYANNA RAINES: I got a speeding ticket! From a motorcycle cop!

JESS MONAY: Why were you speeding?

RYANNA RAINES: I wasn't doing it on purpose! I'm on my way to the jail, listening to Ainsley Coles's latest episode, and I look in the rearview to see flashing reds zoom up behind me. I look down and the speedometer says 88 miles per hour. It's the rental car's fault!

JESS MONAY: I'm so sorry. Where are you right now?

RYANNA RAINES: In the parking lot at the Vista Detention Facility. Trying to compose myself. Luckily, I left my place a half hour early. Thanks for letting me vent, I've got to go now.

JORDAN DE CARLO: You don't have to tell me what she told you, but how is she? How does she look, how does she sound?

RYANNA RAINES: I sit across the table from Jordan in the private visiting room, and he's looking as stringy and malnourished as he did forty-eight hours ago. He opens our visit wanting me to tell him my observations of Victoria.

She looks and sounds worn down, like the experience of six months in jail hasn't been great for her. And by the way, if she asked, I'd tell her the same thing about you.

JORDAN DE CARLO: But she hasn't asked? That's fine. Fine. So let's get back into it, shall we? Where did I leave off?

RYANNA RAINES: That after *Desire Under the Elms*, you and Victoria found "a new pursuit." But before continuing on that, I wanted to ask you about a dinner you went to with Victoria in L.A., where you first introduced her to your parents. Know what I'm referring to?

JORDAN DE CARLO: Victoria told you about that? I thought we were keeping it between us. But all right, let's start there. After they didn't show up to our opening night, Victoria became increasingly curious about Anthony and Lauren. I hadn't spoken about them, but I ended up getting a little emotional over them not being there for my big night—I don't know why, they'd never been interested in my theater work. Victoria kept asking about them and I said, "Let's have you meet them so you can make up your own mind." We set a dinner at the halfway point—L.A.

RYANNA RAINES: Quick question. By the time of the dinner, had you told Victoria about your dad stealing the money from Heaven's Gate?

JORDAN DE CARLO: No. I didn't want to poison the well before she could see him in action for herself. Of course he made a reservation at the most expensive restaurant in Brentwood and got us a private dining room.

Within five minutes, Dad is asking Victoria about her acting, which I knew he would. I'd warned her that my parents were skeptical of actresses. With all respect, Victoria replied there was a general misconception that most actors are narcissists. She said actors channel their self-absorption into the characters they're playing, while true narcissists channel their self-absorption back into themselves. Really smart point, I thought. But my dad leaned forward to challenge her—did she have any real-world experience with narcissists? Before she could answer, he turned to me and declared that as long as I stayed in the theater, he and Mom would not support me financially. Keep in mind, he'd finished four martinis at this point. If I chose a "real career," like in tech or banking, he said they'd buy me a new house. All shit I'd heard before—but Victoria hadn't. She's grabbing my hand under the table, squeezing it to show she can't believe what he's saying, but her face and voice stayed perfectly calm. The dinner plates were cleared, and I went to the restroom to take a breather. When I came back, the table had gone silent and Victoria looked distraught. I didn't want to ask her what happened in front of my parents, so I excused us, saying we had a long drive and had to hit the road. As we left, Dad had gone into a glassy-eyed funk and Mom had a fake smile plastered to her face. The whole thing was a disaster, like I knew it would be.

On the drive back I asked what happened while I was gone from the table. She shook her head and wouldn't talk about it. So we were just driving and streaming our music. And then Victoria started getting, well—amorous. She's kissing my neck and rubbing me as I'm driving and I think, *Okay, let's do this.* I pulled off the freeway away from the lights. I lowered my seat back, she got on me, and it was intense. It wasn't just the sex, I felt closer to this person than to anyone in my life. The contrast between the joy I felt with her and how excruciating it had been at the dinner with my parents was profound. And, I mean, Victoria was absolutely on fire.

As soon as we take a breather, she bursts into tears. Sobbing uncontrollably. I'm like, "What's wrong? Talk to me. Tell me." Took a while before she could get any words out. Tears streaming down her face, she says, "They'll never let us be together." And I say, "We *are* together. Nothing can break us apart."

Finally she got herself calmed down and said, "While you were in the bathroom, your mom said to me: 'You are not what Jordan needs. This is only a fling for him. If you think you're going to stay with him, listen carefully. It'll be over our dead bodies.'"

I know how harsh my parents can be, but that surprised me. I said I was sorry. And then it just all came out of me, the story about my dad and Heaven's Gate, me finding out, and his threat against me. She was shocked—but not shocked. I shared that to show how awful he really was and how I needed to get away from that bad karma. I was never more disgusted by my parents than I was at that moment. And I never felt more in love with Victoria.

Then she said, "I think your mom was right. The only way we can be together—is over their dead bodies." She's looking in my eyes and I can see *she's not joking.*

She's proposing that we kill my parents.

Maybe in my lowest moments, or when I was really angry at them, I'd fantasized about that, but I never crossed the line into actually planning it. I would keep my distance from them, push the bitterness I was feeling out of my mind, focus on the positives. I didn't need their approval. I might be broken inside, but I could channel that into my work. I could turn my family dysfunction into creative energy—like Eugene O'Neill. Now here's this girl I love, who's an amazing person and creative partner, who I want to make a future with, saying we can't be together, *really* together, unless—Anthony and Lauren are dead.

I was quiet for the rest of the night and so was she. She knew I was thinking about it. It couldn't be a rash decision on my part. The next day my dad and mom texted me and said they wanted to talk. I called and they both got on the phone and I let Victoria listen on the speaker. My mom said, "Victoria is using you. She's going to hurt you. All she cares about is herself and her career." Then my dad said they wanted to review our financial arrangement, and the message was: cut that girl loose or we'll cut you off. I couldn't take any more, so I hung up on them.

With total confidence, Victoria said, "We can get away with it. We're smart, we're a great team. Together we made a perfect play. Now we'll make a perfect murder." That was the moment I knew we were going to do it.

We were going to kill my parents.

JESS MONAY: I need a stronger phrase here than *Oh my god*. How about *Holy effing crap*?

RYANNA RAINES: One other detail I want to add. After our time was up and I'm leaving the VDF building, I glimpsed a figure across the parking lot. Just for a moment, because the person turned and started quickly walking away. It was at a distance, but I'm pretty sure I saw a blue hoodie and a flash of red hair. Within five seconds she was out of sight.

JESS MONAY: The FreeJDC follower Jordan warned you about?

RYANNA RAINES: We know that photos of me entering and leaving the jail have surfaced online and can be traced back to #FreeJDC.

JESS MONAY: So they're staking out the Vista Detention Facility. Makes sense.

Getting back to the story Jordan told you, it seems, um, *diametrically opposed* to what Victoria told you.

RYANNA RAINES: She says the murder was Jordan's idea. Jordan says it was her idea.

NATALIE BLOOM: We have a problem, Ryanna.

RYANNA RAINES: That's Natalie Bloom, Jordan's attorney, who got me on the phone moments after she finished listening to my latest interview with her client.

NATALIE BLOOM: My client is making statements that can be incredibly damaging to him and refusing to take my counsel while he's doing it. This is out of control.

RYANNA RAINES: You're concerned about prosecutors subpoenaing the interviews? Because at this point only a few people know what's being said in that room: me, my producer, Jordan, and you.

NATALIE BLOOM: I'm concerned about it all, subpoenas, the interviews leaking to the media and landing online.

RYANNA RAINES: He wants to tell his story and wants it on the record. No one's twisting his arm.

NATALIE BLOOM: But he clearly isn't grasping how much he could be harming himself.

RYANNA RAINES: Write him a note. At our next visit I'll hand-deliver it and urge him to contact you.

NATALIE BLOOM: No, I am suspending your access to him, effective immediately. No more visits until he agrees to meet with me in person. I can't allow him to keep talking to you without advising him of the damage he could be doing. Ryanna, this is not personal against you. It's my job to defend Jordan, and it would be a dereliction of duty not to step in and provide counsel.

RYANNA RAINES: What if you counsel him and he still wants to talk to me?

From jail, Jordan made a call to Natalie, listened to what she had to say, and told her he did still want to keep talking to me. We set my next visit with him for Tuesday, after the Monday I'd be visiting Victoria.

It made the most sense for me to stay the weekend in Oceanside rather than fly back Friday night and then leave again on Sunday. I get up early on Saturday and take the eight-block walk from my Airbnb to the beach. I slip off my shoes, head down to the shoreline, and let the surf wash over my feet. The sun is warm on my skin and there's a cooling breeze. I start walking south and lose myself for a good half hour in the drumming of the surf and the crunch of wet sand underfoot. That's when an idea comes to me. When I get back to my room, I call Jess and pitch it to her. Then together we call Alec Machado, our *Raines Report* sound editor and a key member of our podcast team.

JESS MONAY: So instead of laying down the interviews separately in alternating episodes, the idea is to intercut between the two interviews to do our own compare and contrast.

ALEC MACHADO: So Ryanna asks a question, and we hear each of them answering, highlighting where their stories agree and disagree?

RYANNA RAINES: I don't even think we need me asking questions. Just let the two of them unspool their stories in a continuous "he said, she said" flow.

ALEC MACHADO: I'll be able to exercise muscles I don't get to use all the time. Cool.

RYANNA RAINES: What you're about to hear comes from two separate interviews, conducted on consecutive days. We tried to keep the context of the replies as balanced as possible as Jordan and Victoria each told me their versions of the events leading up to the night of the murders.

JORDAN DE CARLO: She wanted to talk through all the options. Poisoning. Drugging them and burning the house down. Drugging them and suffocating them. Drugging and drowning them in the swimming pool. Beating them to death. And I was trying to be my most rational self, like no, bludgeoning wouldn't be my first choice because the crowbar or baseball bat would be hard to keep hidden and not very efficient. I'm listening to myself say those words and thinking, *Is that really coming out of my mouth?*

VICTORIA BERNE: One of the first major choices was the weapon. Neither of us had experience with guns and we knew they were traceable. Jordan spent hours on the computer doing research, then deleting his browser history.

JORDAN DE CARLO: Ultimately, Victoria thought knives made the most sense. She'd actually been practicing handling knives and daggers in her Stage Combat class. She said she was using that time to "rehearse."

VICTORIA BERNE: We drove across the Nevada state line to a store that sold butterfly knives. It's like a pocketknife with a concealed blade, razor sharp and sturdy. There's a little latch that releases the blade. Jordan paid cash for two of them, and as soon as we got home, he started practicing.

JORDAN DE CARLO: She was reading true-crime books and listening to true-crime podcasts day and night. She said she wanted to see where other killers made their mistakes. She kept saying if we applied our joint brain power, they'd never be able to convict us.

VICTORIA BERNE: He said it was like writing a play together, the same process of plotting. We started with a premise, how to commit a murder and get away with it. And each scene needed to serve that theme and advance us toward the climax. He was so sure we could get away with it.

JORDAN DE CARLO: Victoria had never been to the house in Rancho Santa Fe. She said it was really important to prove she'd been to the house, inside and out, so when they found her DNA there, it could be explained.

VICTORIA BERNE: It was Jordan's idea to drive down to his parents' house for the weekend. I was worried about a repeat of the dinner disaster, but I understood we had to show that I'd been inside that house before. He called his mom and tried to work the plan through her. He told her I was really upset about the first meeting and wanted a second chance. We would be playing the innocent young couple just wanting to be accepted by his parents. It felt gross to me on so many levels. But we had to establish I'd been inside the house.

JORDAN DE CARLO: I practically had to beg my parents to let us come there. I was saying things like, "Don't worry, you're going to see a whole new side to Victoria."

VICTORIA BERNE: The whole way down, Jordan and I were rehearsing. Feeding each other lines, doing improv, practicing being *likable*. He said if we won them over, they might say something positive to a friend or family member. And that would make our alibi stronger.

JORDAN DE CARLO: I was in the swimming pool when Victoria came out of the house. She held her hand behind her back and said, "I had a little accident." Then she showed me her left hand. It was covered in blood. And she was smiling. She'd purposely cut her finger in the kitchen and went around dripping on the floors. I was shocked for a moment. Then I saw how smart that was.

VICTORIA BERNE: Jordan said, "You have to cut yourself and drip some blood around." I didn't want to, I'm squeamish. He offered to cut my finger for me. I said no, I'll do it. I stood in the kitchen and did some breath work. Then I cut a little too deep. My finger started bleeding like crazy. I grabbed a paper towel and went dripping blood all over the place. I was acting the role of a criminal mastermind conspiring with my fellow mastermind. The man I love. The man I would do anything for.

S6:E39

JORDAN DE CARLO: The weekend started with my dad on his best behavior. Mom too—at least she wasn't behaving badly. We slept in the downstairs maid's quarters because Victoria wanted to be as far away from my parents as possible.

VICTORIA BERNE: We're staying in the home where a week later we'll be coming back to kill the people hosting us—yeah, I was feeling massive anxiety. Jordan was acting really sweet and amorous, like it was a turn-on for him. We were in bed and he's whispering in my ear, "If we don't do this, I'll never be safe. And they'll never stop pressuring me to break up with you."

JORDAN DE CARLO: There was definitely something twisted about having sex in the same house where we were planning to kill my mom and dad. It was like two in the morning when suddenly Victoria freezes and says, "Did you hear that?"

VICTORIA BERNE: I heard a sound outside the door of our room. I asked Jordan if he'd check it out. He got up, put on his shorts, opened the door, and went out to look. Suddenly I hear him start shouting and his dad is shouting back.

RYANNA RAINES: I'm Ryanna Raines. And welcome to *The Raines Report*, an audio crime-investigation series produced in association with Amplify. We're in the last phase of our investigation into the De Carlo murders. We're calling this episode "I Don't Think I Can Do This."

JESS MONAY: And I'm Jess Monay, producer of *The Raines Report* and Ryanna's partner in all things crime reporting. We're attempting a seamless transition from the end of our last episode, where we were intercutting between interviews with the two defendants in a double homicide.

RYANNA RAINES: The victims, Anthony and Lauren De Carlo, were the parents of one of those defendants, Jordan De Carlo. The other defendant is Victoria Berne, Jordan's girlfriend. What you are hearing is them both describing a weekend trip they took to Rancho Santa Fe, where they stayed at the De Carlo home. This was one week before the murders.

JORDAN DE CARLO: I didn't hear anything and I'm like, "It's probably nothing," and she's like, "If you're not going to go check, I am." She gets up and puts on my T-shirt. Goes out the door—and a few seconds later I hear her screaming.

VICTORIA BERNE: I go out to the kitchen and find Jordan and his dad squaring off like they're about to get into a physical fight.

JORDAN DE CARLO: I rush out and see her confronting my dad. "What were you doing outside our door? Were you fucking listening to us? Were you?" He's denying it, saying he came down for a glass of water. I get her back into the bedroom to cool her off. This is not part of the plan. When I go back into the kitchen, my dad says, "I want the two of you gone before breakfast."

VICTORIA BERNE: I put myself between them and literally push Jordan back into our room while he's shouting at his dad, calling him a pervert, a creep, and his dad's yelling back that he's going to call the police. I shut Jordan inside and went back to calm Anthony down. I was apologizing and saying we would leave in the morning. At the same time, I'm horrified because I keep seeing myself coming back next weekend and sticking a knife in his chest.

JORDAN DE CARLO: Victoria decided our alibi would be the key, and she was right. We spent hours a day talking it through, making lists, scouting locations. We settled on the library because it has security cameras in some areas and not others. If we parked my SUV in a lot covered by a security camera and got out together, then didn't return until after the murders were committed, it would be proof that we hadn't left campus.

VICTORIA BERNE: We needed another vehicle to drive down and back. We talked about renting a car and giving false information, but that could backfire. We talked about borrowing a friend's car, and that also seemed too risky. We had to make sure my car could be ruled out, so I took it to a body shop and left it to get fixed over the weekend.

JORDAN DE CARLO: There was a guy named Rawlings that I lived with for a quarter during sophomore year. He wasn't in theater and dance. His declared major was electrical engineering—but what he really came to UCSB for was to party. He owned a beater car, an old Ford Focus with over 200,000 miles on it. He kept it in an open carport in Isla Vista and rarely drove it. Because he'd get so drunk and always lose his keys, he rigged a way to hot-wire it.

VICTORIA BERNE: Jordan had seen him do it several times. He said it would be easy.

JORDAN DE CARLO: I bought one of those big party bottles of Grey Goose, stuck it in a gift box, and set it on Rawlings's porch. I left an unsigned note thanking him for some vague favor and asking him to go share the bottle with his bros. I knew he did not have the willpower to wait. Sure enough, he took it right over to a buddy's apartment and got the fun started. The dude's a blackout drunk and wouldn't be driving anywhere that night.

VICTORIA BERNE: We drove Jordan's car to the west end of campus, parked in a lot with security cameras, and locked our phones inside. We left them on so any data pings would show they were in Santa Barbara the whole night.

JORDAN DE CARLO: We took the elevator up to the seventh-floor study room we'd reserved. We got some books off the shelves so it looked like we were there for a long session. We waited until the lobby was empty, then went down the back stairs because they didn't have operating security cameras. It was a Sunday night in summer, so there were very few people around. We walked the long way to Isla Vista, out to the beach and up one of the access stairways to Del Playa Drive.

VICTORIA BERNE: We got to this guy's apartment and made sure he wasn't home. Then we both put on overclothes we'd bought from a thrift shop and plastic gloves. We didn't have to break into the car because he never locked it, wasn't worth stealing. We got in and I lay down on the floor of the back seat. Jordan leaned under the dash to get it started.

But it wasn't working.

JORDAN DE CARLO: Had he changed the wiring? I was sweating bullets, trying different wire combinations, at the same time trying to think of a backup plan. Call an Uber? Drive my Wrangler but take off the license plates?

VICTORIA BERNE: Finally Jordan got the engine to turn on. It was pretty unpleasant on the floor behind the driver's seat, and I'm looking at being there for the next three or four hours. I thought of it as my cosmic punishment. Embrace this suffering, girl, you deserve it!

JORDAN DE CARLO: I thought our biggest risk would be security cameras along the way. I'd filled some gas cans and pulled over on a side street so we could fill up and avoid gas stations. I also unscrewed the license plates. It would mean an added risk of getting pulled over, but against getting caught on a security camera and the plates being traced to Isla Vista, the percentages favored going without them.

VICTORIA BERNE: Jordan wore a black beanie, long sleeves, and yellow-tinted glasses. The plan was to burn our overclothes when we got back to Santa Barbara. The schedule Jordan came up with had no margin for error. As soon as we get on the freeway, the engine starts sputtering.

JORDAN DE CARLO: I had to pull off at the first exit. Victoria was starting to freak. "You said this car would get us down and back!" I told her to chill and let me check it out. Then I remembered Rawlings saying the car wouldn't go over 60 or the engine quit. As long as I kept it under 60, we'd be okay. Which impacted our timing. If we got stopped or broke down along the way, we'd have to call it off. I took the slow lane and prayed—that the car *would* break down.

VICTORIA BERNE: While we were on the freeway I got to move up to the back seat, but I still had to lie down and not lift my head above the windows. I started getting motion sickness. It took every ounce of will-power not to vomit in the car. Actually it was a combination of motion sickness and dread. If I'm being real, I was hoping we wouldn't make it in time and have to bail on the plan.

JORDAN DE CARLO: We were over thirty minutes behind schedule. On the good side, there wasn't much traffic down to L.A. But at LAX we hit a dead stop. And tick tick tick goes the clock.

VICTORIA BERNE: Jordan kept talking over the plan. We'd arrive at his parents' acting humble, apologizing, asking to make a fresh start. We'd lead them into the kitchen and draw them over to the island. We'd all be standing facing each other, and I would start saying how much I love

their son and will always be there for him. When I had their full attention, Jordan would strike. He'd stab his dad, and that's my cue to pull
out my knife and stab his mom. I had to mentally dissociate from the
meaning of those words.

JORDAN DE CARLO: Victoria said they wouldn't expect it coming from
her. She's super strong for her size and really agile. When my parents
were facing me, she'd step around the island and stab my dad first, then
my mom. When both were on the floor, I'd take my knife and slit their
throats.

VICTORIA BERNE: The traffic broke up, but we were more than an hour
behind schedule.

JORDAN DE CARLO: It would be harder to get both my parents into the
kitchen if they'd already gone up to bed. They usually watched TV in
the great room, then went upstairs between nine and ten. We got off the
freeway at quarter after nine, right on the edge.

VICTORIA BERNE: The closer we got, the heavier the weight pressing
down on my chest.

JORDAN DE CARLO: I knew a place to park on the street below. It was
next to an open lot without security cameras. I pulled up, turned off
the lights, but kept the car running. And then I felt this icy coldness
go up my legs and my arms. My throat's like sandpaper, my hands are
shaking.

I said to Victoria, "I don't think I can do this."

VICTORIA BERNE: Jordan got out and opened the back door for me. I
looked out at him. And I just shook my head.

JORDAN DE CARLO: No matter how much I despised my parents, I could
not physically stab them or watch it happen. Victoria stared at me in
disbelief, then disappointment. And that turned into this stoic determi-
nation. She held out her hand. I gave her the knife.

VICTORIA BERNE: I told Jordan, "I thought I could do it, but I can't. I can't." He just stared at me. Then he nodded and said, "Don't get out of the car. Don't turn off the engine. If you see any cars coming, keep your head down."

JORDAN DE CARLO: I watched her cross the road and turn up my parents' driveway. Then she was gone.

VICTORIA BERNE: I wanted to stop him and call it off. But I couldn't get the words to come out. I saw him cross the road to his parents' street. He started up the hill and disappeared in the dark.

JESS MONAY: Well, there's one thing we can be sure of. They can't both be telling the truth.

RYANNA RAINES: It's also possible both are lying.

JESS MONAY: Detective Sanchez was pretty clear when he walked you through the crime scene. There was a single assailant.

RYANNA RAINES: A second person could have been present but not have taken part in the attack. We'll come back to that. So we're at the point in the interviews where the murders are being committed. Each of the defendants is saying the other one went up and committed the murders while they waited in the car parked below. Now we'll hear them talk about the aftermath of the murders. This is also where their accounts diverge, so we'll go back to hearing from one at a time.

VICTORIA BERNE: Worst half hour of my life. Felt like I was having muscle spasms all over my body. I couldn't catch my breath, my stomach kept twisting in knots. I wasn't up there, but my mind was exploding with images of Jordan hurting his parents. When I shut my eyes, these horribly violent animations were playing on a loop. Am I having a brain seizure? It was *unbearable*.

I was lying on the back seat in a fetal position when the driver door opened. He was in his underwear. He'd taken off his clothes and put them in a plastic trash bag. He'd rinsed off in the downstairs shower and was still wet. I didn't see any blood on him, but it was dark. I handed him the clothes we'd brought and he put them on. I said something lame like, "How'd it go?"

He said, "I don't want to talk about it. Please don't ask me. We're behind schedule. Let's focus on dumping this stuff and getting back to the car."

As tense as the ride down was, the ride back was double that. We had to take the gas cans to a station and fill them up, so that took more time. At one point a highway patrol car got behind us on the freeway—Jordan had taken off the license plates. He started to panic. Then some other car went racing past, and the patrol car took off after it. I peeked out the window and he yelled at me to keep my head down. He was so stressed. We both were.

We started singing songs to keep our minds busy. We went decade by decade, starting with the sixties all the way up to the present. My sixties song was "Help." Jordan's was "All You Need Is Love." It was so unreal.

We got back to Isla Vista, parked the car in the carport, cleaned it out best we could. Then we took a roundabout route back to campus. We made it to the parking lot and our timing was still okay. We got in Jordan's SUV and drove back to his place. We showered together and I washed every inch of his body—with a bar of cucumber-mint soap. Then we got in bed and held each other. I kept nodding off and waking up. Jordan was out for ten solid hours. I just lay there not wanting to wake him and thinking, *I'll never sleep through the night again.*

Next came the waiting game for the bodies to be discovered. We knew they had a housekeeper who came during the week, but we weren't sure what day she was working next. That kept us totally on edge, monitoring the news, constantly checking our phones. We had no idea it would take three days until someone found them. I started telling myself it hadn't happened. The whole thing had been a hallucination. The De Carlos were alive and well and life would just go on as normal.

That lasted all day Monday, all day Tuesday, and finally Wednesday morning Jordan got the call from police. Now begins a new phase, we're getting investigated! I had headaches and stomach cramps every day. My mom's calling and texting and I'm not getting back to her—what am I going to say?

Then came the De Carlos' funeral service. I took half a Valium on the way down and it strung me out. After my experimentation days, I'd sworn off drugs completely. So just that little bit of Valium was like getting smacked in the head with a brick. We got there late, everyone was already seated. The officiant was waiting for us to begin the service. We had seats reserved in the front row, so my back was to the room. When the officiant asks if anyone would like to speak about Anthony and Lauren, Jordan gets up and goes to the podium. I just froze. He'd told me he wasn't going to speak—so I had no idea what he was going to say. Had he lost it in the moment? A sudden attack of conscience? Was he going to expose us?

He started in with all the problems he had with his parents and I thought, *Oh shit, he's going to confess here and now and out me as his accomplice.* Suddenly I feel the room start to spin. I get up to go to the bathroom, but instead I pass out and crash on the floor right in front of the podium. I remember nothing until we were in the car headed back to Santa Barbara.

RYANNA RAINES: You fainted during Jordan's eulogy. Did he tell you later what he was intending to say?

VICTORIA BERNE: That he was starting by talking about the conflicts he had with them growing up, but fully intended to bring it around to how things had changed and he'd come to realize how much he loved them. And that more than anything he wanted to see his parents' killer brought to justice.

When we got back to Jordan's house, we shut ourselves off from the outside world. Closed all the window shades and kept them down. Had groceries delivered. Stopped picking up calls. When someone came to the front door, we didn't answer. Then Aunt Frances sent Jordan a text saying detectives at the sheriff's department wanted to talk to him. We drove back down together and I waited for him in the parking lot, right outside there. A few days later I got a message from Detective Sanchez saying they wanted to talk to me. So we drove down again, and this time Jordan waited for me while I was being questioned. A few days after that they asked us to come in together for a double interview. We could see they didn't have much evidence but had zeroed in on us because of the lack of other suspects. When two rich people get killed in a community of rich people, the police are highly motivated to solve the crime. We were like scene partners in a showcase, playing a grieving son and his supportive girlfriend. We thought we nailed it.

But the detectives kept dialing up the pressure, getting search warrants, questioning our families. I woke up every morning feeling like my head was going to explode. At a certain point we realized one or both of us could be arrested, even if they didn't have the evidence to convict. And that meant we'd be separated. Which was the thing I dreaded most. Jordan kept saying it was going to be okay, and I trusted him completely. But my mind was constantly doomscrolling all the ways we could get caught.

Then Jordan finds out he's getting an advance on his inheritance. He shows me a website for a resort in Mexico, this five-star hotel with oceanfront villas and private infinity pools. He figured the advance would get us twenty-six nights, with meals and gratuities. It was Jordan's idea not to tell anyone, to just go. At that point we were still only persons of interest. No one told us we couldn't go on vacation. So within twenty-four hours we booked one-way tickets, Ubered down to LAX, and flew to Los Cabos.

This next part is the last. Mexico and the final act of the homicidal soulmates.

"For never was a story of more woe,
Than this of Juliet and her Romeo."

RYANNA RAINES: I see Victoria's eyes get misty, and I'm reminded of a moment at the end of my interview with Gwen Phan—something I recorded but that never made it into an episode.

When I spoke to your roommate, Gwen, she walked me back to see your apartment in Isla Vista. While she was cleaning out your room, she found a gold neck chain with a heart charm. She thought it was a gift to you from Jordan, so she gave it to me and I sent it to your mom to hold for you.

For a moment Victoria seems not to know what I'm talking about. Then she nods.

VICTORIA BERNE: I'd honestly forgotten about that. That wasn't from Jordan. I got it from a girlfriend in high school. It's gold-plated, not worth much. Can't remember the last time I wore it. Just a little keepsake. Thanks for rescuing it.

RYANNA RAINES: Sure. I wonder why Gwen thought it was from Jordan?

VICTORIA BERNE: I'm not sure. Now that you mention it, Jordan never gave me any jewelry. Not that that means anything.

RYANNA RAINES: So what about the final act?

And then, as if on cue, comes that knock and the door opens.

VICTORIA BERNE: Time's up. It'll have to wait until next time.

RYANNA RAINES: If that leaves you hanging, dear listener, imagine how I felt.

S6:E40

RYANNA RAINES: *Folie à deux* is defined as shared psychotic disorder in leading medical and psychiatric journals. It's a relatively rare clinical syndrome, and its characteristic feature is the transmission of delusions from an inducer, or *primary*, to another person, or *secondary*.

JESS MONAY: So it's like a cult mentality, only instead of the leader's psychological obsessions affecting a group, they affect just one person. Crazy squared. Excuse me, *delusional* squared. Our research shows that folie à deux and parricide go together quite a bit.

RYANNA RAINES: For example, in the case of Pauline Parker and Juliet Hulme, which we mentioned in an earlier season. These two teen girls were convicted of planning and carrying out the murder of one of their mothers in New Zealand in 1954. Everything in their young lives came down to this magical, creative connection the girls shared. The real world was a stage over which they ruled as masters of the dramatic arts, perched high above the lower players, and that included Pauline's mother. When

Mrs. Parker attempted to separate the girls because she suspected their friendship was growing unhealthy, the solution was obvious. Remove the obstacle by killing her.

JESS MONAY: Sounds *eerily* familiar.

RYANNA RAINES: I'm Ryanna Raines. And welcome to *The Raines Report*, an audio crime-investigation series produced in association with Amplify. We're in the last phase of our investigation into the De Carlo murders and we're calling this episode "A Universe of Two."

DR. MARJORIE WEBBER: Folie à deux is a medically recognized psychiatric disorder in which two individuals exhibit simultaneous and identical delusions.

RYANNA RAINES: Dr. Marjorie Webber is a licensed and board-certified forensic psychologist who examined Jordan and Victoria at the Vista Detention Facility prior to my visits with them.

DR. MARJORIE WEBBER: The circumstances of Jordan and Victoria's involvement, the intensity of their creative collaboration and sexual coupling, their near-instant interdependence, then closing themselves off to the outside world, those are optimal conditions for folie à deux to develop.

RYANNA RAINES: One had to be the inducer, right? One initiated the delusional behavior and the other came under their spell?

DR. MARJORIE WEBBER: Not so fast. The behaviors here could also be evidence of narcissistic personality disorder. If one is manipulating the other toward a desired end—say, helping them commit a murder—and what's driving them is past trauma and not delusional thoughts, that isn't psychosis, only a covert effort to deceive and influence. I'll sketch you out a couple of scenarios.

Jordan De Carlo is a golden boy, in looks, talent, accomplishments. He is sought after by women and men and attracts a high degree of romantic attention from his classmates, not just in the theater department. He knows this gives him the power in relationships and he's learned how to use it for his benefit. Along comes shy, inexperienced Victoria who has dreams of becoming a successful actress. She auditions for the first big role in her college career and Jordan chooses her. After that, he chooses her to become his lover. This is a life changer for her, and she quickly develops a profound dependence on him. He validates her acting talent, her physical attractiveness, her sex appeal, all the things an introverted eighteen-year-old sophomore doubts in herself. He listens to her ideas, takes her seriously as a collaborator, and sexually transports her to places she's never been.

Now, Jordan has this problematic relationship with his parents. He despises them. He believes they are actively trying to thwart his career and ruin his life. Over the years, his anger toward them for constantly demeaning his dreams has only intensified. Victoria can relate to this anger because of the sexual misconduct of her own father, so it doesn't take much for Jordan to convince her that his parents are monsters. Because Victoria is an actress, his mom and dad look down on her and are strongly against the union. Jordan keeps hammering home to Victoria that they'll never stop trying to break them apart. The only way he and she can live in peace together is to kill off these horrible people. Her wild infatuation and codependency incite her to bypass any personal moral imperatives and follow him over the cliff. That's hypothesis one.

Hypothesis two has Jordan as a boy-man who harbors deep self-doubts. He's learned to hide them well, but suffers from persistent impostor syndrome. There's always a little voice whispering, *You're not good enough*. These insecurities have only been exacerbated by his parents' negativity toward his passion for the theater. He's been with several women, but never formed a close emotional bond. Now along comes this young acting dynamo, full of talent and promise, and he casts her as the lead in his play. Victoria, ambitious but with her own unresolved trauma, experiences Jordan's interest in her as therapeutic to her damaged self-image. She pulls all of his focus onto her under the guise of an actress needing her director's attention. She starts controlling other people's access to him. She enthralls him sexually. It's all going exactly how she wants—until she meets his parents and sees they're not at all happy about her or her relationship with their son. She obsesses over their disapproval and increasingly views them as a threat. To the point of developing delusions that Mr. and Mrs. De Carlo are actively trying to take Jordan away from her and do her harm. Her accusations against them offer Jordan a validation of his past trauma. Soon he's internalizing Victoria's paranoia that his parents are trying to destroy their bond and they begin mutually reinforcing each other's fears. How can they ever be free to realize their romantic and creative goals while his parents are in the picture? Victoria nudges Jordan to a decision point, and it doesn't take much to push him across the line.

RYANNA RAINES: Which hypothesis do you think is the more plausible?

DR. MARJORIE WEBBER: I didn't have enough time with them to form a well-grounded opinion.

RYANNA RAINES: Your best guess?

DR. MARJORIE WEBBER: Not for a podcast.

RYANNA RAINES: Fair enough.

JESS MONAY: Whether a personality disorder or psychosis, everything Jordan is saying indicates that Victoria was the primary and everything Victoria's saying indicates Jordan was the primary. The piece of the puzzle still missing is what happened in Mexico.

JORDAN DE CARLO: Then there was the reading of my parents' will. And that whole shock.

RYANNA RAINES: I am back in the jail's inner sanctum sitting across from Jordan.

It was a shock? Why?

JORDAN DE CARLO: Anthony and Lauren had written me out of it. Not completely. They left me a hundred thousand to quote *get my career started*. But everything else, their investments and the properties—hundreds of millions of dollars—would all be going to get them nice shiny plaques at universities and hospitals.

RYANNA RAINES: That must've hurt.

JORDAN DE CARLO: To be honest, I never expected to get money from them. I knew I was at the end of their financial support. Because I was pursuing a career they didn't approve of, I wasn't counting on anything more.

RYANNA RAINES: Did Victoria know that was all the money you were getting?

JORDAN DE CARLO: She did not. I didn't lie and say, "Oh, don't worry, I've got millions more coming." I figured that would be her assumption and I didn't want it to be an issue. This might be the last chance we'd have to be together. I was willing to spend the whole advance to have a great last fling on a beach in Mexico. It was never about running away. It was about going somewhere we could be alone and experiencing pure togetherness.

We turned that oceanfront villa into our private utopia. Phones locked in the room safe, no media of any kind. We created our romantic paradise. *A universe of two.* We kept telling each other that no matter what happened, we'd always be connected. Our love was a forever love.

RYANNA RAINES: Were you concerned arrest warrants might be issued back in San Diego?

JORDAN DE CARLO: We put ourselves into a mutual trance. We made each other live in an immediate, moment-to-moment reality. Every day it got a little easier.

RYANNA RAINES: The records show that you were booked for twenty-six nights, but you left the resort after five.

JORDAN DE CARLO: So we had all of our meals delivered by room service. A couple of times we went down to the beach and had to walk past the hotel's restaurants and swimming pool. There are all these older people on vacation, ordering the staff around, boozing it up, being loud. After our fifth night Victoria turns to me and says, "This isn't us. It's for rich people. It's a place your parents would've stayed. We don't want to be your parents, ever."

She was right. It was nice, but it wasn't us. We're artists, we thrive on authentic experience. We need to find the real culture here—not this luxury resort filled with one-percenters. We checked out the next morning and went to a hostel in Los Cabos that was, like, twenty bucks a night. We went to places tourists didn't go, small towns and deserted beaches and restaurants where we were the only non-Mexicans. We watched women hang laundry on clotheslines and men go out in small boats to catch fish to feed their families. It took us to a next level of intimacy. I thought I couldn't love Victoria more than I already did. But I was wrong.

RYANNA RAINES: You've been listening to our podcast since being arrested?

JORDAN DE CARLO: Haven't missed an episode.

RYANNA RAINES: Then you know we found the gift-shop receipt for two journals—purchased forty-eight hours before you flew back to San Diego.

JORDAN DE CARLO: Is it time to talk about the journals? Okay.

Well, in figuring out how much money I'd have left when we got back from Mexico, I noticed the resort had charged me for an extra night. So I wanted to go back there and straighten it out. While I went to the front desk, Victoria went into the gift shop. The desk manager admitted their mistake and removed the charge. I went to meet Victoria outside the entrance. She had a bag from the gift shop and pulled out two journals. We needed a plan for when we got back to the States. A narrative that would speak to our love for each other and make the case for our innocence. It was her idea to backdate the entries. Which I thought was brilliant.

RYANNA RAINES: How did you decide on the dates and all the details?

JORDAN DE CARLO: We tried to capture our real experiences. Like when we went to the church in that small town and got "married." That really happened. We didn't need to invent much. We sat on the beach together and went back and forth to stay in sync and make sure it all flowed together.

RYANNA RAINES: And when did you decide to call *The Raines Report* tip line?

JORDAN DE CARLO: That same day we got the journals. Victoria had listened to you while we were in the planning phase. I told you she listened to a lot of true crime and the stories of other murderers and the mistakes that got them caught.

RYANNA RAINES: So why *The Raines Report*? Why me?

JORDAN DE CARLO: You really listen to people. And you love a good crusade against injustice. We thought our story of star-crossed lovers being wrongfully hounded by police and threatened with being ripped apart would appeal to you.

RYANNA RAINES: And I fell for it.

JORDAN DE CARLO: You weren't the only one.

RYANNA RAINES: Well, no, but it was through me and *The Raines Report* platform that your "innocent lovers" story went out into the public space. I encouraged you to read your journals aloud. Jess and I even read entries on the podcast while the court had a gag order on you.

JORDAN DE CARLO: Some details may have been embellished, but the emotions were a hundred percent real. It was the truth of what I was feeling, what *we* were feeling.

RYANNA RAINES: But you admit you were using me as your megaphone to get #TheRealRomeo&Juliet trending and our listeners to embrace you.

JORDAN DE CARLO: People like your voice and your vibe. You're a wife and mom who lives in Pittsburgh, so you're credible. We knew you wouldn't just roll over. But we believed you'd give us a fair hearing. And you did.

RYANNA RAINES: You targeted me to help you spread lies about your innocence. I'm letting that sink in.

JORDAN DE CARLO: Nothing we did was against you. We like you. I wouldn't have brought you here to tell you the real story if I didn't think you were the best one to put it out into the world.

RYANNA RAINES: So now you're using me to get the most favorable plea deal?

JORDAN DE CARLO: I want the true story out there. I want people to know what really happened. I did not kill my mother and father by my own hand. But I bear responsibility. I could have pulled Victoria back before she walked up that driveway. I was weak. And then I helped her cover it up. All for one reason. Because I was so in love with her. Because I *am* so in love with her.

RYANNA RAINES: If you lied to me before, why should I believe you now?

As a writer of psychological thrillers might say, *The question hung in the air between us.*

JESS MONAY: Did Jordan have an answer for that?

RYANNA RAINES: He said if he was still lying to me, he'd be saying he was innocent. He was now coming clean by confessing to the role he played in his parents' murders. I asked why he was choosing this moment to make his confession.

JORDAN DE CARLO: I've spent six months obsessing over this every minute of every day. What I know is, I deserve to pay a price for my actions.

And I'm ready for that. But people should also know the reality of how it all went down.

RYANNA RAINES: I wanted to ask what price he deserves to pay, but the guard came in and our interview was over.

After leaving the jail, I drove to the airport and took a Thursday-night flight back home. I got back too late to see our kids, but my husband and I had some quality time. Friday morning I made the kids breakfast, drove them to school, and headed to our downtown studio.

As I walk through the door, I notice a text come in from Kurt Nall.

JESS MONAY: The BFA student who played the third major character in *Desire Under the Elms*.

RYANNA RAINES: The one who wouldn't talk to us about that incident with Victoria in Stage Combat class. Well, out of nowhere he's asking me to give him a call. No reason stated.

JESS MONAY: Because we need another twist in this story.

RYANNA RAINES: Hi, is this Kurt Nall? It's Ryanna Raines. Thanks for getting in touch.

Kurt does not consent to being recorded on this call. He first wants to send me "a short video." After I've viewed it, he will agree to speak on the record. He asks how best to send it and I shoot him a link to our encrypted site for audio and video files. The video presumably comes from his phone. It's a ninety-two-second clip, time-stamped in early April of the prior year. This was during the period that Jordan, Victoria, Thad, and Kurt were in rehearsals for *Desire Under the Elms*. I turn my laptop around so Jess and I can view it together. What follows is a detailed description of what we see:

This was recorded inside room 1507 at the UCSB theater and dance complex—where most of the rehearsals for *Desire* had been taking place in the evenings. During the day this studio space is used for other classes. A camera phone is recording video from a fixed position, apparently propped up on a chair or table. Three people are in the frame, one with his back to the camera. This is the instructor who teaches Stage Combat, an elective course for BFA students. It's a popular class for theater majors, with a high enrollment during most quarters.

The two other people we can see are Kurt Nall, a tall, Nordic-looking twenty-year-old junior, and Victoria Berne, wearing a black mock turtleneck and black tights, hair in a ponytail. Each is gripping a stage dagger—one of the props I'd seen when I visited the department last fall. Kurt and Victoria face each other as they practice the choreography of a fight. The teacher can be heard giving instruction. "Three-quarters speed. Right-to-left slash. Downward thrust. Block the attack." The two students follow his verbal cues. This goes on for the first 56 seconds of the video. Then Kurt makes a sudden advance and he and Victoria briefly go off the right side of the frame. A moment later Victoria can be heard crying out as though she's been struck. Then Kurt bursts back into the frame, backpedaling as Victoria goes on the attack, thrusting her dagger at him in what looks like a manic frenzy. Kurt dodges and blocks her blade as Victoria continues to violently stab and slash at him, screaming in fury, out of control. The instructor rushes up behind and wraps her in a bear hug. He disarms her and holds her until she goes still. Kurt stands at the left edge of the frame staring at Victoria. He seems physically unharmed but emotionally shaken. The video ends there.

JESS MONAY: Did we just see what I think we saw?

RYANNA RAINES: We watch it a second time. And a third. And a fourth.

JESS MONAY: I keep hearing Detective Sanchez's graphic description.

DETECTIVE SANCHEZ: Imagine you had a side of beef hanging in front of you and you took a steak knife and with all your strength slashed and stabbed it sixty-five times in under three minutes. That requires a tremendous amount of physical energy.

RYANNA RAINES: No doubt, Victoria is showing a lot of physical energy in this video.

JESS MONAY: As OMG moments go on *The Raines Report*, this has to be top three.

RYANNA RAINES: I think we could rightly classify it as a bombshell.

S6:E41

UPLOADED TUESDAY, SEPTEMBER 5

RYANNA RAINES: I am not a criminal lawyer. Yet my job constantly brings me into contact with defense attorneys, public defenders, and prosecutors. I have not been a defendant or plaintiff in any kind of courtroom trial, never even been picked to sit on a jury. Yet my work frequently takes me into courtroom trials. I know my way around criminal law pretty well. Yet I would not presume to know the value of potential evidence without consulting a real live defense attorney. I may have a well-informed opinion, but I don't have the hands-on experience to understand how the machinery works, especially the behind-the-scenes wrangling. I know my limitations, and I'm cool with them. Then comes human error, unintended consequences, and a certain phrase I learned the meaning of firsthand.

I'm Ryanna Raines. And welcome to *The Raines Report*, an audio crime-investigation series produced in association with Amplify. We're in the last phase of our investigation into the De Carlo murders and we're calling this episode "Involuntarily Viral."

JESS MONAY: You ready to call him back?

RYANNA RAINES: Taking a breath, settling myself.

Kurt, hi, it's Ryanna Raines. Okay, I watched the video. Yes, well, before I say anything, I'm curious about its history and why you sent it to me. First of all, who else has seen it? Oh, and do I have your permission to record this call?

KURT NALL: Yes, you have my permission. No one else has seen this. You're the first. I knew it would be—controversial.

RYANNA RAINES: Who else knows you recorded it?

KURT NALL: Just one other person. At first I didn't know I recorded it. I usually set my phone on a stand, and I record a lot of the stuff I do in classes, so I can play it back and study myself. As an actor, that's helpful for process refinement. That day in Stage Combat, I'd been recording the instructor talking about the historical uses of weapons on the stage that I found interesting and wanted to listen to again. My phone was set up on a table, and when I went to turn it off, I must not have tapped it firmly enough. It was left on by accident. And then I kind of forgot about it. Until the detectives came up here to talk to those of us who'd worked with Jordan and Victoria.

RYANNA RAINES: You didn't share the video with the detectives?

KURT NALL: No, because when they asked me about Victoria, I told them verbally what happened. They also got Brendan's statement about it— the instructor. At that point no one even knew Jordan or Victoria were suspects. To me, Victoria had a meltdown one day. Actors in the BFA program are under a lot of pressure. People snap. They blow off steam and get it out of their systems. That's how I saw the stage combat incident.

RYANNA RAINES: Why did you keep the video on your phone?

KURT NALL: Believe me, I've thought about deleting it every single day. Then, when Jordan and Victoria got arrested, I thought, *Shit, if I delete* *it now, it could look like I'm destroying evidence.* Even if I get it off my phone, it'll still be in the cloud, someone could dig it up and tie it to me.

RYANNA RAINES Why didn't you hand it over to the police after her arrest?

KURT NALL: I didn't want to see it used against her. Like I said, I was directly involved and it wasn't like she was trying to murder me. But I've been stressing over it for months. I confided in Thad Baylor, and he said I should send it to you and that you would know what to do with it.

RYANNA RAINES: Having just watched it minutes ago, I have to be honest—I don't know what I'm going to do with it. How would you feel if it got publicly released?

KURT NALL: Then the world's going to think I was withholding the video to help Victoria. Right?

RYANNA RAINES: Not necessarily. It sounds like you're being truthful. You've been conflicted, not sure what to do with it—and it's not a smoking gun. Correlation doesn't imply causation. By itself it doesn't prove anything.

KURT NALL: It probably won't be admissible in court—I read up on that. But if it got out in social media, the true-crime junkies would lose their minds. They'd turn me into a co-conspirator, a villain. I'd get tainted by association and there goes my shot at an acting career.

RYANNA RAINES: You could get the defense attorneys to vouch for you and put out statements saying you're not to blame. You're really an innocent bystander here. What do you want to see happen with the video?

KURT NALL: Not going to lie, I wish I'd deleted it right after that class. Should it go to the defense attorneys, the prosecutor, the detectives, all three? I'm not the right person to make that call. I just think if this got online, it would negatively impact my life.

RYANNA RAINES: So you're handing off the hot potato and now I've got it.

KURT NALL: Better you than me. You'll do the right thing. Everyone trusts you.

JESS MONAY: You heard him. Everyone trusts Ryanna Raines. So what're you going to do?

RYANNA RAINES: I have to get it to Victoria's defense counsel. He'll advise us on what comes next. So, I'm writing a quick email to AJ.
  Urgent: Please review and let's speak.
  Send.

JESS MONAY: You sent it to his encrypted address, right?

RYANNA RAINES: Yes. Uh. No! I cannot believe it. Ryanna, what did you do!

JESS MONAY: Human error is the number one cause of cybersecurity breaches.

RYANNA RAINES: Is that supposed to make me feel better?

JESS MONAY: AJ has to delete the file immediately.

RYANNA RAINES: I'll text him:
  Sent file by mistake to your regular email. Please delete immediately.

JESS MONAY: You also created a file on your end as the sender. Delete that first.

RYANNA RAINES: My fingers are shaking.

JESS MONAY: Here, let me do it. I'm deleting it from your email. Then emptying your trash. Then resending to his encrypted account and ours.

RYANNA RAINES: I can't believe I did that. There's just so much going on inside my head. Okay, what now?

JESS MONAY: Now we treat ourselves to a nice brunch. And a pitcher of margaritas. I'm kidding. About the margaritas.

RYANNA RAINES: Sitting down in a booth and looking at the menu of Mack's Café, I find myself wanting comfort food—eggs with a breakfast meat. The menu lists several choices, including bacon, sausage, ham steak, ground beef, pork chops, chicken-fried steak, and Angus top sirloin. Yes, Virginia, there is a Pittsburgh. What do I end up ordering? The California omelet with avocado, jack cheese, and fresh salsa. I won't say what Jess orders.

JESS MONAY: Three eggs scrambled with chicken-fried steak, mm-mm!

RYANNA RAINES: Then just before the food arrives, both of our phones blow up. Boom.

JESS MONAY: Un-freaking-real.

RYANNA RAINES: Like invisible bandits in some techno dystopia where digital data is as secure as a Wells Fargo stagecoach in the Wild West, #FreeJDC actors had within minutes swooped in and stolen the stage combat video. It is now spreading across the web like wildfire. Those ninety-two seconds are going *involuntarily viral*.

First thing I do is *not* answer the call that comes shooting in from AJ Novick. Instead, I reach out to Kurt Nall and apologize with profuse and utter humility. I feel awful. He entrusted his explosive phone video to me as a confidential matter, and in less than an hour he could watch himself on every social media platform under a dagger attack by a first-degree-murder defendant.

"I'm so sorry, it's totally my fault. I'll get the attorneys, the prosecutor, the police, all the above to put out statements that you had no involvement in the crime or a cover-up." Kurt Nall is too stunned to say much. I tell him I will do everything I can to make this right. I almost throw in a "trust me," but that seems gratuitous at this point.

A tasty-looking California omelet goes uneaten that day. In an anxious funk, we pay the bill and head back to the studio. I wrap myself in a mental flak jacket and return AJ's call. I can tell he's tense but tries to show understanding.

AJ NOVICK: I won't tell you my ugliest email fails. So. We've already heard from Mark Petrosian, the San Diego D.A. He's predictably furious. He's drafting a motion to go back to the judge and reimpose the gag order, not only on the defendants, but on the attorneys and on you.

RYANNA RAINES: Gag a journalist? Does he know what's been happening in the interviews?

AJ NOVICK: Not yet. Rather than dribble it out, Natalie and I agreed to wait until we had something closer to a complete statement from each before we take a next step. You're visiting Victoria Monday and Jordan on Tuesday?

RYANNA RAINES: Yes. By 4:00 P.M. Tuesday I should have it all: the planning, the crime, and the cover-up.

AJ NOVICK: We know what this movie looks like—the two lovers turning on each other. You're going to crush all those romantics on social media, Ryanna. This is not how they want #TheRealRomeo&Juliet to end.

RYANNA RAINES: The ending has yet to be written. With these two, anything is possible.

JESS MONAY: We should change your flight to an earlier departure.

RYANNA RAINES: I had booked a red-eye out Sunday night so I could spend the maximum amount of time with my family before flying back to California. Now that's been changed to a 1:00 P.M. departure with one stop in Phoenix that will get me into San Diego by 8:00 P.M. local time.

I pack a bigger bag than I need, enough for two weeks without having to do laundry. I gather my recording equipment, and my husband drives me to the airport with our kids in the back seat.

My son cries as I hug him goodbye at the curb outside the terminal. My daughter tries to be stoic. "Your stories help people, Mom," she says. I nearly burst out crying then and there.

Apart from the kids, my husband says in my ear, "I'm never thrilled about you going into rooms with cold-blooded killers. But I trust your judgment. And that gets me through the day."

Yeah, but do I trust my judgment as much as he does? Partings like this make me wonder. I tell him I love him, give the kids a last kiss, then turn and wheel my bag into the terminal. Heading to the security check, I can't hold back my tears. It's never easy leaving my family when I go off on these journeys to find the holy grail of truth. But whether I find it or not, I thank God I have them to come home to.

At the departure gate, I scan a mix of online comments and opinion pieces regarding the hacked stage combat video. While much of it trends toward the video proving Victoria's guilt, I'm also seeing new areas of support for her. On Instagram, pages are now popping up like Victoria Innocent, Victoria Framed, Our Angel Victoria B. That last one has eighty posts and six thousand followers. They've captured frames from the stage combat video and photoshopped angel wings on her body.

When my plane lands in Phoenix, I come off the jetway in a kind of trance, trying to blink myself back to reality. When I check the flight information screen for the gate of my connecting flight to San Diego, I notice the word *canceled* next to the flight number. I look at the clock. Just after 2:30 local time. It seems I'll have more than enough time to catch another flight, land in San Diego, rent a car, and get to the Airbnb before bedtime.

But things don't exactly go smoothly.

JESS MONAY: Where are you?

RYANNA RAINES: Still in Phoenix. All flights are delayed due to lightning storms in the area.

JESS MONAY: I'm seeing the last flight out to San Diego departs at 6:45 tonight?

RYANNA RAINES: It was full. I'm on standby but way down the list. I'm thinking of renting a car here and driving to San Diego. I can make it door to door in five hours. Coming back, I'll fly out of San Diego and drop the car there.

JESS MONAY: That's a long way to drive at night by yourself. Are you sure?

RYANNA RAINES: I think better when I'm driving. It'll be a good way to prepare myself mentally for the week ahead.

JESS MONAY: Be careful. You don't want another speeding ticket. They might take away your driving privileges in California.

RYANNA RAINES: Wouldn't that be tragic.

I rent a little compact with Bluetooth and head west through a desert landscape. The sun is in front of me, I'll be driving straight into it until it sets. As I get onto the I-8, which will take me all the way to the coast in 287 miles, I start listening to a podcast about the De Carlo/Berne case. All this time I've held off from listening to other people's podcasts about the murders because I didn't want to be influenced either way. This one, which I won't name, is a presentation-style true-crime show. Its coverage relies mostly on interviews, articles, and reporting conducted by others. It's a popular tried-and-true format, with the two hosts going back and forth telling a narrative of the case. This podcast has the cohosts each taking Victoria to task, casting her as the true primary. I cringe at some of the graphic language they use to accuse her of a potpourri of sins. Our series is still months from coming out. How different will our portrayal of Victoria be? I tell myself there's a long way to go and to just keep putting one foot in front of the other. Thanks again, Ainsley.

I arrive at my Airbnb just before eleven. It takes me a couple of hours to fall asleep. In my dreams, I once again stand at the bottom of the De Carlo driveway. I can see a figure walking down the hill toward me. This person is in shadows, I can't identify who it is. Suddenly the figure comes under the glow of a streetlight. It's Victoria. Covered head to toe in blood. That's when I wake up.

I pull into the parking lot at the Vista Detention Facility an hour before my scheduled visit and stride across the asphalt to the visitor processing center. The deputy recognizes me—but somehow that doesn't shorten my processing time. Once again, I am escorted to the private meeting room and sit in the same chair, at the same table, facing the same door. I take out my recorder, make sure it's cued up, and set it at the midpoint between our two chairs. I have to believe that Victoria will have heard about, if not seen, the viral stage combat video. I am prepared to launch into an apology right off the bat. "So sorry, it was an accident, I take full responsibility."

The door opens and a corrections officer comes in—alone. She tells me that Victoria isn't feeling well and has to cancel our visit. "She asked me to tell you she's sorry," says the officer.

My face drops in disappointment. I did not expect this. Our next scheduled visit might well be canceled by forces beyond our control. I try not to stutter on the next words out of my mouth: "Did she say anything about our appointment for Wednesday?"

"Not to me."

I am more surprised than I should be. Somehow I had not factored visit cancellations into my linear thinking about these interviews. My subject's final act will have to be postponed. But by then will it be too late? As I head back down the concrete corridor and through the metal doors, I have a strange feeling—a premonition? I might never speak to Victoria Berne again.

As I exit the jail and head to my car, I catch sight of the girl in the blue hoodie. She is standing near a row of trees at the north end of the parking lot, holding up her phone and aiming it at me. I pivot away from my car and start toward her. She notices me coming, immediately turns and heads away.

I call out, "Excuse me, may I talk to you?" Now hoodie girl moves faster—she definitely does not want to talk to me. I pick up my pace and try to gain on her. She hops over a chest-high fence into an adjacent parking lot. I see her run over and get into a white Toyota Camry. I climb over the fence after her and click a photo of her license plate. She turns on the engine and starts toward the street exit. And then I do something really dumb. I rush forward and stand in the path between her car and the exit. She could run me down—but she brakes to a stop.

We're staring into each other's eyes. I can see she's a teenager, probably no older than seventeen. She looks like a child to me. I can't help thinking of my own daughter.

"I know who you are," I say.

"Get out of my way," she says.

"You sent that threatening message to me and my family."

"Good luck proving it."

"Why would you do that? I have a young daughter and son. Why would you want to scare them like that? Just to prove your support for Jordan?"

The redhead in the blue hoodie gives no reply but keeps her eyes on mine. "I could call the police," I say, "but I'm not. Because I am going to trust that someday you'll understand what an awful thing it is to terrorize people. Then maybe you'll lead by example. Still advocating passionately. But not weaponizing that passion to hurt the people you disagree with."

I let my eyes linger on hers. Then I step aside. The Toyota Camry zooms past me and goes screeching out of the parking lot.

S6:E42

RYANNA RAINES: After Victoria canceled our jail visit, I got worried that Jordan would do the same. The prosecution filed a motion with the court that Monday to impose a new gag order, this one including defendants, lawyers, and *The Raines Report*. They asked the judge to expedite his ruling based on the viral video showing one of the defendants going into a stabbing frenzy during a stage combat class. This had been seen by millions of people already and would undoubtedly prejudice the minds of potential jurors ahead of her murder trial.

And it's all Ryanna's fault!

JESS MONAY: You just have to go there and hope he shows up.

RYANNA RAINES: He's already spun out the planning, the murder, and the cover-up. What's left?

JESS MONAY: This is your chance to fill holes, press him on details. He's been the one directing the interviews so far. Now is the time for you to drill down on the things you may not get another chance to ask.

RYANNA RAINES: Like, "If Victoria killed your parents in that horrific way, weren't you concerned about what else she might be capable of?"

JESS MONAY: "Before you went to sleep at night, did you check under her pillow for a knife?"

RYANNA RAINES: Of course, a reasonable amount of paranoia would apply to Victoria, too. I hope I get to ask her the same question.

JESS MONAY: Ask Jordan about the incident in Stage Combat class. Did Victoria tell him about it? Did Kurt Nall? They were in the middle of rehearsals for *Desire Under the Elms* and those were two of his three leads. When did Jordan find out about it and did he do anything?

JORDAN DE CARLO: I had not seen it before. The stage combat video. But now it's out there and it's hurting Victoria. Because everyone can visualize her doing that to my parents.

RYANNA RAINES: I'm Ryanna Raines. And welcome to *The Raines Report*, an audio crime-investigation series produced in association with Amplify. We're in the last phase of our investigation into the De Carlo murders and we're calling this episode "The Truest Truth."

On Monday evening, after having one of our subjects, Victoria Berne, cancel my scheduled jail visit, I spoke to her attorney, AJ Novick.

AJ NOVICK: She won't talk to me, either. She's gone dark. I'm not sure what to make of that, other than her feeling the video is a very bad look for her.

RYANNA RAINES: So she's in despair thinking it'll convince people she committed the murders? And now she has to face the reality of a long time in prison?

AJ NOVICK: I sent her a note saying the video won't be admissible, and in any event, we'd fight like hell to keep it out. She'll come around. Just a matter of when.

RYANNA RAINES: On Tuesday morning, I walk from my Airbnb down to the beach. I sit on the sand staring at the vast ocean and listening to the surf. Does it help clear my mind? A little. It feels like we're coming to some kind of a breaking point in this case. There could still be a trial ahead, which will be its own journey, an ultramarathon with more twists and turns and highs and lows and daily media frenzies. Do I have the stamina for that? It may be another year before we can see the light at the end of the tunnel. This has already been one of the most emotionally draining cases I've ever worked on. And it might not even be half over.

Before going to the jail, I drive down to Rancho Santa Fe to take a look at the De Carlo property again. I find where Jordan and Victoria parked their stolen car the night of the murders. They'd said they stopped next to an empty lot, but now a new home is under construction there. I park off the main road of El Camino Del Norte, facing north toward the De Carlos' street. I get out and walk the same path that Jordan *or* Victoria would have taken to get up to the house. I go to the foot of the De Carlos' driveway and look back toward my car.

It's just beyond the curve in the road. From where I stand, I can't see it, my view is blocked.

VICTORIA BERNE: I saw him cross the road to his parents' street. He started up the hill and disappeared in the dark.

JORDAN DE CARLO: I watched her cross the road and turn up my parents' driveway. Then she was gone.

RYANNA RAINES: There is a streetlight on El Camino Del Norte about fifty yards to the west of this intersection. Which could provide enough light to see a figure cross that road at night. But once Victoria or Jordan got to the other side and started up the De Carlos' street, they would have disappeared around that curve before they got to their driveway. From the vantage point that Jordan is claiming, it would not have been possible to see Victoria *turn up his parents' driveway*. Certainly a discrepancy. But how significant?

As I turn to the wrought-iron gate and look through it up the driveway, I feel my blood chill.

JORDAN DE CARLO: I have a surprise for you today.

RYANNA RAINES: One more in an ongoing series?

JORDAN DE CARLO: The last one from me. I promise. Because today, you will be recording my full and voluntary confession to the murders of Anthony and Lauren De Carlo. Since we now have under twenty-eight minutes left in our visit, I suggest I get started. You ready?

RYANNA RAINES: All I can do is sit up, check the recorder, and pretend that my pulse hasn't started racing. Is this happening? Or is it just another unforeseen detour through this psychologically distorted house of mirrors?

JORDAN DE CARLO: From the day of her audition, my first priority was the play, and to gain Victoria's trust. She had to know that if she put herself in my hands, I could take her to the mountaintop.

When we got together, she was sexually inexperienced, but had great body awareness from all the dance and movement classes. The first time I kissed her, I could feel a shock wave go through her body. I took my time and gently invited her to the deeper pleasures of lovemaking and sexual stimulation. She'd never orgasmed with a man. I showed her how to be multiorgasmic. We were together either making art or making love eighteen to twenty hours a day, every day, for forty-five days. I watched her gaining more and more confidence in her artistic choices. I'd never seen that much raw talent in an actor. I helped her shape and refine it, while still being bold and uncompromising. She put her trust in me as her creative guide, as her advocate, her champion, her lover.

For opening night, I'd bought my parents two tickets. Only, I didn't tell them about it. So I knew they wouldn't show up. And I knew I could use that as a way to transition Victoria to our next big project. I demonstrated how torn up I was by my toxic relationship with my mom and dad. I started telling her things meant to paint them in the worst possible light. For instance, the story that my dad stole money from the Heaven's Gate cult and then threatened to kill me?

I made it up. Completely.

RYANNA RAINES: That never happened? But your dad was working for a bank down the road in Del Mar at the time of the suicides?

JORDAN DE CARLO: True. And so is the anonymous tip the police ignored, as well as Dad's abrupt departure from his job and the area. And so is the house he bought in Rancho Santa Fe being next to the property where those thirty-nine people ended their lives. I took separate strands and wove them together to make him look like a thief and a ruthless opportunist. I wanted her to believe these things because I wanted her to hate my parents as much as I did. And to think I was in mortal danger. I held that back until the right moment.

I encouraged Victoria to share her family secrets with me. We found common ground in our rage against our fathers. We'd both been scarred by their betrayals. We fed off each other's bitterness. Still, Victoria wanted a chance to meet my parents and *win them over*. I saw that as an opportunity. I knew that Anthony and Lauren would play their roles to perfection. They came that night with their minds made up about my girlfriend. I may have helped by planting seeds about her middle-class upbringing and lack of social graces. During dinner, I steered the conversation to where I knew Mom and Dad would reveal their worst selves. It was tense, even excruciating, and Victoria came away deeply troubled by the scorn they showed for her.

On the drive back up to Santa Barbara I threw a tantrum and had to pull off the freeway. That's when I revealed my dad's Heaven's Gate theft and his threat to kill me. When I saw her reaction of fear for my safety and concern they would undermine our relationship, I said to her: "I want you to help me kill them."

RYANNA RAINES: Those were your words? You were the first to bring it up?

JORDAN DE CARLO: Yes. She was shocked but not shocked. I didn't press her. I did tell her I got a follow-up call from my mom, who confirmed that she and my dad did not approve of the *actress* I brought to dinner and would be penalizing me financially. I said normally I wouldn't have passed that on, but I wanted to have total transparency regarding my family. I could see how much that weighed on her. I kept up with subtle but steady inducements. And then one morning I woke up and found her staring at me. The first words out of her mouth were "Okay. I'll help you. I'll help you kill your parents."

Right after that we had one of our most intense lovemaking sessions. We sealed our conspiracy with sexual euphoria. This pact of ours would bring us even closer together than the experience of *Desire Under the Elms*. Over peppermint tea, we began making the plan.

RYANNA RAINES: You took the lead?

JORDAN DE CARLO: As the writer-director, with Victoria in a principal role. I'd been thinking about this project for years. I'd plotted it out a thousand times. I'd done research and studied crimes where the criminals had gone wrong and gotten caught. The one element vital to committing the perfect crime is creating the perfect alibi. Constructing our alibi would be like writing a play together. What's our line of action? What's our motivation? Well, we're passionate lovers exploring the boundaries of our sexuality. Making love in a public place when it's deserted doesn't seem farfetched. The big magnolia on the Commencement Green was ideal.

RYANNA RAINES: But you never really made love there because it was part of your fictional alibi.

JORDAN DE CARLO: Actually we did go and try it out one night at 2:00 A.M. It was a tight fit, but workable. That's why we were able to describe the scene so vividly to those detectives. I also realized we'd need to put Victoria inside my parents' home prior to the murder to explain why her DNA and blood was at the scene. I called my mom and begged her to let us come down for the weekend. It was my idea to have Victoria cut herself in the kitchen and drip blood around. She didn't love that, but knew why it was important, so she did it. I made my mom take a photo of the cut so the evidence would be on her phone. The whole time we were there Victoria felt uneasy, but she acted her role flawlessly. We were scheduled to stay two nights. Then I told her my dad was outside our room listening to us have sex, and that gave us a reason to leave early.

The key to it all was me having watched my former roommate hot-wire his car. There's our vehicle. I drove, Victoria lay down on the back seat. She expressed last-minute doubts. I reassured her it was the right thing for us, and no one would ever be able to prove we did it.

When we finally got there, I was ready. I'd bought two butterfly knives and I put one in my pocket and held out the other one to Victoria. She just shook her head and wouldn't take the knife. She said, "I can't do that to another human being. I'm sorry, I'm so sorry." And I realized I'd be on my own. But as I headed up the street to their driveway, I began feeling it was the right way to go. They were *my* parents. I couldn't force Victoria to do something she'd regret the rest of her life. The day would come when she'd blame me for pressuring her and I didn't want that. So I felt a certain lightness as I came up to the front door and knocked.

I knew my parents would be surprised to see me and full of questions, so when my dad opened the door, I just told him I needed to talk to him and Mom and that it was important. When I got inside, I said I needed a glass of water. I led the two of them into the kitchen. I let my mom pour me the glass and didn't touch it because I didn't want my fingerprints on it.

RYANNA RAINES: A warning to listeners. This next part has Jordan describing his violent assault on his parents. It's pretty rough. If you're squeamish or feel it might be triggering, you can skip ahead about three minutes.

JORDAN DE CARLO: I knew my dad kept a gun in the bedroom, so I had to catch them by surprise. To get them to relax their guard, I told them I'd broken up with Victoria. That I saw what they were telling me about her. I even squeezed out a few tears. They actually started speaking words of compassion, something I'd rarely experienced from them. That itself was triggering for me: *Oh, now you're being nice? On the night I'm going to kill you?*

My dad even came toward me, like to physically console me. That was the moment. I pulled the knife, slid it open, and stabbed him in the stomach. He looked down at the blade, then up into my eyes—only time in my life I saw him a hundred percent vulnerable. I heard my mom scream, and I turned on her. I became a stabbing machine, plunging the knife in over and over. My dad came up behind me, so I whirled and stabbed him in the neck and top of the chest. Wham-wham-wham-wham! Blood flying everywhere. It even splashed in my mouth. It had this warm salty taste. I turned back to my mom down on the floor. You know, when you stab a person, your hand can feel their organs being penetrated. I saw my dad going off to get his gun. I caught him and he turned to face me and I stabbed and stabbed and he fell on the floor. I kept stabbing until he stopped moving. Then I lifted his head and used the edge of the blade to slash his throat. I went back to my mom, lifted her head—she's still alive. She looks in my eyes. Not questioning me or begging me to spare her—her eyes are saying, *I hope you burn in hell for this.*

I slit her throat.

And it was done. I stood there in my parents' house with their blood all over me. On my face, in my hair. I was soaked with it. And you know what? It didn't feel the way I thought it would. I thought I'd have this tremendous feeling of release and relief. Of freedom. But I felt absolutely nothing. Not happy, not sad, not up, not down—just numb.

RYANNA RAINES: Jordan goes quiet a moment, his eyes focused on some unspeakable memory.

Why are you telling me this now?

JORDAN DE CARLO: I'm not just telling you. This will be going out to the world. A lot of ears are going to be hearing this.

RYANNA RAINES: Not before there's a sentencing order. The thing is, Jordan, you've told me a few different versions of this story. First, you claimed innocence. The version you told more recently cast Victoria as taking the lead in the murders. You told me she went up to your parents' house alone that night and committed the murders herself. Now you're telling me you were the one driving this all along. That you used your influence over Victoria to draw her in and help you commit the killings of your parents. Why should I believe you now?

JORDAN DE CARLO: Because I'm ready to take responsibility for my actions.

RYANNA RAINES: Why?

JORDAN DE CARLO: Because I'm guilty of killing my parents.

RYANNA RAINES: But you've had all these opportunities to tell the truth. What is it about now, today, this visit that made you change your mind?

JORDAN DE CARLO: Is this the Ryanna Raines third degree? You're in full interrogator mode?

RYANNA RAINES: I'm asking a fair question, Jordan. Going back to last October, my mission has been to get the truth from you. It's taken months of research and following leads and staying in Airbnbs and talking to lots of people. And today of all days, you decide to wipe out everything you've told me prior to this and tell a new story that could get you locked up for life.

JORDAN DE CARLO: I'm ready to change my plea to guilty.

RYANNA RAINES: Are you afraid of losing at trial?

For the first time since he entered the room, I hear his voice choke with emotion.

JORDAN DE CARLO: Of *Victoria* losing. And suffering the same punishment that I get. Which would not be right. Which I could not live with. Knowing she received the same penalty as the person who pulled her in, lied to her, manipulated her—that would weigh heavier on me than anything.

RYANNA RAINES: So you're confessing because you don't want to drag Victoria down with you?

JORDAN DE CARLO: Her participation came only because of my influence over her.

RYANNA RAINES: Yet she did participate every step of the way. Including when you came back from Mexico and you both lied on the record, lied extensively, not just to me, but to the world. I wasn't aware you were pressuring her to do that. I saw no gun being held to her head.

JORDAN DE CARLO: I was directing her. She was playing the role I cast her to play. And she's a fantastic actor, so your listeners believed her. And so did you.

RYANNA RAINES: I *wanted* to believe you weren't acting. I wanted to believe that two young people who were so talented and conscientious would be incapable of committing such a horrific crime. And then using me as the amplifier to tell the world they were innocent.

JORDAN DE CARLO: You could choose to be flattered. We selected you with great care. And let's be honest. Our case lifted your podcast into the big leagues. You profited from telling our story.

RYANNA RAINES: And a lot of those profits will be channeled into the victims' groups we support. To women and children survivors of domestic violence. To organizations working to reverse wrongful convictions.

JORDAN DE CARLO: Seizing the opportunity for a podcaster PSA, bravo. Hey, if writing checks makes you feel better, knock yourself out. In the meantime, after we finish here, I'll be calling my lawyer and having her start a conversation with the court. I'll be going away for a long time, I know that. And I'm not saying Victoria should be released without any consequences—that's not going to happen. But the court should be lenient, because this is on me. My future is history. Victoria should get a second chance down the line. She's not a killer and never will be.

RYANNA RAINES: You really love her, don't you?

JORDAN DE CARLO: My feelings for her are not the point. If you really believe in capital J justice, put me away and toss the key. But let her out while she's still relatively young.

RYANNA RAINES: The knock comes and the guard enters. Jordan stands and lets himself be reshackled.

JORDAN DE CARLO: When you see her, please tell her I said I love her. And that I'm sorry. That's the truest truth. Goodbye, Ryanna.

RYANNA RAINES: And the door shut on my final interview with Jordan De Carlo.

JESS MONAY: That last part he said to pass on to Victoria? I believe him.

RYANNA RAINES: Why?

JESS MONAY: Not because I'm a romantic, but I think Victoria touched Jordan's heart in a way he never expected. And he's proving it by sacrificing himself to decades in prison so that she can get a lighter sentence. He doesn't have to do that. He could go to trial and take his chances.

RYANNA RAINES: If they were both convicted, they'd likely get equal sentences. And at that point, it would be too late for him to take the blame in a way that gets her a lesser punishment.

JESS MONAY: You know who's not going to be happy about this at all? Jordan's attorney, Natalie Bloom.

RYANNA RAINES: She's beyond not happy. She gave Jordan an ultimatum. If he confesses to the charges and agrees to take a long prison sentence, she'll quit.

JESS MONAY: He's already confessed to you, on tape.

RYANNA RAINES: He's got to do it all over again for the prosecutor and they have to take that to the judge. The judge has to approve it and settle on a sentence for both of them before it can be final. So we still have a ways to go here.

Next up, our final episode for this season. And there will be at least one more big twist that none of us saw coming.

S6:E43

RYANNA RAINES: I'm Ryanna Raines. And welcome to *The Raines Report*, an audio crime-investigation series produced in association with Amplify. We're in the last phase of our inquiry into the De Carlo murders and we're calling this season's finale "The Judgment of This Court."

Season 6 got kicked off when my producer and I came upon a message left on *The Raines Report*'s tip line. Reaching out to us from Mexico were the two main suspects in a vicious double murder. I returned the call and spoke for the first time to twenty-two-year-old Jordan De Carlo and his eighteen-year-old girlfriend, Victoria Berne. That began an eleven-month odyssey that we will be bringing to an end—or at least to a pause—with this episode.

JESS MONAY: It's been quite a ride, for you, for me, and for the team. That initial call came in last October tenth. On October eleventh you flew out and met the couple as they arrived back in San Diego. They believed they were about to be arrested on murder charges and wanted to tell you their side of the story before being taken into custody.

RYANNA RAINES: I'd get a first-person, up-close view into their lives by spending time with them, asking questions, sharing meals, and observing them.

JESS MONAY: Over social media there was an outpouring of sympathy for Jordan and Victoria during their last nine days of freedom. When a warrant was issued for their arrests, you ended up driving them 200 miles to the Vista sheriff's station, where the couple surrendered.

RYANNA RAINES: The two were promptly arraigned on first-degree murder charges and had a gag order placed on them. That caused a shift in our strategy. By phone and in person, I conducted some two dozen interviews with Jordan and Victoria's families, friends, faculty, and classmates.

JESS MONAY: After months of putting out weekly episodes devoted to investigating the suspects and their victims, we struck a deal with the court. Ryanna would interview the defendants in jail, on the condition that our reporting be held back from the public until there was a legal resolution to the case. Jordan and Victoria had signaled they were ready to disclose new information. They had their own condition: they would speak only to Ryanna, who they'd gotten to know and trust.

RYANNA RAINES: It was during these jailhouse interviews, conducted six months after their arrests, that Jordan and Victoria began telling me a very different story. Limited to thirty-minute visits on alternating weekdays, they separately confessed to plotting the killings of Jordan's mother and father and orchestrating a cover-up. However, each pointed to the other as the instigator, lead planner, and sole perpetrator of the murders.

JESS MONAY: Then a video came to us, through a fellow theater student of Jordan and Victoria's, that showed Victoria lose her temper during a practice dagger fight in Stage Combat class. That video ended up getting hacked by a pro-Jordan online faction and going viral.

RYANNA RAINES: Thanks for not mentioning my screw-up that gave the hackers their way in. But I fully own that. The stage combat video set a number of things in motion. Victoria declined to participate in any further interviews. Jordan completely reversed course and took full responsibility for the murders. He admitted to grooming and manipulating Victoria into conspiring with him to kill his parents. He declared that he alone entered his parents' home that Sunday night in June and he alone stabbed Anthony and Lauren to death. He told me he was going to plead guilty and accept a sentence that fit his crime—given Victoria received a lesser sentence.

JESS MONAY: At that point, we anticipated the case might get resolved pretty quickly and our news embargo would be lifted.

RYANNA RAINES: But Judge Elliott Rendell, the California superior court judge overseeing *The People v. De Carlo and Berne*, put the brakes on a fast resolution. He ordered Jordan and Victoria to undergo a series of evaluations by court-appointed psychologists. He wanted experts to analyze and report on the extent to which one defendant influenced and/or induced the other to become involved in plotting and carrying out the murders.

JESS MONAY: In addition, all parties and the court agreed to having Jordan and Victoria take individual polygraph tests. This is somewhat unusual for a California court.

RYANNA RAINES: Polygraph evidence is admissible only when defendants are willing to be tested and there is agreement between defense and prosecution to enter the results into the record.

It's time to say my piece about polygraph tests. To start, the instrument known as a polygraph is not a lie detector. It measures changes in the subject's physiology as the subject is asked and answers questions posed by the examiner. While the study of lie detection is advancing in areas such as eye and body scanning, these newer technologies are still being tested. Currently, the subject's bio-recordings are processed through a computer program that uses algorithms to chart changes in breathing, heart rate, and electrodermal activity—sweat glands.

The traditional title of polygraph examiner has been upgraded to *forensic psycho-physiologist*—FP for short. The instrument itself can measure only a subject's physical responses. It cannot look inside a subject's mind. So everything depends on how the FP calibrates their questions to a specific person and a specific set of circumstances.

Defense attorneys AJ Novick and Natalie Bloom brought in a top FP from Los Angeles, and the prosecution secured the services of an experienced San Diego FP, someone they had a history with. That's two tests for Jordan and two for Victoria. Each test lasted two hours. The sheriff's department has adjacent rooms with a soundproof glass divider, and both the prosecutors and defense attorneys were present to witness the tests as they took place.

All four tests saw these forensic psychophysiologists reach similar conclusions. On the matter of Jordan taking the lead in the planning and carrying out the murders and Victoria following along, the subjects showed no deception.

JESS MONAY: Then Jordan and Victoria were subjected to hours of examinations by court-appointed psychologists. Here are some excerpts from their reports:

"Ms. Berne gave a clear and consistent account of how she was first drawn in by Mr. De Carlo as a creative collaborator and a lover, then recruited by him as a partner in a plot to kill his parents. Her examples of how he methodically programmed her are numerous and highly detailed."

RYANNA RAINES: "Mr. De Carlo stated his grievances against his parents go back as far as he can remember. He described his relationship with them as a ticking time bomb that he kept looking for an opportunity to detonate."

JESS MONAY: "Ms. Berne submerged her personality into Mr. De Carlo's because of her deep-seated need for his love and approval. Given her own childhood trauma, she was at risk for developing unhealthy emotional attachments that could result in her being manipulated and exploited."

RYANNA RAINES: "Mr. De Carlo said he perceived Ms. Berne's vulnerabilities and became consciously intentional in making her psychologically dependent on him."

JESS MONAY: "Ms. Berne's warped judgment can be seen when she stopped calling and consulting with her mother. As Mr. De Carlo took on the roles of creative Svengali, master lovemaker, and trauma sympathizer, Ms. Berne became isolated from everyone else in her life."

RYANNA RAINES: In her summation, one psychologist wrote: "Having skipped a grade in middle school, Ms. Berne was younger, less experienced, and susceptible to the predations of an older, more experienced, and seductive upperclassman with a deep-rooted hatred of his parents."

JESS MONAY: I find it remarkable all four psychologists reached essentially the same conclusion.

RYANNA RAINES: This was the independent confirmation the judge needed to accept the defendants' change of pleas and to move ahead with their sentencing.

Jess and I decided we'd fly together to San Diego to attend the hearing. The media circus in the parking lot of the San Diego Superior Court was bigger and noisier than the one in front of Jordan's house in Santa Barbara. Did you hear people calling out your name as we passed through the gauntlet into the building?

JESS MONAY: That was surreal.

I'd never seen Jordan or Victoria in person. Not going to lie, I was a little nervous waiting with you in the gallery for the defendants to arrive. They'd become these global true-crime superstars. I know, a lot of that was because of us.

RYANNA RAINES: Let's describe what was going on inside the courtroom. Predictably, every seat was filled and two deputies were posted at the doorways. The anticipation was palpable within those walls. We knew Jordan would be receiving a long sentence. There was more suspense about what Victoria would get. Everything pointed to her being Jordan's accomplice in planning and committing the murders. Legally, she didn't have to be present during the commission of the crime. To be guilty of first-degree murder, it's enough that she accompanied Jordan, knew what he planned to do, and helped him get rid of evidence. It would have been normal for her to get an equal sentence to his. But the court found what it calls "mitigating" circumstances. Not only had Jordan admitted his manipulations of her, but experts agreed that he'd used his power and control over Victoria to convert her into his partner in crime.

JESS MONAY: But she still has a free will. Doesn't she bear some responsibility for continuing to follow his lead?

RYANNA RAINES: And that played into the judge's calculations. Now, we were not allowed to record the proceeding, but we both made extensive notes. Jordan and Victoria were last to enter the courtroom and they were brought in through separate entrances. Every person there leaned forward trying to read their behavior toward each other.

JESS MONAY: For the hearing, the defendants were permitted to change out of their jail uniforms. Jordan wore a black blazer with a thin tie and Victoria a white dress with a low heel. In terms of how they presented themselves, they lived up to their reputations.

RYANNA RAINES: True, they looked like they were ready to play themselves in the Netflix series. I caught a few sighs from behind us. Victoria entered first and kept her head down all the way to the defense table. Then Jordan came in and he was looking all around, making eye contact with friends and family who were there to support him. When he got to the defense table, he looked very intentionally at Victoria.

JESS MONAY: But she would not meet his eyes. She kept her gaze either on the table in front of her or on the judge.

RYANNA RAINES: After the judge entered and took the bench, both defense attorneys got up to speak to the court. AJ Novick spoke on behalf of Victoria, and Jordan's new attorney, Martin Lancaster, on behalf of Jordan. Lancaster detailed the emotional abuse that his parents inflicted on Jordan during his childhood and adolescence. Jordan sat expressionless, mostly tuned out.

JESS MONAY: Tuned out of what his attorney was saying, but trying to tune in Victoria.

RYANNA RAINES: She had the air of someone who'd broken free of her bad influence. She didn't want to be Juliet to his Romeo anymore. She wanted to show the world an independent identity.

JESS MONAY: Her attorney worked that theme hard, saying she participated in the crime under the influence of a powerful personality who groomed her, first as a performer in his fictional production, then as a performer in his real-life murder plot.

RYANNA RAINES: All of this was courtroom theater because the judge had already determined the offenders' sentences. He started with Jordan and cited that his crime of first-degree murder involved excessive violence and aggravated harm to his victims. It displayed, quote, "an extreme degree of viciousness." Judge Rendell said, "The blood covering you was your family's blood." Although it didn't rise to the level of "special circumstances" as defined by California sentencing law, the judge did find the combination of violence and the enlisting of an accomplice through lies and manipulation justified two consecutive sentences of life in prison—*without the possibility of parole.*

JESS MONAY: You could hear gasps all over the courtroom. Jordan's back was to us, so we couldn't see his immediate reaction. Life without parole? Wow.

RYANNA RAINES: In taking responsibility for brutally murdering his parents as well as seducing Victoria into joining his plot to get rid of them, Jordan sacrificed his entire future. Talk about a dramatic gesture. He might have blamed his actions on some mental illness, but he wouldn't go there. He was grimly determined to pay the full price for his actions.

JESS MONAY: The ultimate price short of capital punishment, which the State of California has placed a moratorium on. By accepting the most severe penalty, Jordan had given Victoria cover that helped justify a lesser sentence. I could feel the tension in the gallery when the judge turned to sentencing the female defendant.

RYANNA RAINES: Judge Rendell started right in on the mitigating factors in Victoria's guilty plea to the double murder. The defendant participated in the crime under an insidious psychological and emotional influence. He used that word *insidious*, defined as "intending to entrap." He cited that Victoria had no prior criminal record and an excellent academic record. He cited that Victoria voluntarily changed her plea and acknowledged wrongdoing well ahead of her murder trial. He emphasized the point that the person who physically committed the crimes was already receiving the maximum sentence under the law.

Here are the words the judge spoke: "Having reviewed all the findings from court-appointed psychologists and examiners and in consideration of the mitigating factors, it is the judgment of this court that for the violation of Penal Code 187, the unlawful killing of a human being with malice aforethought, Victoria Camille Berne shall be confined to a state correctional facility for a term of twelve years."

JESS MONAY: Meaning with time already served and reductions for good behavior, she'll probably be out in eight. Victoria will likely be free again before she turns thirty.

RYANNA RAINES: I looked over and met eyes with her mother, Gail. She was dabbing tears that came from a mix of sorrow and relief.

JESS MONAY: We should note that Jordan's aunt Frances, his champion inside the family, was absent from the courtroom.

RYANNA RAINES: I can't really blame her for not showing up. The outcome was a foregone conclusion. I feel for her, for all of Jordan's extended family. For them, it was a double tragedy.

JESS MONAY: When the judge concluded the hearing, they took Victoria out first. Jordan had his eyes on her the whole way.

RYANNA RAINES: And then, just before exiting, and likely the last time she'd ever be in the same room with him, she looked back and met Jordan's eyes.

JESS MONAY: I wish someone had gotten a photo of her face at that moment. How did you read her?

RYANNA RAINES: Maybe I'm the romantic, but I saw a flash of gratitude. I mean, Jordan did take full responsibility and exonerated her the best he could. And it worked, because she'll have most of her life ahead of her when she gets out of prison.

JESS MONAY: I am not a romantic, but I have to agree. It was just for a moment, but you could see this glimmer in her eye.

RYANNA RAINES: I looked back at Jordan and saw his shoulders lift when she looked at him. And then drop after she exited. Then it was his turn to get escorted out by the deputies. He went straight out the door without looking back.

After the sentencing, we ran into Detective Sanchez in the hallway of the courthouse. There were still some things we wanted to know. What was the evidence the state had that made them so sure they could win at trial? Sanchez declined to be recorded, but made several on-the-record remarks that helped fill in the gaps.

The lead investigator and his team had painstakingly put together surveillance and security camera footage that tracked the white Ford Focus

Jordan and Victoria had used to drive from Isla Vista to Rancho Santa Fe and back. Inside the car they discovered fibers that matched with clothing found inside Jordan's house through search warrants. They also found Victoria's DNA in the back seat, despite the car owner's statement that he had no knowledge she'd ever been inside the car. All those hours of reviewing video footage accounted for the delay in the arrests of Jordan and Victoria. After they had it pieced together, the department gave me a tour of the crime scene because they wanted the public to understand the brutality of the crime. Then, because they knew they could disprove Jordan and Victoria's alibi, they shared the video of their double interview with us to expose the extent to which the couple was lying.

One never knows how a trial will turn out, but based on what we learned from Detective Sanchez, Jordan and Victoria would probably have been convicted and both given life sentences. Which means in this version of the story, Romeo did save Juliet from suffering his same fate.

JESS MONAY: So our platform was used not only by the guilty to claim innocence, but also by law enforcement to put out their own narrative. And this roller coaster isn't over yet, is it?

RYANNA RAINES: Not quite. We have one more account to report on. This one caused us to do a lot of soul-searching in deciding whether we should bring it to you. We had to think hard about our role as journalists and how appropriate and relevant the information we received was to this case as we've been reporting it.

JESS MONAY: We had a spirited internal debate. To include it here was not an easy decision.

RYANNA RAINES: *"You remember me," I say.*
He shakes his head. "I don't."
"Well, I remember you. I'm the journalist who was up here with Jordan De Carlo and Victoria Berne before they got arrested. You came up to me and said there was something you had to tell me."
"Sorry, I think you're mistaken."

"Were you in front of his house when all the media was camped out there?"

"No."

"On the UCSB campus a couple Saturdays ago, watching me?"

"You must be confusing me with someone else."

I had that exchange in a Santa Barbara coffeehouse at the end of last October. Two weeks after Jordan and Victoria had surrendered to authorities.

JESS MONAY: He worked as a server at Café Bloomsday and his name was Daniel Mazzoli. Since then, we hadn't heard anything from him or about him.

RYANNA RAINES: I'd more or less forgotten him. And then, a few hours after the prison sentences for Jordan and Victoria were announced, my phone rang.

DANIEL MAZZOLI: Hi, yeah, my name is Daniel. You came into Café Bloomsday in Santa Barbara last fall. I was your server. You asked if I remembered you and I said no. Well, that wasn't true.

RYANNA RAINES: Jess and I are staying overnight in Oceanside before flying home in the morning. Daniel, aka Blackbeard, is calling me on my cell. He says he has something he wants to get off his chest and is willing to speak to me on the record. He's currently in San Diego and asks if I'd meet him for coffee. I say okay—and that my producer is coming with me.

JESS MONAY: This is the guy you thought might be stalking you. Good thing I brought pepper spray.

RYANNA RAINES: An hour later, Jess and I walk into a coffee shop on Coast Highway.

DANIEL MAZZOLI: Thanks for meeting me. I'm glad I got a chance to talk to you in person. I thought you'd probably be in town for the sentencing.

RYANNA RAINES: Turns out Daniel has listened to all of Season 6 and followed the case closely. He goes back to our exchange at Café Bloomsday.

DANIEL MAZZOLI: I knew who you were. And I had been following you. Trying to work up the courage to tell you some information I had about Victoria.

RYANNA RAINES: What about Victoria?

DANIEL MAZZOLI: I was in a relationship with her. An intimate relationship. We'd been—hooking up for about six months before the murders.

RYANNA RAINES: Define *hooking up.*

DANIEL MAZZOLI: Having sex.

RYANNA RAINES: And you're saying this *hooking up* ended six months before the murders?

DANIEL MAZZOLI: I'm saying it lasted six months, up until a few days before the murders.

RYANNA RAINES: Jess and I exchange a glance, then lean a little closer to Mr. Mazzoli.

You mean during the time she was with Jordan and working on the play?

DANIEL MAZZOLI: Yes.

RYANNA RAINES: Our understanding is Jordan and Victoria were together constantly, day and night. When would she have had time to get together with you?

DANIEL MAZZOLI: It varied. A half hour here, forty-five minutes there. She never stayed over, not after she started on the play. She came to my place once, twice a week.

RYANNA RAINES: And the two of you would have sex each time?

DANIEL MAZZOLI: That's pretty much what the relationship was about. Sometimes we'd get on the phone late at night and talk dirty.

RYANNA RAINES: Did you know she was also having sex with Jordan?

DANIEL MAZZOLI: She never mentioned him. I had no reason to think we were exclusive. It didn't really matter if she was having sex with someone else. It was a "don't ask, don't tell" kind of thing.

RYANNA RAINES: Did she talk to you about anything that was going on with her life?

DANIEL MAZZOLI: When she came into the café to study, we'd talk a little. I knew she was a BFA student and serious about her acting.

RYANNA RAINES: So, how would you describe your relationship?

DANIEL MAZZOLI: I mean, we were sex partners. Not exclusively, but she came off to me as very experienced. Enthusiastic and confident in the bedroom. When I heard her being described on your podcast, it didn't fit with what I knew about her. She loved to take charge.

RYANNA RAINES: Can you verify this relationship you had with her?

DANIEL MAZZOLI: I have her texts scheduling our hookups. Time-stamped selfies of us together. And my roommate saw her come and go several times. He said he would talk to you.

RYANNA RAINES: When was the last time you spoke to Victoria?

DANIEL MAZZOLI: The last time she came over, like three days before the murders. We had sex, but it felt bittersweet. Then she told me she couldn't see me anymore. I asked why. She just said it was complicated. But she was sweet about it. I walked her to her car and we had a good long hug. And that was it. Never heard from her again.

RYANNA RAINES: What made you decide to come forward now?

DANIEL MAZZOLI: It all came back to me when I started listening to your podcast. I wanted to tell you then, but I was torn because I didn't want to get her in any more trouble. As time went on, I felt guilty about not saying anything. Now that she's been sentenced and the case is settled, I want to tell my truth. It's also important for me to say that . . . I cared about her.

RYANNA RAINES: Right then I have a flash. Call it a journalist's intuition. Daniel, did you ever give Victoria a gift? Like a keepsake, something to show you cared?

DANIEL MAZZOLI: Yes. I gave her this gold neck chain with a little heart strung on it. Wasn't expensive or anything, I put it on her as she was leaving one time. I guess I wanted to show her she meant more to me than just sex.

RYANNA RAINES: Victoria lied to me. Straight up.

JESS MONAY: She did. Straight up.

RYANNA RAINES: That hurts. Which kind of surprises me. Not that she lied, but that it hurts.

JESS MONAY: To give some perspective, this disclosure from Daniel Mazzoli came before we'd dropped our last nine episodes. So he wouldn't have heard how Jordan initially described his sexual experiences with Victoria. But here's the issue, journalistically. Daniel's account really doesn't make a difference in the legal outcome for Victoria. There's no correlation between Victoria's sexual activities outside of Jordan and the crime of murder that she pled guilty to.

RYANNA RAINES: You're right. But Daniel's account does go to the issue of Victoria's truthfulness and credibility. We checked those texts and photos and we spoke to Daniel's roommate. We confirmed his story of their affair and the timeline.

JESS MONAY: We are not here to judge Victoria for carrying on another relationship while she was with Jordan. Really, that's her private business. But throughout your questioning of her and of those who know her, this kind of behavior wasn't on the radar.

RYANNA RAINES: Except in the first version of Jordan's confession.

JORDAN DE CARLO: Not only was she a fantastic actress who transcended my vision for *Desire Under the Elms*, she was a magical lover. She knew exactly where to touch me, how to move, what to say. She took charge.

RYANNA RAINES: We immediately reached out to Victoria to get her comment on Daniel's story. I would've been happy to sit down with her for a follow-up interview. But we received no response. Except from her attorney, AJ Novick, who told us, "Victoria is focused on putting this tragedy behind her." She wouldn't be commenting or speaking to any journalists in the foreseeable future.

JESS MONAY: Which is her right.

RYANNA RAINES: It absolutely is.

JESS MONAY: So we're anticipating getting comments about our decision to report what this source had to tell us. And possibly a fair amount of blowback.

RYANNA RAINES: Had we gotten this information and not reported it, we would've been presenting an incomplete picture. The spine of this investigation turned into dueling accounts that went to the core of who these people are. Is Jordan an insidious Svengali? Is Victoria a devious Jezebel? Did Jordan ultimately lie about what happened on the night of his parents' murders because of his love for Victoria?

JESS MONAY: The psychologists and polygraph examiners believed Jordan was the one who initiated the plot to kill his parents. And that he manipulated Victoria into participating with him. The court locked that down as the *official* finding in this case.

RYANNA RAINES: And we accept that finding. But at the same time we have unanswered questions. Questions that will linger in our minds whenever we think about *The De Carlo Murders*.

We're already at work on Season 7 of *The Raines Report*, and we'll be announcing our new schedule soon. Until then, for Jess Monay, for our whole team here, and for me, Ryanna Raines, take care, stay safe, and we look forward to being back with you.

BONUS CONTENT

RYANNA RAINES: This is a piece I'm recording for *The Raines Report* Instagram. Before I was ready to do this, I needed some distance from *The De Carlo Murders* to more fully reflect on my experience during those eleven months of reporting. Now that the final episodes are out and we're pursuing new cases, I want to get personal and talk about how this case affected me and what I'm taking away from it.

When I'm in investigative mode, I process my experiences as a journalist, as a podcast host, someone doing a job the best I know how. But there is another Ryanna, with a life outside the podcast, who is a daughter, wife, mother, and friend. I used to think I had to compartmentalize that person, to wall her off from my professional side. When I realized how much energy that was taking, how exhausting it was to keep making that shift, I made a conscious decision to integrate those two sides of my life. This more unified Ryanna can be both a better journalist and a more compassionate person.

No longer do I draw a hard line between my work and my family—our listeners know I talk pretty freely about my husband and kids on the podcast. This season, that led to a head-on collision when, because of my reporting, I received a death threat that included them as targets. This was shocking and upsetting to me and a consequence I hadn't factored into my more blended approach to my work. My husband was great about it and I thank him so much for his courage and support.

All my angst about this came to a head when I confronted hoodie girl in that parking lot outside the jail. Whether she was directly responsible for the threat, I don't know. She may not have been, but if she was, I hope she gets a new life. Because bullying solves nothing, ever. Since Jordan changed his plea to guilty, I can report that we have received no more threats and a dwindling amount of hate mail. But my trauma from that attack remains.

I have to say that, and this will surprise nobody, I feel a deep sadness

for Jordan De Carlo and Victoria Berne. This case was about twin trag-
edies. The murder of two people who in no way deserved that abrupt
and horrific ending. And the murder convictions of two people who
had such a promising road ahead of them. Four lives utterly wasted.

I got closer to Jordan and Victoria than anyone during their post-
murder phase. Did I ever really know them? What part of their opening
up to me was a performance and what part was genuine? How can I be
sure where their truth-telling ended and their lie-telling began? From
the moment I stepped on the path to becoming a journalist, the truth
has been my north star. Did I reach that destination in *The De Carlo
Murders*? Can we ever know whose hand really held the knife that
plunged over and over into Anthony and Lauren De Carlo? Yes, there
has been a legal resolution and a murderer is going to prison for life. But
has there been a finding of moral certainty? I'm still pondering those
questions, aware I may never get the answers.

This season was the first time *The Raines Report* has taken up a
crime of parricide, the killing of one's parents. Victims of violence by a
stranger, an acquaintance, a coworker, to me those somehow seem less
terrible than violence within the sacred space of family. I know families
can be toxic and rife with cruelty and abuse. All families have their dark
places. But beyond the victim's physical pain, to be violently attacked
by a parent, sibling, or child would add a cellular-level sense of betrayal.

The other day our daughter broke one of our house rules and my husband and I decided to punish her. Not physical punishment—we don't
believe in that. But we did temporarily take away her TV time and tab-
let privileges. This made her angry and led to a verbal argument. In the
middle of it, I felt myself stepping outside my body and watching the
scene play out. I became acutely aware of how a relationship between a
parent and a child might at any time shift in a negative direction. I could
make parenting decisions that send my relationship with my child into
a bad place with lingering consequences. I saw up close the fallout from
such a downward spiral.

That night I went into my daughter's room and sat on her bed. She turned away to the wall and pretended not to notice me. I told her I loved her and that her dad and I were trying to be the best parents we could be. Our taking her privileges away was not out of meanness or selfishness or disrespect. We want to help her be the best person she can be. I rubbed her back and told her the most important thing as a family is to support one another. Even when it's hard, even when we disagree. After a minute she turned back to me with tears in her eyes and reached up to hug me. As I hugged her back, my eyes teared up, too.

Crisis averted. But what about next time? And when she becomes a teenager? I did not feel these apprehensions before becoming involved with those two brilliant and doomed drama students. In my family, when the inevitable confrontations between parent and child come, will I ever not flash on what happened at the top of that driveway inside that home on a night in early June?

This I do know. It's going to take some work for me to let go of those apprehensions.

AUTHOR NOTE

Over the past few years, we've listened to a lot of crime-investigation podcasts, hosted by a new generation of audio journalists. Many of these podcasters stand independent from traditional news organizations, but share that timeless reporter's zeal to go forth, find the truth, and put it out into the world. Our podcasting crime journalist, Ryanna Raines, was born out of these fresh voices bringing to the culture a new style of crime narrative. Creating *The Raines Report* and the team behind it seemed like a novelistically opportune way to explore the true-crime phenomenon while utilizing it as a framework through which to tell a shocker of a crime story.

The crime story we wanted to explore and dramatize had its roots in a real-life murder case. What happened inside the Virginia home of Derek and Nancy Haysom that spring night in 1985 may never be completely known. What is known is that this affluent middle-aged couple died from a hyper-violent knife attack. Eventually their twenty-one-year-old daughter, Elizabeth, and her boyfriend, Jens Soering, were arrested, charged, and convicted of the murders. Since first hearing of this baffling crime, by way of an investigative podcast, we couldn't get it out of our heads. Because nothing about these brainy college lovers fit with the savagery of the attack. That either (or both) could have acted with such a level of brutality defied our imaginations. That is, until we worked out a fictional version probing the psychological complexities of two brilliant but emotionally scarred young people doomed to fall into each other's orbit.

In what feels like a golden era for storytelling, filled with a diversity of voices speaking across multiple mediums and platforms, we wanted to take a fresh approach to the traditions of crime fiction and give voice to a new kind of investigator. In writing our last novel, *The Anatomy of Desire*, a 2022 finalist in the Audie Awards Multi-Voice Performance category, we fell in love with the multi-voice narrative form and were eager to do it again in *With a Kiss We Die*. Our journey to Ryanna Raines and *The Raines Report* Season 6 combined identifying a culture shift, following our passions, and applying our best story instincts. We hope our novel can amplify the voices of those who report on crime as well as showcase the changing ways in which today's crime stories are being told.

We couldn't do what we do without the contributions of those who supported us through each draft of the manuscript, at each production milestone, and at our publication launch (when we finally get to exhale and uncork the bubbly). Many thanks to our literary agent, Paul Bresnick, for his steadfast encouragement and optimism. To our phenomenal team at William Morrow/HarperCollins: our editors, David Highfill, who offered invaluable wisdom in shaping our vision through early drafts, and Julia Elliott, who enthusiastically shepherded us to completion. To Jessica Rozler, our diligent production editor; Nancy Inglis, who skillfully copyedited our words; Leah Carlson-Stanisic for our stylish page designs; and Yeon Kim, who gave us a chillingly cool cover design.

For the crucial task of marketing and promoting our book, we especially thank Martin Wilson and Taylor Turkington. Thank you to Kate Falkoff for handling foreign rights. And to our publisher, Liate Stehlik, and associate publisher, Jennifer Hart, our deepest gratitude for believing in us.

To the HarperAudio team, especially Caitlin Garing and Suzanne

Mitchell, thank you for once again rocking it and producing a stellar audiobook.

To our early readers who provided greatly appreciated feedback, thank you Sean O'Shea, Sierra Hastings, Julie Buehler, Steph Tenyak, and Beth Ludwig. For those who personally supported us in their own important ways, thanks for your generosity to Wayne Alexander and Lance Bogart. And to all the raters, reviewers, bookstagrammers, book tokkers, booksellers, librarians, and our readers and listeners, we're so grateful to you for helping us get this story and these characters out into the world.

Lastly, this book begins and ends with a dedication and a very special thanks to the many fans of true crime and crime fiction and to the piece in each of us that believes in truth and justice.

Thank you so much for reading . . . and listening!

L. R. Dorn is the pen name for Matt Dorff and Suzanne Dunn. **Matt** is a Southern California native and graduate of the USC School of Cinema who has written, produced, and/or directed over sixty hours of dramatic television (CBS, NBC, ABC, Showtime, HBO, Lifetime). He is a member of the Writers Guild of America West. **Suzanne** is a two-time Emmy Award winner for interactive programming who has written two movies for television. She grew up in Bucks County, Pennsylvania, and earned degrees from Penn State and the University of Chicago. She is a member of the Producers Guild of America and the Academy of Television Arts & Sciences.